"Do you still think you're not sexy?"

Neil's tone was infinitely tender, and the look Deirdre returned was just as soft.

"With you?" she whispered. "I feel downright seductive."

"That's good." He moved his hand to cover her bottom and pressed her hips close. "Because I think I'm needing you again."

Deirdre slowly trailed her fingers down his chest. "The needing is mutual," she murmured. "I only wish I could get rid of this cast for an hour . . . or two."

"It does present a challenge. I didn't hurt your leg last time, did I?"

Fascinated by the whorl of hair around his navel, she replied distractedly, "Did I sound like I was in pain?"

Barbara Delinsky needs no introduction to romance readers—she's one of the most popular authors writing today. No wonder, when she spins such warm, sensuous and totally involving tales as *The Real Thing*.

Temptation editors, always delighted when Barbara's latest manuscript comes in, became enthralled with the character of Victoria Lesser, matchmaker *extraordinaire*. In response to such enthusiasm, Barbara is planning two more Temptations in which this fascinating lady plays Cupid.

Books by Barbara Delinsky

FINGER PRINTS
WITHIN REACH

HARLEQUIN TEMPTATION

JASMINE SORCERY
98–STRAIGHT FROM THE HEART
116–FIRST, BEST AND ONLY

These books may be available at your local bookseller.

Don't miss any of our special offers. Write to us at the following address for information on our newest releases.

Harlequin Reader Service
901 Fuhrmann Blvd., P.O. Box 1397, Buffalo, NY 14240
Canadian address: P.O. Box 603,
Fort Erie, Ont. L2A 5X3

The Real Thing

BARBARA DELINSKY

Harlequin Books

TORONTO • NEW YORK • LONDON
AMSTERDAM • PARIS • SYDNEY • HAMBURG
STOCKHOLM • ATHENS • TOKYO • MILAN

Published November 1986

ISBN 0-373-25230-7

Printed in Canada

1

IT WASN'T EARTH-SHATTERING in the overall scheme of things. Nor was it unexpected. Yet coming as it did topping six weeks' worth of unpleasantness, it was the final straw.

Neil Hersey glared out the window of his office. He saw neither Constitution Plaza below him, nor anything else of downtown Hartford. The anger that blinded him would have spilled into his voice had not frustration already staked its claim there.

"Okay, Bob. Let me have it. We've been friends for too long to beat around the bush." He kept his fists anchored in the pockets of his tailored slacks. "It's not just a question of preferring someone else. We both know I'm as qualified for the job as any man. And we both know that Ryoden's been courting me for the past year. For some reason there's been an eleventh-hour reversal." Very slowly he turned. "I have my suspicions. Confirm them."

Robert Balkan, executive vice president of the Ryoden Manufacturing conglomerate, eyed the ramrod-straight figure across from him. He and Neil Hersey went back a long way. Their friendship was based on mutual admiration and genuine affection, and Bob respected Neil far too much to lie.

"Word came directly from Wittnauer-Douglass," he stated defeatedly. "Your release as corporate counsel there was a compassionate move. It was either let you go or bring you to trial."

Neil swore softly and bowed his head. "Go on."

"They alleged you were responsible for some transactions that were unethical, some that were downright illegal. For your own protection, the details remain private. The corporation is taking internal measures to counter the damage."

"I'll bet."

"What can I say, Neil? The charge was totally unsubstantiated, but it was enough to get the chairman of our board up in arms. One word in the old coot's ear and it became a crusade with him. Someone at Wittnauer-Douglass knew exactly what he was doing when he made that call. Then Ned Fallenworth got in on the act and that was that."

Fallenworth was the president of Ryoden. Bob had had reason to regret that fact in the past, but never as vehemently as he did now. "I've been spitting bullets since Ned gave me his decision. Ned's always been a coward, and what he's doing is a sad reflection on Ryoden. I gave it all I had, but his mind was closed. Narrow minds, Neil. That's what we're dealing with. Narrow minds."

Neil deliberately unclenched his jaw. "Narrow minds with a hell of a lot of power" was his own bleak assessment of the situation.

Leaving the window, he prowled the room, moving from parquet floor to Oriental rug and back, continuing the circle until he reached his gleaming mahogany desk. He leaned against the edge, his long legs extended and crossed at the ankles. His arms were folded over his chest. The pose might have been one of casual confidence under other circumstances. "Six weeks, Bob," he gritted. "This hell's being going on for six weeks. I'm being blackballed and it's touched every blessed aspect of my life. Something's got to give!"

"Do you need money? If it's a question of finances, I'd be glad to—"

"No, no." Neil waved aside the suggestion, then gentled his expression into a half smile of thanks. "Money's no problem. Not for now, at least." With the measured breath he took, the remnants of his half smile vanished. "The way things stand, though," he resumed, unable to stem his irritation, "my future as a lawyer in this town is just about nil, which is exactly what Wittnauer-Douglass intended."

"I think you should sue."

"Are you kidding?" Straightening his arms, he gripped the edge of the desk on either side of his lean hips. "Listen, I appreciate your vote of confidence, but you don't know that company as I do. A, they'd cover everything up. B, they'd drag the proceedings on so long that I would run out of money. C, *regardless* of the outcome, they'd make such a public issue of a suit that what little is left of my reputation would be shot to hell in the process. We're talking piranhas here, Bob."

"So why did you represent them?"

"Because I didn't *know,* damn it!" His shoulders slumped. "And that's the worst of it, I think. I just . . . didn't . . . know." His gaze skittered to the floor, dark brows lowered to hide his expression of deep self-dismay.

"You're human. Like the rest of us."

"Not much by way of encouragement."

Bob rose. "I wish I could do more."

"But you've done what you came to do and it's time to leave." Neil heard the bitterness in his voice, and while he detested it, he couldn't bring himself to apologize.

"I have an appointment at three." Bob's tone verged on apologetic, and Neil was quickly wary. He'd witnessed six weeks of defections, of so-called friends falling by the wayside.

Testing the waters, he extended his hand. "I haven't seen Julie in months. Let's meet for dinner sometime soon?"

"Sure thing," Bob said, smiling a little too broadly as the two shook hands.

Bob was relieved, Neil mused. The dirty work was done. And a "sure thing" for dinner was as noncommittal as Neil had feared it might be.

Moments later he was alone with an anger that approached explosive levels. Slumping into the mate of the chair Bob had just left, he pressed a finger to the crease in the center of his forehead and rubbed up and down. His head was splitting; he had to keep it together somehow. But how to remain sane when everything else was falling apart . . . Where was justice? Where in the hell was the justice in life?

Okay, he could understand why his working relationship with Wittnauer-Douglass would be severed after the abysmal scene six weeks ago. There had been, and was a difference of opinion. A rather drastic difference of opinion. He wouldn't have wanted to continue serving as counsel for the corporation any more than they'd wanted him to. But should he be punished this way?

His entire life was twisted. Damn it, it wasn't right!

Okay, so he'd lost Ryoden. He could have lived with that if it hadn't been for the fact that he'd also lost three other major clients in as many weeks. He was being blackballed within the corporate community. How the hell could he counter it, when the enemy was so much larger, so much more powerful?

He took several slow, measured breaths, opened his eyes and looked around the office. Ceiling-high mahogany bookshelves filled with legal tomes; an impressive collection of diplomas and brass-framed citations; a state-of-the-art telephone system linking him to his secretary and the world beyond; a credenza filled with important forms and personal papers—all worthless. What counted was in his head. But if he couldn't practice law his mind was worthless, too; it was hammering at his skull now, hammering mercilessly.

Neil Hersey had never felt so furious, so bitter—so utterly helpless—in his entire life. He knew that something had to be done, and that he was the one who was going to have to do it. For the life of him, though, he didn't know what action to take. His thoughts were mired in that fury and bitterness. He couldn't think clearly.

Muttering a dark oath, he bolted from his seat. He needed a break, a change of scenery. More than anything at the moment, he needed out.

Rounding the desk, he snatched his personal phone book from the top right-hand drawer and flipped to the *L*s. Landry. Lazuk. Lee. Lesser. He set the book down, marking the place with his finger. Lesser. Victoria Lesser. Within seconds he'd punched out the number that would connect him with the stylish Park Avenue co-op high above the hustle of Manhattan.

A very proper maid answered. "Lesser residence."

"This is Neil Hersey. Is Mrs. Lesser in?"

"Please hold the phone."

Neil waited, tapping his foot impatiently. He massaged the throbbing spot on his forehead. He squeezed his eyes shut. Only when he pictured Victoria breezing toward the phone— wending her way through the most elegant of furnishings while, very likely, wearing jeans and an oversized work shirt—did he give a small smile.

Victoria Lesser was a character. Thanks to the husband she'd worshipped until his death six years earlier, she was extremely wealthy and influential. She was also a nonconformist, which was what Neil adored about her. Though never outrageous, she did what she wanted, thumbing her nose at the concept of a staid and proper fifty-two-year-old widow. She traveled. She entertained. She took up ballet dancing. She fantasized herself a painter. She was interesting and refreshing and generous to the core.

It was that generosity Neil was counting on.

"Neil Hersey... fine friend you are!" A good-natured tirade burst from the other end of the line. "Do you know how long it's been since I've heard from you? It's been months! *Months!*"

"I know, Victoria. And I'm sorry. How are you?"

"How I am is beside the point," Victoria said more softly. "The question is, how are *you*?"

Neil hadn't been sure how far word had spread, but he should have realized Victoria would have heard. The mutual friend through which they'd originally met was an executive at Wittnauer-Douglass.

"You're speaking to me," he answered cautiously, "which makes me feel better already."

"Of course I'm speaking to you. I know what happened there, Neil. I know that board of directors. That is, I know how to recognize snakes. I also know what kind of lawyer you are—I haven't forgotten what you did for my niece—and I know the bind you're in right now."

"Then you know I need to get away." He broached the topic quickly. He was in no mood, even with Victoria, to pussyfoot around. "I can't think here. I'm too angry. I need peace and quiet. And seclusion."

"Something like a remote and uninhabited island off the coast of Maine?"

Neil's mouth lifted slightly at the corners. "Something like that."

"It's yours."

"No one's there?"

"In October?" She snorted. "People nowadays are sissies. Once Labor Day's passed, you'd think going north to an island was tantamount to exploring the Arctic. It's yours, Neil, for as long as you want it."

"Two weeks should do it. If I can't come up with some solutions by then . . ." There wasn't much more he could say.

"You haven't called me before, and knowing you, you'll want to work this out for yourself. But if there's anything I can do, will you let me know?"

Neil found solace in her words. She had the courage that others lacked. Not only was she unswayed by smear tactics, she would root for the underdog any day. "Use of the island is more than enough," he said gratefully.

"When were you thinking of going?"

"As soon as possible. Tomorrow, I guess. But you'll have to tell me how to get there."

Victoria did so. "Once you get to Spruce Head, ask for Thomas Nye. Big fellow. Bushy red beard. He lobsters from there. I'll call ahead and alert him. He'll take you out to the island."

With brief but heartfelt thanks, plus a promise to call her when he returned, Neil hung up the phone. He spent the rest of the afternoon working with his secretary to clear his calendar for the next two weeks. It was a relatively easy feat, given the amount of work he'd recently lost. He met in turn with each of his two young associates, giving them enough direction to keep them marginally occupied during his absence.

For the first time in his memory, when he left the office his briefcase remained behind. He carried nothing more than a handful of Havana cigars.

If he was going to escape it all, he decided belligerently, he'd go all the way.

DEIRDRE JOYCE glowered at the thick white cast that sheathed her left leg from thigh to toe. It was a diversionary tactic. If she looked into the urgent faces that circled her hospital bed, she was sure she'd explode.

"It was an act of fate, Deirdre," her mother was saying. "A message. I've been trying to get it across for months now, but you've refused to listen, so someone higher up is spelling it out. Your place is in the business with your sister, not teaching aerobics."

"My teaching aerobics had nothing to do with this, Mother," Deirdre declared. "I tripped on the stairs in my own town house. I fell. I broke my leg. I don't see any message there, except that I was careless. I left a magazine where it shouldn't have been and slipped on it. It could as easily have been *Forbes* as *Runner's World*."

"The message," Maria Joyce went on, undaunted, "is that physical fitness will only get you so far. For heaven's sake, Deirdre, you'll be sidelined for weeks. You can't teach your precious dance even if you want to. What better time is there to help Sandra out?"

Deirdre looked at her sister then. Once upon a time she'd have felt compassion for her, but that was before six months of nonstop pressure had taken its toll. "I'm sorry, Sandra. I can't."

"Why not, Dee?" Tall and dark-haired, Sandra took after their mother, while Deirdre was more fair and petite. She had been different from the start. "You have the same education I do, the same qualifications," Sandra pressed.

"I don't have the temperament. I never did."

Maria was scowling. "Temperament has nothing to do with it. You decided early on that you preferred to take the easy way out. Well, you have, and look where it's gotten you."

"Mother..." Deirdre closed her eyes and sank deeper into the pillows. Four days of confinement in a bed had left her weak, and that annoyed her. It had also left her craving a hot shower, but that was out of the question. To say that she was testy was putting it mildly.

Her voice was quiet, but there was clear conviction in her words. "We've been through this a hundred times. You and Dad may have shared the dream of a family corporation, but it's your dream, not mine. I don't want it. I'm not suited for it. It's too structured, too demanding. I gave it a try once and it was a disaster."

"Eight months," Maria argued, "years ago."

"Your mother's right, Deirdre." The deep, slightly gravelly voice belonged to Deirdre's uncle. He had been standing, silent and innocuous up to that point, at the foot of the bed. "You'd only just graduated from college, but even then you showed potential. You're a doer, like your father, but you were young and you let things overwhelm you. You left too soon. You didn't give it a fair shot."

Deirdre shook her head. "I knew myself then," she insisted, scrunching folds of the coarse white sheet between tense fingers, "and I know myself now. I'm not cut out for the business world. Having a technical aptitude for business is one thing. Maybe I do have that. But emotionally—what with board meetings, conferences, three-martini lunches, client dinners, being constantly *on*—I'd go stark raving mad!"

"You're being melodramatic," her mother scoffed.

"Right. That's the way I am, and there's no place for melodrama in Joyce Enterprises. So please," she begged, "please leave me out of it."

Sandra took a step closer. "We need you, Dee. *I* need you. Do you think I'm any more suited to heading a corporation than you are?"

"At least you want to do it."

"Whether I do or not is irrelevant. Things have been a mess since Dad died."

Since Dad died. That was the crux of it. Six months before, Allan Joyce had died in his sleep, never knowing that what he'd done so peacefully had created utter havoc.

Deirdre closed her eyes. "I think this conversation's going nowhere," she stated quietly. "The only reason things have been a mess since Dad died is that not one of you—of us—has the overall vision necessary to head a corporation. What Joyce Enterprises needs is outside help. It's as simple as that."

"We're a family-run company—" her mother began, only to stop short when Deirdre's eyes flew open, flashing.

"And we've run out of family. You can't run a business, Mother. Apparently neither can Sandra. Uncle Peter is as helpless as Uncle Max, and I'm the only one who's willing to acknowledge that the time has come for a change." She gave an exasperated sigh. "What astounds me most is that the corporation is still functioning. It's been running itself, coasting along on Dad's momentum. But without direction it's only a matter of time before it grinds to a halt. *Sell it*, Mother. And if you won't do that, hire a president and several vice presidents and—"

"We have a president and several vice presidents," Maria informed her unnecessarily. "What we lack is someone to coordinate things. You're the organizer. You're what we need. You're the one who's put together all kinds of functions."

"Charity functions, Mother. One, maybe two, a year. Benefit road races and sports days," she replied wearily. "We're not talking heavy business here."

"You're your father's daughter."

"I'm not my father."

"But still—"

"Mother, I have a wicked headache and you're not helping. Uncle Peter, will you please take Mother home?"

Maria held her ground. "Now just a minute, Deirdre. I won't be dismissed. You're being selfish. You've always put your own needs first. Don't you have any sense of responsibility toward this family?"

The guilt trip. It had been inevitable. "I'm not up to this," Deirdre moaned.

"Fine." Maria straightened. "Then we'll discuss it tomorrow. You're being discharged in the morning. We'll be here to pick you up and drive you to the house—"

"I'm not going to the house. I'm going to my place."

"With a broken leg? Don't be absurd, Deirdre. You can't climb those stairs."

"If I can't handle a flight of stairs, how can I possibly run a multimillion-dollar corporation from a seventeenth-floor office?"

"There are elevators."

"That's not the point, Mother!" Deirdre threw an arm over her eyes. She felt tired and unbelievably frustrated. It was nothing new. Just worse. "All I know," she managed stiffly, "is that I'm checking out of here tomorrow morning and going to my own town house. Where I go from there is anyone's guess, but it won't be to Joyce Enterprises."

"We'll discuss it tomorrow."

"There's nothing to discuss. It's settled."

Maria's chin gave a little twitch. It was a nervous gesture, one that appeared when she wasn't getting her way. Deirdre had caused it more times than either of them could count. "You're upset. It's understandable, given what you've been through." She patted her daughter's cheek. "Tomorrow. We'll talk tomorrow."

Deirdre said nothing. Lips set in a grim line, she watched her visitors pass one by one through the door. Alone at last, she pressed her finger hard on the call button.

Her head throbbed. Her leg throbbed. She needed aspirin.

She also needed a magic carpet to sweep her up, up and away.

This time when she glowered at her cast, there was no diversion intended. How could she have been so careless as to slip on that magazine? Why hadn't she caught herself, grabbed the banister? Why hadn't she just sat down and bumped her way to the bottom of the stairs?

But that would have been too simple. Deirdre the athlete had had to tumble head over heels. She'd had to catch her ankle in the banister, breaking her leg in three places.

Given the picture of coordination she'd projected day in day out for the past five years, it was downright embarrassing. Given the physical exertion her body was used to, her body craved, her present state was downright stifling.

It was also depressing. Her future was a huge question mark. Rather than a simple break, what she'd done to her leg had required intricate surgery to repair. She'd been trussed up in the hospital for four days. She'd be in the cast for six weeks more. She'd have to work her way through several weeks of physical therapy after that, and only *then* would she learn whether she'd be able to teach again.

As if her own problems weren't enough to bear, there was the matter of her family... and Joyce Enterprises. That provoked anger. Ever since her initial eight-month fiasco of a professional introduction to the company, she'd insisted that she wanted no part of it.

While he'd been alive, her father had put in repeated plugs. *Try it again, Deirdre. You'll grow to like it, Deirdre. If the business isn't for my children, who is it for, Deirdre?* After his death, her mother had picked up the gauntlet. Her sister and her uncles in turn had joined in later. And as the company had begun to fray at the edges, the pressure had increased.

Deirdre loved her own career. It was an outlet—demanding, creative and rewarding. She took pride in the fact that she was a good teacher, that she'd developed a loyal following, that her classes were packed to overflowing and that she'd become known as the queen of aerobics at the health club.

Her career had also been a convenient excuse, and now she was without.

A pair of aspirin eased the pain in her leg and, to some extent, her headache. Unfortunately, it did nothing to ease her dilemma. The prospect of leaving the hospital in the morning, and by doing so putting herself at the mercy of her family, was dismal. She could see it now—the phone calls, the drop-in visits, the ongoing and relentless campaign to draft her. Dismal. Unfair. *Unbearable.* If only there were someplace quiet, distant, secluded . . .

Sparked by a sudden determination, she grabbed the phone, dealing first with the hospital operator, then New York City information, then the hospital operator once more. At last her call went through.

A very proper maid answered. "Lesser residence."

"This is Deirdre Joyce. Is Mrs. Lesser in?"

"Please hold the phone."

Deirdre waited, tapping her finger impatiently against the plastic receiver. She shifted her weight from one bed-weary hip to the other. She squeezed her eyes shut, relieving herself of the sight of the sickroom. And she pictured Victoria, dressed no doubt in an oversized shirt and jeans, wending her way through the most elegant of surroundings to pick up the phone. Would she be coming from the music room, having just set down her cello? Or from tending African violets in her rooftop greenhouse?

Victoria was neither a musician nor a gardener, if skill was the measure. But whatever she did she loved, which was more than enough measure for Deirdre. Of all the family friends Deirdre had come to know in her twenty-nine years, Victoria Lesser was the one she most admired. Victoria was a freethinker, an individual. Rather than withering when the husband she'd loved had died, she'd blossomed and grown. She shunned parochialism and put protocol in its place. She did what she wanted, yet was always within the boundaries of good taste.

Deirdre enjoyed and respected her. It had been far too long since they'd seen each other.

"Hey, stranger," came the ebullient voice from the other end of the line, "where *have* you been?"

Deirdre gave a wan half smile. "Providence, as always, Victoria. How are you?"

"Not bad, if I do say so myself."

"What were you doing just now? I've been trying to imagine. Was it music? Gardening? Tell me. Make me smile."

"Oh-oh. Something's wrong."

For an instant Deirdre's throat grew tight. She hadn't spoken with Victoria in months, yet they could pick up a conversation as though it had been left off the day before. Despite the more than twenty years separating them, their relationship was honest.

Deirdre swallowed the knot. "What were you doing?"

"Stenciling the bathroom ceiling... Are you smiling?"

"A little."

"What's wrong, Dee?"

"I've always hated that nickname. Did you know? The only people who use it are members of my family... and you. When they do it, I feel like a child. When you do it, I feel like... a friend."

"You are," Victoria said softly, "which is why I want you to tell me what's wrong. Are they at it again?"

Deirdre sighed and threw an arm across the mop of sandy hair on her forehead. "With a vengeance. Only this time I'm operating from a position of weakness. I broke my leg. Can you believe it? Super athlete hits the dust."

Silence.

Deirdre's voice dropped an octave. "If you're laughing at me, Victoria, so help me . . ."

"I'm not laughing, sweetheart. I'm not laughing."

"You're smiling. I can hear it."

"It's either that or cry. The irony of it is too much. Of all the people to break a leg, you can stand it the least . . . no pun intended. Are you going stir-crazy?"

"I can see it coming fast. It's bad enough that I can't work out. Lord only knows when—or if—I'll be able to teach again. But they're closing in on me, and they're not about to let up until I either give in and go to the office or flip out completely." She took an uneven breath. "I need to get away, Victoria. There'll be no peace here and I have to think about what I'm going to do if . . . if I can't . . ." She didn't need to finish; Victoria felt her fear.

There was a pause. "You're thinking of Maine."

"If it'd be all right with you. You've mentioned it so often, but the timing's never been right. It might be just what I need now—distant enough, quiet, undemanding."

"And there's no phone."

"You do understand."

"Uh-huh." There was another pause, then a pensive, "Mmmm. Maine might be just what you need. When were you thinking of going?"

For the first time since her fall down the stairs, Deirdre felt a glimmer of spirit. "As soon as I can." Definitely. "Tomorrow, I guess." Why not! "But you'll have to tell me how to get there."

Victoria did so, giving her route and exit numbers. "Can you get someone to drive you?"

"I'll drive myself."

"What about your broken leg?"

"It's my left one."

"Ahhh. Be grateful for small favors."

"Believe me, I am. Okay, once I get to Spruce Head, what do I do?"

"Look for Thomas Nye. Big fellow. Bushy red beard. He lobsters from there. I'll call ahead and alert him. He'll take you out to the island."

Deirdre managed a smile then. "You are a true friend, Victoria. A lifesaver."

"I hope so," Victoria replied cautiously. "Will you give me a call when you get back to let me know how things went?"

Deirdre agreed, adding heartfelt thanks before she finally hung up the phone and lay back on the bed.

Victoria, on the other hand, merely pressed the disconnect button. When the line was clear, she put through her second call in as many hours to Thomas Nye. She wore a distinct look of satisfaction when she finally returned the receiver to its cradle.

IT WAS STILL RAINING. Strike that, Neil amended sourly. It was pouring.

He scowled past his streaming windshield to the rain-spattered road ahead. The storm had followed him north, he decided. Just his luck. From Connecticut, through Massachusetts, to New Hampshire, then Maine—four-plus hours of nonstop rain. Leaden skies promised more of the same.

His windshield wipers flicked from left to right and back in double time, yet the passing landscape blurred. He hadn't minded the lack of visibility when he'd been on the super-highway—there hadn't been much to see. But he was well off the turnpike now, following Route 1 through towns such as Bath, Wiscasset and Damariscotta. He would have welcomed the diversion of an occasional "down east" sight.

But all he saw was the dappling and redappling sweep of grays and browns, in the middle of which—demanding his constant attention—was the road. The only sounds he heard were the steady beat of rain on the roof of the car and the more rhythmic, if frantic, pulse of the wipers. The world smelled wet. He was tired of sitting. And his mind... His mind persisted in rummaging through the baggage it had brought along on the trip.

Shortly before three in the afternoon, his mood as dark as the clouds overhead, Neil pulled his black LeBaron to a stop alongside the weathered wharf at Spruce Head. He should have been relieved that the arduous drive was over. He should have felt uplifted, filled with anticipation, eager to be nearing his destination.

What he felt was dismay. The docks were mucky. Visibility beyond the moored but wildly bobbing boats was practically nil. And the stench in the air, seeping steadily into the car, was nearly overpowering.

Distastefully he studied the large lobster tanks lined up on the wharf, then the nearby vats filled with dead fish, rotting for use as lobster bait. His own fondness for lobster meat in no way made the smell easier to take.

A gust of wind buffeted the car, driving the rain against it with renewed fury. Neil sat back in the seat and swore softly. What he needed, he decided, were a fisherman's oilskins. As far as he could see, though, not even the fishermen were venturing outside.

Unfortunately he had to venture. He had to find Thomas Nye.

Retrieving his Windbreaker from the back seat, he struggled into it. Then, on a single sucked-in breath, he opened the car door, bolted out, slammed the door behind him and raced to the nearest building.

The first door he came to opened with a groan. Three men sat inside what appeared to be a crude office, though Neil doubted he'd interrupted serious work. Each man held a mug filled with something steaming. Two of the chairs were tipped back on their hind legs; the third was being straddled backside-to.

All three men looked up at his entrance, and Neil was almost grateful for his disheveled appearance. His hair was damp and mussed; a day's worth of stubble darkened his cheeks. His Windbreaker and worn jeans were rain spattered, his running shoes mud spattered, as well. He felt right at home.

"I'm looking for Thomas Nye," he announced straightaway. Fishermen were laconic; that suited him fine. He was in no mood for polite chitchat. "Big fellow with a bushy red beard?"

One chair and one chair only hit the floor. Its occupant propped his elbows on his knees and gestured with a single hand. "Down a block . . . feust left . . . second house on y'or right."

Nodding, Neil left. Head ducked low against the torrent, he dashed back to the car and threw himself inside. Rain dripped from his Windbreaker onto the leather seats, but he paid no heed. In the short minutes since he'd arrived at Spruce Head, his focus had narrowed. Reaching Victoria's island and shutting himself inside her house to avail himself of that highly acclaimed master bedroom with its walls of glass, its huge stone fireplace and its quilt-covered king-size bed seemed all-important.

Taking a minute to decide which way was "down" the block, he started the car and set off. One left later he turned, then pulled up at the second house on the right. It was one of several in a row on the street, and he might have said it had charm had he been in a better mood. It was small, white with gray shutters and, with its paint peeling sadly, looked as aged as he felt.

Loath to waste time, he ran from the car and up the short front walk. Seeing no doorbell, he knocked loudly enough to make himself heard above the storm. Shortly the door was opened by a big fellow with a bushy red beard.

Neil sighed. "Thomas Nye."

The man nodded, held the door wide and cocked his head toward the inside of the house. Neil accepted his invitation instantly.

LESS THAN AN HOUR LATER, Deirdre pulled up at the same house. She looked in turn at the humble structure, then at the sporty black car parked in front of her. Even had she not seen the Connecticut license plate she would have bet it wasn't the car of a lobsterman.

Thomas Nye apparently had guests and the thought didn't thrill her. She wasn't exactly at her best—an assessment, she realized, that was decidedly kind.

She'd been lucky. A passerby at the wharf had given her directions, sparing her a dash from the car. Not that she could dash. Or even walk. Hobble was more like it.

But her luck had run out. She was at Thomas Nye's house and there was no way she could speak to the man without leaving the haven of her car. That meant hauling out her crutches, extricating her casted leg from the hollow to the left of the brake and maneuvering herself to a standing position. It also meant getting wet.

Well, why not! she snapped to herself. The day had been a nightmare from the start. What was a little more grief?

Tugging her hip-length Goretex parka from the back seat, she struggled into it. Then, taking a minute to work out the logistics of dealing with cast, crutches and rain, she opened the car door and set to it.

By the time she reached Thomas Nye's front door, she was gritting her teeth in frustration. What might have taken ten seconds, had she been operating on two strong legs, had taken nearly two minutes—long enough for the storm to drench her. Her hair was plastered to her head and dripping in her eyes. Her sweatpants were noticeably heavier. Her wet grip on the crutches was precarious. And her armpits ached.

Tamping down her irritation as best she could, she shifted her weight to one crutch and knocked. As the small porch overhang offered some protection from the gusting rain, she wedged herself closer to the door.

She twitched her nose. The rank odor that had hit her full force at the wharf was less pungent here, diluted by the fresh salty air and the rain.

She tugged at her collar. She was cold. Impatient, she knocked again, louder this time. Within seconds, the door was opened by a big fellow with a bushy red beard.

Deirdre sighed. "Thomas Nye."

Eyes skittering away, he nodded, held the door wide and cocked his head toward the inside of the house. She hitched her way into the narrow front hall, and at another silent gesture from the large man, into the small living room.

The first thing she saw was a low table spread with papers, charts and what looked to be bills. The second was the television set, broadcasting *Wheel of Fortune* in living color. The third was the dark, brooding figure of a man slouched in a chair in the far corner of the room.

The fourth thing she noticed, unfortunately, was that Thomas Nye had calmly settled into a seat by the table, returning to the work her knock had apparently interrupted.

She cleared her throat. "You were expecting me."

"That's right," he said. He had already lifted several papers, and didn't look up. "Want to sit?"

"Uh . . . are we . . . going?"

"Not now."

She ingested that information with as much aplomb as she could, given that the last thing she wanted was a delay. "It's the weather, I take it?" The possibility had been niggling at the back of her mind for the past hour. She'd done her best to ignore it.

The man in the corner grunted.

Thomas Nye nodded.

"Do you have any idea when we *will* be able to go?" she asked, discouraged; it seemed like forever since she'd awoken that morning. She now had to admit that making the trip on the same day as her discharge from the hospital may have been taking too much upon herself. But it was done. The best she could hope for was that the delay would be minimal.

In answer to her question, the bearded man shrugged. "As soon as it lets up."

"But it could rain for days," she returned. When a second grunt came from the man in the corner, she darted him a scowl. At the moment all she wanted was to be dry and warm beneath a heavy quilt on that king-size bed in the house on Victoria's island. Alone. With no one to stare at the sorry sight she made and no one to make her feel guilty about anything.

She willed her concentration on Nye. "I thought you went lobstering rain or no rain."

"The wind's the problem." At precisely that moment a gust howled around the house.

Deirdre shuddered. "I see." She paused. "Is there a forecast? Do you have any idea when it will let up?"

Nye shrugged. "An hour, maybe two, maybe twelve."

She leaned heavily on the crutches. An hour or two she could live with. But twelve? She doubted she could last twelve hours without that warm, dry bed and heavy quilt. And where would she be waiting out the time?

She glanced again at the man in the corner. He sat low in his chair, one leg stretched out, the other ankle crossed over his knee. His elbows were propped on the arms of the chair, his mouth pressed flush against knuckle-to-knuckle fists. His eyebrows were dark, the eyes beneath them even darker. He, too, was waiting. She could sense his frustration as clearly as she felt her own.

"Uh, Mr. Nye," she began, "I really have to get out there soon. If I don't get off this leg, I'm apt to be in trouble."

Nye was jotting something on the top of one of the papers that lay before him. He lifted his gaze to the game show and gestured with his pencil toward a faded sofa. "Please. Sit."

Deirdre watched as he resumed his work. She contemplated arguing further but sensed the futility of it. He looked calm, satisfied...and utterly immovable. With a grimace she plodded to the sofa. Jerking off her wet parka, she thrust it over the back of the worn cushion, coupled her crutches to one side of her and eased her way down.

When she lifted her eyes once more, she found the man in the corner staring at her. Irritated, she glared back. "Is something wrong?"

He arched a brow, lowered his fists and pursed his lips. "That's quite an outfit." It wasn't a compliment.

"Thank you," she said sweetly. "I rather like it myself." Actually, when they were dry, the roomy pink sweatpants were the most comfortable ones she owned, and comfort was a high priority, what with a cast the size of hers. Unfortunately, while dressing, she'd also been fighting with her mother, and consequently she'd pulled on the first sweatshirt that came to hand. It was teal colored, oversized and as comfortable as the pants, though it did clash slightly. And if the man had an argument with her orange leg warmers, that was his problem. The left one, stretched out and tucked into itself beyond her foot, had kept her toes warm and her cast dry. Her lone sneaker on the other foot, was pitifully wet.

So she didn't look like Jaclyn Smith advertising makeup. Deirdre didn't care. In the immediate future, she was going to be all alone on an island. No one would see her. No one would care what she wore. Practicality and comfort were the two considerations she'd made when deciding what to bring with her. The man with the dark, brooding eyes could thank his lucky stars he wouldn't have to see her beyond this day.

Muted pandemonium broke loose on the television screen as a player won a shiny red Mercedes. Looking up, Thomas grinned at the victory, but Deirdre merely lowered her head and pressed chilled fingers to the bridge of her nose. She hated game shows almost as much as she hated soap operas. On occasion when she passed through the lounge of the health club, the set would be tuned to one or the other. Invariably she'd speed on by.

Now she was speeding nowhere. That fact was even more grating than the sound of the show. Disgruntled, she shoved aside the wet strands of hair on her brow and focused on Thomas Nye.

Head tucked low once again, he was engrossed in his paperwork. He looked almost preppy, she reflected, appraising his corduroy pants, the shirt and sweater. A man of few words, and those spoken with a New York accent, he was apparently a transplant. Deirdre wondered about that. Was he antiestablishment? Antisocial? Or simply...shy? He seemed unable to meet her gaze for more than a minute, and though he was pleasant enough, he made no attempt at conversation. Nor had he introduced her to the man in the corner.

Just as well, she decided as she shifted her gaze. The man in the corner didn't appear to be anyone she'd care to meet. He was frowning toward the window now, his fist propped back against his cheek. The furrow between his brows was marked. His lips held a sullen slant. And if those signs of discontent weren't off-putting enough, the heavy shadow of a beard on his lower face gave him an even less inviting appearance.

Just then he looked her way. Their eyes met and held, until at last she turned her head. No, he wasn't anyone she'd care to meet, because he looked just as troubled as she was, and there was precious little room in her life for compassion at the moment.

At the moment, Neil Hersey was thinking similar thoughts. It had been a long time since he'd seen anyone as pathetic-looking as the woman across the room. Oh, yes, the weather had taken its toll, soaking her clothes and matting her short, brown hair in damp strands that grazed her eyelids. But it was more than that. The weather had nothing to do with the fact that she had one fat leg and an overall shapeless figure. Or that she was pale. Or that her crossness seemed to border on orneriness. He assumed Nye was shuttling her to one of the many islands in the Gulf of Maine. But he had woes enough to keep him occupied without bothering about someone else's.

His immediate woe was being landlocked. Time was passing. He wanted to be moving out. But Thomas Nye was calling the shots, a situation that only exacerbated Neil's dour mood.

He shifted restlessly and absently rubbed his hand over the rough rag wool of his sweater. Was that heartburn he felt? Maybe an incipient ulcer? He took a disgusted breath, shifted again and was about to glance at his watch, when he saw the woman do it.

"Mr. Nye?" she asked.

"Thomas," Nye answered without looking up.

"Thomas. How long will the crossing take?"

"Two hours, give or take some."

She studied her watch again, making the same disheartening calculations Neil did. "But if we're held up much longer, we won't make it before dark." It would be bad enough negotiating rugged terrain in daylight with her crutches, but at night? "That . . . could be difficult."

"Better difficult than deadly," Thomas replied gently. "As soon as the wind dies down, we'll go. We may have to wait till morning."

"Morning! But I don't have anywhere to stay," she protested.

Thomas tossed his head toward the ceiling. "I've got room."

She gave an exaggerated nod, which said *that* solved everything, when in fact it didn't. It wasn't what she wanted at all! She wanted to be on Victoria's island, comfortably settled in that spectacular master bedroom she'd heard so much about. She pictured it now—huge windows, an elegant brass bed, dust ruffles, quilt and pillows of a country-sophisticate motif. Silence. Solitude. Privacy. Oh, how she wanted that.

The awful fatigue she was fighting now she did not want. Or the ache in her leg that no amount of shifting could relieve. Or the fact that she was in a room with two strangers and she couldn't throw back her head and scream . . .

Neil had returned his attention to the window. What he saw there wasn't pleasing; the thought of spending the night in this tiny fisherman's house was even less so. *I've got room.* It was a generous enough offer, but hell, he didn't want to be here! He wanted to be on the island!

He was exhausted. The day's drive through the rain had been a tedious cap to six tedious weeks. He wanted to be alone. He wanted privacy. He wanted to stretch out on that king-size bed and know that his feet wouldn't hang over the edge. Lord only knew most everything else had gone wrong with his life lately.

"Does the boat have radar?" he asked on impulse.

"Yes."

"So we're not limited to daylight."

"No."

"Then there's still a chance of getting out today?"

"Of course there's a chance," Deirdre snapped, testy in her weariness. "There's always a chance."

Neil shot her a quelling look. "Then let's put it in terms of probability," he stated stubbornly, returning his attention to Thomas. "On a scale of one to ten, where would you put the chances of our making it out today?"

Deirdre scowled. "How can he possibly answer that?"

"He's a fisherman," Neil muttered tersely. "I'm asking for his professional estimate based on however many number of years he's worked on the sea."

"Three," Thomas said.

Deirdre's eyes were round with dismay. "On a scale of one to ten, we only get a *three*?"

Neil eyed her as though she were daft. "He's only been lobstering for three years."

"Oh." She then focused on Thomas. "What *are* the chances?

Thomas straightened a pile of papers and stood. "Right now I'd give it a two."

"A two," she wailed. "That's even worse!"

Neil glowered toward the window. Thomas stood. The Wheel of Fortune spun, gradually slowing, finally stopping on "bankrupt." The groans from the set reflected Deirdre's feelings exactly.

But she wouldn't give up. "How do you decide if we can leave?"

"The marine report."

"How often does that change?"

"Whenever the weather does."

The man in the corner snickered. Deirdre ignored him. "I mean, are there periodic updates you tune in to? How can you possibly tell, sitting here in the house, whether the wind is dying down on the water?"

Thomas was heading from the room. "I'll be back."

She looked at the man. "Where's he going?" He stared back mutely. "You're waiting to get out of here, too. Aren't you curious?"

Neil sighed. "He's getting the forecast."

"How can you tell?"

"Can't you hear the crackle of the radio?"

"I can't hear a thing over this inane show!" Awkwardly she pushed herself up, hopped to the television and turned the volume down, then hopped back. She was too tired to care if she looked like a waterlogged rabbit. Sinking into a corner of the sofa, she lifted her casted leg onto the cushions, laid her head back and closed her eyes.

Moments later Thomas returned. "Raise that to a seven. The wind's dying."

Neil and Deirdre both grew alert, but it was Neil who spoke. "Then we may make it?"

"I'll check the report in another half-hour." The lobsterman said no more, immersing himself back in his work.

The next half-hour seemed endless to Deirdre. Her mind replayed the events of the day, from her hospital discharge through the cab ride to her town house, then on to the unpleasant scene with her mother, who had been positively incensed that Deirdre would even think of leaving Providence. Deirdre would have liked to believe it was maternal concern for her health, but she knew otherwise. Her refusal to tell Maria where she was headed had resulted in even stronger reprisals, but Deirdre couldn't bear the thought that some-how her mother would get through to her on the island.

She needed this escape. She needed it badly. The way she felt, she doubted she'd get out of bed for days . . . when she finally reached the island.

Neil didn't weather the half-hour any better. Accustomed to being constantly on the move, he felt physically confined and mentally constrained. At times he thought he'd scream if something didn't happen. Everything grated—the lobster-man's nonchalance, the flicker of the television, the sight of the woman across the room, the sound of the rain. Too much of his life seemed dependent on external forces; he craved full control. Misery was private. He wanted to be alone.

At long last Thomas left the room again. Deirdre raised her head and held her breath. Neil waited tensely.

From the look on the fisherman's face when he returned, it seemed nothing had changed. Yet the first thing he did was flip off the television, then he gathered up his papers.

Aware that the man in the corner was holding himself straighter, Deirdre did the same. "Thomas?"

He said nothing, simply gestured broadly with his arms. Deirdre and Neil needed no more invitation. Within seconds, they were up and reaching for their jackets.

2

THE STORM MIGHT HAVE ABATED over the water, but Deirdre saw no letup on shore. The rain soaked her as she limped on her crutches to her car, which, at Thomas's direction, she moved to the deepest point in the driveway. Transferring her large duffle bag to the pickup was a minor ordeal, eased at the last minute by Thomas, who tossed her bag in, then returned to stowing boxes of fresh produce in the back of the truck. The other man was preoccupied, parking his own car, then loading his bag.

Gritting her teeth, she struggled into the cab of the truck. No sooner was she seated than the two men—the dark one, to her chagrin, had turned out to be every bit as large as the lobsterman—boxed her in, making the ensuing ride to the wharf damp and uncomfortable. By the time she was aboard Thomas's boat, propped on a wood bench in the enclosed pilothouse, she felt stiff and achy. Her sneaker was soggy. Her jacket and sweatpants were wet. She was chilled all over.

The nightmare continued, she mused, but at least its end was in sight. She'd be at Victoria's island, alone and in peace, by nightfall. It was this knowledge that kept her going.

The engine chugged to life and maintained an even growl as the boat left the wharf and headed seaward. Deirdre peered out the open back of the pilothouse for a time, watching Spruce Head recede and finally disappear in the mist. Burrowing deeper into her jacket, she faced forward then and determinedly focused on her destination. She pictured the island forested with pines, carpeted with moss, smelling of earth, sea and sky, kissed by the sun. She envisioned her own recovery there, the regaining of her strength, the rebirth of her spirit. And serenity. She conjured images of serenity.

Just as Neil did. Serenity...solitude... Soon, he told himself, soon. He'd wedged himself into a corner of the pilothouse, not so much to keep a distance from Nye's other passenger as to keep his body upright. It had been a long day, a long night before that. He'd grown accustomed to sleeplessness over the past weeks, but never had its effects hit him as they did now.

Though his fatigue was in large part physical, there was an emotional element as well. He was away from the office, relieved of his duties, distanced from his profession. This wasn't a vacation; it was a suspension. Brief, perhaps, but a letdown. And more than a little depressing.

A tiny voice inside accused him of running away; his abrupt departure from Hartford was sure to be seen by some as just that. Maybe he had run away. Maybe he was conceding defeat. Maybe...maybe... It was very depressing.

His pulse was steadily accelerating, as it always did when he pursued that particular line of thought. He wondered if he had high blood pressure yet. It wouldn't have surprised him, given the kind of nervous tension he'd been living with for days on end. He needed an outlet. Any outlet.

His gaze settled on the woman just down the bench. "Don't you think it's a little stupid going out in all this like that?" He jerked his chin toward the fat leg she'd painstakingly hauled up beside her on the hard bench.

Deirdre had been wondering apprehensively if the rhythmic plunge of the boat, noticeable now that they'd left the harbor behind, was going to get worse. She looked at him in disbelief. "Excuse me?"

"I said, don't you think it's a little stupid going out in all this like that?" He found perverse satisfaction in the verbatim repetition.

"That's what I thought you said, but I couldn't believe you'd be so rude." She had no patience. Not now. Not here. "Didn't your mother ever teach you manners?"

"Oh, yes. But she's not here right now, so I can say exactly what I want." Ah, the pleasure in blurting words out at will. He couldn't remember the last time he'd done it as freely. "You haven't answered my question."

"It's not worth answering." She turned her head away and looked at Thomas, who stood at the controls, holding the wheel steady. His body swayed easily with the movement of the boat. Deirdre wished she could go with the flow that way, but her own body seemed to buck the movement. She was glad she hadn't eaten recently.

In an attempt to divert her thoughts from various unpleasant possibilities, she homed in on the baseball hat Thomas had been wearing since they'd left the house. It had fared unbelievably well in the rain. "Are you a Yankees' fan, Thomas?" she called above the rumble of the motor.

Thomas didn't turn. "When they win."

"That's honest enough," she murmured under her breath, then raised her voice again. "You're originally from New York?"

"That's right."

"What part?"

"Queens."

"Do you still have family there?"

"Some."

"What were you doing before you became a lobsterman?"

A grumble came from the corner. "Leave the man alone. He's hardly encouraging conversation. Don't you think there's a message in that?"

Deirdre stared back at him. "He's a Maine fisherman. They're all tight-lipped."

"But he's not originally from Maine, which means that he *chooses* not to speak."

"I wish *you* would," she snapped. "I've never met anyone as disagreeable in my life." She swung back to the lobsterman. "How'd you get saddled with this one, Thomas? He's a peach."

Thomas didn't answer, but continued his study of the white-capped waves ahead.

Neil propped his elbow on the back of the bench, rested his cheek in his palm and closed his eyes.

Deirdre focused on a peeling panel of wood opposite her and prayed that her stomach would settle.

Time passed. The boat had the ocean to itself as it plowed steadily through the waves amid an eerie air of isolation. The smell of fish mingled with a decidedly musty odor, whether from wet clothing, wet skin or aged wood Deirdre didn't know, but it did nothing for the condition of her insides. She took to doing yoga breathing, clearing her mind, concentrating on relaxation. She wasn't terribly successful.

At length she spoke again, clearly addressing herself to Thomas. "Two hours, more or less, you said. Will it be more, in weather like this?" The rain hadn't let up and the sea was choppy, but, to her untrained eye, they were making progress.

"We're in luck. The wind's at our back."

She nodded, grateful for the small word of encouragement. Then she shifted, bending her good knee up and wrapping her arms around it.

"You look green," came an unbidden assessment from the corner.

She sighed. "Thank you."

"Are you seasick?"

"I'm fine."

"I think you're seasick."

Lips thinned, she swiveled around. "You'd like that, wouldn't you? You'd like to see me sick. What's the matter? Are *you* feeling queasy?"

"I'm a seasoned sailor."

"So am I," she lied, and turned away. Straightening her leg, she sat forward on the bench. Then, fingers clenched on its edge, she pushed herself up and hopped toward Thomas.

"How much longer?" she asked as softly as she could. She didn't want the man in the corner to hear the anxiety in her words. Unfortunately Thomas didn't hear the words at all. When he tipped his head toward her, she had to repeat herself.

"We're about halfway there," he replied eventually. On the one hand it was reassuring; halfway there was better than nothing. On the other hand, it was depressing; another full hour to endure.

"His island's near Matinicus, too?" The slight emphasis on the "his" told Thomas who she meant.

"There are several small islands in the area."

She moved closer and spoke more softly again. "Will you drop me first? I'm not sure I can take much more of this."

"I'm heading straight for Victoria's island."

She managed a wan smile and a grateful "Thank you" before maneuvering back to her seat. She avoided looking at the man in the corner. He raised her hackles. She didn't need the added aggravation, when so much of the past week had been filled with it.

Neil was brooding, thinking of the last time he'd been on a boat. A seasoned sailor? He guessed it was true. Nancy had had a boat. She loved boats. Supposedly she'd loved him, too, but that had been when he'd had the world on a string. At the first sign of trouble she'd recoiled. Granted, her brother was on the board at Wittnauer-Douglass, so she'd been in an awkward position when Neil had been summarily dismissed. Still . . . love was love . . . Or was it?

He hadn't loved Nancy. He'd known it for months, and had felt guilty every time she'd said the words. Now he had a particularly sour taste in his mouth. Her words had been empty. She hadn't loved him—she'd loved what he was. She'd been enthralled by the image of a successful corporate attorney, the affluence and prestige. With all that now in doubt, she was playing it safe. And it was just as well, he knew, a blessing in disguise, perhaps. A fair-weather lover was the last thing he needed.

He looked over at the woman on the bench. She was another can of worms entirely. Small and shapeless, unpolished, unsociable, unfeminine—quite a switch from Nancy. "What did you do to your leg?" he heard himself ask.

Deirdre raised her head. "Are you talking to me?"

He glanced around the pilothouse. "I don't see anyone else with crutches around here. Did you break it?"

"Obviously."

"Not 'obviously.' You could have had corrective surgery for a congenital defect, or for a sports injury."

A sports injury. If only. There might have been dignity in that. But falling down a flight of stairs? "I broke it," she stated curtly.

"How?"

"It doesn't matter."

"When?"

Deirdre scowled. "It doesn't *matter*."

"My Lord, and you called *me* disagreeable!"

She sighed wearily. "I'm not in the mood for talking. That's all."

"You still look green." He gave a snide grin. "Stomach churning?"

"My stomach is fine!" she snapped. "And I'm not green...just pale. It's the kind of color you catch when you've been surrounded by hospital whites for days."

"You mean you were just released?" he asked with genuine surprise.

"This morning."

"And you're off racing through the rain to get to a remote island?" Surprise gave way to sarcasm once more.

"It's only a broken leg! The rest of me is working fine." Not quite true, but an understandable fib. "And, in case you're wondering, I didn't personally request the rain. It just came!"

"You were crazy to come out. Didn't your mother try to stop you?"

She heard the ridicule in his tone and was reminded of her earlier shot at him. Hers had been offered facetiously, as had his, yet he'd unwittingly hit a raw nerve. "She certainly did, but I'm an adult, so I don't have to listen to her!" She turned her head away, but it did no good.

"You don't look like an adult. You look like a pouting child."

Her eyes shot back to him reproachfully. "Better a pouting child than a scruffy pest! Look, why don't you mind your own business? You don't know me, and I don't know you, and before long, thank goodness, this ride will be over. You don't need to take out your bad mood on me. Just stay in your corner and brood to yourself, okay?"

"But I enjoy picking on you. You rise to the occasion."

That was the problem. She was letting him get to her. The way to deal with a man of his ilk was to ignore him, which she proceeded to do. Whether it worked or not she wasn't sure, because she suspected he had freely chosen not to speak further.

But he continued to look at her. She could feel his eyes boring into her back, and she steadfastly refused to turn. The man had gall; she had to hand it to him. He wasn't spineless, as Seth had been....

Seth. Sweet Seth. Parasitic Seth. He'd slipped into her world, taken advantage of her home, her job, her affections, and then turned tail and run when the family pressure had begun. Seth hadn't wanted ties. He hadn't wanted responsibility. And the last thing he'd wanted was a woman whose career demands and family responsibilities took precedence over his own needs.

The irony of it, Deirdre reflected, was that he'd had such little understanding of her. She'd never wanted Joyce Enterprises, and she'd told him so repeatedly. But he'd still felt threatened, so he'd left. In hindsight, she was better off without him.

She was drawn from her reverie when the man in the corner rose from the bench, crossed the pilothouse and positioned himself close by Thomas. He spoke in a low murmur, which, try as she might, Deirdre couldn't hear over the guttural drone of the engine.

"How much longer?" Neil asked.

Thomas glanced at one of his dials. "Half an hour."

"Where's she going?" He put a slight emphasis on the "she."

"Near Matinicus."

"Lots of islands, are there?"

"Some."

"Who gets dropped off first?"

"I'm heading straight for Victoria's island."

Neil considered that. "Look, it's okay with me if you drop her off first. She's really pretty pathetic."

Thomas's eyes remained on the sea. "I thought you didn't like her."

"I don't. She bugs the hell out of me. Then again—" he ran a hand across his aching neck "—just about anyone would bug the hell out of me right about now. She just happens to be here." He was feeling guilty, but was torn even about that. On the one hand, arguing with the woman was thoroughly satisfying. He needed to let off steam, and she was a perfect patsy. On the other hand, she was right. He'd been rude. It wasn't his normal way.

Head down, he started back toward his corner.

Deirdre, who'd been thinking just then about how badly she wanted, *needed* a bath, and what an unbelievable hassle it was going to be trying to keep her cast out of the water, stopped him mid-way. She was feeling particularly peevish. "If you think you can con Thomas into dropping you off first, don't hold your breath. He's already set a course and it happens that *my* island's up there at the top of the list."

"Shows how much *you* know," Neil mumbled under his breath. He passed her by, slid down into his corner of the bench, crossed his arms over his chest and stared straight ahead.

Deirdre passed his comment off as a simple case of sour grapes. He was an ill-humored man. Soon enough she'd be free of his company. Soon enough she'd be at the island.

"There it is," Thomas called over his shoulder a little while later. "Victoria's island."

Deirdre pushed herself to her good knee and peered through the front windshield. "I can't see a thing."

Neil, too, had risen. "No harm," he muttered.

"Do you see anything?"

"Sure. There's a dark bump out there."

"There's a world of dark bumps out there. How do you tell which one's a wave and which one's an island?"

"The island has trees."

The logic was irrefutable. "Swell," she said, sinking back into her seat. When they reached the island they'd reach the island. She'd have plenty of time to see it, time when she wouldn't be tired and uncomfortable and thoroughly out of sorts.

Neil stood by Thomas, watching the dark bump swell and rise and materialize into an honest-to-goodness land mass. It wasn't large, perhaps half a mile square, but it was surprisingly lush. Neither the rain, nor the clouds, nor the approach of dusk could disguise the deep green splendor of the pines. And the house was there, a rambling cape-style structure of weathered gray clapboard, nestling in a clearing overlooking the dock.

Deirdre was on her knee again. "That . . . is . . . beautiful," she breathed.

Neil, who was feeling rather smug at the perfection of his destination, darted her an indulgent glance. "I agree."

"For once. I was beginning to wonder if you had any taste at all."

His indulgence ended. "Oh, I've got taste, all right. Problem is that I haven't seen a thing today that even remotely appealed to it." His eyes didn't stray from her face, making his meaning clear.

It was an insult Deirdre simply couldn't let pass. "The feeling is mutual. In fact—"

"Excuse me," Thomas interrupted loudly, "I'll need everyone's help here. And it's still pouring, so we'd better work quickly." He was already cutting the engine and guiding the boat alongside the short wooden dock. "Neil, you go outside and throw the lines onto the dock, one at the bow, one at the stern. Then hop ashore and tie us up on those pilings. I'll pass supplies to you and Deirdre. Watch yourself on the dock, Deirdre. It'll be slippery."

Deirdre nodded and worked at the wet zipper of her parka, thinking what a waste it was to give a nice name like Neil to such an obnoxious man. But at least he was helping. She'd half expected him to insist on staying dry while Thomas got her set up on shore.

Neil zipped up his jacket and headed for the open pit of the boat's stern, thinking how ironic it was that a woman with as flowing a name as Deirdre should prove to be so thorny. But at least she'd agreed to help. That surprised him. Of course, Thomas hadn't exactly given her a choice.

"The line, Neil. We're here." Thomas's call ended all silent musings.

Head ducked against the rain, Neil raced to tie up the boat, bow and stern.

Biting her lip against a clumsiness foreign to her, Deirdre managed to lumber onto the dock with only a helping hand from Thomas. When she would have thanked him, he'd already turned away to begin off-loading. He handed things, first to her, then to Neil when he reached her side.

"I'll be back in a week with fresh supplies," instructed the lobsterman hurriedly. "These should be more than enough until then. Keys to the front door are in an envelope tucked in with the eggs. If you run into a problem, any kind of emergency, you can reach me on the ship-to-shore radio in the den. The directions are right beside it."

Deirdre nodded, but she was too busy concentrating on keeping her balance to answer. When her large duffel bag came over the side of the boat, she rearranged her crutches and somehow managed to hook the wide strap of the bag over her shoulder, then return the crutches to their pre-scribed position without falling.

Neil, busy piling boxes of supplies atop one another to keep them as dry as possible, looked up briefly when Thomas handed over his canvas cargo bag. He set it down on the dock, finished up with the supplies, put a box in one arm and the cargo bag's broad strap over his other shoulder, then turned back to thank Thomas.

The boat was already drifting away from the dock, which didn't surprise Neil. Thomas had said they'd work quickly. But there was something that did surprise him....

Deirdre, whose eyes had gone wide in alarm, cleared her throat. "Uh, Thomas?" When the boat slipped farther away, she tried again, louder this time. "Thomas?"

The engine coughed, then started.

This time it was Neil who yelled. "Nye! You've forgotten someone! Get back here!"

The boat backed around the tip of the dock, then turned seaward.

"Thomas!"

"Nye!"

"There's been a mistake!" Deirdre shrieked, shoving her dripping hair from her eyes, then pointing to Neil. "*He*'s still here!"

Neil rounded on her. His face was soaked, but his eyes were hard as steel. "Of course I'm still here! This is my friend's island!"

"It's *Victoria's* island, and Victoria is *my* friend."

"*My* friend, and she didn't mention you. She said I'd have the place all to myself!"

"Which was exactly what she told me!"

They glared at each other amid the pouring rain. "Victoria who?" Neil demanded.

"Victoria Lesser. Who's your Victoria?"

"The same."

"I don't believe you. Tell me where she lives."

"Manhattan. Park Avenue."

"She is Mrs. Arthur Lesser. Tell me about Arthur."

"He's dead. She's a widow, a wonderful . . . wacky. . ."

"Conniving . . ."

Scowling at each other amid encroaching darkness on that windswept dock in the rain, Deirdre and Neil reached the same conclusion at once.

"We've been had," he stated, then repeated in anger, "we've been had!"

"I don't believe it," Deirdre murmured, heart pounding as she looked out to sea. "Oh, damn," she breathed. "He's going!"

Simultaneously they began to yell.

"Thomas! Come back here!"

"Nye! Turn around!"

"Thomas! Don't do this to me, Thomas! Thomas!" But Thomas was well beyond earshot and moving steadily toward the mainland.

"That creep!" Neil bellowed. "He was in on it! Victoria must have known precisely what she was doing, and he went along with it!"

Deirdre didn't remember ever being as miserable in her life. All that she'd faced at home, all that she'd escaped was nothing compared to this having been manipulated. Her frustration was almost paralyzing. She took a ragged breath and tried to think clearly. "I've come all this way, gone through hell . . ." She brushed the rain from her cheek and looked at Neil. "You can't stay! That's all there is to it!"

Neil, who felt rain trickling down his neck, was livid. "What do you mean, I can't stay? I don't know what brought you here, but whatever it was, I need this island more, and I have no intention of sharing it with a sharp-tongued, physically disabled . . . urchin!"

She shook her head, sure she was imagining it all. "I don't have to take this," she spat. Turning, she set her crutches before her and started along the murky dock toward the even murkier path.

Neil was beside her. "You're right. You *don't* have to take it. I'll put through a call to Thomas and get him to come back tomorrow to pick you up."

Deirdre kept her eyes on the wet boarding, then the muddy dirt path. "I have no intention of being picked up, not until I'm good and ready to leave! You can put through that call to Thomas and have him pick *you* up!"

"No way! I came here for peace and quiet, and that's exactly what I'm going to get."

"You can get peace and quiet somewhere else. You sure can't get it with me around, and I sure can't get it with you around, and I don't know how you know Victoria, but she's been a friend of my family's for years and I'm sure she'll give me the right to this place—"

"*Right* to this place? Look at you! You can barely make it to the door!"

He wasn't far off the mark. The path was wet and slippery, slowing her progress considerably. It was sheer grit that kept her going. "I'll make it," she fumed, struggling to keep her footing on the slick incline. "And once I'm inside I'm not budging."

They reached the front steps. Deirdre hobbled up, then crossed the porch to the door. Neil, who'd taken the steps by twos, was standing there, swearing. "Tucked in beside the eggs . . ." He dropped his bag under the eaves, out of the rain, set down the box he'd carried and began to rummage through it. He swore again, then turned and retraced his steps at a run.

Weakly Deirdre leaned against the damp clapboard by the door. Pressing her forehead to the wood, she welcomed its chill against her surprisingly hot temple. The rest of her felt cold and clammy. She was shaking and perilously close to tears. How could the perfect solution have gone so wrong?

And there was nothing to be done about it, at least not until tomorrow. That was the worst of it.

Then again, perhaps it wasn't so bad. Once inside the house, she intended to go straight to bed. She didn't care if it was barely seven o'clock. She was beat and cold, perhaps feverish. Neil whoever-he-was could do whatever he wanted; she was going to sleep through the night. By the time she got up tomorrow, she'd be able to think clearly.

Neil dashed up the steps, his arms laden with boxes.

"I can't believe you did that," she cried. "You've got every last one of them piled up. It's a miracle you didn't drop them on the path, and then where would I be?"

He tossed his head back, getting his hair out of his eyes and the rain out of his hair. "Be grateful I did it myself. I could have asked you to help."

She wasn't in the mood to be grateful. "The key. Can you find the key?"

He'd set the bundles down and was pushing their contents around. "I'm looking. I'm looking." Moments later he fished out an envelope, opened it, removed the key and unlocked the door.

Deirdre, who feared that if she waited much longer she'd collapse on the spot, limped immediately inside. It was dark. She fumbled for a light switch and quickly flipped it on. In one sweeping glance she took in a large living room and an open kitchen off that. To the left was a short hall, to the right a longer one. Calculating that the hall to the right would lead to bedrooms, she single-mindedly headed that way.

There were three open doors. She passed the first, then the second, correctly surmising that they were the smaller guest bedrooms. The third... She flipped another light switch. Ah, she'd been right. It was much as she'd imagined it—a sight for sore eyes.

Swinging inside, she slammed the door shut with her crutch and made straight for the bed. She'd no sooner reached it than her knees buckled and she sank down, letting her crutches slip unheeded to the floor. Hanging her head, she took several deep, shaky breaths. Her limbs were quivering from weakness, exhaustion or chill, or all three. She was wet, and remedying that situation had to take first priority. Though the room was cold, she simply didn't have the wherewithal to confront that problem yet.

With unsteady fingers, she worked down the zipper of her jacket, struggled out of the soggy mass and dropped it on the rag rug by the side of the bed. She began to apologize silently to Victoria for making a mess, then caught herself. After what Victoria had done, she didn't owe her a thing!

She kicked off her sodden sneaker and tugged the wet leg warmer off her cast. The plaster was intact. Gingerly she touched the part that covered her foot. Damp? Or simply cold? Certainly hard enough. So far, so good.

Bending sharply from the waist, she unzipped her duffel bag and began pushing things around in search of her pajamas. Normally the neatest of packers, she'd been in the midst of the argument with her mother that morning when she'd thrown things into the bag. She'd been angry and tired. Fortunately everything she'd brought was squishable.

She'd finally located the pajamas, when the door to the bedroom flew open and Neil burst in. He'd already taken off his jacket, shoes and socks, but his jeans were soaked up to the thigh. Tossing his cargo bag onto the foot of the bed, he planted his hands on his hips.

"What are you doing in here? This is my room."

Deirdre clutched the pajamas to her chest, more startled than anything by his sudden appearance. "I didn't see your name on the door," she argued quietly.

"This is the largest bedroom." He pointed at the bed. "That is the largest bed." He jabbed his chest with his thumb. "And I happen to be the largest person in this house."

Deirdre let her hands, pajamas and all, fall to her lap. She adopted a blank expression, which wasn't hard, given her state of emotional overload. "So?"

"So . . . I want this room."

"But it's already taken."

"Then you can untake it. The two other rooms are perfectly lovely."

"I'm glad you feel that way. Choose whichever you want."

"I want this one."

For the first time since she'd entered the room, Deirdre really looked around. Nearly two complete walls were of thick, multi-paned glass, affording a view that would no doubt be spectacular in daylight. The large, brass-framed bed stood against a third wall; out of the fourth was cut the door, flanked by low, Colonial-style matching dressers, and, at one end, the pièce de résistance; a large raised hearth. Over it all was a warm glow cast by the bedside lamp.

Deirdre looked Neil straight in the eye. "So do I."

Neil, who'd never been in quite this situation before, was thrown off balance by her quiet determination. It had been different when she'd been yelling. This was, strangely, more threatening. Deirdre whoever-she-was was a woman who knew what she wanted. Unfortunately he wanted the same thng.

"Look," he began, carefully guarding his temper, "it doesn't make sense. I need this bed for its length alone. I'm six-three to your, what, five-one, five-two? I'll be physically uncomfortable in any of the other rooms. They all have twin beds."

"I'm five-three, but that's beside the point. I have a broken leg. I need extra space, too...not to mention a bathtub. From what I've been told, the master bath is the only one with a tub. I can't take a shower. It'll be enough of a challenge taking a bath."

"Try," Neil snapped.

"Excuse me?"

"I said, try."

"Try what?"

"To take a bath."

"And what is that supposed to mean?"

"What do you think it means?" he asked rhetorically. "You're filthy." He hadn't been able to resist. When he'd tried logic on her, she'd turned it around to suit herself. He didn't like that, particularly when he had no intention of giving in when it came to the master bedroom.

She looked down at her mud-spattered orange leg warmer and plucked at the odious wet wool. "Of course I'm filthy. It's muddy outside, and that boat was none too clean." She raised her head, eyes flashing. "But I don't have to apologize. Look at you. You're no prize, yourself!"

Neil didn't have to look at himself to know she was right. He'd worn his oldest, most comfortable jeans and heavy sweater, and if she could see the T-shirt under the sweater.... The stormy trip had taken its toll on him, too. "I don't give a damn how I look," he growled. "That was the whole purpose in coming here. For once in my life I'm going to do what I want, when I want, where I want. And that starts with this bed."

Jaw set, Deirdre reached for her crutches. "Over my dead body," she muttered, but much of the fight had gone out of her. Whatever energy she'd summoned to trade barbs with Neil had been drained. Draping the pajamas over her shoulder, she stood. "I have to use the bathroom. It's been a long day."

Neil watched her hobble into the bathroom and close the door. Again he found himself wishing she'd yell. When she spoke quietly, wearily, he actually felt sorry for her. She looked positively exhausted.

But damn it, so was he!

Taking his cargo bag from the foot of the bed, he put it where Deirdre had been sitting. He then lifted her soaked jacket by its collar, grabbed her duffel bag by its strap and carried them down the hall to the more feminine of the two guest bedrooms.

She'd get the hint. With luck, she'd be too tired to argue. Either that, or she'd come after him once she left the bathroom, and they could fight it out some more.

He sighed, closed his eyes and rubbed that throbbing spot on his forehead. Aspirin. He needed aspirin. No. He needed a drink. No. What he really needed was food. Breakfast had been a long time ago, and lunch had been a Whopper, eaten in sixty seconds flat at a Burger King on the turnpike.

Stopping briefly in the front hall to adjust the thermostat, he returned to the kitchen, where he'd left the boxes of food piled up. Plenty for two, he mused dryly. He should have been suspicious when Thomas had continued to hand out supplies. But it had been rainy and dim, and he hadn't thought. They'd been rushing. He'd simply assumed the girl would get back on the boat when the work was done.

He'd assumed wrong. Thrusting splayed fingers through his hair, he stared at the boxes, then set about unloading them. Soon he had a can of soup on to heat and was busy making a huge ham-and-cheese sandwich.

The kitchen was comfortable. Though small, it was modern, with all the amenities he enjoyed at home. He hadn't expected any less of Victoria. At least, not when it came to facilities. What he hadn't expected was that she'd foist company on him, not when he'd specifically said that he needed to be alone.

What in the devil had possessed her to pull a prank like this? But he knew. He knew. She'd been trying to fix him up for years.

Why now, Victoria? Why now, when my life is such a goddamned mess?

The house was quiet. He wondered about that as he finished eating and cleaned up. Surely Deirdre would be finished using the bathroom. He hadn't heard a bath running. Nor had he heard the dull thud of crutches in the hall.

Not liking the possible implications of the silence, he headed for the smaller bedroom where he'd left her things.

It was empty.

Nostrils flaring, he strode down the hall to the master bedroom. *"Damn it,"* he cursed, coming to a sudden halt on the threshold. She was in bed, albeit on the opposite side from his bag. She was in his bed!

His feet slapped the wood floor as he crossed the room and came to stand on the rug by that other side of the bed. "Hey, you! What do you think you're doing?"

She was little more than a series of small lumps under the quilt. None of the lumps moved. The bedding was pulled to her forehead. Only her hair showed, mousy brown against the pillow.

"You can't sleep here! I told you that!"

He waited. She gave a tiny moan and moved what he assumed to be her good leg.

"You'll have to get up, Deirdre," he growled. "I've moved your things to the other bedroom."

"I can't," came the weak and muffled reply. "I'm...too tired and...too...cold."

Neil glanced helplessly at the ceiling. *Why me? Why here and now?* He lowered his gaze to the huddle of lumps. "I can't sleep in any of the other beds. We've been through this before."

"Mmm."

"Then you'll move?"

There was a long pause. He wondered if she'd fallen asleep. At last, a barely audible sound came from beneath the covers.

"No."

He swore again and shoved another agitated hand through his hair as he stared at the bundle in the bed. He could move her. He could bodily pick her up and cart her to the next bedroom.

"Don't try to move me," the bundle warned. "I'll cry rape."

"There'll be no one to hear."

"I'll call Thomas. I'll make more noise than you've ever heard."

Rape. Of all the stupid threats. Or was it? There were just the two of them in the house. It would be her word against his, and "date rape" had become the in thing. If she was cruel enough to go through with it, she could really make a scene. And a scene of that type was the last thing he needed at this point in his life.

Furious and frustrated, he wheeled around and stormed from the room. When he reached the living room, he threw himself into the nearest chair and brooded. He threw every name in the book at Victoria, threw many of the same names at Thomas, then at the woman lying in *his* bed. Unfortunately, all the name-calling in the world didn't change his immediate circumstances.

He was bone tired, yet there was enough adrenaline flowing through him to keep him awake for hours. Needing to do something, he bolted from the chair and put a match to the kindling that had so carefully been placed beneath logs in the fireplace. Within minutes, the fire was roaring. It was some comfort. Even greater comfort came from the bottle of Chivas Regal he fished from the bar. Several healthy swallows, and he was feeling better; several more, and his anger abated enough to permit him to think.

After two hours he was feeling far more mellow than he would have imagined. He wandered into the den off the shorter of the two halls and studied the directions taped beside the ship-to-shore radio. *Piece of cake.*

Unfortunately no one responded from Thomas's house. *Bastard.*

Okay, Hersey. Maybe he's not back yet. After all, it was still raining, and the man was working in total darkness. No sweat. He'll be there tomorrow. And in the meantime...

Neil banked the fire, nonchalantly walked back to the master bedroom and began to strip. *Let her cry rape*, declared his muzzy brain.

Wearing nothing but his briefs—a concession that later he'd marvel he'd been sober enough to make—he turned off the light, climbed into his side of the bed and stretched out.

"Ah..." The bed was firm, the sheets fresh. He might have imagined himself in his own bed at home had it not been for the faint aroma of wood smoke that lent an outdoorsy flavor to the air. Rain beat steadily against the roof, but it, too, was pleasant, and beyond was a sweet, sweet silence.

He was on a remote island, away from the city and its hassles. Taking a deep breath, he smiled, then let his head fall sideways on the pillow and was soon sound asleep.

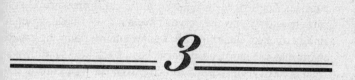

3

SEVERAL HOURS LATER Neil's sleep was disturbed. Brow puckering, he turned his head. The mattress shifted, but he hadn't been the one to move. He struggled to open an eye. The room was pitch-black.

When the mattress shifted again, he opened the other eye. Was it Nancy? No, Nancy never stayed the night, and he wasn't seeing Nancy anymore. Then . . .

It took him a minute to get his bearings, and by the time he did, a dull pounding had started at the back of his head. He rolled to his side, tucked his chin down and pulled his knees up. He'd fall back to sleep, he told himself. He'd keep his eyes closed, breathe deeply and steadily, and fall back to sleep.

A soft moan came from the far side of the bed, followed by another shift in the mattress.

Eyes flying open, Neil swore silently. Then, gritting his teeth, he moved nearer his edge of the bed and closed his eyes again.

For a time there was silence. He was nearly asleep, when another moan came. It was a closed-mouth moan, more of a grunt, and, as before, was followed by the rustle of bedding and the shimmy of the mattress.

His head throbbed. Cursing, he threw back the covers and stalked into the bathroom. The sudden light was glaring; he squinted against it as he shoved the medicine chest open. Insect repellent . . . Caladryl lotion . . . antihistamine . . .

aspirin. Aspirin. He fought with the child-proof cap for a minute and was on the verge of breaking the bottle, when it finally opened. Shaking three tablets into his palm, he tossed them into his mouth, threw his head back and swallowed, then bent over and drank directly from the tap. Hitting the light switch with a blind palm, he returned to bed.

The aspirin had barely had time to take effect, when Deirdre moaned and turned again. Neil bolted upright in bed and scowled in her direction, then groped for the lamp. Its soft glow was revealing. She was still buried beneath the covers, but her side of the quilt was pulled up and around every which way. Even as he watched, she twisted, lay still for several seconds, then twisted again.

"Deirdre!" He grasped what he calculated to be a handful of her shoulder and shook her. "Wake up, damn it! I can't sleep with that tossing and turning."

There was movement, independent of his shaking, from the lumps beneath the quilt. One hand emerged, slim fingers clutching the quilt, lowering it until a pair of heavily shadowed and distinctly disoriented brown eyes met his.

"Hmm?"

"You'll have to settle down," he informed her gruffly. "It's bad enough that I have to share this bed, but I refuse to do it with a woman who can't lie still."

Her eyes had suddenly widened at the "share this bed" part; they fell briefly to the shadowed expanse of his naked chest, then flew back up. Slowly, slowly they fluttered shut.

"I'm sorry," she whispered with a sincerity that momentarily took the wind from his sails.

"Were you having a nightmare?"

"No. My leg kills."

He studied the thick wedge that had to be her cast. "Is there something you're supposed to do for it? Didn't the doctor give you any instructions? Shouldn't you elevate it or something?"

Deirdre felt groggy and exceedingly uncomfortable. "They kept it hitched up in the hospital—to minimize swelling—but I thought that was over."

"Great." Neil threw off the covers and headed for the door. "I'm stuck here with a dimwit whose leg may swell to twice its normal size." His voice was loud enough to carry clearly back to her from the hall. "And if that happens your circulation may be cut off by the cast, and if *that* happens, gangrene may set in. Terrific." He stomped back into the master bedroom, carrying two pillows under each arm, went straight to her side of the bed and unceremoniously hauled back the quilt.

"What are you doing?" she cried, blinking in confusion.

"Elevating your leg." He had two of the pillows on the bed and was trying to sort out the legs of her pajamas. "There's so much damned material here . . . Can you move your good leg? There, I've got it." With surprising gentleness, he raised her casted leg just enough to slip the pillows underneath.

"Gangrene won't set in," she argued meekly. "You don't know what you're talking about."

"At least I know enough to prop up your leg." With a flick of his wrist, he tossed the quilt back over her as he rounded the bed to reach his side. "That feels better, doesn't it?"

"It feels the same."

"Give it a minute or two. It'll feel better." He turned off the light and climbed back into bed, dropped his head to the pillow and massaged his temple. Seconds later he was up again, this time heading back to the bathroom. When he returned, he carried a glass of water and two pills. "Can you sit up?"

"Why?"

"Because I think you should take these."

The only light in the room was the sliver that spilled from the bathroom. The dimness made Deirdre feel at a marked disadvantage to the man who loomed above her. "What are they?"

"Aspirin."

He was so large...shadowed...ominous. He wasn't wearing much. What did he intend? "I don't take pills."

"These are harmless."

"If they're harmless, why should I bother to take them?"

"Because they may just help the ache in your leg, and if that happens you'll lie quietly, and then maybe I'll be able to sleep."

"You can always try another bedroom."

"No way, but that's beside the point. Right now we're discussing your taking two innocent aspirin."

"How do I know they're innocent? How do I know they're aspirin at all? I don't know you. Why should I trust anything you give me?"

Amazed that Deirdre whoever-she-was could be as perverse in the middle of the night as she was during the day, he gave an exasperated sigh. "Because, A, I took these pills from a bottle marked Aspirin, which I found in Victoria's medicine chest. B, I took three of them myself a little while ago, and I'm not up, down or dead yet. And C, I'm Victoria's friend, and that's about as good a character reference as you're going to get." He sucked in a breath. "Besides, it works both ways, you know."

"What does?"

"Character references. I have to trust that you're clean—"

"What do you mean, clean?"

"That you don't have any perversions, or addictions, or contagious diseases..."

"Of course I don't!"

"How can I be sure?"

"Because I'm Victoria's friend—"

"And Victoria knowingly stuck us together, so we have to trust that neither of us is an unsavory character, because we both do trust Victoria. At least I do. Or did." He threw his clenched fist in the air. "I don't believe I'm standing here arguing. Do you, or do you not, want the damn aspirin?" His fist dropped and opened, cradling the tablets.

"I want them."

Neil let out an exaggerated breath. "Then we're back where we started. Can you sit up?" He spoke the last very slowly, as though she might not understand him otherwise.

Deirdre was beyond taking offense. "If I can't, I have no business doing what I do," she muttered to herself, and began to elbow her way up. With her leg elevated, the maneuvering was difficult. Still, she was supposedly agile, an athlete, an expert at bending and twisting...

Neil didn't wait to watch her fall. He came down on a knee on the bed, curved his arm beneath her back and propped her up. "The pills are in my right hand. Can you reach them?"

His right hand was by her waist; his left held the glass. She took the tablets, pressed them into her mouth and washed them down with the water he offered.

Neither of them spoke.

Neil lowered her to the sheets, removed his knee from the bed and walked back to the bathroom. Quietly he set the glass by the sink, switched off the light and returned to bed.

Deirdre lay silent, unmoving, strangely peaceful. Her leg felt better; her entire body felt better. She closed her eyes, took a long, slow breath and drifted into a deep, healing sleep.

When she awoke it was daylight—overcast still, raining still, but daylight nonetheless. She lay quietly, gradually assimilating where she was and what she was doing there. As the facts crystallized, she realized that she wasn't alone in the bed. From its far side came a quiet breathing; she turned her head slowly, saw the large quilt-covered shape of Victoria's other friend, turned her head back. Then the crux of her dilemma hit her.

She'd fled Rhode Island, driven for hours in the pouring rain, been drenched, mud spattered, nearly seasick—all to be alone. But she wasn't. She was marooned on an island, some twenty miles from shore, with a grump of a man. Now what was she going to do?

Neil was asking himself the same question. He lay on his side with his eyes wide open, listening to the sounds of Deirdre's breathing, growing more annoyed by the minute. He did believe what he'd said the night before. If she was Victoria's friend—and she knew a convincing amount about Victoria—she couldn't be all bad. Still, she was disagreeable, and he wanted to be alone.

Pushing back the quilt, he swung his legs to the floor, then paused to give his head a chance to adjust to the shift in position. His head ached, though he was as ready to blame it on Deirdre as on the amount of Scotch he'd drunk the evening before.

"Don't you have something decent to wear?" came a perturbed voice from beneath the quilt.

His head shot around. Mistake. He put the heels of his hands on his temples and inch by inch faced forward. "There's nothing indecent about my skin," he gritted.

"Don't you have pajamas?"

"Like yours?"

"What's wrong with mine? They're perfectly good pajamas."

"They're men's pajamas." Even as he said it his arm tingled. It was his right arm, the one he'd used to prop her up. Sure, she'd been wearing men's pajamas, but beneath all the fabric was a slender back, a slim waist and the faintest curve of a hip.

"They're comfortable, and warm."

"I don't need warmth," he growled roughly.

"It's freezing in here. Isn't there any heat?"

"I like my bedroom cold."

"Great." It was an argument to be continued later. For the moment, there was something more pressing. Vividly she recalled the sight of his chest, the corded muscles, the dark swirls of hair. "It might have been considerate of you to put *something* on when you decided to crawl into bed with me."

"Be grateful for the consideration I did make. I usually sleep in the buff."

She clenched a fistful of quilt by her cheek. "So macho."

"What's the matter?" he shot back. "Can't handle it?"

"There's nothing to handle. Macho has never turned me on."

"Not enough woman for it?"

The low blow hit hard, causing her to lash out in self-defense. "Too much of a woman. I hate to disillusion you, but machismo is pretty shallow."

"Ah, the expert."

"No. Simply a modern woman."

Muttering a pithy curse, Neil pushed himself from bed. "Save it for Thomas when he comes back for you later. Right now, I need a shower."

She started to look up, but caught herself. "I need a bath."

"You had your chance last night and you blew it. Now it's my turn."

"Use one of the other bathrooms. They've got showers."

"I like this one."

"But it's the only one with a tub!"

"You can have it as soon as I'm done."

"What happened to chivalry?"

"Talk of chivalry from a modern woman?" he chided, and soundly closed the bathroom door behind him.

Deirdre did look up then. He'd had the last word . . . so he thought. Rolling to her side, she grabbed her crutches from the floor and hobbled from the bedroom. Off the short hall on the other side of the living room was a den, and in the den was the ship-to-shore radio.

She checked her watch. Ten-forty-five. *Ten-forty-five*? She couldn't believe she'd slept round the clock and then some! But she'd needed it. She'd been exhausted. And she'd slept soundly once she'd been settled with her leg propped up and aspirin dispersing through her system.

Ten-forty-five. Had she missed Thomas? Would he be home or out on the boat? It was rainy, true, but windy?

She studied the directions beside the radio and, after several unsuccessful attempts, managed to put through the call. A young man responded, clearly not the lobsterman.

"It's urgent that I reach Thomas," she said.

"Is there an emergency?" the young man asked.

"Not exactly an emergency in the critical sense of the word, but—"

"Are you well?"

"Yes, I'm well—"

"And Mr. Hersey?"

Hersey. "Neil? He's well, too, but it really is important that I speak with Thomas."

"I'll have him call you as soon as he can."

She tightened her fingers on the coiled cord of the speaker. "When do you think that will be?"

"I don't know."

"Is he on the boat?"

"He's in Augusta on business."

"Oh. Is he due back today?"

"I believe so."

Frustration. She sighed. "Well, please give him the message."

After the young man assured her he would, Deirdre replaced the speaker and turned off the set. In Augusta on business. She wondered. Thomas would know precisely why she was calling; he'd known precisely what he was doing yesterday when he left both of his unsuspecting passengers on Victoria's island together.

She thought back to the things he'd said. He'd been smooth. She had to hand it to him. He'd been general enough, vague enough. He'd never lied, simply given clever, well-worded answers to her questions.

She wasn't at all sure she could trust him to call back.

Scowling, she turned at the sound of footsteps in the hall. So Neil had finished his shower, had he? And what was he planning to do now? She listened. The footsteps receded, replaced by the sound of the refrigerator door opening, then closing. He was in the kitchen. Good. Now she'd take her bath, and she'd take her sweet time about it.

In truth, she couldn't have rushed if she'd wanted to. Maneuvering herself into the tub was every bit the hassle she'd expected. Particularly awkward—and annoying—was the fact that the tub was flush against one wall, and in order to drape her casted leg over its lip she had to put her back to the faucets. Her decision to climb in before she ran the water resulted in a considerable amount of contortion, not to mention the fact that when she tried to lie back, the spigot pressed into her head. She finally managed to wedge herself into a corner, which meant that she was lying almost diagonally in the tub.

It was better than nothing, or so she told herself when she gave up the idea of relaxing to concentrate on getting clean. That, too, was a trial. With both hands occupied soaping and scrubbing, she slid perilously low in the water. Just as well,

she reasoned. Her hair needed washing as badly, if not more
than the rest of her. How long had it been since she'd had a
proper shampoo? A week?

"Yuk."

Tipping her head back, she immersed her hair, doused it
with shampoo and scrubbed. Unfortunately she'd used too
much shampoo. No amount of dipping her head in the water
removed it completely, and by then the water was dirty. She
was thoroughly disgusted. In the end she drained the tub,
turned on fresh warm water, sharply arched her back to put
her head in the stream and hoped for the best.

By the time she'd awkwardly made her way out of the tub,
she was tense all over. So much for a refreshing bath, she
mused. But at least she was clean. There was some satisfaction in that. There was also satisfaction in rubbing moistur-
izing lotion over her body, a daily ritual that had been
temporarily abandoned during her stay in the hospital. The
scent of it was faint but familiar. When she closed her eyes
she could imagine that she was back home, in one piece,
looking forward to the day.

She couldn't keep her eyes closed forever, though, and
when she opened them, the truth hit. She was neither home,
nor in one piece, nor looking forward to the day. Rather, she
was in self-imposed exile on Victoria's island. Her left leg was
in a heavy cast, her face was decidedly pale and she was
pathetically weak. And she was not looking forward to the
day, because *he* was here.

Angrily she tugged on her underwear, then the mint green
warm-up suit she'd brought. It was loose, oversized and
stylish, and the top matched the bottom. He couldn't complain about her clothes today.

Propping herself on the toilet seat, she worked a pair of
white wool leg warmers over her cast, then her good leg, put
a single white crew sock on the good foot, then a single white

sneaker. She towel-dried her hair with as much energy as she could muster, then, leaning against the sink, brushed it until it shone.

She studied her face. A lost cause. Squeaky clean, but a lost cause nonetheless. It was pale, bland, childlike. She'd always looked younger than her years. When she'd been in her late teens and early twenties, she'd hated it. Now, with women her age doing their best to look younger, she had her moments of self-appreciation. This wasn't one of them. She looked awful.

A pouting child? Perhaps, but only because of *him*. With a deep breath, she turned from the mirror and began to neaten the bathroom. *Him.* What an unpleasant man, an unpleasant situation. And a remedy? There was none, until she reached Thomas, until she convinced him that, for her sanity alone, Neil Hersey should be removed from the island.

A few minutes later, she entered the kitchen to find the remnants of bacon smoke in the air, two dirty pans on the stove, the counter littered with open cartons of juice and milk, a bowl of eggs, a tub of margarine, an open package of English muffins and miscellaneous crumbs. Neil Hersey was nonchalantly finishing his breakfast.

"You're quite a cook," she remarked wryly. "Does your skill extend to cleaning up after yourself, or were you expecting the maid to come in and do it?"

Neil set down his fork, rocked back in his chair and studied her. "So that's why Victoria sent you along. I knew there had to be a reason."

Deirdre snickered. "If you think I'm going to touch this disaster area, you're crazy. You made the mess, you clean it up."

"And if I don't?"

"Then you'll have spoiled juice and milk, stale muffins and dirty dishes to use next time." She stared at the greasy pans. "What did you make, anyway?"

"Bacon and eggs. Sound tempting?"

Her mouth was watering. "It might if you didn't use so much fat. I'd think that at your age you'd be concerned about that, not to mention the cholesterol in however many eggs you ate."

"Four. I was hungry. Aren't you? You didn't have supper."

"I had other things on my mind last night." She sent him a look of mock apology and spoke in her sweetest tone. "I'm sorry. Were you waiting for me to join you for dinner?"

His lips twisted. "Not quite. I had better company than you could ever be."

"A bottle of Scotch?" At his raised brows, she elaborated. "It's sitting right there in the living room with a half-empty glass beside it. Now that was brilliant. Do you always drown your sorrows in booze?"

The front legs of his chair hit the floor with a thud. "I don't drink," he stated baldly.

"Then we must have a little gremlin here who just happened to get into the liquor cabinet."

Faint color rose on Neil's neck. "I had a couple of drinks last night, but I'm not a drinker." He scowled. "And what's it to you? I came here to do what I want, and if that means getting drunk every night, amen."

He was being defensive, and Deirdre found she liked that. Not just because she was momentarily on top. There was something else, something related to that hint of a blush on his neck. "You know, you're really not all that bad-looking." Her gaze fell to take in his large, maroon-and-white rugby shirt and slimmer fitting jeans. "Aside from a receding hairline and all that crap you've got on your face—"

Neil reacted instantly. His eyes narrowed and his jaw grew tight. "My hairline is not receding. It's the same one I've had for years, only I don't choose to hide it like some men do. And as for 'all that crap' on my face, they're whiskers, in case you didn't know."

"You could have shaved."

"Why should I?"

"Because I'm here, for one thing."

"Through no choice of mine. This is my vacation you're intruding on, and the way I see it, you don't have any say as to what I do or how I look. Got that?"

Deirdre stared mutely back at him.

"Got that?" he repeated.

"I'm not hard of hearing," she said quietly.

He rolled his eyes. "Thank goodness for that, at least."

"But you've got it wrong. You're the one who's intruding on my time here, and I'll thank you to make yourself as invisible as possible until Thomas comes to pick you up."

Neil stood then, drew himself up and slowly approached her. "Make myself invisible, huh? Just how do you suggest I do that?"

He came closer and closer. Even barefoot he towered over her. Deirdre tipped back her head, stubbornly maintaining eye contact, refusing to be cowed. "You can clean up the kitchen when you're done, for one thing."

"I would have done that, anyway... when I was done."

"For another, you can busy yourself exploring the island."

"In the rain?"

"For a third, you can take yourself and your things to one of the other bedrooms."

His voice suddenly softened. "You didn't like my taking care of you last night?"

His question hung in the air. It wasn't that the words were shocking, or even particularly suggestive, but something about his nearness made Deirdre's breath catch in her throat. Yes, he was large, but that wasn't it. Yes, he looked roguish, but that wasn't it, either. He looked...he looked... warm...gentle...deep?

Neil, too, was momentarily stunned. When he'd come up so close, he hadn't quite expected—what? That she should smell so fresh, so feminine? That the faint, nearly transparent smattering of freckles on the bridge of her nose should intrigue him? That she should have dusty brown eyes, the eyes of a woman?

Swallowing once, he stepped back and tore his gaze from hers. It landed on the littered counter. With but a moment's pause, he began to close containers and return them to the refrigerator. "How does your leg feel?"

"Okay," Deirdre answered cautiously.

"Any worse than yesterday?"

"No."

He nodded and continued with his work.

Deirdre took a breath, surprised to find herself slightly shaky. "I, uh, I tried to call Thomas. He wasn't in."

"I know."

So he'd tried, too. She should have figured as much. Hobbling on her crutches to the stool by the counter peninsula, she propped herself on its edge. "We have to find a solution."

"Right."

"Any thoughts on it?"

His head was in the refrigerator, but his words carried clearly. "You know them."

She certainly did. "Then we're stalemated."

"Looks that way."

"I guess the only thing to do is to dump the problem in Victoria's lap. She caused it. Let her find a solution."

The refrigerator door swung shut. Neil straightened and thrust a hand on his hip. "That's great. But if we can't reach Thomas, how in the hell are we going to reach Victoria?"

"We'll just have to keep trying."

"And in the meantime?"

She grinned. "We'll just have to keep fighting."

Neil stared at her. It was the first time he'd seen her crack a smile. Her teeth were small, white and even; her lips were soft, generous. "You like fighting."

"I never have before, but, yeah, I kinda like it." She tilted her head to the side, tipped her chin up in defiance. "It feels good."

"You are strange, lady," he muttered as he transferred the dirty pans to the sink with more force than necessary. "Strange."

"Any more so than you?"

"There's nothing strange about me."

"Are you kidding? I haven't been arguing in a vacuum, you know. You even admitted that you enjoy picking on me. I dare you to tell me how that's any different from my saying I like fighting."

He sent a leisurely stream of liquid soap onto a sponge. "Give me a break, will you?"

"Give *me* a break, and hurry up, will you? I'm waiting to use the kitchen, or have you forgotten? It's been twenty-four hours since I've eaten—"

"And whose fault is that? If you'd stayed home where you belonged, you wouldn't have missed any meals."

"Maybe not, but if I'd stayed home, I'd have gone crazy!"

Neil stared at her over his shoulder; Deirdre stared back. The question was there; he was on the verge of asking it. She dared him to, knowing she'd take pleasure in refusing him.

In the end he didn't ask. He wasn't sure he wanted to know what she'd left that was so awful. He wasn't sure he wanted to think of someone else's problems. He wasn't sure he wanted to feel sympathy for this strange woman-child.

Perversely disappointed, Deirdre levered herself from the stool, fit her crutches under her arms and swung into the living room. Though it was the largest room in the house, it had a feel of coziness. Pine, dark stained and rich, dominated the decor—wall paneling; rafters and pillars; a large, low hub of a coffee table, and the surrounding, sturdy frames of a cushioned sofa and chairs. The center of one entire wall was bricked into a huge fireplace. Deirdre thought she'd very much like to see the fire lit.

Propping her hip against the side of one of the chairs, she gave the room a sweeping overview. No doubt about it, she mused sadly. The room, the house, the island—all had high potential for romance. Miles from nowhere . . . an isolated, insulated retreat . . . fire crackling mingled with the steady patter of rain. At the right time, with the right man, it would be wonderful. She could understand why so many of Victoria's friends had raved about the place.

"It's all yours," Neil said. Momentarily confused, Deirdre frowned at him. "The kitchen. I thought you were dying of hunger."

The kitchen. "I am."

"Then it's yours."

"Thank you."

He stepped back, allowing more than ample room for her to pass. "There's hot coffee in the pot. Help yourself."

"Thank you."

Just as she was moving by, he leaned forward. "I make it thick. Any objections?"

She paused, head down. "What do you think?"

"I think yes."

"You're right. I like mine thin."

"Add water."

"It tastes vile that way."

"Then make a fresh pot."

"I will." She looked up at him. His face was inches away. Dangerous. "If you don't mind . . ."

Taking the hint, he straightened. She swung past him and entered the kitchen, where she set about preparing a meal for the first time in a week.

It was a challenge. She began to remove things from the refrigerator, only to find that she couldn't possibly handle her crutches and much else at the same time. So she stood at the open refrigerator, balancing herself against the door, taking out one item, then another, lining each up on the counter. When she'd removed what she needed, she balanced herself against the counter and, one by one, moved each item in line toward the stove. A crutch fell. Painstakingly she worked her way down to pick it up, only to have it fall again when she raised her arm a second time.

For a woman who'd always prided herself on economy of movement, such a production was frustrating. She finally gave up on the crutches entirely, resorting alternately to leaning against counters and hopping. Each step of the preparation was an ordeal, made all the worse when she thought of how quickly and effortlessly she'd normally do it. By the time she'd finally poured the makings of a cheese omelet into the pan, she was close to tears.

Lounging comfortably on the sofa in the living room, Neil listened to her struggles. It served her right, he mused smugly. She should have stayed at home—wherever that was. Where was it? He wondered what would have driven her crazy had she not left, then he chided himself for wondering when he had worries aplenty of his own.

He thought of those worries and his mood darkened. Nothing had changed with his coming here; the situation would remain the same in Hartford regardless of how long he stayed away. He had to think. He had to analyze his career, his accomplishments and aspirations. He had to decide on a positive course of action.

So far he was without a clue.

The sound of shattering glass brought his head up. "What the hell . . ." He was on his feet and into the kitchen within seconds.

Deirdre was gripping the stove with one hand, her forehead with another. She was staring at the glass that lay broken in a puddle of orange juice on the floor. "What in the devil's the matter with you?" he yelled. "Can't you manage the simplest little thing?"

Tear-filled eyes flew to his. "No, I can't! And I'm not terribly thrilled about it!" Angrily she grabbed the sponge from the sink and knelt on her good knee.

"Let me do that," Neil growled, but she had a hand up, warding him off.

"No! I'll do it myself!" Piece by piece, she began gathering up the shards of broken glass.

He straightened slowly. She was stubborn. And independent. And slightly dumb. With her cast hooked precariously to the side, her balance was iffy at best. He imagined her losing it, falling forward, catching herself on a palm, which in turn would catch its share of glass slivers.

Grabbing several pieces of paper towel, he knelt, pushed her hands aside and set to work cleaning the mess. "There's no need to cry over spilled milk," he said gently.

"It's spilled orange juice, and I'm not crying." Using that same good leg, she raised herself. Her thigh muscles labored, and she cringed to think how out of shape she'd become in a mere week. "You don't have to do that."

"If I don't, you're apt to do even worse damage."

"I can take care of myself!" she vowed, then turned to the stove. The omelet was burning. "Damn!" Snatching up a spatula, she quickly folded the egg mixture in half and turned off the heat. "A crusty omelet. Just what I need!" Balling her hands against the edge of the stove, she threw her head back. "Damn it to hell. Why me?"

Neil dumped the sodden paper towels in the wastebasket and reached for fresh ones. "Swearing won't help."

"Wanna bet!" Her eyes flashed as she glared at him. "It makes me feel better, and since that's the case, I'll do it as much as I damn well please!"

He looked up from his mopping. "My, my, aren't we in a mood."

"Yes, we are, and you're not doing anything to help it."

"I'm cleaning up."

"You're making me feel like a helpless cripple. I told you I'd do it. I'm not totally incapacitated, damn it!"

He sighed. "Didn't anyone ever tell you that a lady shouldn't swear?"

Her lips twisted. "Oh-ho, yes. My mother, my father, my sister, my uncles—for years I've had to listen to complaints." She launched into a whiny mimic and tipped her head from one side to the other. "'Don't say that, Deirdre,' or 'Don't do that Deirdre,' or 'Deirdre, smile and be pleasant,' or 'Behave like a lady, Deirdre.'" Her voice returned to its normal pitch, but it held anger. "Well, if what I do isn't ladylike, that's tough!" She took a quick breath and added as an afterthought, "And if I want to swear, I'll do it!"

With that, she hopped to the counter stool and plopped down on it with her back to Neil.

Silently he finished cleaning the floor. He poured a fresh glass of juice, toasted the bread she'd taken out, lightly spread it with jam and set the glass and plate before her. "Do you want the eggs?" he asked softly.

She shook her head and sat for several minutes before slowly lifting one of the slices of toast and munching on it.

Neil, who was leaning against the counter with his ankles crossed and his arms folded over his chest, studied her defeated form. "Do you live with your family?"

She carefully chewed what was in her mouth, then swallowed. "Thank God, no."

"But you live nearby."

"A giant mistake. I should have moved away years ago. Even California sounds too close. Alaska might be better—northern Alaska."

"That bad, huh?"

"That bad." She took a long, slow drink of juice, concentrating on the cooling effect it had on her raspy throat. Maybe she was coming down with a cold. It wouldn't surprise her, given the soaking she'd taken the day before. Then again, maybe she'd picked up something at the hospital. That was more likely. Hospitals were chock-full of germs, and it would be just her luck to pick one up. Just her luck. "Why are you being so nice?"

"Maybe I'm a nice guy at heart."

She couldn't bear the thought of that, not when she was in such a foul mood herself. "You're an ill-tempered, scruffy-faced man."

Pushing himself from the counter, he muttered, "If you say so," and returned to the living room, where he sat staring sullenly at the cold hearth while Deirdre finished the small breakfast he'd made for her. He heard her cleaning up, noted the absence of both audible mishaps and swearing and found himself speculating on the kind of person she was at heart. He knew about himself. He wasn't really ill-tempered, only a victim of circumstance. Was she the same?

He wondered how old she was.

By the time Deirdre finished in the kitchen, she was feeling a little better. Her body had responded to nourishment; despite her sulky refusal, she'd even eaten part of the omelet. It was more overcooked than burned and was barely lukewarm by the time she got to it, but it was protein. Her voice of reason said she needed that.

Turning toward the living room, she saw Neil sprawled in the chair. She didn't like him. More accurately, she didn't want him here. He was a witness to her clumsiness. That, on top of everything else, embarrassed her.

In the back of her mind was the niggling suspicion that at heart he might well be a nice guy. He'd helped her the night before. He'd helped her this morning. Still, he had his own problems; when they filled his mind, he was as moody, as curt, as churlish as she was. Was he as much of a misfit as she sometimes felt?

She wondered what he did for a living.

With a firm grip on her crutches, she made her way into the living room, going first to the picture window, then retreating until she was propped against the sofa back. From this vantage point she could look at the world beyond the house. The island was gray and wet; its verdancy made a valiant attempt at livening the scene, but failed.

"Lousy day," Neil remarked.

"Mmm."

"Any plans?"

"Actually," she said with a grand intake of breath, "I was thinking of getting dressed and going to the theater."

He shook his head. "The show's sold out, standing room only. You'd never make it, one-legged."

"Thanks."

"Don't feel bad. The show isn't worth seeing."

"Not much is nowadays," she answered. If she was going to be sour, she mused, she might as well do it right. By nature she was an optimist, choosing to gloss over the negatives in life. But all along she'd known the negatives were there. For a change, she wanted to look at them and complain. It seemed to her she'd earned the right.

"I can't remember the last time I saw a good show, or, for that matter, a movie," she began with spirited venom. "Most of them stink. The stories are either so pat and contrived that you're bored to tears, or so bizarre that you can't figure out what's happening. The settings are phony, the music is blah and the acting is pathetic. Or maybe it's the casting that's pathetic. I mean, Travolta was wonderful in *Saturday Night Fever*. He took Barbarino one step further—just suave enough, just sweet enough, just sensitive enough and born to dance. But a newspaper reporter in *Perfect*? Oh, please. The one scene that might have been good was shot in the exercise class, but the camera lingered so long on Travolta's pelvis it was disgusting!"

Neil was staring at her, one finger resting against his lips. "Uh, I'm not really an expert on Travolta's pelvis, disgusting or otherwise."

"Have *you* seen anything good lately?"

"In the way of a pelvis?"

"In the way of a movie."

"I don't have time to go to the movies."

"Neither do I, but if there's something I want to see—a movie, an art exhibit, a concert—I make time. You never do that?"

"For basketball I do."

She wondered if he himself had ever played. He had both the height and the build. "What team?"

"The Celtics."

"You're from Boston?"

"No. But I got hooked when I went to school there. Now I just drive up whenever I can get my hands on tickets. I also make time for lectures."

"What kind of lectures?"

"Current affairs-type talks. You know, by politicians or business superstars—Kissinger, Iacocca."

Her eyes narrowed. "I'll bet you'd go to hear John Dean speak."

Neil shrugged. "I haven't. But I might. He was intimately involved in a fascinating period of our history."

"He was a criminal! He spent time in prison!"

"He paid the price."

"He named his price—books, a TV miniseries, the lecture circuit—doesn't it gall you to think that crime can be so profitable?"

Moments before, the conversation had been purely incidental; suddenly it hit home. "Yes," he said stiffly, "it galls me."

"Yet you'd pay money to go hear someone talk about his experiences on the wrong side of the law?"

Yes, he would have, and he'd have rationalized it by saying that the speaker was providing a greater service by telling all. Now, though, he thought of his experience at Wittnauer-Douglass and felt a rising anger. "You talk too much," he snapped.

Deirdre was momentarily taken aback. She'd expected him to argue, either for her or against her. But he was cutting the debate short. "What did I say?"

"Nothing," he mumbled, sitting farther back in his seat. "Nothing important."

"Mmm. As soon as the little lady hits a raw nerve, you put her down as 'nothing important.'"

"Not 'nothing important,' as in you. As in what you said."

"I don't see much difference. That's really macho of you. Macho, as in coward."

Neil surged from his chair and glared at her. "Ah, hell, give me a little peace, will ya? All I wanted to do was to sit here quietly, minding my own business."

"You were the one who talked first."

"That's right. I was trying to be civil."

"Obviously it didn't work."

"It would have if you hadn't been spoiling for a fight."

"Me spoiling for a fight? We were having a simple discussion about the ethics involved in giving financial support to convicted political criminals, when you went off the handle. I asked you a simple question. All you had to do was to give me a simple answer."

"But I don't have the answer!" he bellowed. A vein throbbed at his temple. "I don't have answers for lots of things lately, and it's driving me out of my mind!"

Lips pressed tightly together, he stared at her, then whirled around and stormed off toward the den.

4

WITH NEIL'S EXIT, the room became suddenly quiet. Deirdre listened, knowing that he'd be trying to reach Thomas again. She prayed he'd get through, for his sake as well as hers. She and Neil were like oil and water; they didn't mix well.

Taking advantage of the fact that she had the living room to herself, she stretched out on the sofa, closed her eyes and pretended she was alone in the house. It was quiet, so quiet. Neither the gentle patter of rain nor the soft hum of heat blowing through the vents disturbed the peaceful aura. She imagined she'd made breakfast without a problem in the world, and that the day before she'd transferred everything from Thomas's boat without a hitch. In her dream world she hadn't needed help, because her broken leg was good as new.

But that was her dream world. In reality, she had needed help, and Neil Hersey had been there. She wondered what it would be like if he were a more even-tempered sort. He was good-looking; she gave that to him, albeit begrudgingly. He was strong; she recalled the arm that had supported her when he'd brought her aspirin, remembered the broad chest she'd leaned against. He was independent and capable, cooking for himself, cleaning up both his mess and hers without a fuss.

He had potential, all right. He also had his dark moments. At those times, given her own mood swings, she wanted to be as far from him as possible.

As she lay thinking, wondering, imagining, her eyelids slowly lowered, and without intending to, she dozed off. A full hour later she awoke with a start. She'd been dreaming.

Of Neil. A lovely dream. An annoying dream. The fact that she'd slept at all annoyed her, because it pointed to a physical weakness she detested. She'd slept for fourteen hours the night before. Surely that had been enough. And to dream of *Neil*?

She'd been right in her early assessment of him; he was as troubled as she was. She found herself pondering the specifics of his problem, then pushed those ponderings from her mind. She had her own problems. She didn't need his.

What she needed, she decided, was a cup of coffee. After the breakfast fiasco, she hadn't had either the courage or the desire to tackle coffee grounds, baskets and filters. Now, though, the thought of drinking something hot and aromatic appealed to her.

Levering herself awkwardly to her feet, she went into the kitchen and shook the coffeepot. He'd said there was some left but that it was thick. She didn't like thick coffee. Still, it was a shame to throw it out.

Determinedly she lit the gas and set the coffee on to heat.

Meanwhile, Neil was in the den, staring out the window at the rain, trying to understand himself. Deirdre Joyce—the young man who'd answered at Thomas's house had supplied her last name—was a thorn in his side. He wanted to be alone, yet she was here. It was midafternoon. He still hadn't spoken with Thomas, which meant that Deirdre was going to be around for another night at least.

What annoyed him most were the fleeting images that played tauntingly in the corners of his mind. A smooth, lithe back...a slim waist...the suggestion of a curve at the hip...a fresh, sweet scent...hair the color of wheat, not mousy brown as he'd originally thought, but thick, shining wheat. Her face, too, haunted him. She had the prettiest light-brown eyes, a small, almost delicate nose, lips that held promise when she smiled.

Of course, she rarely smiled. She had problems. And the fact of the matter was that he really did want to be alone. So why was he thinking of her in a way that would suggest that he found her attractive?

From the door came the clearing of a throat. "Uh, excuse me?"

He turned his head. Damn, but the mint-green of her warm-up suit was cheerful. Of course, she still looked lumpy as hell. "Yes?"

"I heated up the last of the coffee, but it really is too strong for me. I thought you might like it." Securing her right crutch with the muscles of her upper arm, she held out the cup.

Neil grew instantly wary. It was the first attempt she'd made at being friendly. Coming after nonstop termagancy, there had to be a reason. She had to want something. "Why?" he asked bluntly.

"Why what?"

"Why did you heat it up?"

She frowned. "I told you. I thought you might like it."

"You haven't been terribly concerned with my likes before."

"And I'm not now," she replied defensively. "It just seemed a shame to throw it out."

"Ah. You're making a fresh pot, so you heated the dregs for me."

"I don't believe you," she breathed. She hadn't expected such instant enmity, and coming in the face of her attempted pleasantness, it set her off. "You would have had me drink the dregs, but suddenly they're not good enough for you?"

"I didn't say they weren't good enough." His voice was smooth, with an undercurrent of steel. "I reheat coffee all the time because it saves time, and yes, it is a shame to throw it out. What I'm wondering is why the gesture of goodwill from you. You must have something up your sleeve."

"Boy," she remarked with a wry twist of her lips, "have *you* been burned."

His eyes darkened. "And just what do you mean by that?"

"For a man to be as suspicious of a woman, he'd have to have been used by one, and used badly."

Neil thought about that for a minute. Funny, it had never occurred to him before, but he had been used. Nancy had been crafty—subtle enough so the fact had registered only subliminally in his brain—but crafty nonetheless. Only now did he realize that often she'd done small things for him when she'd wanted something for herself. It fit in with the nature of her love, yet he hadn't seen it then. Just as he hadn't seen the potential for treachery at Wittnauer-Douglass.

"My history is none of your damned business," he ground out angrily.

"Fine," she spat. "I just want you to know that it's taken a monumental effort on my part to get the dumb coffee in here without spilling it. And if you want to know the truth, my major motivation was to find out where you were so I'd know what room to avoid." She set the mug on a nearby bookshelf with a thud. "You can have this or not. I don't care." She turned to leave, but not fast enough to hide the hint of hurt in her expression.

"Wait."

She stopped, but didn't turn back. "What for?" she asked. "So you can hurl more insults at me?"

He moved from the window. "I didn't mean to do that. You're right. I've been burned. And it was unfair of me to take it out on you."

"Seems to me you've been taking an awful lot out on me."

"And vice versa," he said quietly, satisfied when she looked over her shoulder at him. "You have to admit that you haven't been the most congenial of housemates yourself."

"I've had . . . other things on my mind."

He took a leisurely step closer. "So have I. I've needed to let off steam. Yelling at you feels good. It may not be right, but it feels good."

"Tell me about it," she muttered rhetorically, but he took her at face value.

"It seems that my entire life has been ruled by reason and restraint. I've never spouted off quite this way about things that are really pretty petty."

She eyed him askance. "Like my using the master bedroom?"

"Now that's not petty. That's a practical issue."

"Then what about heat? The bedroom is freezing, while the rest of the house is toasty warm. You purposely kept the thermostat low in that room, didn't you?"

"I told you. I like a cool bedroom."

"Well, I like a warm one, and don't tell me to use one of the other bedrooms, because I won't. You'll be leaving—"

"*You'll* be leaving." His voice had risen to match the vehemence of hers, but it suddenly dropped again. "Only problem is that Thomas still isn't in, so it looks like it won't be today."

"He's avoiding us."

"That occurred to you, too, hmm?"

"Which means that we're stranded here." Glumly she looked around. "I mean, the house is wonderful. Look." She gestured toward one wall, then another. "Hundreds of books to choose from, a stereo, a VCR, a television—"

"The TV reception stinks. I tried it."

"No loss. I hate television."

"Like you hate movies?"

"I didn't say I hated movies, just that lately they've been awful. The same is true of television. If it isn't a corny sit-com, it's a blood-and-guts adventure show, or worse, a prime-time soap opera."

"Opinionated urchin, aren't you?"

Her eyes flashed and she gripped her crutches tighter. "Yes, I'm opinionated, and I'm in the mood to express every one of those opinions." Silently she dared him to stop her.

Neil had no intention of doing that. He was almost curious as to what she'd say next. Reaching for the mug she'd set down, he leaned against the bookshelf, close enough to catch the fresh scent that emanated from her. "Go on. I'm listening."

Deirdre, too, was aware of the closeness, aware of the breadth of his shoulders and the length of his legs, aware of the fact that he was more man than she'd been near for a very long time. Her cheeks began to feel warm, and there was a strange tickle in the pit of her stomach.

Confused, she glanced around, saw the long leather couch nearby, and inched back until she could sink into it. She raked her lip with her teeth, then looked up at him. "What was I saying?"

"You were giving me your opinion of the state of modern television."

"Oh." She took a breath and thought, finally saying, "I hate miniseries."

"Why?"

"They do awful things to the books they're adapted from."

"Not always."

"Often enough. And they're twice as long as they need to be. Take the opening part of each installment. They kill nearly fifteen minutes listing the cast, then reviewing what went before. I mean, the bulk of the viewers know what went before, and it's a waste of their time to rehash it. And as for the cast listings, the last thing those actors and actresses need is more adulation. Most of them are swellheaded as it is!" She was warming to the subject, enjoying her own perversity. "But the worst part of television has to be the news."

"I like the news," Neil protested.

"I do, too, when it is news, but when stations have two hours to fill each night, a good half of what they deliver simply isn't news. At least, not what I'd consider to be news. And as for the weather report, by the time they've finished with their elaborate electronic maps and radar screens, I've tuned out, so I miss the very forecast I wanted to hear."

"Maybe you ought to stick to newspapers."

"I usually do."

"What paper do you read?"

"The *Times.*"

"New York?" He was wondering about her connection to Victoria. "Then you live there?"

"No. I live in Providence."

"Ah, Providence. Thriving little metropolis."

"What's wrong with Providence?"

"Nothing that a massive earthquake wouldn't fix." It was an exaggeration that gave him pleasure.

She stared hard at him. "You probably know nothing about Providence, much less Rhode Island, yet you'd stand there and condemn the entire area."

"Oh, I know something about Providence. I represented a client there two years ago, in the middle of summer, and the air conditioning in his office didn't work. Since it was a skyscraper, we couldn't even open a window, so we went to what was supposed to be the in restaurant. The service was lousy, the food worse, and to top it all off, some bastard sideswiped my car in the parking lot, so I ended up paying for that, too, and *then* my client waited a full six months before settling my bill."

Deirdre was curious. "What kind of client?"

"I'm a lawyer."

"A lawyer!" She pushed herself to the edge of the seat. "No wonder you're not averse to criminals on the lecture circuit. The proceeds could well be paying your fee!"

"I am not a criminal attorney," Neil stated. The crease between his brows grew pronounced. "I work with corporations."

"That's even worse! I hate corporations!"

"You hate most everything."

Deirdre's gaze remained locked with his for a moment. He seemed to be issuing a challenge, asking a question about her basic personality and daring her to tell the truth. "No," she said in a quieter tone. "I'm just airing certain pet peeves. I don't—I can't do it very often."

He, too, had quieted. "What do you do?"

"Hold it in."

"No. Work-wise. You do work, don't you? All modern women work."

Deirdre dipped one brow. "There's no need for sarcasm."

He made no apology. "You pride yourself on being a modern woman. So tell me. What do you do for a living?"

Slowly she gathered her crutches together. She couldn't tell him what she did; he'd have a field day with it. "That—" she rose "—is none of your business."

"Whoa. I told you what I do."

"And I told you where I live. So we're even." Leaning into the crutches, she headed for the door.

"But I want to know what kind of work you do."

"Tough."

"I'll bet you don't work," he taunted, staying close by her side. "I'll bet you're a very spoiled relative of one of Victoria's very well-to-do friends."

"Believe what you want."

"I'll bet you're here because you really wanted to be in Monte Carlo, but Daddy cut off your expense account. You're freeloading off Victoria for a while."

"Expense account?" She paused midway through the living room and gave a brittle laugh. "Do fathers actually put their twenty-nine-year-old daughters on expense accounts?"

Neil's jaw dropped. "Twenty-nine. You're pulling my leg."

"I wouldn't pull your leg if it were attached to Mel Gibson!" she vowed, and continued on into the kitchen.

"Twenty-nine? I would have given you twenty-three, maybe twenty-four. But twenty-nine?" He stroked the stubble on his face and spoke pensively. "Old enough to have been married at least once." He started after her. "Tell me you're running away from a husband who beats you. Did he cause the broken leg?"

"No."

"But there is a husband?"

She sent him an impatient look. "You obviously don't know Victoria very well. She'd never have thrown us together if one of us were already married."

He did know Victoria, and Deirdre was right. "Okay. Have you ever been married?"

"No."

"Are you living with someone?" When she sent him a second, even more impatient look, he defended himself. "It's possible. I wouldn't put it past Victoria to try to get you to forget him if he were a creep.... Okay, okay. So you're not living with someone. You've just broken up with him, and you've come here to lick your wounds."

"Wrong again." Seth had left four months before, and there had been no wounds to lick. Propping her crutches in a corner, she hopped to the cupboard. She was determined to make herself a cup of coffee. "This is sounding like *Twenty Questions*, which reminds me of what I *really* hate, and it's game shows like the one Thomas was watching yesterday. I mean, I know why people watch them. They play along, getting a rush when they correctly guess an answer before the contestant does. But the contestants—jumping all over the place, clapping their hands with glee when they win, kissing an emcee they don't know from Adam . . ." She shook her head. "Sad. Very sad."

Neil was standing close, watching her spoon coffee into the basket. Her hands were slender, well formed, graceful. There was something about the way she tipped the spoon that was almost lyrical. His gaze crept up her arm, over one rather nondescript shoulder to a neck that was anything but nondescript. It, too, was graceful. Strange, he hadn't noticed before. . . .

Momentarily suspending her work, Deirdre stared at him. Her eyes were wider than normal; her pulse had quickened. It occurred to her that she'd never seen so many textures on a man—from the thick gloss of his hair and the smooth slope of his nose to the furrowing of his brow and the bristle of his beard. She almost wanted to touch him . . . almost wanted to touch . . .

She tightened her fingers around the spoon. "Neil?"

He met her gaze, vaguely startled.

"I need room. I'm, uh, I'm not used to having someone around at home."

His frown deepened. "Uh, sure." He took a step back. "I think I'll . . . go take a walk or something."

Deirdre waited until he'd left, then slowly set back to work. *Take a walk. In the rain?* She listened, but there was no sound of the door opening and closing. So he was walking around the house. As good an activity as any to do on such a dismal day. She wondered when the rain would end. The island would be beautiful in sunshine. She'd love to go outside, find a high rock to sit on, and relax.

Surprisingly, when she thought of it, she wasn't all that tense, at least not in the way she'd been when she'd left Providence. In spite of the hassles of getting here, even in spite of the rain, the change of scenery was good for her. Of course, nothing had changed; Providence would be there when she returned. Her mother would be there, as would Sandra and the uncles. They'd be on her back again, unless she thought of some way to get them off.

She hadn't thought that far yet.

Carefully taking the coffee and a single crutch, she made her way into the den. She could put some weight on the cast without discomfort, which was a reassuring discovery. Carrying things such as coffee became a lot easier. Of course, it was a slow trip, and that still annoyed her, but it was better than being stuck in bed.

Leisurely sipping the coffee, she sat back on the leather sofa. Her duffel bag held several books, yarn and knitting needles, plus her cassette player and numerous tapes. None of these diversions appealed to her at the moment. She felt in limbo, as though she wouldn't completely settle down until Neil left.

But would he leave? Realistically? No. Not willingly. Not unless Victoria specifically instructed him to. Which she wouldn't.

Victoria had been clever. She'd known she was dealing with two stubborn people. She'd also known that once on the island, Neil and Deirdre would be virtually marooned. Thomas Nye was their only link with the mainland, and Thomas, while alert to any legitimate physical emergency, appeared to be turning a deaf ear to their strictly emotional pleas.

It was Neil and Deirdre versus the bad guys. An interesting prospect.

On impulse, she set down her cup and limped from the den. The house was quiet. She wondered what Neil was doing and decided that it was in her own best interest to find out. He hadn't returned to the living room while she'd been in the den, and he wasn't in the kitchen.

He was in the bedroom. The master bedroom. Deirdre stopped on the threshold and studied him. He lay on his back on the bed, one knee bent. His arm was thrown over his eyes.

Grateful she hadn't yet been detected, she was about to leave, when the whisper of a sound reached her ears. It was a little louder than normal breathing, a little softer than snoring. Neil was very definitely asleep.

Unable to help herself, she moved quietly forward until she stood by his side of the bed. His chest rose and fell in slow rhythm; his lips were faintly parted. As she watched, his fingers twitched, then stilled, and correspondingly something tugged at her heart.

He was human. When they'd been in the heat of battle, she might have tried to deny that fact, but seeing him now, defenseless in sleep, it struck her deeply. He was tired, perhaps emotionally as well as physically.

She found herself once again wondering what awful things he'd left behind. He was a lawyer; it was a good profession. Had something gone wrong with his career? Or perhaps his troubles related to his having been burned by a woman. Maybe he was suffering the effects of a bad divorce, perhaps worrying about children the marriage may have produced.

She actually knew very little about him. They'd been thrown together the moment she'd arrived at Spruce Head, and he'd simply provided a convenient punching bag on which to vent her frustrations. When she was arguing with him, she wasn't thinking of her leg, or aerobics, or Joyce Enterprises. Perhaps there was merit to his presence, after all.

He really wasn't so bad; at times she almost liked him. Moreover, at times she was physically drawn to him. She'd never before had her breath taken away by a man's nearness, but it had happened several times with Neil. For someone who'd always been relatively in control of her emotions, the experience was frightening. It was also exciting in a way....

Not trusting that Neil wouldn't awaken and lash out at her for disturbing him, she silently left the room and returned to the den. Her gaze fell on the ship-to-shore radio. She approached it, eyed the speaker, scanned the instructions for its use, then turned her back on both and sank down to the sofa. Adjusting one of the woven pillows beneath her head, she yawned and closed her eyes.

It was a lazy day. The sound of the rain was hypnotic, lulling, inducing the sweetest of lethargies. She wondered at her fatigue and knew that it was due only in part to her physical debilitation. The tension she'd been under in Providence was also to blame.

She needed the rest, she told herself. It was good for her. Wasn't that what a remote island was for? Soon enough she'd feel stronger, and then she'd read, knit, listen to music, even exercise. Soon enough the sun would come out, and she'd be able to avail herself of the island's fresh air.

But for now, doing nothing suited her just fine.

She was sleeping soundly when, some time later, Neil came to an abrupt halt at the door to the den. He was feeling groggy, having awoken only moments before. He wasn't used to sleeping during the day. He wasn't used to doing nothing. Oh, he'd brought along some books, and there were tapes here and a vast collection of old movies to watch, but he wasn't up to any of that just yet. If the weather were nice, he could spend time outdoors, but it wasn't, so he slept, instead.

Rationally he'd known that it was going to take him several days to unwind and that he badly needed the relaxation. He'd known that solutions to his problems weren't going to suddenly hit him in the face the moment he reached the island. Nevertheless, the problems were never far from consciousness.

Ironically Deirdre was his greatest diversion.

Deirdre. Looking down at her, he sucked in his upper lip, then slowly released it. Twenty-nine years old. He thought back to when he was that age. Four years out of law school, he'd been paying his dues as an associate in a large Hartford law firm. The hours had been long, the work boring. Frustrated by the hierarchy that relegated him to doing busywork for the partners, he'd set out on his own the following year. Though the hours had been equally long, the work had been far more rewarding.

Now, ten years later, he was approaching forty, sadly disillusioned. He knew where he'd been, saw his mistakes with vivid clarity... but he couldn't picture the future.

If Deirdre was disillusioned about something at the age of twenty-nine, where would she be when she reached his age? What did she want from life? For that matter, what had she had?

Lying there on her side, with her hands tucked between her thighs and her cheek fallen against the pillow, she was the image of innocence. She was also strangely sexy-looking.

He wondered how that could be, when there was nothing alluring about her in the traditional sense. She wore no make-up. Her hair was long in front, short at the sides and back, unsophisticated as hell. Her warm-up suit was a far cry from the clinging things he'd seen women wearing at the racquet club. The bulky fabric was bunched up in front, camouflaging whatever she had by the way of breasts, and yet... and yet... the material rested on a nicely rounded bottom—he could see that now—and she looked warm and vaguely cuddly. He almost envied her hands.

With a quick headshake, he walked over to the ship-to-shore radio, picked up the speaker, shifted it in his hand, frowned, then set it back down. Ah, hell, he told himself, Thomas wouldn't be there; he was conspiring with Victoria. Short of a legitimate physical emergency, he wouldn't be back soon. And that being the case, it behooved Neil to find a way to coexist in relative peace with Deirdre.

But what fun would that be?

Deirdre was, for him, a kind of punching bag. He felt better when he argued with her. She provided an outlet and a diversion. Perhaps he should just keep swinging.

Smiling, he sauntered into the living room. His gaze fell on the fireplace; the ashes from last night's fire lay cold. Taking several large logs from the nearby basket, he set them atop kindling on the grate and stuck a match. Within minutes the kindling caught, then the logs. Only when the fire was crackling heatedly did he settle back in a chair to watch it.

Strange, he mused, but he'd never come to the wilderness to relax before. He'd been to the beach—southern Connecticut, Cape Cod, Nantucket—and to the snow-covered mountains of Vermount. He'd been to the Caribbean and to Europe. But he'd never been this isolated from the rest of the world. He'd never been in the only house on an island, dependent solely on himself to see to his needs.

Nancy would die here. She'd want the option of eating out or calling room service. She'd want there to be people to meet for drinks. She'd want laundry service.

And Deirdre? Broken leg and all, she'd come looking for solitude. Perhaps stupidly, with that leg, but she'd come. Was she indeed a spoiled brat who had run away from all that had gone wrong in her life? Or was she truly self-sufficient? It remained to be seen whether she could make a bed....

"Nice fire."

He looked up. Deirdre was leaning against the wall by the hall, looking warm and still sleepy and mellow. He felt a lightening inside, then scowled perversely. "Where's the other crutch?"

Her eyes grew clearer. "In the kitchen."

"What's it doing there?"

She tipped her chin higher. "Holding up the counter."

"It's supposed to be under your arm. You're the one who needs holding up."

"I've found I can do just fine with one."

"If you put too much strain on the leg," he argued, "you'll slow the healing process."

"You sound like an expert."

"I broke my own leg once."

"How?"

"Skiing."

She rolled her eyes. "I should have guessed. I'll bet you sat around the ski lodge with your leg on a pedestal—the wounded hero basking in homage."

"Not quite. But what I did is beside the point. What you're doing is nuts. The doctor didn't okay it, did he?"

"*She* told me to use common sense. And what's it to you, anyway? You're not my keeper."

"No, but it'll be my job to do something if you fall and crack the cast, or worse, break the other leg."

She smiled smugly. "If anything happens to me, your problems will be solved. You'll get through to Thomas, zip, zip, and he'll be out to fetch me before you can blink an eye."

Neil knew she was right. He also knew that she had momentarily one-upped him. That called for a change of tactics. He took a deep breath, sat back in his chair and propped his bare feet on the coffee table. "But I don't want him to come out and fetch you. I've decided to keep you."

Her smile faded. "You've what?"

"I've decided to keep you."

"Given the fact that you don't *have* me, that's quite a decision."

He waved a hand. "Don't argue semantics. You know what I mean."

She nodded slowly. "You've decided to let me stay."

"That's right."

"And if I decide I want to leave?"

"Thomas won't give us the time of day, so it's a moot point."

"Precisely, which means that you're full of hot air, Neil Hersey. You can't decide to keep me, any more than I can decide to keep you, or either of us can decide to leave. We're stuck here together, which means—" Her mind was working along pleasurable lines. The grin she sent him had a cunning edge. "That you're stuck with me, bad temper and all." The way she saw it, he'd given her license to fire at will, not to mention without guilt. Battling with him could prove to be a most satisfying pastime.

"I think I can handle it," he said smugly.

"Good." Limping directly between Neil and the fire, she took the chair opposite his. "So," she said, sitting back, "did you have a good sleep?"

"You spied on me?"

"No. I walked into my bedroom and there you were. Snoring."

He refused to let her get to him. "Is that why you took your nap in the den?"

"You spied on me."

"No. I walked in there intending to call Thomas. Then I decided not to bother. So I came in here and built a fire. It is nice, isn't it?"

"Not bad." She levered herself from the chair and hopped into the kitchen. A bowl of fresh fruit sat on the counter; she reached for an orange, then hopped back to her seat.

"You're a wonderful hopper," Neil said. "Is it your specialty?"

She ignored him. "What this fire needs is a little zip." Tearing off a large wad of orange peel, she tossed it into the flame.

"Don't do that! It'll mess up my fire!"

"It adds a special scent. Just wait." She threw in another piece.

Neil stared into the flames. "I hate the smell of oranges. It reminds me of the packages of fruit my grandparents used to send up from Florida every winter. There was so much of it that my mother worried about it spoiling, so we were all but force-fed the stuff for a week." His voice had gentled, and his lips curved at the reminiscence. "Every year I got hives from eating so many oranges."

She pried off a section and held it ready at her mouth. "You said 'we.' Do you have brothers and sisters?" The orange section disappeared.

"One of each."

"Older or younger?"

"Both older."

"Are you close?"

"Now? Pretty close." He shifted lower in his seat, so that his head rested against its back, and crossed his ankles. "We went our separate ways for a while. John is a teacher in Minneapolis, and Sara works for the government in Washington. They're both married and have kids, and all our lives seemed so hectic that we really didn't push reunions."

"What changed that?" Deirdre asked.

"My mother's death. Something about mortality hit us in the face—you know, life-is-so-short type of thing. That was almost seven years ago. We've been much closer since then."

"Is your father still living?"

"Yes. He's retired."

"Does he live near you?"

"He still lives in the house where we grew up in Westchester. We keep telling him to move because it's large and empty but for him most of the time. He won't sell." Neil was grinning. "He travels. So help me, nine months out of twelve he's galavanting off somewhere. But he says he needs the house. He needs to know it's there for him to come home to. Personally—" He lowered his voice "—I think he just doesn't want to displace the couple who live above the garage. They've been overseeing the grounds for nearly twenty years. They oversee *him* when he's around, and he loves it."

Absently Deirdre pressed another piece of fruit into her mouth. She chewed it, all the while looking at Neil. It was obvious that he felt affection for his family. "That's a lovely story. Your father sounds like a nice man."

"He is."

She took a sudden breath. "So how did he get a son like you? By the way, aren't your feet freezing? I haven't seen you with socks on since we got here, but it's cold."

He wiggled his toes. "I'm warm-blooded."

"You're foolhardy. You'll get splinters."

"Are you kidding? The floor's been sanded and waxed. Only the walls have splinters, and, thank you, I don't walk on walls." He swung his legs down and stood. "So you'll have to find something else to pick on me for."

"I will," she promised. "I will." She watched him escape into the kitchen. "What are you doing?"

"Contemplating dinner."

"We haven't had lunch!"

"Breakfast was lunch." He flipped on a light in the darkening room. "Now it's dinnertime."

She glanced at her watch. It was well after six o'clock. She supposed she was hungry, though the thought of preparing another meal was enough to mute whatever hunger pangs she felt. So she remained where she was, looking at the fire, telling herself that she'd see to her own needs when Neil was done. She didn't want an audience for her clumsiness. Besides, between her hopping and Neil's size, they'd never be able to work in the kitchen at the same time.

She listened to the sounds of his preparations, wondering how he'd come to be so handy. Various possible explanations passed through her mind, but in the end the question remained. Then she heard the sizzle of meat and began to smell tantalizing aromas, and her admiration turned to annoyance. Why *was* he so good in the kitchen? Why wasn't he as clumsy as she? The men she'd known would have been hollering for something long before now—help in finding the butter or sharpening a knife or preparing vegetables for cooking. Why didn't he need her for something?

Pushing herself from the chair, she limped peevishly to the kitchen. What she saw stopped her cold on the threshold. Neil had set two places at the table and was in the process of lowering one brimming plate to each spot.

He looked up. "I was just about to call you." Her expression of shock was ample reward for his efforts, though his motives went deeper. If he helped Deirdre with things he knew she found difficult, he wouldn't feel so badly when he picked on her. Good deeds for not-so-good ones; it seemed a fair exchange. Not to mention the fact that keeping her off balance seemed of prime importance. "Steak, steamed broccoli, dinner rolls." He beamed at the plates. "Not bad, if I do say so myself."

"Not bad," she echoed distractedly. "You'd make someone a wonderful wife."

He ignored the barb and held out her chair. "Ms Joyce?"

At a loss for anything better to do, particularly when her mouth was watering, she came forward and let him seat her. She stared at the attractive plate for a minute, then looked up as he poured two glasses of wine. "Why?" she asked bluntly.

"Why wine? It's here for us to drink, and I thought it'd be a nice touch.

"Why me? I didn't ask you to make my dinner."

"Are you refusing it?"

She glanced longingly at her plate. Hospital food was nearly inedible; it had been days since she'd confronted anything tempting. "No. I'm hungry."

"So I figured."

"But you must have something up your sleeve."

He sat at his place, nonchalantly shook out his napkin and spread it on his lap. "Maybe I'm thinking of Victoria's kitchen. You broke a glass this morning. Another few, and we'll run low."

"It's not the glass, and you know it. What is it, Neil? I don't like it when you're nice."

He arched a brow as he cut into his steak. "Prefer the rough stuff, do you? A little pushing and shoving turns you on." He put a piece of steak into his mouth, chewed it and closed his eyes. "Mmmm. Perfect." His eyes flew open in mock innocence. "I hope you like it rare."

"I like it medium."

"Then you can eat the edges and leave the middle." He gestured with his fork. "Go ahead. Eat. On second thought—" He set down the fork and reached for his wine "—a toast." When Deirdre continued to stare at him, he dipped his head, coaxing. "Come on. Raise your glass."

Slowly, warily, she lifted it.

He grinned. "To us." The clink of his glass against hers rang through the room.

5

TO US. Deirdre thought about that through the evening as she sat pensively before the fire. She thought about it that night when she lay in bed, trying her best to ignore the presence of a large male body little more than an arm's length away. She thought about it when she awoke in the morning. By that time she was annoyed.

Victoria had fixed them up. Deirdre had always resented fix-ups, had always fervently avoided them. She'd never been so hard up for a man that she'd risk taking pot luck, and she wasn't now. Who was Neil Hersey, anyway? She asked herself that for the umpteenth time. After spending thirty-six hours with the man, she still didn't know. She did know that she'd been aware of him in some form or another for the majority of those thirty-six hours, and that her body was distinctly tense from that awareness.

She turned her head to study him. Sleeping, he was sprawled on his back with his head facing her. His hair was mussed; his beard sported an additional day's growth. Sooty eyelashes fanned above his cheekbones. Dark swirls of hair blanketed his chest to the point where the quilt took over.

One arm was entirely free of the covers. Her gaze traced its length, from a tightly muscled shoulder, over a leanly corded swell to his elbow, down a forearm that was spattered with hair, to a well-formed and thoroughly masculine hand. As though touched by that hand, she felt a quiver shoot through her.

Wrenching her head to the other side, she took a shallow breath, pushed herself up and dropped her legs over the side of the bed. For a minute she simply sat there with her head bowed, begrudging the fact that she found Neil attractive. She wanted to hate the sight of him after what he'd done to her dreams of solitude. But the sight of him turned her on.

She didn't want to be turned on.

Slowly she began to roll her head in a half circle, concentrating on relaxing the taut muscles of her neck. She extended the exercise to her shoulders, alternately rolling one, then the other. Clasping her hands at the back of her head, she stretched her torso, first to the left, then to the right. The music played in her mind, and she let herself move to its sound, only then realizing what she'd missed during the past week, finding true relaxation in imagining herself back at the health club, leading a class.

"What in the hell are you doing?" came a hoarse growl from behind her.

Startled from her reverie, she whirled around, then caught herself and tempered the movement. "Exercising."

"Is that necessary?"

"Yes. My body is tense."

"So is mine, and what you're doing isn't helping it." He'd awoken with the first of her exercises and watched her twist and stretch, watched the gentle shift in her absurdly large pajamas. And he'd begun to imagine things, which had quickly affected his own body. In other circumstances he'd have stormed from bed right then. As things stood—literally—he didn't have the guts.

"Then don't look," she said, turning her back on him and resuming her exercises. It was spite that drove her on, but all petty thoughts vanished when a strong arm seized her waist and whipped her back on the bed. Before she knew what had happened, Neil had her pinned and was looming over her.

"I think we'd better get something straight," he warned in a throaty voice. "I'm a man, and I'm human. If you want to tempt me beyond my limits, you'd better be prepared to take the consequences."

Deirdre's trouble with breathing had nothing to do with exercising. Neil's lunge had dislodged the quilt, leaving his entire upper body bare. The warmth of his chest reached out to her, sending rivulets of heat through her body, while the intensity of his gaze seared her further.

"I didn't know you were tempted," she said in a small voice. "I'm a bundle of lumps to you. That's all." She'd been a bundle of lumps to most men, lumps that were conditioned by steady exercise, lumps that were anything but feminine. She'd always known she couldn't compete with the buxom beauties of the world, and she fully assumed Neil was used to buxom beauties. The way he'd looked at her that first day had left no doubt as to his opinion of her body. Then again, there had been other times when he'd looked at her . . .

"You are a bundle of lumps," he agreed, dropping his gaze to her pajama front. "That's what's so maddening. I keep wondering what's beneath all this cover." His eyes made a thorough survey of the fabric—she felt every touch point—before lazily meeting hers. "Maybe if I see, I won't be tempted. Maybe what we need here is full disclosure."

Deirdre made a reflexive attempt at drawing in her arms to cover herself, but he had them anchored beneath his and gave no quarter.

"Maybe," he went on, his voice a velvety rasp, "what I ought to do is to unbutton this thing and take a good look at all you're hiding."

"There's not much," she said quickly. Her eyes were round in a pleading that she miraculously managed to keep from her voice. "You'd be disappointed."

"But at least then I wouldn't have to wonder anymore, would I?"

Her heart was hammering, almost visibly so. She was frightened. Strangely and suddenly frightened. "Please. Don't."

"Don't wonder? Or don't look?"

"Either."

"But I can't help the first."

"It's not worth it. Take my word for it. I'm an athletic person. Not at all feminine."

Neil was staring at her in growing puzzlement. He heard the way her breath was coming in short bursts, saw the way her eyes held something akin to fear. He felt the urgency in his body recede, and slowly, gently he released her. Instantly, she turned away from him and sat up.

"I'd never force you," he murmured to her rigid back.

"I didn't say you would."

"You were talking, rationalizing as though you thought I would. I scared you."

She said nothing to that. How could she explain what she didn't understand herself: that her fear had been he'd find fault with her body? She didn't know why it should matter what he thought of her body. . . .

"You didn't scare me."

"You're lying."

"Then that's another fault to add to the list." She fumbled for her crutches and managed to get herself to her feet. "I'm hungry," she grumbled, and started for the door.

"So am I," was his taunting retort.

"Tough!"

DEIRDRE MADE her own breakfast, grateful to find such easy fixings as yogurt and cottage cheese in the refrigerator. She waited in the den until she heard Neil in the kitchen, then retreated to the other end of the house for a bath.

At length she emerged, wearing the same bulky green top she'd worn during the drive up. This time she had gray sweatpants on, and though the outfit didn't clash, it was less shapely than yesterday's warm-up suit had been.

Reluctant to face Neil, she busied herself cleaning up the bedroom. Making a king-size bed by hobbling from one side to the other and back took time, but for once she welcomed the handicap. She went on to unpack her duffel bag. It wasn't that she hadn't planned on staying, simply that she hadn't had the strength to settle in until now. Yes, she did feel stronger, she realized, and found some satisfaction in that. She also found satisfaction in placing her books, cassette player and tapes atop the dresser. Neil had put his things on the other dresser; she was staking her own claim now.

Under the guise of housekeeping, she crossed to that other dresser and cursorily neatened Neil's things. He'd brought several books, a mix of fiction and nonfiction, all tied in some fashion to history. A glass case lay nearby, with the corner of a pair of horn-rimmed spectacles protruding. Horn-rimmed spectacles. She grinned.

Completing the gathering on the dresser was a scattered assembly of small change, a worn leather wallet and a key ring that held numerous keys in addition to those to his car. She wondered what the others unlocked, wondered where his office was and what it was like, wondered where he lived.

Moving quickly into the bathroom, she wiped down the sink and shower, then the mirror above the sink. She'd put her own few things in one side of the medicine chest. Curious, she slid open the other side. Its top shelf held a number of supplies she assumed were Victoria's. Far below, after several empty shelves, were more personal items—a comb, a brush, a tube of toothpaste and a toothbrush.

Neil's things. He traveled light. There was no sign of a razor. He'd very obviously planned to be alone.

Strangely, she felt better. Knowing that Neil was as unprepared for the presence of a woman as she was for the presence of a man was reassuring. On the other hand, what would she have brought if she'd known she'd have company? Makeup? Aside from mascara, blusher and lip gloss, she rarely used it. A blow dryer? She rarely used one. Cologne? Hah!

And what would Neil have brought? She wondered.

Sliding the chest shut with a thud, she returned to the bedroom, where a sweeping glance told her there was little else to clean. She could always stretch out on the bed and read, or sit in the chaise by the window and knit. But that would be tantamount to hiding, and she refused to hide.

Discouraged, she looked toward the window. It was still raining. Gray, gloomy and forbidding. If things were different, she wouldn't have been stopped by the rain; she'd have bundled up and taken a walk. All too clearly, though, she recalled how treacherous it was maneuvering with crutches across the mud and rocks. She wasn't game to try it again soon.

Selecting a book from those she'd brought, she tucked it under her arm alongside the crutch, took a deep breath and headed for the living room. Neil was there, slouched on the sofa, lost in thought. He didn't look up until she'd settled herself in the chair, and then he sent her only the briefest of glances.

Determinedly she ignored him. She opened the book, a piece of contemporary women's fiction and began to read, patiently rereading the first page three times before she felt justified in moving on to the second. She was finally beginning to get involved in the story, when Neil materialized at her shoulder.

Setting the book down, she turned her head, not far enough to see him, just enough to let him know he had her attention. "Something wrong?" she asked in an even tone.

"Just wondering what you were reading," he said just as evenly.

Leaving a finger to mark her place, she closed the cover so he could see it.

"Any good?" he asked.

"I can't tell yet. I've just started."

"If it doesn't grab you within the first few pages, it won't."

"That's not necessarily true," she argued. "Some books take longer to get into."

He grunted and moved off. She heard a clatter, then another grunt, louder this time, and, following it, a curse that brought her head around fast. "Goddamn it. Can't you keep your crutches out of the way?" He had one hand on the corner of her chair, the other wrapped around his big toe.

"If you were wearing shoes, that wouldn't have happened!"

"I shouldn't have to wear shoes in my own home."

"This isn't your own home."

"Home away from home, then."

"Oh, please, Neil, what exactly would you have me do? Leave the crutches in the other room? You were the one who was after me to use them."

He didn't bother to answer. Setting his foot on the floor, he gingerly tested it. Then he straightened and limped across the room to stand at the window. He tucked his hands in the back pockets of his jeans, displacing the long jersey that would have otherwise covered his buttocks. The jersey itself was black and slim cut, fairly broadcasting the strength and breadth of his shoulders, the leanness of his hips. She wondered if he'd chosen to wear it on purpose.

Returning her eyes to her book, she read another two pages before being interrupted again.

"Crummy day" was the information relayed to her from the window.

She set the book down. "I know."

"That's two in a row."

"Three."

"Two full days that we've been here."

She conceded the point. "Fine. Two in a row." She picked up the book again. Several pages later, she raised her head to find Neil staring at her. "Is something wrong?"

"No."

"You look bored."

"I'm not used to inactivity."

"Don't you have anything to do?"

With a shrug he turned back to the window.

"What would you do at home on a rainy day?" she asked.

"Work."

"Even on a weekend?"

"Especially on a weekend. That's when I catch up on everything I've been too busy to do during the week." At least, it had been that way for years, he mused. Of course, when one was losing clients right and left, there was a definite slackening.

"You must have a successful practice," she remarked, then was taken aback when he sent her a glower. "I meant that as a compliment."

He bowed his head and rubbed the back of his neck. "I know. I'm sorry."

Deirdre glanced at her book, and realized she wasn't going to get much reading done with Neil standing there that way. She was grateful he hadn't made reference to what had happened earlier, and wondered if he was sorry for that, too. If so, she reflected, he might be in a conciliatory mood. It was as good a time as any to strike up a conversation.

"How do you know Victoria?" she asked in as casual a tone as she could muster.

"A mutual friend introduced us several years ago."

"Are you from the city?"

"Depends what city you mean."

For the sake of civility, she stifled her impatience. "New York."

"No." He was facing the window again, and for a minute she thought she'd have to prod, when he volunteered the information she'd been seeking. "Hartford."

A corner of her mouth curved up. She couldn't resist. "Ah, Hartford. Thriving little metropolis. I went to a concert there last year with friends. The seats were awful, the lead singer had a cold and I got a flat tire driving home."

Slowly Neil turned. "Okay. I deserved that."

"Yes, you did. Be grateful I didn't condemn the entire city."

He wasn't sure he'd have minded if she had. At the moment he felt the whole of Hartford was against him. "My allegiance to the city isn't blind. I can see her faults."

"Such as...?"

"Parochialism. Provinciality."

"Hartford?"

"Yes, Hartford. Certain circles are pretty closed."

"Isn't that true of any city?"

"I suppose." Casually he left the window and returned to the sofa. Deirdre took it as a sign of his willingness to talk.

"Have you lived there long?"

"Since I began practicing."

"You mentioned going to school in Boston. Was that law school, or undergraduate?"

"Both."

"So you went from Westchester to Boston to Hartford?"

He had taken on an expression of amused indulgence. "I did a stint in San Diego between Boston and Hartford. In the Navy. JAG division."

"Ah. Then you missed Vietnam."

"Right." He had one brow arched, as though waiting for her to criticize the fact that he hadn't seen combat.

"I think that's fine," she said easily. "You did something, which is more than a lot of men did."

"My motive wasn't all that pure. I would have been drafted if I hadn't signed up."

"You could have run to Canada."

"No."

The finality with which he said it spoke volumes. He felt he'd had a responsibility to his country. Deirdre respected that.

"How did you break your leg?" he asked suddenly.

The look on her face turned sour. "Don't ask."

"I am."

She met his gaze and debated silently for a minute. He'd opened up. Perhaps she should, too. Somehow it seemed childish to continue the evasion. She gave him a challenging stare. "I fell down a flight of stairs."

He held up a hand, warding off both her stare and its unspoken challenge. "That's okay. I'm not laughing."

Averting her gaze, she scowled at the floor. "You would if you knew the whole story."

"Try me. What happened?"

She'd set herself up for it, but strangely she wasn't sorry. It occurred to her that she wanted to tell the story. If he laughed, she'd have reason to yell at him. In some ways, arguing with him was safer than . . . than what had happened earlier.

Taking a breath, she faced him again. "I slipped on a magazine, caught my foot in the banister and broke my leg in three places."

He waited expectantly. "And . . . ? There has to be a punch line. I'm not laughing yet."

"You asked what I did for a living." She took a breath. "I teach aerobic dance."

His eyes widened fractionally. "Ah. And now you can't work."

"That's the least of it! I've always been into exercise of one sort or another. I'm supposed to be ultracoordinated. Do you have any idea how humiliating it is to have done this slipping on a magazine?"

"Was the magazine worth it?" he asked, deadpan.

"That's not the point! The point is that I'm not supposed to fall down the stairs! And if I do, I'm supposed to do it gracefully, with only a black-and-blue mark or two to show for it." She glared at her leg. "Not a grotesque cast!"

"How does the leg feel, by the way?"

"Okay."

"The dampness doesn't bother it?"

"My thigh is more sore from lugging the cast around, and my armpits hurt from the crutches."

"That'll get better with time. How long will the cast be on?"

"Another five weeks."

"And after that you'll be good as new?"

Her anger was replaced by discouragement. "I wish I knew. The doctor made no promises. Oh, I'll be able to walk. But teach?" Her shrug was as eloquent as the worry in her eyes.

Neil surprised himself by feeling her pain. Wasn't it somewhat akin to his own? After all, his own future was in limbo, too.

Leaning forward, he propped his elbows on his thighs. "You'll be able to teach, Deirdre. One way or another you will, if you want to badly enough."

"I do! I have to work. I mean, it's not a question of money. It's a question of emotional survival!"

That, too, he understood. "Your work means that much to you."

It was a statement, not a question, and Deirdre chose to let it rest. She wasn't ready to go into the issue of Joyce Enterprises, which was so much more complex and personal. Besides, Neil was a corporate attorney. He'd probably take *their* side.

"Well," she said at last, "I guess there's nothing I can do but wait."

"What will you do in the meantime?"

"Stay here for as long as I can."

"There's nothing else to keep you busy in Providence while your leg mends?"

"Nothing I care to do."

Neil wondered at her mutinous tone, but didn't comment. "What had you planned to do here? Besides read."

Still scowling, she shrugged. "Relax. Knit. Listen to music. Work up some routines. It may be a waste of time if it turns out I can't teach, but I suppose I have to hope."

"You could have done all that in Providence. I'd have thought that with a broken leg and all, you'd be more comfortable there. The drive up couldn't have been easy, and if Thomas had dumped you on that dock alone, you'd have had a hell of a time getting everything to the house."

Her scowl deepened. "Thomas knew what he was doing. *You* were here. Otherwise he'd probably have helped me himself."

"Still, to rush up here the day you left the hospital... What was the rush?"

"The telephone! My family! It was bad enough when I was in the hospital. I had to get away!"

"All that, just because you were embarrassed?"

Deirdre knew that she'd be spilling the entire story in another minute. Who in the devil was Neil Hersey that he should be prying? She hadn't asked *him* why he'd been in such a foul mood from day one. "Let's just say that I have a difficult family," she concluded, and closed her mouth tightly. Between that and the look she gave him, there was no doubt that she was done talking.

Neil took the hint. Oh, he was still curious, but there was time. Time for . . . lots of things.

She opened her book again and picked up where she'd left off, but if her concentration had been tentative before, it was nonexistent now. She was thinking of that difficult family, wondering what was going to change during the time she was in Maine that would make things any better when she returned.

From the corner of her eye she saw Neil get up, walk aimlessly around the room, then sit down. When a minute later he bobbed up again, she sighed.

"Decide what you want to do, please. I can't read with an active yo-yo in the room."

He said nothing, but took off for the bedroom. Moments later he returned, threw himself full length on the sofa and opened a book of his own. He read the first page, turned noisily to the last, then began to flip through those in between.

"Are you going to read or look at the pictures?" Deirdre snapped.

His face was the picture of innocence when he looked up. "I'm trying to decide if it's worth reading."

She was trying to decide if he was purposely distracting her. "You brought it along, didn't you?"

"I was in a rush. I took whatever books I had around the house and threw them in the bag."

"Then you must have decided it was worth reading when you bought it. What's it about?" She wondered which he'd chosen.

"World War I. History fascinates me."

"I know."

His eyes narrowed. "How would you know?"

"Because I saw the books lying on your dresser, and every one of them dealt with history in some form. You know, you really should wear your glasses when you read. Otherwise you'll get eye strain."

"I only wear them when I *have* eye strain, and since I haven't had much to look at for the past two days, my eyes are fine." He turned his head on the sofa arm to study her more fully. "You're pretty nosy. Did you look through my wallet, too?"

"Of course not! I was cleaning, not snooping. I've never liked living in a pigpen."

"Could've fooled me, what with the way you've been dropping clothes around."

"That was only the first night, and I was exhausted." She noticed a strange light in his eyes and suspected he was enjoying the sparring. It occurred to her that she was, too. "What's in your wallet, anyway? Something dark and sinister? Something I shouldn't see?"

He shrugged. "Nothing extraordinary."

"Wads of money?"

"Not quite."

"A membership card to a slinky men's club?"

"Not quite."

"A picture of your sweetheart?"

"Not . . . quite."

"Who is she, anyway—the one who burned you?"

The day before he wouldn't have wanted to talk about Nancy. Now, suddenly, it seemed less threatening. "She's someone I was seeing, whom I'm not seeing now."

"Obviously," Deirdre drawled. "What happened?"

Neil pursed his lips and thought of the best way to answer. He finally settled on the most general explanation. "She decided I didn't have enough potential."

"What was she looking for? An empire builder?"

"Probably."

"You don't sound terribly upset that she's gone."

"I'm getting over it," he said easily.

"Couldn't have been all that strong a relationship, then."

"It wasn't."

Deirdre settled her book against her stomach and tipped her head to the side. "Have you ever been married?"

"Where did that come from?"

"I'm curious. You asked me. Now I'm asking you."

"No. I've never been married."

"Why not?"

He arched a brow. "I never asked you that. It's impolite."

"It's impolite to ask a woman that, because traditionally she's the one who has to wait for the proposal. A man can do the proposing. Why haven't you?"

It occurred to Neil that there was something endearing about the way Deirdre's mind worked. It was quick, unpretentious, oddly refreshing. He smiled. "Would you believe me if I said I've been too busy?"

"No."

"It is true, in a way. I've spent the past fifteen years devoted to my career. She's a very demanding mistress."

"Then she's never had the right competition, which means that the old cliché is more the case. You haven't met the right woman yet."

He didn't need to ponder that to agree. "I have very special needs," he said, grinning. "Only a very special woman can satisfy them."

Deirdre could have sworn she saw mischief in his grin. She tried her best to sound scornful. "That I can believe. Any woman who'd put up with a face full of whiskers has to be special. Do you have any idea how...how grungy that looks?"

The insult fell flat. To her dismay, he simply grinned more broadly as he stroked his jaw. "It does look kinda grungy. Nice, huh?"

"Nice?"

"Yeah. I've never grown a beard in my life. From the time I was fifteen I shaved every blessed morning. And why? So I'd look clean. And neat. And acceptable. Well, hell, it's nice to look grungy for a change, and as for acceptability—" He searched for the words he wanted, finally thrust out his chin in defiance. "Screw it!"

Deirdre considered what he'd said. He didn't look unclean, or unneat, or unacceptable, but rather...dashing. Particularly with that look of triumph on his face. Helpless against it, she smiled. "That felt good, didn't it?"

"Sure did."

"You're much more controlled when you work."

"Always. There's a certain, uh, decorum demanded when you're dealing with corporate clients."

"Tell me about it," she drawled, bending her right leg up and hugging it to her chest.

Once before, he'd taken her up on the offer. This time he let it ride, because he didn't really want to talk about corporate clients. He wanted to talk about Deirdre Joyce.

"What about you, Deirdre? Why have you never married?"

"I've never been asked."

He laughed. "I should have expected you'd answer that way. But it's a cop-out, you know," he chided, then frowned and tucked in his chin. "Why are you looking at me that way?"

"Do you know that that's the first time I've heard you laugh, I mean, laugh, as in relaxed and content?"

His smile mellowed into something very gentle, and his eyes bound hers with sudden warmth. "Do you know that's the first time I've heard such a soft tone from you. Soft tone, as in amiable." As in womanly, he might have added, but he didn't. He'd let down enough defenses for one day.

For a minute Deirdre couldn't speak. Her total awareness centered on Neil and the way he was looking at her. He made her feel feminine in a way she'd never felt before.

Awkward, she dropped her gaze to her lap. "You're trying to butter me up, being nice and all. I think you're looking for someone to do the laundry."

Laundry was the last thing on his mind. "I don't think I've ever seen you blush before."

The blush deepened. She didn't look up. She didn't trust the little tricks her hormones were playing on her. She felt she was being toasted from the inside out. It was a new and unsettling sensation. Why *Neil*?

Lips turning down in a pout, she glared at him.

"Aw, come on," he teased. "I liked you the other way."

"Well, I didn't." It smacked of vulnerability, and Deirdre didn't like to think of herself as vulnerable. "I'm not the submissive type."

His laugh was gruffer this time. "I never thought you were. In fact, submissive is the last word I'd use to describe you. You prickle at the slightest thing. I'd almost think that *you*'d been burned."

The directness of her gaze held warning. "I have. I was used once, and I didn't like the feeling."

"No one does," he said softly. "What happened?"

She debated cutting off the discussion, but sensed he'd only raise it another time. So she crossed her right leg over her cast and slid lower in the chair in a pose meant to be nonchalant

"I let myself be a doormat for a fellow who had nothing better to do with his life at the time. The minute he sensed a demand on my part, he was gone."

"You demanded marriage?"

"Oh, no. It was nothing like that. Though I suppose he imagined that coming. My family would like to see me married. They don't think much of my. . . life-style."

"You're a swinger?"

She slanted him a disparaging glance. "Just the opposite. I avoid parties. I can't stand phony relationships. I hate pretense of any kind."

"What does pretense have to do with marriage?"

"If it's marriage for the sake of marriage alone, pretense is a given."

Neil couldn't argue with that. "Do you want to have children?"

"Someday. How about you?"

"Someday."

They looked at each other for a minute longer, then simultaneously returned to their books. Deirdre, for one, was surprised that she was talking about these things with Neil. She asked herself what it was about him that inspired her to speak, and finally concluded that it was the situation, more than the man, that had brought her out. Hadn't she come here to soul-search, to ponder the direction her life was taking?

Neil was brooding about his own life, his own direction, and for the first time that brooding was on a personal bent. Yes, he'd like to be married, but only to the right person. He was as averse to pretense as Deirdre was. Nancy—for that matter, most of the women he'd dated over the years—had epitomized pretense. One part of him very much wanted to put his law practice in its proper perspective, to focus, instead, on a relationship with a woman, a relationship that was intimate, emotionally as well as physically, and rewarding. And yes, he'd like to have children.

Absently he turned a page, then turned it back when he realized he hadn't read a word. He darted a glance at Deirdre and found her curled in the chair, engrossed in her book. She was honest; he admired her for that. She didn't have any more answers than he did, but at least she was honest.

Settling more comfortably on the sofa, Neil refocused on his book and disciplined himself to read. It came easier as the morning passed. The rain beat a steady accompaniment to the quiet activity, and he had to admit that it was almost peaceful.

Setting the book down at last, he stood. "I'm making sandwiches. Want one?"

Deirdre looked up. "What kind?"

His mouth turned down at the corner. "That's gratitude for you, when someone is offering to make you lunch."

"I can make my own," she pointed out, needing to remind him—and herself—that she wasn't helpless.

"Is that what you'd rather?"

"It depends on what kind of sandwiches you know how to make."

"I know how to make most anything. The question is what have we got to work with?" He crossed into the kitchen, opened the refrigerator and rummaged through the supplies. Straightening, he called over his shoulder, "You can have ham and cheese, bologna and cheese, grilled cheese, grilled cheese and tomato, grilled cheese and tuna, a BLT, egg salad, peanut butter and jelly, cream cheese and jelly—" he sucked in a badly needed breath "—or any of the above taken separately."

Any of the above sounded fine to Deirdre, who'd never been a picky eater. She tried not to grin. "That's quite a list. Could you run through it one more time?"

The refrigerator door swung shut and Neil entered her line of vision. His hands were hooked low on his hips and his stance was one of self-assurance. "You heard it the first time, Deirdre."

"But there are so many things to choose from . . . and it's a big decision." She pressed her lips together, feigning concentration. "A big decision . . ."

"Deirdre . . ."

"I'll have turkey with mustard."

"Turkey wasn't on the list."

"No? I thought for sure it was."

"We don't have any turkey."

"Why not? Thomas should have known to pick some up. Turkey's far better for you than ham or cheese or peanut butter."

Hands falling to his sides, Neil drew himself up, shoulders back. He spoke slowly and clearly. "Do you, or do you not, want a sandwich?"

"I do."

"What kind?"

"Grilled cheese and tuna."

He sighed. "Thank you." He'd no sooner returned to the refrigerator, when he heard her call.

"Can I have it on rye?"

"No, you cannot have it on rye," he called back through gritted teeth.

"How about a roll?"

"If a hamburg roll will do."

"It won't."

"Then it's white bread or nothing. Take it or leave it."

"I'll take it."

He waited a minute longer to see if she had anything else to add. When she remained silent, he tugged open the refrig-

erator and removed everything he'd need. He'd barely closed
the door again, when Deirdre entered the kitchen.

"If you've changed your mind," he warned, "that's tough.
Your order's already gone to the cook. It's too late to change."

She was settling herself on the counter stool. "Grilled
cheese and tuna's fine." Folding her hands in her lap, she
watched him set to work.

He opened a can of tuna, dumped its contents into a bowl
and shot her a glance as he reached for the mayonnaise. A
glob of the creamy white stuff went the way of the tuna. He
was in the process of mixing it all together with a fork, when
he darted her another glance. "Anything wrong?"

"No, no. Just watching. You don't mind, do you? I'm fascinated. You're very domestic for a man."

"Men have to eat."

"They usually take every shortcut in the book, but grilled
cheese and tuna . . . I'm impressed."

"It's not terribly difficult," he scoffed.

"But it takes more time than peanut butter and jelly."

"Tastes better, too."

"I *love* peanut butter and jelly."

"Then why'd you ask for grilled cheese and tuna?"

She arched a brow, goading him on. "Maybe I wanted to
see what you could do."

Neil, who'd been slathering tuna on slices of bread,
stopped midstroke, put down the knife and slowly turned.
"You mean you purposely picked what you thought was the
hardest thing on the menu?"

Deirdre knew when to back off. "I was only teasing. I really
do feel like having grilled cheese and tuna."

With deliberate steps, he closed the small distance between them. "I don't believe you. I think you did it on purpose, just like you asked for turkey when you knew damn
well we didn't have it."

She would have backed up if there'd been anywhere to go, but the counter was already digging into her ribs. "Really, Neil." She held up a hand. "There's no need to get upset. Unless you're having ego problems with my being in the kitchen this way—"

The last word barely made it from her mouth, when Neil scooped her up from the stool, cast and all, and into his arms.

"What are you doing?" she cried.

He was striding through the living room. "Removing you from my presence. You wanted to get my goat. Well, you got it. Picking the most complicated sandwich. *Ego* problems." They were in the hall and moving steadily. "If you want to talk, you can do it to your heart's content in here." He entered the bedroom and went straight to the bed, his intent abundantly clear to Deirdre, who was clutching the crew neckline of his jersey.

"Don't drop me! My cast!"

Neil held her suspended for a minute, enjoying the fact of his advantage over her. Then, in a single heartbeat, his awareness changed. No longer was he thinking that she'd goaded him once too often. Rather, he was suddenly aware that her thigh was slender and strong beneath one of his hands, and that the fingertips of the other were pressed into an unexpectedly feminine breast. He was thinking that her eyes were luminous, her lips moist, her cheeks a newly acquired pale pink.

Deirdre, too, had caught her breath. She was looking up at Neil, realizing that his eyes, like her hair, weren't black at all, but a shade of charcoal brown, and that his mouth was strong, well formed and very male. She was realizing that he held her with ease, and that he smelled clean, and that the backs of her fingers were touching the hot, hair-shaded surface of his chest and he felt good.

Slowly he lowered her to the bed, but didn't retreat. Instead he planted his hands on either side of her. "I don't know what in the hell is going on here," he breathed thickly. "It must be cabin fever." His gaze fell from her eyes to her lips, declaring his intent even before he lowered his head.

6

His MOUTH TOUCHED hers lightly at first, brushing her lips, sampling their shape and texture. Then he intensified the kiss, deepening it by bold degrees until it had become something positively breathtaking.

Deirdre could barely think, much less respond. She'd known Neil was going to kiss her, but she'd never expected such force in the simple communion of mouths. He drank from her like a man who was dying of thirst, stumbling unexpectedly upon an oasis in the desert. From time to time his lips gentled to a whisper, touching hers almost timidly in reassurance that what he'd found wasn't a mirage.

His hands framed her face, moving her inches away when his mouth would have resisted even that much. "Kiss me, Deirdre," he breathed, studying her through lambent eyes.

His hoarse command was enough to free her from the spell she'd been under. When he brought her mouth back to his, her lips were parted, curious, eager, and she returned his kiss with growing fervor. She discovered the firmness of his lips, the evenness of his teeth, the texture of his tongue. She tasted his taste and breathed his breath, and every cell in her that was woman came alive.

"Deirdre," he whispered, once again inching her face from his. He pressed his warm forehead to hers and worked at catching his breath. "Why did you *do* that?"

Deirdre, who was having breathing difficulties of her own, struggled to understand. "What?"

"*Why did you do that?*"

"Do what?"

"Kiss me!"

The haze in her head began to clear, and she drew farther away. "You told me to kiss you."

His brows were drawn together, his features taut. "Not like that. I expected just a little kiss. Not . . . not that!"

He was angry. She couldn't believe it. "And who was kissing whom first like that?"

His breath came roughly, nostrils flaring. "You didn't have to do it back!" Shoving his large frame from the bed, he stormed from the room, leaving Deirdre unsure and bewildered and, very quickly, angry.

She sat up to glare in the direction he'd gone, then closed her eyes and tried to understand his reaction. Though she'd never, never kissed or been kissed that way, she wasn't so inexperienced that she couldn't see when a man was aroused. Neil Hersey had been aroused, and he'd resented it.

Which meant he didn't want involvement any more than she did.

Which meant they had a problem.

She'd enjoyed his kiss. More than that. It had taken her places she'd never been before. Kissing Neil had been like sampling a rich chocolate with a brandy center, sweet and dissolving—yet potent. He went straight to her head.

She touched her swollen lips, then her tingling chin. Even his beard had excited her, its roughness a contrast to the smoothness of his mouth. Yes, he was smooth. Smooth and virile and stimulating, damn him!

Dropping her chin to her chest, she took several long, steadying breaths. With the fresh intake of oxygen came the strength she needed. Yes, they were stuck under the same roof. They were even stuck, thanks to a matching stubbornness, in the same bed. She was simply going to have to remember that she had problems enough of her own, that *he*

HARLEQUIN GIVES YOU SIX REASONS TO CELEBRATE!

MAIL THE BALLOON TODAY!

INCLUDING

**1.
4 FREE
BOOKS**

**2.
AN ELEGANT
MANICURE SET**

**3.
A SURPRISE
BONUS**

AND MORE!

TAKE A LOOK . . .

Yes, become a Harlequin home subscriber and the celebration goes on forever.

To begin with we'll send you:

- **4 new Harlequin Temptation novels – Free**
- **an elegant, purse-size manicure set – Free**
- **and an exciting mystery bonus – Free**

And that's not all! Special extras – Three more reasons to celebrate

4. Money-Saving Home Delivery That's right! When you become a Harlequin home subscriber the excitement, romance and far-away adventures of Harlequin Temptation novels can be yours for previewing in the convenience of your own home **at less than retail prices.** Here's how it works. Every month we'll deliver four new books right to your door. If you decide to keep them, they'll be yours for only $1.99! That's 26¢ less per book than what you pay in stores. And there is **no charge for shipping and handling.**

5. Free Monthly Newsletter – It's "Heart to Heart" – **the** indispensable insider's look at our most popular writers and their up-coming novels. Now you can have a behind-the-scenes look at the fascinating world of Harlequin! It's an added bonus you'll look forward to every month!

6. More Surprise Gifts – Because our home subscribers are our most valued readers, we'll be sending you additional free gifts from time to time – as a token of our appreciation.

This beautiful manicure set will be a useful and elegant item to carry in your handbag. Its rich burgundy case is a perfect expression of your style and good taste. And it's yours **free** in this amazing Harlequin celebration!

HARLEQUIN READER SERVICE
FREE OFFER CARD

BUSINESS REPLY CARD

First Class   Permit No. 717   Buffalo, NY

Postage will be paid by addressee

Harlequin Reader Service
901 Fuhrmann Blvd.,
P.O. Box 1394
Buffalo, NY 14240-9963

NO POSTAGE
NECESSARY
IF MAILED
IN THE
UNITED STATES

had problems enough of his own. And that he could be a very disagreeable man.

Unfortunately Neil chose that moment to return to the bedroom. He carried her crutches and wore an expression of uncertainty. After a moment's hesitation on the threshold, he started slowly toward the bed.

"Here," he said, quietly offering the crutches. "The sandwiches are under the broiler. They'll be ready in a minute."

Deirdre met his gaze, then averted her own, looking to the crutches. She reached for them, wrapped her hands around the rubber handles and studied them for a minute before raising her eyes again.

The corners of his mouth curved into the briefest, most tentative of smiles before he turned and left the room.

Leaning forward, Deirdre rested her head against the crutches. Oh, yes, Neil was a very disagreeable man. He also had his moments of sweetness and understanding, which, ironically, was going to make living with him that much more of a trial.

She sighed. It had to be done. Unless she was prepared to capitulate and leave the island by choice. Which she wasn't.

Struggling to her feet, she secured the crutches under her arms and, resigned, headed for the kitchen.

Lunch was a quiet, somewhat awkward affair. Neil avoided looking at Deirdre, which she had no way of knowing, since she avoided looking at him. She complimented him on the sandwiches. He thanked her. When they were done, he made a fresh pot of coffee—medium thick—and carried a cup to the living room for her. She thanked him. And all the while she was thinking of that kiss, as he was. All the while she was wondering where it might have led, as he was. All the while she was asking herself why, as was he.

Knowing she'd never be able to concentrate on her book, she brought her knitting bag from the bedroom, opened the instruction booklet and forced her attention to the directions.

Neil, who was in a chair drinking his second cup of coffee, was as averse to reading as she was, but could think of nothing else he wanted to do. "What are you making?" he asked in a bored tone.

She didn't look up. "A sweater."

"For you?"

"Hopefully." She reached for a neatly wound skein of yarn, freed its end and pulled out a considerable length. Casting on—that sounded simple enough.

Neil noted the thick lavender strand. "Nice color."

"Thank you." With the book open on her lap, she took one of the needles and lay the strand against it.

"That's a big needle."

She sighed. Concentration was difficult, knowing he was watching. "Big needle for a big sweater."

"For you?"

Her eyes met his. "It's going to be a bulky sweater."

"Ah. As in ski sweater?"

She pressed her lips together in angry restraint. "As in warm sweater, since it looks like I won't be skiing in the near future."

"Do you ski?"

"Yes."

"Are you good?"

She dropped the needle to her lap and stared at him. "I told you I was athletic. I exercise, play tennis, swim, ski . . . At least, I used to do all of those things. Neil, I can't concentrate if you keep talking."

"I thought knitting was an automatic thing."

"Not when you're learning how."

One side of his mouth twitched. "You haven't done it before?"

"No, I haven't."

"Was it the broken leg that inspired you?"

"I bought the yarn several months ago. This is the first chance I've had to work with it."

He nodded. She lifted the needle again, studied the book again, brought the yarn up and wound it properly for the first stitch. It took several attempts before she'd made the second, but once she'd caught on, she moved right ahead. Before long she had enough stitches cast on to experiment with the actual knitting.

When Neil finished his coffee, he returned the cup to the kitchen and started wandering around the house. At last, all else having failed to divert him, he picked up his book again.

By this time Deirdre was painstakingly working one knit stitch after another. The needles were awkward in her hands, and she continually dropped the yarn that was supposed to be wrapped around her forefinger. Periodically she glanced up to make sure Neil wasn't witnessing her clumsiness, and each time she was frowning when she returned to her work. Simply looking at him turned her inside out.

He was stretched full length on the couch . . . so long . . . so lean. The sleeves of his jersey were pushed back to reveal forearms matted with the same dark hair she'd felt on his chest. *Felt.* Soft, but strong and crinkly. The texture was permanently etched in her memory.

From his position on the sofa, Neil was also suffering distractions. His curiosity as to what Deirdre hid beneath her bulky sweatshirt had never been greater. He'd felt the edge of her breast. *Felt.* Strong and pert, but yielding beneath his fingertips. He'd carried her; she was light as thistledown and every bit as warm. He'd tasted her. That was his worst mistake, because there'd been a honeyed sweetness to her that he never would have imagined. Did the rest of his imaginings pale by comparison to the real thing?

From beneath half-lidded eyes he slanted her a look. Her hands gripped the needles, the forefinger of each extended. She was struggling, he saw, but even then the sweep of her fingers was graceful. Athletic? Perhaps. But if so, in a most healthy, most fitting, most feminine way.

Slapping the book shut, he sat bolt upright. Deirdre's questioning eyes shot to him.

"I can't read with that clicking," he grumbled. "Can't you be any quieter?"

"I'm having trouble as it is. Do you want miracles?"

"Not miracles. Just peace and quiet." Dropping the book on the sofa, he began to prowl the room.

"Book didn't grab you?"

"No." He ran a hand through his hair. "How about playing a game? Victoria has a bunch of them in the other room."

The knitting fell to Deirdre's lap. She wasn't sure she was up to playing games with Neil. "What did you have in mind?" she asked warily.

"I don't know. Maybe Monopoly?"

"I hate Monopoly. There's no skill involved."

"What about Trivial Pursuit?"

"I'm no good at history and geography. They make me lose."

"You make you lose," he argued. "The game doesn't do it."

"Whatever. The result's the same."

"Okay. Forget Trivial Pursuit. How about chess?"

"I don't know how."

"Checkers."

She scrunched up her nose in rejection.

"Forget a game," he mumbled.

"How about a movie?" she asked. It was a rainy day; the idea held merit. Her fingers were cramped, anyway.

"Okay."

"What do we have to choose from?"

In answer he started off toward the den. Deirdre levered herself up and followed, finding him bent over a low shelf in contemplation of the video tapes. She came closer, trying not to notice how snugly his jeans molded his buttocks, how they were slightly faded at the spot where he sat.

"*Magnum Force?*" he suggested.

"Too violent."

"*North by Northwest?*"

"Too intense." Leaning over beside him, she studied the lineup. "How about *Against All Odds?*"

"That's a romance."

"So?"

"Forget it."

"Then *The Sting*. Unromantic, but amusing."

"And boring. The best part's the music."

Her gaze moved across the cassettes, eyes suddenly widening. "*Body Heat*. That's a super movie. William Hurt, Kathleen Turner, intrigue and—"

"—Sex." Neil's head was turned, eyes boring into her. "I don't think we need that."

He was right, of course. She couldn't believe she'd been so impulsive as to suggest that particular movie.

"Ah." He drew one box out. "Here we go. *The Eye of the Needle*. Now that was a good flick."

It had action, intrigue, and yes, a bit of sex, but Deirdre felt she could take it. "Okay. Put it on." She set her crutches against the wall and hopped to the leather couch.

Removing the cassette from its box, Neil inserted it in the VCR, pressed several buttons, then took the remote control and sank onto the couch an arm's length from Deirdre. The first of the credits had begun to roll, when he snapped it off and jumped up.

"What's wrong?" she asked.

"We need popcorn. I saw some in the kitchen cabinet."

"But it takes time to make popcorn, and we're all set to watch."

"We've got time. Besides, it doesn't take more than a couple of minutes in the microwave." He rubbed his hands together. "With lots of nice melted butter poured on top—"

"Not butter! It's greasy, and awful for you."

"What's popcorn without butter?" he protested.

"Healthier."

"Then I'll put butter on mine. You can have yours without."

"Fine." She crossed her arms over her chest and sat back while he went to make the popcorn. Gradually her frown softened. It was rather nice being waited on, and Neil wasn't complaining. She supposed that if she'd had to be marooned with a man, she could have done worse. She *knew* she could have done worse. She could have been stuck with a real egomaniac. True, Neil had his moments. It occurred to her that while she'd given him a clue as to what caused her own mood swings, as yet she had no clue to his motivation. She'd have to work on that, she decided, merely for the sake of satisfying her curiosity. Nothing else.

Neil entered the room carrying popcorn still in its cooking bag. He resumed his seat, turned the movie back on and positioned the bag at a spot midway between them.

"Did you add butter?" she asked cautiously.

"No. You're right. I don't need it."

"Ah. Common sense prevails."

"Shh. I want to watch the movie."

She glanced at the screen. "I'm only disturbing the credits."

"You're disturbing me. Now keep still."

Deirdre kept still. She reached for a handful of popcorn and put one piece, then another in her mouth. The movie progressed. She tried to get into it but failed.

"It's not the same watching movies at home," she remarked. "A theater's dark. It's easier to forget your surroundings and become part of the story."

"Shh." Neil was having trouble of his own concentrating. It wasn't the movie, although as he'd seen it before, it held no mystery. What distracted him was Deirdre sitting so close. Only popcorn separated them. Once, when he reached into the bag, his hand met hers. They both retreated. And waited.

"You go first," he said.

She kept her eyes on the small screen. "No. That's okay. I'll wait."

"I've already had more. Go ahead."

"I don't need it. I'll get fat."

"You won't get fat." From what he'd seen, she wasn't a big eater; as for getting fat, from what he'd felt she was slender enough. Still, he couldn't resist a gibe. "On second thought, maybe you're right. You will get fat. You're smaller than I am, and I'm the one who's getting all the exercise around here. I'll wear it off easier."

He reached for the popcorn, but Deirdre already had her hand in the bag. She withdrew a full fist, sent him a smug grin and with deliberate nonchalance popped several pieces into her mouth.

Neil, who'd almost expected she'd do just that, wasn't sure whether to laugh or scream. Deirdre was impetuous in a way that was adorable, and adorable in a way that was bad for his heart. She had only to look at him with those luminous brown eyes and his pulse raced. He never should have kissed her. Damn it, he never should have kissed her!

But he had, and that fact didn't ease his watching of the rest of the movie. He was constantly aware of her—aware when she shifted on the couch, aware when she dropped her head back and watched the screen through half-closed eyes, aware when she began to massage her thigh absently.

"Leg hurt?" he asked.

She looked sharply his way, then shrugged and looked back at the screen.

"Want some aspirin?"

"No."

"Some Ben-Gay?"

"There is no Ben-Gay."

His lips twitched. "I'd run to the island drugstore for some if you'd let me rub it on."

She glared at the movie, but carried on the farce. "The island drugstore's out. I checked."

"Oh. Too bad."

Deirdre clamped her lips tightly, silently cursing Neil for his suggestion. *Let me rub it on.* Her insides tingled with a heat that, unfortunately, didn't do a whit to help her thigh.

Neil, too, cursed the suggestion, because his imagination had picked up from there, and he'd begun to think of rubbing far more than her thigh. He wondered whether her breasts would fit his hand, whether the skin of her belly would be soft....

He shifted away from her on the couch, and made no further comments, suggestive or otherwise. The movie was ruined for him. He was too distracted to follow the dialogue; the intrigue left him cold; the sex left him hot. The only thing that brought him any relief from the build-up of need in his body was the thought of Hartford, of work, of Wittnauer-Douglass. And because that upset him all the more, he was truly between a rock and a very hard place, where he remained throughout the evening.

He and Deirdre ate dinner together. They sat together before the fire. They pretended to read, but from the way Deirdre's eyes were more often on the flames than her book, he suspected that she was accomplishing as little as he was. He also suspected that her thoughts were running along similar lines, if the occasional nervous glances she cast him were any indication.

There was an element of fear in her. He'd seen it before; he could see it now. And it disturbed him. Was she afraid of sex? Was she afraid of feeling feminine and heated and out of control?

Even as he asked himself those questions, his body tightened. What in the hell was *he* afraid of? Certainly not sex. But there was something holding him back, even when every nerve in his body was driving him on.

He sat up by the fire long after Deirdre had taken refuge in bed. When at last he joined her, he was tired enough to fall asleep quickly. By the time the new day dawned, though, he was wondering whether he should relent and sleep in another room. Twice during the night he'd awoken to find their bodies touching—his outstretched arm draped over hers, the sole of her foot nestled against his calf.

What *was* it that made them gravitate toward each other? Each had come to Maine in search of solitude, so he'd have thought they'd have chosen to pass the time in opposite corners of the house. That hadn't been the case. Spitting and arguing—be it in the bedroom, the kitchen, the living room or den—they'd been together. And now . . . still . . . the bed.

He saw Deirdre look over her shoulder at him, then curl up more tightly on her side. Rolling to his back, he stared up at the ceiling, but the image there was of a disorderly mop of wheat-colored hair, soft brown eyes still misty with sleep, soft cheeks bearing a bed-warmed flush and lips that were slightly parted, unsure, questioning.

He had to get out. Though there was still the intermittent patter of rain and the air beyond the window was thick with mist, he had to get out. Without another glance at Deirdre, he flew from the bed, pulled on the dirty clothes he'd been planning to wash that day, laced on the sneakers that still bore a crust of mud from the day of his arrival on the island, threw his Windbreaker over his shoulders and fled the room, then the house.

Surrounded by the silence left in his wake, Deirdre slowly sat up. Being closed in had finally gotten to him, she mused. It had gotten to her, too. Or was it Neil who'd gotten to her? She'd never spent as uncomfortable an evening or night as those immediately past, her senses sharpened, sensitized, focused in on every nuance of Neil's physical presence. He breathed; she heard it. He turned; she felt it. Once, when she'd awoken in the middle of the night to find her hand tucked under his arm, she'd nearly jumped out of her skin, and not from fear of the dark.

Her body was a coiled spring, taut with frustration. She wanted to run six miles, but couldn't run at all. She wanted to swim seventy-two laps, but couldn't set foot in a pool, much less the ocean. She wanted to exercise until she was hot and tired and dripping with sweat, but . . . but . . . Damn it, yes, she could!

Shoving back the covers, she grabbed her crutches, took a tank top and exercise shorts from the dresser drawer and quickly pulled them on. She sat on the bed to put on her one sock and sneaker and both leg warmers, then pushed herself back up, tucked her cassette player and several tapes under one arm and her crutch under the other, and hobbled into one of the spare bedrooms. Within minutes the sounds of Barry Manilow filled the house.

Deirdre took a deep breath and smiled, then closed her eyes and began her familiar flexibility exercises. Her crutches lay on the spare bed; she discovered she could stand perfectly well without them. And the fact that various parts of the routine had to be altered in deference to her leg didn't bother her. She was moving.

In time with the music, she did body twists and side bends. She stretched the calf and ankle muscles of her right leg, and the inner thigh muscles of both legs. It felt good, so good to be feeling her body again. She took her time, relaxed, let the music take her where it would.

After several minutes, she moved into a warm-up, improvising as she went to accommodate her limited mobility. The music changed; the beat picked up, and she ventured into an actual dance routine. Though she couldn't dance in the true sense of the word, her movements were fluid and involved her entire upper torso as well as her good leg. By the time she'd slowed to do a cool-down routine, she'd broken into a healthy sweat and felt better than she had in days.

So immersed was she in the exercise that she didn't hear the open and closing of the front door. Neil, though, heard her music the minute he stepped into the house. He was incensed; it was loud and far heavier than the music he preferred. Without bothering to remove his wet jacket, he strode directly toward the sound, intent on informing Deirdre that as long as they were sharing the house, she had no right to be so thoughtless.

He came to an abrupt halt on the threshold of the spare bedroom, immobilized by the sight that met him. Eyes closed, seeming almost in a trance, Deirdre was moving in time to the music with a grace that was remarkable given her one casted leg. But it wasn't the movement that lodged his breath in his throat. It was her. Her body.

If he'd wondered what she'd been hiding beneath her oversized clothes, he didn't have to wonder any longer. She wore a skimpy tank top that revealed slender arms and well-toned shoulders. Her breasts pushed pertly at the thin fabric, their soft side swells clearly visible when she moved her arms. Her waist was small, snugly molded by the elasticized band of her shorts, and the shorts themselves were brief, offering an exaggerated view of silken thighs.

He gave a convulsive swallow when she bent over, his eyes glued to crescents of pale flesh. Then she straightened and stretched, arms high over her head, dipping low and slow from one side to the other. He swallowed again, transfixed by the firmness of her breasts, which rose with the movement.

Neil realized then that Deirdre's shapelessness had belonged solely to her bulky sweat clothes. Deirdre Joyce was shapely and lithe. With her hair damp around her face, her skin gleaming under a sheen of perspiration, with her arms flexing lyrically, her breasts bobbing, her hips rocking, she looked sultry, sexy and feminine.

He was in agony. His own body was taut, and his breath came raggedly. Turning, he all but ran down the hall, through the master bedroom, directly into the bathroom. He was tugging at his clothes, fumbling in his haste, knowing only that if he didn't hit a cold shower soon he'd explode.

His clothing littered the floor, but he was oblivious to the mess. Stepping into the shower, he turned on the cold tap full force, put his head directly beneath the spray, propped his fists against the tile wall and stood there, trembling, until the chill of the water had taken the edge of fever from his body. He thought of Hartford, of Wittnauer-Douglass, of his uncle who'd died the year before, of basketball—anything to get his mind off Deirdre. Only when he felt he'd gained a modicum of control did he adjust the water temperature to a more comfortable level for bathing.

Deirdre, who was totally unaware of the trial Neil had been through, finished her cool-down exercises and did several final stretches before allowing herself to relax in a nearby chair. Feeling tired but exhilarated, she left the music on; it was familiar, comfortable and reassuring.

At length she sat forward and reached for her crutches, knowing that if she didn't dry off and change clothes, her perspiration-dampened body would soon be chilled.

She turned off the music and listened. The house was still silent, which meant, she reasoned, that Neil was still outside, which meant, she reasoned further, that she could have the bathroom to herself without fear of intrusion. A warm bath sounded very, very appealing.

The smile she wore as she swung her way down the hall was self-congratulatory. She was proud of herself. She'd exercised, and in so doing had not only proved that she could do it, but had worked off the awful tension she'd awoken with that morning. So much for Neil Hersey and his virility, she mused. She could handle it.

Intending to fill the tub while she undressed, she passed straight through the master bedroom to the bathroom. The door was closed. Without a thought, she shouldered it open and let the rhythm of her limp carry her several feet into the room. There she came to a jarring halt.

Neil stood at the sink. His head was bowed and he was bent slightly at the waist, his large hands curving around the edges of the porcelain fixture. He was stark naked.

The breath had left her lungs the instant she'd seen him, and Deirdre could do no more than stare, even when he slowly raised his head and looked at her. He had a more beautifully male body than she'd ever have dreamed. His back was broad and smooth, his flanks lean, his buttocks tight. Seen in profile, his abdomen was flat, his pelvic bones just visible beneath a casement of flesh, his sex heavy and distinct.

"Deirdre?" His voice was husky. Her eyes flew to his when, without apparent modesty, he straightened and turned to face her. Two slow steps brought him close enough to touch. He repeated her name, this time in a whisper.

She was rooted to the spot, barely able to breathe, much less speak. Her eyes were wide and riveted to his.

He brought up a hand to brush the dots of moisture from her nose, then let his thumb trail down her cheek, over her jaw to her neck and on to the quivering flesh that bordered the thin upper hem of her tank top. Her breath was suddenly coming in tiny spurts that grew even tinier when he slipped his hand beneath her shoulder strap and brushed the backs of his fingers lower, then lower. She bit her lip to stifle a cry when he touched the upper swell of her breast, and though she kept her eyes on his, she was aware of the gradual change in his lower body.

"I didn't know you looked like this," he said hoarsely. "You've kept it all hidden."

Deirdre didn't know what to say. She couldn't quite believe he was complimenting her, not when he was so superbly formed himself. Surely the other women who'd seen him this way had been far more desirable than she. And though she knew he was aroused, her insecurities crowded in on her.

The backs of his fingers were gently rubbing her, dipping ever deeper into her bra. "Take off your clothes," he urged in a rough murmur, eyes flaming with restrained heat. "Let me see you."

She shook her head.

"Why not?"

She swallowed hard and managed a shaky whisper. "I'm sweaty."

"Take a shower with me." His baby finger had reached the sensitive skin just above her nipple, coaxing.

Pressing her lips together to hold in a moan, she shook her head again. "I can't take a shower." Her voice was small, pleading.

"Then a bath. Let me bathe you."

She wasn't sure if it was the sensuality of his words, or the fact that his finger had just grazed the hard nub of her nipple, but her good knee buckled, and she would have fallen had not her crutches been under her arms. His finger moved again, then again, sending live currents through her body. This time she couldn't contain the soft moan that slipped from her throat.

"Feel good?" he whispered against her temple, his own breath coming quicker.

"I don't want it to," she cried.

"Neither do I, but it does, doesn't it?"

It felt heavenly—his touching her, his being so near, so naked. She wanted to be naked beside him, too, but she was frightened. He'd be disappointed. She was sure of it. She was an athlete, "boyish" by her family's definition, and that description had haunted her doggedly over the years. She wasn't soft and fragile and willowy.

And even if Neil wasn't disappointed looking at her, he'd be let down by what would come after that. She felt the ache, the emptiness crying out inside of her, and knew she'd want to make love. And then he'd be disappointed, and the illusion would be broken.

She hobbled back a step, dislodging his hand. "I have to go. I have to go, Neil." Without waiting for his reply, she turned and fled from the bathroom, taking refuge in the bedroom where she'd exercised, collapsing in the chair and cursing her failings. *So much for handling Neil's virility.* Hah!

She didn't know how long she sat there, but the sweat had long since dried from her skin and she was feeling chilled when Neil appeared at the door. He wore a fresh pair of jeans and a sweater, and was barefoot, as usual. She wished she could believe that things were back to normal between them, but she knew better.

Neil felt neither anger nor frustration as he looked at her, but rather a tenderness that stunned him. Padding slowly into the room, he took an afghan from the end of the bed, gently draped it over her shoulders, then came down on his haunches beside her chair. "What frightens you, Deirdre?" he asked in a tone that would have melted her if the sight of him hadn't already done so.

It was a minute before she could speak, and then only brokenly. "You. Me. I don't know."

"I'd never hurt you."

"I know."

"Then what is it? You respond to me. I can feel it in your body. Your breath catches, and you begin to tremble. Is that fear, too?"

"Not all of it."

"You do want me."

"Yes."

"Why don't you give in and let go? It'd be good between us."

She looked down at her hands, which were tightly entwined in her lap. "Maybe for me, but I'm not sure for you."

"Why don't you let me be the judge of that?"

"I'm an athlete, not soft and cuddly like some women."

"Just because you're athletic doesn't mean you're not soft and cuddly. Besides, if it was a cushiony round ball I wanted, I'd go to bed with a teddy bear."

As he'd intended, his comment brought a smile to her face. But it was a tentative smile, a nervous one. "Somehow I can't picture that."

"Neither can I, but, then, I can't picture myself being disappointed if you let me hold you . . . touch you . . . make love to you."

His words sent a ripple of excitement through her, and there was clear longing in her gaze as she surveyed his face. "I'm scared" was all she could manage to say.

Neil studied her a minute longer, then leaned forward and kissed her lightly. "I'd never hurt you. Just remember that." Standing, he left the room.

His words were in Deirdre's mind constantly as the day progressed. She believed that he'd meant what he'd said, but she knew that there were different kinds of hurt. Physical hurt was out of the question; Neil was far too gentle for that. But emotional hurt was something else. If their relationship should take the quantum leap that lovemaking would entail...and he should be let down...she'd be hurt. How it had happened, she didn't know, particularly since they'd spent most of their time together fighting, but Neil had come to mean something to her. She wasn't up to analyzing the exact nature of that something; all she knew was that she was terrified of endangering it.

If he'd thought long and hard, Neil couldn't have come up with a better way to goad Deirdre that day than by being kind, soft-spoken and agreeable. Without a word he prepared their meals. Without a word he did the laundry. He was indulgent when she tackled her knitting again, abiding the noise without complaint. He was perfectly amenable to watching her choice of movie on the VCR. He didn't start a single argument, but, then, neither did she. It was the quietest day they'd spent on the island.

Deirdre was as aware as he of that fact. She was also aware that, by denying her any cause to bicker, Neil was allowing her time to think about what he'd said and what she was going to do about it. If the issue had been entirely cerebral, she might have had a chance to resist him. But her senses refused to be reasoned with and were constantly attuned to his presence. That side of her she'd never paid much heed to was suddenly clamoring for attention. Though all was peaceful on the outside, inside she was a mass of cells crying for release from a tension that radiated through her body in ever-undulating waves.

By the time they'd finished dinner and had spent a quiet hour before the fire, she had her answer. Yes, she was frightened and very, very nervous, but she'd decided that if Neil approached her again, she wouldn't refuse him. The sensual side of her nature wouldn't allow her to deny herself.

Head bowed, she quietly got to her feet, secured her crutches under her arms and left the living room. Once in the bedroom, she slowly changed into her pajamas, then sat on the side of the bed and reviewed her decision. She was taking a chance, she knew. A big one. If things didn't go well, the atmosphere in the house would be worse than ever. Then again, maybe not. They might be able to settle into a platonic relationship for the rest of their time here. Then again, Neil might not even come to her. . . .

Even as she pondered that possibility, she sensed his presence in the room. Her head swiveled toward the door, eyes following his silent approach. Every one of her insecurities found expression in her face. Her back was straight. Her hands clutched the rounded edge of the bed.

More than anything at that moment, Neil wanted to alleviate her fear. It tore at him, because he knew he was its cause, just as he knew that her fear was unfounded. If she worried that she wouldn't please him, she worried needlessly. Deirdre turned him on as no other woman had, turned him on physically and in a myriad of other ways he'd only begun to identify.

Hunkering down, he raised his eyes to hers. He wanted to ask, but couldn't find the words. One part of him was frightened, too—frightened of being turned down when the one thing he wanted, the one thing he needed just then, was to be accepted, to be welcomed. So his question was a wordless one, gently and soulfully phrased.

Deirdre's insides were trembling, but she wasn't so wrapped up in apprehension that she didn't hear his silent request. It was a plea that held its share of unsureness, and that fact, more than anything, gave her the courage she needed.

Of its own accord, her hand came up, touching his cheek, inching back until her fingers wove gently into his hair. Tentatively, nervously, she let her lips soften into the beginnings of a smile.

Neil had never seen anything as sweet. He felt relief, and a kind of victory. But more, a well of affection rose inside, spreading warmth through him. Whatever Deirdre's fears were, she was willing to trust him. That knowledge pleased him every bit as much as the prospect of what was to come.

Holding her gaze, he brought his hands up to frame her face. His thumbs stroked her lips for a minute before he came forward and replaced them with his mouth. His kiss was sure and strong, the sealing of a pact, but it was every bit as gentle in promise, and Deirdre was lost in it. It was almost a shock when he set her back and she remembered that there was more to lovemaking than kisses alone. Her expression reflected her qualms, and Neil was quick to reassure her.

"Don't be frightened," he whispered. "We'll take it slow." Sitting back on his haunches, he slid his hands to her neck, then lower to the first button of her pajamas, which he released. He moved on to the second button, working in such a way that some part of his hand constantly touched her flesh. For him, the touch point reflected sheer greed; for Deirdre it was a sensually electric connection that served as a counterpoint to her apprehension.

Only when the last of the buttons was released did Neil lower his gaze. With hands that trembled slightly, he drew back the voluminous pajama fabric, rolling it outward until her breasts were fully exposed. The sight of them, small and high, but well rounded, shook him deeply. He'd been right; imagination did pale against reality. Or maybe it was that he hadn't dared dream. . . .

The cool air of the bedroom hit Deirdre simultaneously with trepidation, but when her arms would have moved inward, he gently held them still.

"You're beautiful, Deirdre," he breathed. "What could ever have made you think that you wouldn't be right for me?"

She didn't answer, because the light in his eyes was so special, so precious, that she was afraid of distracting him lest his fascination fade. So she watched, mesmerized, as he brought both hands to her breasts. Long fingers circled them, tracing only their contours before growing bolder. A soft sigh slipped through her lips when he began to knead her fullness, and the feeling was so right and so good that she momentarily forgot her fears.

When the pads of his fingers brushed her nipples, she stiffened her back, but it was a movement in response to the surge of heat, not a protest. She had to clutch his shoulders then, because he had leaned forward and opened his mouth over one tight nub, and the sensation was jolting her to her core.

His tongue dabbed the pebbled tip. His teeth toyed with it. And all the while his hand occupied her other breast, caressing it with such finesse that she bit her lip to keep from crying out.

At last, when she simply couldn't help herself, she began to whimper. "Neil . . . I don't think I can stand this. . . ."

"If I can, you can," he rasped against her skin.

"I feel like I'm on fire. . . ."

"You are."

"I can't sit still. . . ."

"Sure you can. Let it build."

"It's been building for three days!"

"But it has to be slow, has to be right."

He drew back only long enough to whip the sweater over his head. Then he came up to sit beside her and take her in his arms. That first touch, flesh to flesh, was cataclysmic. Deirdre's entire body shook when her breasts made contact with his chest. Her arms went around him, holding him tightly, as though otherwise she'd simply shatter.

Neil's grip on her was no less definitive. His large body shuddered at the feel of her softness pressing into it. His breath came raggedly by her ear, while his hands hungrily charted every inch of her bare back, from her shoulders, over her ribs, to the dimpled hollows below her waist. Her pajama bottoms hung around her hips; he took advantage of their looseness to explore the creamy smoothness of her belly, the flare of her hips, the conditioned firmness of her bottom.

Deirdre, whose body all but hummed its pleasure, was finding a second heaven touching Neil. She loved the broad sweep of his back, the textured hollows of his collarbone, the sinewed swells of his chest. Slipping her hands between their bodies, she savored his front as she'd done his back. It was hairier, enticingly so, and his nipples were every bit as taut, if smaller, than hers were.

"What you do to me, Deirdre," he murmured dazedly, recapturing her face with his hands and taking her lips in a fevered kiss. "I think I agree with you. I'm not sure how much more I can stand, either."

She'd been right, he realized. Though they hadn't known it at the time, they'd endured three days of foreplay. From the very first there'd been curiosity. And it had grown more intense, despite every argument they'd had, despite every scathing comment they'd exchanged. Later he would wonder how much of the fighting had been caused by that basic attraction between them, but for now all he could think about was that their mutual desire was on the verge of culmination.

Coming up on one knee, he grasped her under the arms and raised her gently to the pillow. He eased the quilt from under her until she was lying on the bare sheet, then, unsnapping her pajama bottoms, he worked them down her legs and over her cast, finally dropping them to the floor.

Deirdre experienced a resurgence of anxiety when he sat back and looked at her, but his gaze was filled with such reverence that those fears receded once again. The hand he skimmed up her leg was worshipful, and when he reached the nest of pale hair at the juncture of her thighs, he touched her with care that bordered on awe.

She felt totally exposed, yet treasured. Looking at Neil, seeing the way his large frame quivered with restrained desire, she marveled that fate had brought him to her.

"Neil...please..." she begged in a shaky whisper. "I want you."

He needed no more urging. Sitting back, he unsnapped his jeans and thrust them down his legs along with his briefs. Within seconds he was sliding over her, finding a place for himself between her thighs, threading his fingers through hers and anchoring them by her shoulders.

Bearing his weight on his elbows, he rubbed his hot body back and forth over hers. He made no attempt to penetrate her, simply sought the pleasure of his new level of touching. But the pleasure was galvanic, causing them both to breathe quickly and unevenly.

Deirdre had never before known such anticipation. She wasn't thinking about her fears, wasn't thinking about what would happen if Neil didn't find her lovemaking adequate. She was only thinking of the burning deep within her, knowing that she needed his possession now.

Eyes closed, she arched upward, hips straining toward his in a silent plea that dashed the last of his resistance. Nudging her legs farther apart, he positioned himself, then tightened his fingers around hers.

"Look at me, Deirdre," he whispered. "Look at me, babe."

Her eyes opened, then grew wider when, ever so slowly, he entered her. She felt him clearly, slidırg deeper and deeper; it was as though each individual cell inside her responded to his presence, transmitting one heady message after another to her brain. By the time he filled her completely, she knew that she'd never, never be the same again.

Neil closed his eyes and let out a long and tremulous sigh. Satisfaction was so clearly etched on his features that Deirdre would have breathed a sigh of relief, too, had she been able to. But he'd begun to move inside her, and breathing became increasingly difficult. All she could do was to give herself up to the spiral of passion he created.

The heat built steadily. Neil set a pace that maximized her pleasure, knowing precisely when to slow, precisely when to speed up. She moved to his rhythm, following his lead with a flair of her own that drove him on and up.

Then, when the fire within her became too hot for containment, she arched her back a final time, caught a sudden deep breath and dissolved into a seemingly endless series of spasms. Somewhere in the middle, Neil joined her, holding himself at the very entrance of her womb while his body pulsed and quivered.

It was a long time before either of them could speak, a long time during which the only sounds in the room were the harsh gasping for air and the softer, more gentle patter of the rain. Only when they'd begun to breath more normally did Neil slide to the side, but he brought her with him, settling them face to face on the pillow.

"Well," he asked softly, "what do you think?"

For an instant, Deirdre's old fears crowded in on her. "What do *you* think?" she whispered.

"I think," he said slowly, reining in a smug smile, "that for a lady with a sharp tongue and a questionable disposition, you're one hell of a lover."

7

RELIEF WASHED OVER HER, this time thoroughly wiping away whatever lingering doubts she'd had. A smile lit her face, unwaveringly, even as she raised her voice in mock protest.

"Sharp tongue? Questionable disposition? It was all because of you, Neil Hersey. You were the one who wasn't supposed to be here!"

Neil was undaunted. His own euphoria was too great. "And if I hadn't been," he ventured naughtily, "just think of all we'd have missed."

Deirdre had no suitable answer for that, so she simply continued to smile, and he was content to bask in her sunshine. After a time, he tenderly brushed a damp wisp of hair from her cheek.

"You're looking happy."

"I am . . . happy . . . satisfied . . . relieved."

"Was it that awful—the thought of our making love?" he chided.

"Oh, no, Neil," she answered quickly. "It was exciting. But you knew I was frightened."

"I'm still not sure why. It couldn't have been the athletic thing alone. Did it have something to do with the fellow who burned you once?"

She thought about that. "Indirectly, I suppose." Her gaze dropped. "Things were okay between us . . . sexually. It's just that when he got the urge to leave, he up and left, like there really wasn't anything worth sticking around for. On a subconscious level, I may have taken it more personally than I should have." She lapsed into silence as she considered why that had been. Her fingers moved lightly over the hair on Neil's chest in a reminder of what had just passed between them, and it gave her the courage to go on.

"I think it relates more to my family than Seth. I've always been the black sheep, the one who didn't fit in. My mother is the epitome of good manners, good looks and feminine poise. My sister takes after her. I've always been different, and they've made no secret of their opinion of me."

He cupped her throat in the vee of his hand, while his thumb drew circles on her collarbone. "They don't think you're feminine enough?"

"No."

His laugh was a cocky one. "Shows how much they know."

She rewarded him with a shy smile. "You're talking sex, which is only one part of it, but you're good for my ego, anyway."

"And you're good for mine. I don't think I've ever had a woman want me as much as you did just now. I know damn well that sex was the last thing on your mind when you got here, and that makes your desire so precious. I'd like to think it wasn't just any man who could turn you on like that."

"It wasn't!" she exclaimed, then lowered her voice. "There's only been one man, and that was Seth. I'm not very experienced."

"Experienced women are a dime a dozen. You're worth far more."

"I've never been driven by sexual need. I've never seen myself as a sexual being."

"We're all sexual beings."

"To one degree or another, but those degrees can vary widely." She moved her thigh between his, finding pleasure in the textural contrast of their bodies. "I guess what I'm saying is that I've always assumed myself to be at the lower end of the scale."

"Do you still?" he asked softly.

The look she gave him was every bit as soft. "With you? No."

He ran his hand down her spine, covered her bottom and pressed her hips intimately close. "That's good," he said, and sucked in a loud breath. "Because I think I'm needing you again."

Deirdre couldn't have been more delighted. Not only was he proving once again that her fears had been unfounded, but he was mirroring the state of her own reawakening desire. She followed the progress of her hand as it inched its way down his chest. "I think the needing is mutual."

"Any regrets?" he asked thickly.

"Only that I can't wrap both legs around you."

"It is a challenge with your cast. I didn't hurt you before, did I?"

She was fascinated by the whorl of hair around his navel. "Did I sound like I was in pain?" she asked distractedly.

"Dire pain."

"It had nothing to do with my leg." Her hand crept lower, tangling in the dark curls above his sex.

"Deirdre?" He was having trouble breathing again.

She was too engrossed in her exploration to take pity on him. "You have a beautiful body," she whispered. Her fingers grazed his tumescence. "I didn't have time to touch you before."

"Oh, God," he breathed when she took him fully into her grasp. His hand tightened on her shoulder, and he pressed his lips to her forehead. "Oh . . ."

"Do you like that?" she asked, cautiously stroking him.

"Oh, yes…harder…you can do it harder." His body was straining for her touch; when she strengthened it, he gave a moan of ecstasy. "Almost heaven—that's what it is."

"Almost?"

He opened his eyes and gazed at her then. "True heaven is when I'm inside." Inserting his leg between hers, he brought her thigh even higher. "You're hot and moist and tight, so tight. The way I slip in—" he put action to words "—shows how perfectly you…ummmmmm…how perfectly you were made…for me."

It was Deirdre's turn to gasp, then moan. He was lodged deeply within her, while his hand was caressing the rest of her with consummate expertise. When he withdrew, then surged back, she thought she'd explode.

The explosion wasn't long in coming. His mouth covered hers and he filled her with his tongue, as his manhood already filled her. One bold thrust echoed the other in a rhythm that repeated itself until all rhythm was suspended in a climactic surge.

This time when they tumbled back from that pyrotechnic plane, they had neither the strength nor the need to talk. Fitting Deirdre snugly into the curve of his body, Neil held her until her breathing was long and even. Soon after, he, too, was asleep.

THE NEXT DAY was the most glorious one Deirdre had ever known. She awoke in Neil's arms with a smile on her face, and if the smile ever faded, it was never for long. He instructed her to stay in bed while he showered, then he returned and carried her in for a bath. By the time he'd washed her to his satisfaction, they were both in need of satisfaction of another sort. So he carried her back to bed, where he proceeded to adore every bare inch of her body.

He taught her things about herself she'd never known, banishing any modesty she might have had and reaping the benefits. With deft fingers, an agile tongue and pulsing sex, he brought her to climax after climax, until she pleaded for mercy.

"A sex fiend!" she cried. "I'm stranded on an island with a sex fiend!"

"Look who's talking!" was all he had to say. Not only had she been as hungry as he, but she'd taken every one of the liberties with his body that he had with hers.

They didn't bother to get dressed that day. It seemed a waste of time and effort. The weather was as ominous as the thought of putting clothing between them. When they left the bedroom, they shared Deirdre's pajamas—the top was hers, the bottom his. He teased her, claiming that she'd brought along men's pajamas with precisely that goal in mind, but he wasn't about to complain when he knew all he had to do— whether in the kitchen, the living room or the den—was to raise her top, lower his bottom, and enter her with a fluid thrust.

Deirdre let his presence fill her, both body and mind. She knew they were living a dream, that reality lurked just beyond, waiting to pounce. But she refused to be distracted by other, more somber thoughts when she was feeling so complete. Neil accepted her. He'd seen her at her worst, yet he accepted her. His attraction to her wasn't based on who she was, what she did for a living, or what she wore; he liked her as the person she was.

Neil was similarly content. The realization that he was avoiding reality did nothing to temper his feelings about Deirdre. He refused to dwell on the fact that she didn't know about the downturn his life in Hartford had taken, because it didn't seem to matter. She was happy; he'd made her happy.

She didn't care about his financial prospects or his reputation. She was satisfied to accept him as he was.

And so they didn't think about the future. One day melded into the next, each filled with relaxation, leisure activity, lovemaking. Deirdre finished one book and started a second. She got the hang of knitting well enough to begin work on the actual sweater, and made commendable headway on it. She exercised each day but made no attempt to devise new routines, loath to do something that might start her brooding on whether she'd be able to teach again.

Neil did his share of reading. He continued to take responsibility for most of the household chores, and it was his pleasure to do so. From time to time Deirdre tried to help, but he saw the frustration she suffered with her cast, and it was enough to tell him that he wasn't being used.

The bickering they'd done during those first three days was, for all intents and purposes, over. This was not to say that they agreed on everything, but compromise became the mode. Neil accepted the loud beat of Deirdre's music, while she accepted the drone of his radio-transmitted Celtics games. She subjected herself to a clobbering at Trivial Pursuit, while he endured the gyrations in *Saturday Night Fever*.

One night, when he was feeling particularly buoyant, he took a Havana cigar from his bag, lit it and sat back on the sofa in bliss. Deirdre, who'd watched in horror his elaborate ceremony of nipping off the end of the cigar, then moistening the tip, simply sat with one finger unobtrusively blocking her nose. It was an example of how far they'd come; as disgusting as she found the smell, she wasn't about to dampen his obvious pleasure.

He'd been smoking for several minutes before he cast her a glance and saw her pose. "Uh-oh. Bad?"

She shrugged. "Are't dose tings illegal in dis country?" she asked, careful to breathe through her mouth.

"It's illegal to import them. But if a foreigner brings them in for his own personal use and shares them with his friends, it's okay."

"Is dat how you got it?"

"I have a client from Jordan who has business interests here. He gave me a box several months ago." Neil eyed the long cigar with reverence. "I'm not usually a smoker, but I have to admit that if you want to smoke a cigar, this is the way to go."

"Da Mercedes of cigars?"

"Yup." Eyes slitted in pleasure, he put the cigar to his mouth, drew on it, then blew out a narrow stream of thick smoke. "Should I put it out?"

"Dot on my accou't. But do't ask me to kiss you later, commie breath."

His lips quirked at the corners. Leaning forward, he carefully placed the cigar in an ashtray, then stood and advanced on her.

She held up a hand. "Do't come closer. I dow what you're goi'g to do."

He propped his hands on the arm of her chair and bent so that his face was inches from hers. He was grinning. "I'll kiss you if I want to, and you'll like it, commie breath and all."

"Deil, I'm warding you—"

Her warning was cut short by his mouth, which took hers in a way that was at once familiar and new. After the initial capture, his lips softened and grew persuasive, coaxing hers into a response she was helpless to withhold.

When at last he ended the kiss, he murmured softly, "You can breathe now."

Deirdre's eyes were closed, and the hand that had protected her nose had long since abandoned that post and moved from the rich texture of his beard up into his thick, brown hair. "How can I do that . . . when you take my breath away...." When she pulled him back to her, he was more than willing to accede to her demands.

As time passed the cigar burned itself out, but neither of them noticed

EARLY IN THE MORNING of their one-week anniversary on the island, Thomas called them from shore. Neil was the one to talk to him, but Deirdre, standing by, heard every word.

"How're you folks making out?"

Neil grinned, but made sure his voice was suitably sober. "Okay."

"I got your messages, but I've been away most of the week. I figured that you'd keep trying if there was any kind of emergency."

"He feels guilty," Deirdre whispered mischievously. "Serves him right."

Neil collared her with a playful arm as he spoke grimly back into the receiver. "We'll live."

"Deirdre's doing all right with that leg of hers?"

Neil hesitated before answering. Meanwhile, he toyed gently with Deirdre's earlobe. "The house has taken a beating. She's not very good with her crutches."

Deirdre kicked at his shin with her cast. He side-stepped her deftly.

"Oh," Thomas said. "Well, that's Victoria's problem. Are you two getting along?"

"Getting along?" Deirdre whispered. She slid her hand over Neil's ribs and tucked her fingers in the waistband of his jeans.

Neil cleared his throat and pulled a straight face. "We're still alive."

"You'll drive him crazy," she whispered. "He's dying of curiosity."

"Let him die," Neil whispered back, eyes dancing.

During the brief interlude, Thomas had apparently decided that what was happening between Neil and Deirdre was Victoria's problem, too. "Well," came his staticky voice, "I just wanted to let you know that you've got a store of fresh supplies on the dock."

"On the dock?" Neil looked at his watch. It was barely nine. "You must have been up before dawn."

"I left them last night."

"Coward."

"What's that?" came the static. "I didn't get that last word?"

Deirdre snickered noisily. Neil clamped a hand on her mouth. "I said, thank you," he yelled more loudly than necessary into the handset.

"Oh. Okay. I'll be out next week to pick you up, then. If there's any change in plans, give me a call."

For the first time, Neil's hesitation was legitimate. Looking down, he saw that Deirdre's too, was suddenly more serious. His fingers grew tighter on the handset.

"Will do" was all he said before switching off the instrument and replacing it on its stand. He stood silent for a minute with his arm still around Deirdre. Then, with a squeeze of her shoulder, he took a fast breath. "Hey, do you see what I see?"

She was ready for a diversion. Any diversion. Thomas's last comment had been a depressant. "I don't know. What do you see?"

He raised his eyes to the window. "The sun. Well, maybe not the sun itself, but it's brighter out there than it's been in a week, and it hasn't rained since yesterday, which means that the paths will have begun to dry out, which means that I can get the things in from the dock pretty quick, which means—" He gave her shoulder another squeeze. "—that we can take a walk."

Deirdre followed his gaze, then looked back up at him. "I'd like that," she said softly. "I'd like it a lot."

THE BREAK IN THE WEATHER offered new realms of adventure for them. As though determined to restake its claim after a long absence, the sun grew stronger from one day to the next. The air remained cool, and Deirdre's mobility was limited by her crutches, but she and Neil managed to explore most of the small island. When they weren't wandering in one direction or another, they were perched atop high boulders overlooking the sea. They watched the sun rise one morning, watched the sun set one evening, and in between they agreed that neither of them had ever visited as serene a place.

Unfortunately, with greater frequency as the days passed, their serenity was disturbed by the memory of Thomas's parting words. He'd be by to pick them up at the end of a week, and that week seemed far too short. Deirdre began to brood more and more about Providence, Neil about Hartford, and though the making up was always breathtaking, they began to bicker again.

Finally, three days before they were to leave, things came to a head. They'd finished dinner and were seated side by side in the den, ostensibly watching *Raiders of the Lost Ark*, but in truth paying it little heed. With an abruptness that mirrored his mood, Neil switched off the set.

Deirdre shot him a scowl. She'd been thinking about leaving the island, and the prospect left her cold. "What did you do that for?"

"You're picking your fingernail again. The sound drives me crazy!" What really drove him crazy was the thought of returning to Hartford, but Deirdre's nail picking was as good a scapegoat as any.

"But I wanted to watch the movie."

"How can you watch the movie when you're totally engrossed in your nail?"

"Maybe if you weren't rubbing that damned beard of yours, I'd be able to concentrate."

His eyes darkened. "You haven't complained about my beard for days." In fact, she'd complimented him on it. It was filling in well, she'd said, and looked good. He'd agreed with her assessment. "And maybe I'm rubbing it to drown out the sound of your picking! Why do you *do* that?"

"It's a nervous habit, Neil. I can't help it."

"So why are you nervous? I thought you were supposed to be calm and relaxed."

"I am!" she cried, then, hearing herself, dropped both her gaze and her voice. "I'm not."

Silence hung in the air between them. When Deirdre looked up at last, she found Neil studying her with a pained expression on his face.

"We have to talk," he said quietly.

"I know."

"Thomas will be here soon."

"I know."

"You'll go back to Providence. I'll go back to Hartford."

"I *know*."

"So what are we going to do about it?"

She shrugged, then slanted him a pleading glance. "Tell him we're staying for another week?" Even more frightening to her than the prospect of returning to Providence was the prospect of leaving Neil.

He snorted and pushed himself from the sofa, pacing to the far side of the room before turning on his heel. "I can't do that, Deirdre. Much as I wish it, I can't."

"Then what do you suggest?"

He stood with one hand on his hip, the other rubbing the back of his neck. His gaze was unfocused, alternately shift-

ing from the wall to the floor and back. "I don't know, damn
it. I've been trying to think of solutions—No, that's wrong.
I've avoided thinking about going back since I arrived, and
as a result, I have no solutions. Then there's *this* complication."

Deirdre didn't like the sound of his voice. "What complication?"

He looked her in the eye. "Us."

It was like a blow to her stomach. Though she knew he was
right, she couldn't bear to think of what they'd shared in
negative terms. "Look," she argued, holding up a hand in
immediate self-defense. "*We* don't have to be a complication. You can go your way, I can go mine. *Fini.*"

"Is that how you want it?"

"No."

"How do you want it?"

"I don't know," she cried in frustration. "You're not the
only one who's avoided thinking about going back. I haven't
found any more solutions than you have."

"But we do agree that we want to keep on seeing each
other."

"Yes!"

His shoulders sagged in defeat. "Then it is a complication,
Deirdre. On top of everything else, what we have is very
definitely a complication." He turned to stare out the window.

Deirdre, in turn, stared at him. "Okay, Neil," she began
softly. "You're right. We have to talk. About everything."
When he didn't move, she continued. "When we first came
here, you were as bad-tempered as I was. I know my reasons, but I've never really known yours. At first I didn't want
to know, because I have enough problems of my own. Then
when things got...better between us, I didn't want to ask for
fear of upsetting the apple cart." She was sitting forward on

the couch, a hand spread palm down on each thigh. "But I'm asking now. If we're going to figure anything out, I have to know. What happened, Neil? What happened in Hartford that brought you up here in such a temper? Why did you need to escape?"

Neil dropped his chin to his chest, her questions echoing in his brain. The moment of truth had come. He gnawed on the inside of his cheek, as though even doing something so pointless would be an excuse for not answering. But it wasn't. Deirdre was curious, and intelligent. As much as he wished he didn't have to tell her, she more than anyone deserved to know.

He turned to face her but made no move to close the distance between them. "I have," he said with a resigned sigh, "a major problem back home. It involves one of my principal clients—strike that, one of my prinicipal *ex*-clients, a very large corporation based in Hartford." He hesitated.

"Go on," she urged softly. "I'm with you."

"I've been chief counsel for the corporation for three years, and during that time I've come to be increasingly familiar with various aspects of the business. Last summer, quite inadvertently, I stumbled onto a corruption scheme involving the president of the corporation."

Deirdre held her breath and watched him with growing apprehension. She refused to believe that he'd knowingly condone corruption, yet, as corporate counsel, his job was to side with his client.

"No," he said, reading her fear, "I didn't demand a cut—"

"I never thought you would! But you must have been put in an awful position."

He was relieved by her obvious sincerity, but in some ways that made his task all the more difficult. He would have liked to be able to tell her that his practice was successful and growing even more so. He would have liked to have shone in her eyes. But the facts were against him.

Deirdre didn't deserve this. Hell, *he* didn't deserve it!

"Awful is putting it mildly," he declared. "I could have chosen to look the other way, but it went against every principle I'd ever held. So I took the matter before the board of directors. That was when things fell apart."

"What do you mean?"

"They were involved! All of them! They knew exactly what was going on, and their only regret was that I'd found out!"

Deirdre felt her anger rising on his behalf. "What did you do?"

"I resigned. I had no other choice. There was no way I'd sit back and watch them pad their own pockets at the expense of not only their stockholders but their employees. Their employees! The last people who could afford to be gypped!"

"But I don't understand, Neil. If you resigned, isn't it all over? You may have lost one client, but you have others, don't you?"

"Oh, yes," he ground out with more than a little sarcasm. "But those others have dwindled with a suddenness that can't possibly be coincidental." His jaw was tight. "It seems that Wittnauer-Douglass wasn't satisfied simply with my resignation. The executive board wanted to make sure I wouldn't do anything to rock a very lucrative boat."

She was appalled. "They blackballed you."

"Worse. They passed word around that I'd been the mastermind behind the corruption scheme. According to the chairman of the board—and I got this from a reliable source—if I hadn't left, they'd have leveled charges against me."

"But they can't say that!"

"They can say anything they damn well please!"

"Then they can't *do* it!"

"I'm not so sure. There's a helluva lot of murky paper-work in the archives of any large corporation. That paper-work can be easily doctored if the right people give the go-ahead."

"But why would the board at Wittnauer-Douglass want to even mention corruption? Wouldn't it spoil their own scheme?"

"Not by a long shot. They simply reorganize, shift out-lets, juggle a few more documents. When you've got power, you've got power. It's as simple as that."

"And you can't fight them." It was a statement, a straight follow-up to Neil's. Unfortunately it touched a nerve in him that was all too raw.

"What in the hell can I do?" he exploded, every muscle in his body rigid. "They've spread word so far and so fast that it's become virtually impossible for me to practice law in Hartford! The major corporations won't touch me. The me-dium-sized ones are leery. And it's gone way beyond my profession. Nancy—the woman I was seeing—quickly opted out, which was okay, because it was only a matter of time before we'd have split, anyway. But before I knew what had happened, I'd been replaced as chairman of the hospital fund-raising drive. That did hurt. Word is that I'm a crook, and even if some people believe in my innocence, there are still appearances to uphold. Hell, I can't even find a squash part-ner these days. I've become a regular pariah!"

"They can't do that!"

"*They've done it*," he lashed back. His anger was com-pounding itself, taking on even greater force than it had held in Hartford, mainly because he detested having to dump this on Deirdre. "I've worked my tail off to build a successful practice, and they've swept it away without a care in the world. And do you know what the worst part is?" He was livid now, furious with himself. "I didn't see it coming! I was naive . . . stupid!"

Deirdre was on her feet, limping toward him. "It wasn't your fault—"

He interrupted, barely hearing her argument over the internal din of his self-reproach. "How could I have possibly spent so much time working with those people and not have seen them for what they are? I'm too trusting! I've always been too trusting! Good guys finish last, isn't that what they say? Well, it's true!"

She took his arm. "But trusting is a good way to be, Neil," she argued with quiet force. "The alternative is to be an eternal skeptic, or worse, paranoid, and you couldn't live that way."

"My friends. They even got to my *friends*."

"A real friend wouldn't be gotten to."

"Then I've been a poor judge of character on that score, too."

"You're being too harsh on yourself—"

"And it's about time! Someone should have kicked me in the pants years ago. Maybe if they had, I wouldn't have been such a damned optimist. Maybe I would have seen all this coming. Maybe I wouldn't be in such a completely untenable position now."

"You can find new clients," she ventured cautiously.

"Not the kind I want. My expertise is in dealing with large corporations, and those won't come near me now."

"Maybe not in Hartford—"

"Which means relocating. Damn it, I don't want to relocate. At least, not for that reason."

"But things aren't hopeless, Neil. You have a profession that you're skilled in—"

"And look where it's gotten me," he seethed. "I have a great office, two capable associates and a steadily diminishing clientele. I have a condominium, which the people I once called friends won't deign to visit. I have a record for charity work that's come to a dead halt. I have squash gear and no partner."

Deirdre dropped her hand from his stiff arm. "You also think you have a monopoly on self-pity. Well, you don't, Neil. You're not the only one who has problems. You're not the only one who's frustrated."

"Frustrated?" He raked rigid fingers through his hair. "Now *that's* the understatement of the year. And while we're at it, you can add guilt to the list of my transgressions. I came up here and took every one of those frustrations out on you!"

"But you weren't the only one to do it! I used you for that too, Neil, so I'm as guilty as you are."

"Yeah." His voice was calm now. "Only difference is that your problem has a solution in sight. Once the cast is off—"

"It's not only my leg," Deirdre snapped, turning away from him. "I wouldn't have been in such a lousy mood if it was simply a question of my leg. There's a whole other story to my life, and if you think that in its own way my situation isn't as frustrating as yours, you can add egotistical to that list you're drawing up."

There was silence behind her. For the first time since he'd begun his tirade, Neil's thoughts took a tangent. *A whole other story to my life*, she'd said. He was suddenly more nervous than he'd been angry moments before, inexplicably fearful that his world was about to collapse completely.

"What is it—that other story?"

Head down, she hobbled over to rest her hip against the desk. A dry laugh slipped from her throat. "It's ironic. There you are, without a corporation to represent. Here I am, with a corporation I don't want."

"What are you talking about?"

Slowly she raised her head. Almost reluctantly she replied, "Joyce Enterprises. Have you ever heard of it?"

"I've heard of it. It's based in..." The light dawned. "Providence. You're that Joyce? It's yours?"

"Actually, my family's. My father died six months ago, and my sister took over the helm."

Neil frowned. "I didn't make the connection...I never...it doesn't fit."

"With who I am?" She smiled sadly. "You're right. It doesn't fit. I don't fit, and that's the problem. My parents always intended that the business stay in the family. Sandra—my sister—just can't handle it. I have two uncles who are involved, but they're as ill-equipped to run things as my mother is."

Neil had come to stand before her. "So they want you in."

"Right."

"But you don't want in."

"Right again. I tried it once and hated it. I'm just not the type to dress up all day and entertain, which is largely what the head of a business like that has to do. I don't take to diplomatic small talk, and I don't take to being a pretty little thing on display."

"That I can believe," he quipped.

Deirdre responded to his teasing with a scowl. "I wish my family could believe it, but they won't. They keep insisting that I'm their only hope, and maybe I would be able to handle the management end of the business, but the political end would drive me up a tree! For six months now they've been after me, and while I was busy doing my own thing I had an excuse. At least, it was one I could grasp at. I've always known that sooner or later, as I got older, I'd slow down, but I thought I had time to find a substitute. Now I don't. Suddenly I can't do my own thing, and they've started hounding me to do theirs. Even before I left the hospital they were on me." She paused for a breath, then continued.

"They think I'm selfish, and maybe I am, because I want to be happy, and I know I won't be if I'm forced to be involved in the business. It's really a joke—their pushing me this way. I've always been odd in their minds. I'm a failure. They look down their noses at the work I do. And even beyond that, I don't have a husband, or children, which compounds my sin. What good am I? Nothing I do is right, so they say. Yet they stand over me and insist that I help run Joyce." She rubbed a throbbing spot on her forehead, then looked up at Neil.

"The family needs me. The business needs me. Can I stand by and let it all go down the tubes? Because it will, Neil. I keep telling them to bring in outside help, but they refuse, and if they continue to do that, the whole thing is doomed. Oh, it may take a while. The corporation is like a huge piece of machinery. It's showing signs of wear and tear right now, but the gears are still turning. When it comes time to oil them, though, and there's no one capable of doing the job, things will slow down, then eventually grind to a halt."

She gave a quick, little headshake, more of a shiver. "Talk of guilt, I've got it in spades. I have a *responsibility*, my mother keeps reminding me. And that's the worst part, because as much as I can't bear the thought of having anything to do with the business, I do feel the responsibility. I deny it to them. I've denied it to myself. But it's there." She looked down at her fingers and repeated more softly, "It's there."

Neil wrapped his hand around her neck and kneaded it gently. "We're a fine twosome, you and I. Between us, we've got a pack of ills and no medicine."

She gave a meek laugh. "Maybe the island drugstore has something?"

He sighed. "The island drugstore filled the prescription for two souls who needed a break, but I'm afraid it doesn't have anything for curing the ills back home."

"So," she breathed, discouraged. "We're back where we started. What are we going to do?"

He looked at her intently, then dipped his head and took her lips with a sweetness that wrenched at her heart. "We are going to spend the next three days enjoying each other. That is, if you don't mind dallying with a man who has a very dubious future . . ."

It was at that moment, with Neil standing close, looking at her as though her answer were more important to him than anything else in the world, that Deirdre knew she loved him.

She smiled softly. "If you don't mind dallying with a woman who would rather spend the rest of her life on this island than go back to the mainland and face up to her responsibilities . . ."

His answer was a broad smile and another kiss, this one deeper and more soul reaching than anything that had come before. It was followed by a third, then a fourth, and before long, neither Neil nor Deirdre could think of the future.

THEIR FINAL DAYS on the island were spent much as the preceding ones had been, though now there was direction to their thoughts, rather than a random moodiness. For his part, Neil was relieved to have told Deirdre everything, even if the telling hadn't solved a thing. She'd accepted his quandary without criticism, and her affection—yes, he was sure it was that—for him seemed, if anything, to have deepened.

For her part, Deirdre was relieved to have shared her burden with an understanding soul. Neil hadn't jumped on her for her failings; if anything, his affection—yes she was sure it was that—for her seemed stronger than ever.

If that affection took on a frantic quality at times, each attributed it to the fact that the clock was running out.

Thomas had arranged to pick them up at eight o'clock in the morning on that last day. So the night before they found themselves cleaning the house, making sure that everything was as it had been when they'd arrived two weeks before. Tension suddenly surrounded them, reducing them to nearly the same testy state they'd been in when they'd arrived.

Neil did a final round of laundry, inadvertently tossing Deirdre's teal green sweatshirt into the wash with the towels, half of which were an electric blue not far different from her sweatshirt, half of which were pure white. When the white towels emerged with a distinct green tinge, he swore loudly.

"Goddamn it! I thought you'd packed this thing already!"

"I haven't packed anything yet." She'd been putting that particular chore off for as long as possible. Now, studying the once-white towels, she scowled. "Didn't you see the sweatshirt when you put the towels in?"

"How could I see it in with these blue ones?"

"The sweatshirt's green!"

"That's close enough."

"You must be color-blind."

"I am not color-blind."

They were glaring at each other over the washing machine. Deirdre was the first to look away. "Okay," she said, sighing. "We can put the white towels through again, this time with bleach."

"The little tag says not to use bleach."

Fiery eyes met his. "I've used bleach on towels before, and it does the trick. If you don't want to take the risk, you find a solution." Turning, she swung back to her cleaning of the refrigerator, leaving Neil to grudgingly add bleach to a second load.

Not long after, intent on doing the packing she'd put off, Deirdre was headed for the bedroom, when her crutch caught on the edge of the area rug in the living room. She stumbled and fell, crying out in annoyance as well as surprise.

"Who put that stupid rug there?" she screamed.

Neil was quickly by her side, his voice tense. "That 'stupid' rug has been in exactly the same spot since we got here. Weren't you watching where you were going?"

"It's the damned rubber tips on these crutches!" She kicked at them with her good foot. "They catch on everything!"

Rescuing the crutches, he put an arm across her back and helped her up. "They haven't bothered you before. Are you okay?"

"I'm fine," she snarled, rubbing her hip.

"Then you're lucky. Damn it, Deirdre, are you trying to kill yourself? Why don't you watch where you're going next time?"

"Watch where I'm going? I was watching!"

"Then you were going too fast!"

"I wasn't going any faster than I ever go!"

"Which is too fast!"

Deirdre, who had returned the crutches to their rightful place, backed away from him, incensed. "I don't need advice from you! I've taken care of myself for years, and I'll do it again! Just because you've helped me out this week doesn't give you the right to order me around. If you really wanted to help me, you'd offer to take that damned corporation off my back!"

"If you really wanted to help *me*, you'd *give* me the damned corporation!" he roared back.

For long minutes they stood glaring at each other. Both pairs of eyes flashed; both pairs of nostrils flared. Gradually both chests stopped heaving, and their anger dissipated.

"It's yours," Deirdre said quietly, her eyes glued to his.

"I'll take it," he countered, but his voice, too, was quiet.

"It's a bizarre idea."

"Totally off the wall."

"But it could offer an out for both of us."

"That's right."

They stood where they were for another long minute. Then, resting a hand lightly on her back, Neil urged her toward the sofa. When they were both seated, he crossed one leg over his knee, propped his elbow on the arm of the sofa and chafed his lower lip with his thumb.

"I've done a lot of thinking since we talked the other night," he began, hesitating at first, then gaining momentum. "I've been over and over the problem, trying to decide what I want to do. There are times when I get angry, when the only thing that makes any sense to me is revenge. Then the anger fades, and I realize how absurd that is. It's also self-defeating, when what I really want to do is to practice law." He paused, lowered his hand to his lap and looked at her. "You have a corporation that you don't want. I could make good use of it."

Nervously she searched his features. "For revenge?"

"No. Maybe it'd be a sort of reprisal, but that wouldn't be my main objective. I need something, Deirdre. It kills me to have to say that, especially to you. It's hard for a man—for anyone, I suppose—to admit that he's short on options. But I'm trying to face facts, and the sole fact in this case is that Hartford is no longer a viable place for me to work."

"You said you didn't want to relocate."

"I said I didn't want to relocate because of Wittnauer-Douglass. Maybe it's convoluted logic, but I'm beginning to think that Joyce Enterprises would have attracted me regardless of the problems in Hartford. No matter what you see happening now within the company, Joyce has a solid reputation. I wouldn't be afraid to put my stock in it. And it may be the highest form of conceit, but I do think that I have something to offer. I'm a good lawyer. I'm intimately familiar with the workings of large corporations. I may not be an entrepreneur, but I know people who are. And I know of a headhunter who could help me find the best ones to work with.

"Unfortunately—" he took a breath and his eyes widened as he broached the next problem "—that would mean bringing in an outsider. From what you say, your family has been against that from the start, which raises the even more immediate issue of whether or not they'd even accept me."

Deirdre tipped up her chin in a gesture of defiance. "I hold an equal amount of stock to my mother and sister. If you were to enter the corporation alongside me, they wouldn't dare fight."

"But you don't want to enter the corporation. Wasn't that the point?"

"Yes, but if we were . . ." She faltered, struggling to find the least presumptive words. "If we were together. . . . I mean, if I made it clear that we were . . . involved . . ."

"That we were a steady couple, as in lovers?"

"Yes."

He gave his head a quick shake. "Not good enough. It'll have to be marriage."

"Marriage?" She'd wanted to think that they'd be tied somehow, but marriage was the ultimate in ties. "Isn't that a little radical?"

Neil shrugged, but nonchalance was the last thing he felt. He'd been searching for a way to bind Deirdre to him. He loved her. Somewhere along the line that realization had dawned, and it had fit him so comfortably that he hadn't thought of questioning it. He couldn't say the words yet; he felt too vulnerable. Marriage might be sudden, but it served his purposes well. "Radical only in that we've known each other for such a short time. We get along, don't we?"

"We fight constantly!" she argued, playing the devil's advocate. If she knew that Neil loved her she wouldn't have had an argument in the world. But he hadn't said those words, and she didn't have the courage to lay herself bare by saying them herself, so she felt obligated to resist.

"Not constantly. Only when we're frustrated by problems that seem beyond our control. We've had our smooth times, haven't we?"

"Yes," she admitted, albeit reluctantly.

"And if this whole plan solves our problems, we won't have cause to fight, will we?"

"Every married couple fights."

"Then we wouldn't be any different. Look at it objectively, Deirdre. We have similar values and interests. We've already proved that we can live with each other. If we survived these past two weeks, being together twenty-four hours a day, we've got one foot up on many other couples who marry."

She didn't want to look at it objectively. Love wasn't objective. "But we've known each other in such a limited sphere. This isn't the real world. It's possible that we could return to Providence and find that we *hate* each other."

"That's your insecurity talking."

"Okay, maybe it is. I don't think I'm cut out to be a corporate wife any more than I'm cut out to head that corporation." She waved a hand back and forth. "I'm not the prissy little hostess. I'm not the adorable little lady who always wears and says the right things."

"I'm not complaining about who you are. And I wouldn't ask you to do anything you're uncomfortable with. If we entertain—and I assume there'd be some of that—you'd look as beautiful as any woman in the room. And rather than having you cook we could take people out or have something catered."

"In my modest town house?" she squeaked.

"In the house I'd buy for us." He sat forward, determination strong in the gaze he sent her. "I'm not a gigolo, Deirdre. I wouldn't go into this if I felt I was getting a free ride. You may not know it yet, but I do have my pride. If we agree to go ahead with this scheme, I'll work my tail off in the business. I'll be the one to support us, and that means providing the kind of home for you that I think you deserve. I guess I'm old-fashioned in that way."

"Does that mean I can't work or do whatever else I want?"

"You can do anything you want. I'm not *that* old-fashioned. And if you think I'm bothered by the thought of your teaching aerobics, think again. I adore your athletic body. Don't you know that by now?"

She simply slanted him a wry glance.

"Exercise is the way to go nowadays," he continued. "I'll be proud to have a wife who keeps her body toned."

"If I can," she muttered. "Whether I teach or not is still a big question."

"You'll teach. I told you that. When the cast comes off, you'll have physical therapy or whatever else it takes to get that leg working right."

"But . . . even if that happens, many of my classes are evening ones. How will you feel when you come home to an empty house after a hard day's work and there isn't even a hot meal ready?"

"I can cook. You know that. I'll be proud of you, Deirdre. My wife will be doing something that's constructive, something she enjoys." He paused for a breath, sobering. "And while we're talking of pride, if you agree to marry me, I'll insist on a prenuptial agreement."

Deirdre couldn't conceal a quick flare of hurt. "I don't want your money!"

"You've got it backside-to. It's you I want to protect. If you agree to marry me, I'll draw up a paper stating that your holdings in Joyce Enterprises—and anything else you now have to your name—will remain solely yours. If you should decide, at any point, that you want out of the marriage, you'll have everything you had when you entered into it. And if, at any point, you decide that I'm a detriment to Joyce Enterprises, you'll have the full right to can me."

She couldn't imagine that ever happening. For that matter, she couldn't imagine ever wanting out of a marriage to Neil. Unless he wanted it. "But what about your interests? They won't be protected if you sign a document like that. You thought you'd been naive regarding Wittnauer-Douglass. Isn't your plan now equally shortsighted?"

"I'd rather think of it as a challenge, one I'm approaching with my eyes wide open. I think I can make a go of running Joyce Enterprises, and if I do that, you won't have any cause to let me go. Like I said before, I'm not looking for a handout. I'm prepared to do the job. Yes, you'd be doing me a favor by giving me the chance, but I'd be doing you every bit as big a favor by relieving you of a responsibility you don't want."

He took her hand and studied the shape of her slender fingers. "You'd have a husband, which would please your family. And don't you think it's about time, anyway? I know it is for me. I'm not getting any younger. I'm more than ready to settle down."

But love? What about love? Deirdre pleaded silently. "Somehow it seems very. . . calculated."

"Sometimes the best things are."

"You don't have to marry me. We could still work all of this out."

"I'm sure we could, but marriage will be expedient when it comes to your family. They don't have to know about any agreement we sign. As far as they're concerned, what is yours is mine. I'll be a member of your family. The 'family business' will stay intact." He curved his fingers around hers and lowered his voice. "And I *want* to marry you. I wouldn't be suggesting it if that weren't the case."

But why do you want to marry me? she ached to ask, but didn't. He could give her the answer she craved, which would thrill her, or he could repeat the practical reasons he'd listed earlier, which would distress her. Rather than take the risk, she simply accepted his statement without prodding.

"Will you marry me, Deirdre?" he asked softly.

She met his gaze, knowing that love shone in her own with a strength she was helpless to dim. Silently she nodded, and closed her fingers around his.

8

AS HE'D PROMISED, Thomas was at the dock bright and early the next morning to pick them up. His curiosity was evident in the surreptitious glances he cast toward Deirdre, then Neil, at well-spaced intervals. They simply smiled at each other, feeling smug, but more than that, pleased with what lay ahead. If they'd dreaded the day they'd have to leave their island refuge, the knowledge that they were going to be together reduced that dread to a small twinge of sentimentality as the island faded behind them.

Neil had wanted to drive Deirdre back to Providence, but she insisted, with reason, he finally agreed, that it made no sense for her to leave her car in Maine when she'd want to use it at home. So he followed her on the highway, making sure she stopped periodically to stretch, then later, eat lunch.

It was mid-afternoon when they pulled up at Deirdre's mother's house. They'd discussed that, too, agreeing that the sooner they broke the news of their impending marriage to Maria Joyce the better. And, anticipating that the woman might give Deirdre a hard time, given her history of doing just that, Neil was vehement that he be present.

Maria was in the library when Deirdre called out from the front door. She came quickly, exclaiming loudly even before she entered the hall, "Deirdre! It's about time! I've been worried sick about where you were and how you were making out. If I hadn't thought to call Victoria—" She stopped short when she caught sight of her daughter, leaning on her crutches, beside a tall, bearded man in jeans. "Good Lord," she whispered, staring at the pair, "what have you brought home this time?"

Deirdre felt a movement by her elbow and knew that Neil was trying not to laugh. For that matter, so was she. In her eyes, Neil looked positively gorgeous, but she knew that her mother was wondering what the cat had dragged in.

"Mother. I'd like you to meet Neil Hersey. Neil, Maria Joyce '

Neil stepped forward and extended a firm hand, which Maria had no choice but to meet. "It's my pleasure, Mrs. Joyce. Deirdre has told me a lot about you."

Maria didn't take the time to wonder about the nature of that telling. She was too concerned about retrieving her hand from what was a far-too-confident grip. She nodded at Neil, but her focus was quickly on Deirdre.

"Victoria finally admitted that you'd gone to Maine. I can't believe you did that, Deirdre. The place is totally isolated, and in your condition—"

"My condition is fine. And Neil was there with me." Before her mother could pounce on that, she rushed on. "Neil is a friend of Victoria's, too. Now he's a friend of mine. Furthermore—" she looked at Neil "—we're going to be married. We wanted you to be the first to know." She took perverse delight in her mother's stunned expression.

For a minute the older woman was speechless. Then, pressing a hand to her heart, she revived.

"You can't be serious."

"We are. Very."

"Deirdre, you don't know this man!" She gave Neil a once-over that was disapproving at best.

"You'd be surprised, mother. Two weeks on an island, with no one else around—you can get to know a man pretty well."

Neil rolled his eyes at her smug tone and quickly sought to make amends to Maria. "What Deirdre means is that we had a chance to talk more than many people do in months. We shared responsibility for the house and everything to do with our daily lives. We feel that our marriage would be a good one."

Maria, who'd been eyeing him warily during his brief speech, closed her fingers around the single strand of pearls she was wearing with her very proper silk dress. "I think I need a drink," she said, and turned toward the living room.

Deirdre took off after her, with Neil following in her wake. "It's the middle of the afternoon! You don't need a drink in the middle of the afternoon!"

"Oh, yes, I do," came Maria's voice. She was already at the elegant cherrywood bar, fishing ice from a bucket. "When a woman hears that, after years of nagging, her daughter has decided on the spur of the moment to get married—and to a man she thinks she knows, but can't possibly, since she met him a mere two weeks ago—she needs a drink, *regardless* of the time of day!"

Deirdre took a deep breath and sent Neil a helpless glance before lowering herself to a nearby ottoman. "I think you ought to listen to the rest of what I have to tell you before you pass judgment. You may say something you'll later regret."

"I doubt that," Maria stated. She'd poured a healthy dose of bourbon into the glass and was standing stiffly by the bar. "I don't know where I failed with you, Deirdre, but I very definitely have failed. I've tried to instill in you certain values, and you've rejected every one of them. I tried to raise a lady, but you insist on running around in leotards—"

"Not leotards, mother. A tank top and running shorts. Leotards cut off my circulation."

She waved that aside. "Whatever. The point's the same. I tried to raise you with a sense of family, but you've insisted in going your own way. I've tried to make you see that you have an obligation to the business, but you won't hear of that.

And now, when you've got nothing better to do with your time, instead of giving us a hand, you run off, meet up with a passing . . . hippie, and decide to marry him."

Neil, who'd been standing quietly at Deirdre's shoulder, felt that he'd heard enough. He didn't mind the insults to him, but they were a smaller part of insults to Deirdre, and he wouldn't have that. "I don't think you understand the situation, Mrs. Joyce," he said with such authority that Maria was forced to listen. "I am not a hippie, nor am I passing. If you've formed an opinion of me based on the way I look, I think you should remember that I've just come from a two-week vacation. The bulk of my life is spent in tailored suits, suits that would hold their own—" he looked at the bench before the grand piano "—with that Dunhill tapestry." He shifted his gaze to the small painting to the left of the bar. "Or that Modigliani." He dropped his eyes to the marble coffee table by Deirdre's knees. "Or that Baccarat vase."

Deirdre looked up at him. "I'm impressed," she mouthed.

He nudged her hip with his knee, shushing her with a frown.

Maria arched a well-shaped brow, but she wasn't about to be fully appeased. "The slickest of con men pick up a wealth of knowledge about fine accessories, Mr. Hersey. What is it you do for a living?"

"I'm a lawyer. I head my own firm in Hartford, specializing in corporate work. I can give you a full list of my credits, starting with law review at Harvard, but I don't think that's necessary. Suffice it to say that in recent years I've done work for Jennings and Lange, KronTech, and the Holder Foundation, as well as the Faulkner Company here in Providence." He was confident that the corporations he'd named would give him solid recommendations. He was equally confident that Maria Joyce had heard of them. She would have also heard of Wittnauer-Douglass. There was always the possibility that if the woman ran a check on him, she'd come across that problem, but it was a risk he'd have to take. And besides, by the time she learned anything, his marriage to Deirdre would be a fait accompli.

Maria dipped her head in reluctant acknowledgment of his credentials. "All right. I'll admit that my judgment may have been premature, but the fact remains that this marriage is very sudden. When was it going to take place?"

Deirdre opened her mouth, but Neil spoke first. "As soon as the law will allow. I believe there's a three-day waiting period once the license has been taken out and the blood tests done. I know a judge here in Providence who might cut even that down."

Maria studied her bourbon, pressing her lips together as she ingested that information. "Is there a rush?" She sent Deirdre a meaningful glance. "I know that there are home tests on the market that can give instant results—"

"I am not pregnant, mother," Deirdre interrupted. "And even if I were, I'd have thought you'd be pleased. You've been harping on having grandchildren since I was old enough to vote."

"Every woman wants grandchildren," Maria countered in self-defense.

"So you've said many times. And here's your chance. I don't know why you're complaining. Even if I *were* pregnant, Neil and I will be married before anyone is the wiser. At most, the baby would be born two weeks early, so to speak, which no one would think twice about. You wouldn't have any cause for embarrassment."

Maria scowled at her daughter. "All right," she said crossly. "Forget a pregnancy." Her annoyance broadened to include Neil. "You'll get married and take off for Hartford, leaving Joyce Enterprises in the lurch yet again. Honestly, Deirdre, is that fair?"

Neil answered. "We won't be living in Hartford. We'll be living here."

Maria arched a skeptical brow. "You'd walk away from that successful law practice?"

"I can practice law anywhere," he returned, tamping down a moment's discomfort. "Providence is as good a place as any."

"The fact is, Mother," Deirdre spoke up, "that we are going to bail you out, after all. Neil has agreed to help me with Joyce Enterprises."

For the second time in a very short period, Maria Joyce was speechless. She looked from Deirdre to Neil and back, then raised her glass and took a bolstering drink. By the time she'd lowered the glass, she'd regained a small measure of her composure, though not enough to keep the glass from shaking in her hand. She set it carefully on the bar.

"That," she began slowly, "is an unexpected turn."

"So is our wedding," Deirdre pointed out, "but it all makes sense. You've been after me for years to help with the business. I've been convinced that I'm not right for the job, but I'm equally convinced that Neil is." And she was. She had no doubts but that Neil could handle Joyce Enterprises. "You've wanted to keep things in the family. Neil will be in the family. What more could Dad have asked for than a son-in-law who could take over where his daughters left off?"

"But he's a lawyer," Maria argued, though more meekly this time. "He's not trained in this type of work."

"Neither am I—nor Sandra, for that matter."

Neil joined in. "I've worked closely with large corporations like Joyce for years, so I'm starting with a definite advantage. And I've had the benefit of seeing how other corporations function, which means that I can take the best of the systems and strategies I've seen and implement them at Joyce." He paused. "I think it could work out well for all of us, Mrs. Joyce. I assure you that I wouldn't be putting my career on the line if I didn't feel that the odds were in my favor."

Maria appeared to have run out of arguments. She raised both brows and nervously fingered her pearls. "I . . . it looks like you've thought things out."

"We have," Deirdre said.

The older woman shook her head, for the first time seeming almost confused. "I don't know, Deirdre. It's so sudden. . . . I was hoping that when my daughters got married they'd have big weddings, with lots of flowers and music and people."

Deirdre's shoulders rose with the deep breath she took. "I've never wanted that, Mother. I'll be perfectly happy with something small and private."

Maria looked at them both. "You will be happy? This is what you truly want?" They knew she wasn't referring to the wedding, but to the marriage itself.

Neil's hand met Deirdre's at her shoulder. "It is," Deirdre said softly.

Neil echoed the sentiment. "We'll be happy, Mrs. Joyce. You can take my word for it."

FEELING AS THOUGH they'd overcome their first hurdle, they left Maria, stopped for their marriage license and blood tests, then went to Deirdre's town house. Though Neil agreed that it was on the small side, he was charmed with the way she'd decorated it. Whereas old-world elegance had been the word at her mother's house, here everything was light and airy. The furniture was modern, low and cushiony. One room opened into another with barely a break. There were no Dunhill tapestries, no Modiglianis, no pieces of Baccarat crystal, but a small and carefully chosen selection of work by local artists and artisans.

"I feel very much at home here," Neil said to Deirdre as they lay in bed that night.

Chin propped on his chest, she smiled at him. "I'm glad."

"It's pretty and bright, uncluttered and unpretentious. Like you."

She tugged at his beard. "I think you want something. What is it?"

He smiled back and wrapped an arm around her waist. "Just that when we find the right home, you do it like this. I don't want to live in a museum or . . . or in a shrine to a decorator."

Deirdre narrowed her eyes. "Is that what your place is like?"

"A shrine to a decorator? Yes, it is, and I never thought twice about it until now, but I don't want that, Deirdre. There's a sophistication in the simplicity here. That's what I want. Okay?"

"Okay."

"No argument?"

"No argument."

"Good."

THEY HEADED for Hartford the next day. Neil had a long list of things to take care of, the most pressing and difficult of which was informing his associates that he'd be leaving. Both men were talented lawyers, but being young they hadn't yet developed reputations that would attract new business. Neil gave them the choice of joining other firms or taking over his practice themselves. When they opted for the latter, he assured them that he'd do everything he could to help them out, which included drawing up a letter to send his clients, telling them of the change and assuring them that they'd be in good hands if they remained with the firm.

The second order of business was putting his condominium on the market. The real estate agent, who had a list of people waiting for openings in that particular building, was delighted.

"Are you sure you want to sell it?" Deirdre asked timidly.

"Why not? I won't be living here."

"But if you find that you don't like Providence . . . or that things don't go well . . ."

He took her firmly by the shoulders. "I will like Providence, and things will go well. I'm making a commitment, Deirdre. There's no point in doing it halfway."

She didn't argue further, particularly since his confidence buoyed her. So they returned to Providence and went house hunting. Once again luck was on their side. They found a charming colonial on the outskirts of the city, not far from Deirdre's mother's house ironically, but in a younger neighborhood. The property encompassed three acres of land, with a wealth of trees and lush shrubbery, and though the house needed work, the previous owners had vacated several weeks before, and the work could begin immediately.

Three days after they arrived back from Maine, Deirdre and Neil were married in the church Deirdre had attended as a child. Her mother had made the arrangements—Deirdre felt it was as good a consolation prize as any—and there were more people, more flowers, more food than Deirdre might have chosen herself. But she was too happy that day to mind anything.

Neil looked breathtaking in his dark suit, white shirt, striped tie and cordovans. He'd had his beard professionally trimmed, along with his hair, and she decided that he looked far more like a successful businessman than a conservative corporate lawyer.

Deirdre, who'd had a walking cast put on to replace the original, wore a long white dress, the simplicity of which was a perfect foil for her natural good looks. She'd applied a minimum of makeup—touches each of blusher, mascara, eyeliner and shadow—and though never one to lean heavily toward jewelry, she'd taken pride in wearing the pearl earrings and matching necklace that her father had given her for her twenty-first birthday.

The ceremony was short and sweet, and Deirdre was all smiles as she circulated through the luncheon reception on the arm of her new husband. He'd given her a stunning gold wedding band, as simple as her gown, with a tracing of diamond chips forming a central circle, but she would have been happy with something from the five-and-dime, as long as it told her they were married. Though he still hadn't said the words, she was sure she'd seen love in his eyes throughout that day, and it was the proverbial frosting on the cake.

THE NEXT FEW WEEKS were hectic ones. Neil threw himself fully into Joyce Enterprises, determined to familiarize himself with every aspect of the business. Sandra readily accepted him; not only was she relieved to have the brunt of the load taken from her shoulders, but Deirdre suspected that she was enthralled by Neil. And rightly so. He exuded confidence and was charming not only to Sandra, but to the uncles, as well. If he came home exhausted at night, Deirdre was more than willing to understand. She was also more than willing to make a challenge out of reviving him, which she did with notable success.

He kept her abreast with what was happening at work, sharing his observations, discussing his plans. And he was even eager to hear about the progress at the house, the redecorating of which she was orchestrating with an enthusiasm that surprised her. She'd never seen herself as a decorator. When she'd moved into her town house she'd simply papered and carpeted to suit herself. Knowing that

Neil approved of her taste was a major stimulant—that and knowing the house she now decorated was for the two of them.

By the time they moved in three weeks after the wedding, Deirdre was reeling with confidence. A week later her cast came off, and if that confidence faltered when she experienced a fair amount of pain, Neil was the one to offer encouragement. He personally helped her with the exercises the doctor had outlined, and when those exercise sessions ended more often than not in lovemaking, Deirdre wasn't about to complain. In lieu of verbally professing their love for each other, this physical bonding was crucial to her.

Deirdre put off returning to work, knowing that her leg wasn't ready. Strangely, she didn't miss it as much as she'd thought she would, but, then, between setting up the house and joining Neil for those social engagements he'd warned her would be inevitable, she had little time to miss much of anything.

Strangely, she didn't mind the social engagements, either. But, then, she was with Neil. He never failed to compliment her on the way she looked; as a result, she found that dressing up wasn't as odious as it had been in the past. Moreover, he was the perfect host, drawing her into conversations with their guests such that she experienced far less pain on that score than she'd anticipated.

Neil was exceedingly satisfied with the way things had worked out. Deirdre was as wonderful a wife as she'd been a lover, and as they'd left most of the bickering behind in Maine, he found her to be a thoroughly amiable companion. The only thing that bothered him from time to time was his awareness of the agreement they'd struck. He wanted to think that they were together out of love, not simply taking advantage of a mutually beneficial arrangement. Since the latter was what had brought about this marriage, he went through passing periods of doubt regarding Deirdre's feelings for him.

He had no such self-doubt when it came to Joyce Enterprises. The work was interesting and challenging, and he seemed to have a natural affinity for it. As he'd intended, he brought in a highly experienced executive from a Midwest corporation. Together they mapped out a strategy for keeping Joyce Enterprises not only running smoothly but growing, as well. Between them, they provided the vision that had been lacking since Deirdre's father's death.

Deirdre was thrilled. Her faith in Neil had been justified.

Maria Joyce was likewise pleased, though she made sure Deirdre knew of the risks involved. "I checked up on Neil," she informed her daughter when the two were having lunch at a downtown restaurant one day. "Neither of you was fully honest with me about his past."

Deirdre, who'd been savoring her victory, paused. "We were honest."

"You didn't tell me about Wittnauer-Douglass."

"There wasn't anything to tell. He had a bad experience with one client and was forced to terminate that particular relationship, but it was an isolated incident. He did the same kind of quality work for Wittnauer-Douglass that he did for the rest of his clients."

"According to my friend Bess Hamilton, whose husband is on the board at Wittnauer-Douglass, Neil took part in some unethical dealings."

Deirdre's anger was quick to rise. "If Bess Hamilton's husband was on the board, *he* was involved in the unethical dealings. Neil resigned because he wouldn't have anything to do with it!"

"That wasn't what Bess said."

"And who do you choose to believe, your friend or your son-in-law?"

Maria's gaze didn't waver. "I don't have much choice, do I? Neil is firmly entrenched in the running of our business—"

"And he's doing an excellent job. You can't deny it."

"But I have to wonder what his motives are. From what Bess said, he was washed out in Hartford."

"He wasn't *washed out*. His two associates are doing fantastically well with the business he left them, and if it hadn't been for his own urgings, those clients would have left in a minute and gone elsewhere. They had faith in Neil, which is why they followed his recommendation and stayed with the firm."

Maria wasn't about to be fully convinced. "Still, he got a good thing going for him when he married you. It was a shrewd move."

"What are you trying to say, Mother?" Deirdre asked through gritted teeth.

"Just that I think you ought to be careful. I think we all ought to be careful. He may be trying to take over Joyce Enterprises and sweep it away from us."

"Neil wouldn't do that."

"How do you know?"

"Because I'm *married* to him. Because I *know* him."

"You love him, and love sometimes clouds people's judgment."

"Not in this case. I trust him." She also knew of the papers she'd signed before she and Neil had been married, but she didn't feel that was any of her mother's business. "And I'd think that if you can't find it in yourself to trust him, as well, the least you can do is appreciate him. He's taken a load off all our backs, and what he's doing with Joyce Enterprises would have made Dad proud."

Maria had nothing to say on that score, so she changed the subject. Her words, however, lingered for a long time in Deirdre's mind.

Deirdre had meant what she'd said—that she trusted Neil. There were times, though, when she wondered about the energy he was pouring into the business. Rarely did a night pass when he didn't bring a project of some form home from the office with him. The enthusiasm he had for his work seemed boundless. . . .

Perhaps, Deirdre mused, she was simply jealous. She recalled the days they'd spent in Maine, and there were times when she wished for them again. Neil had been totally devoted to her there; here she had to share him with a very demanding job. She recalled his saying that he'd never married before because the law was such a demanding mistress. At the time she'd argued that the right woman had simply never come along.

Now she wondered if *she* was the right woman, and let her insecurities suggest that she might not be. Yes, Neil was warm and affectionate. Yes, he put aside his work when she came to talk with him. Yes, he was patient with her frustration when her leg seemed to take inordinately long in healing.

But he went off to work quite happily each morning. And he never said that he loved her.

Then again, she realized, maybe her unease was reflective of nothing more than the changes her life had undergone in a few short months. The work on the house was now finished. It was furnished to their mutual satisfaction in the style of understated sophistication that Deirdre had never before thought of as a style; it was merely the way she wanted to live. She wasn't one to spend hours simply looking at the finished product or wandering from one room to another, and the demands Neil made on her for evening engagements weren't enough to occupy her time.

As time passed she grew restless.

She started going to the health club. Though she probably could have taught, she didn't want to. She felt tired. Her leg, though better, still bothered her. She began to wonder whether her compulsion to teach had been directly tied to her need to escape Joyce Enterprises. Since that need was no longer there the compulsion had faded.

She sat at home for long hours, missing Neil, wondering what to do with herself. She lunched with friends, but that brought no lasting relief from her malaise. She took part in the planning of a ten-kilometer charity run, but that occupied far too little of her time.

Finally, on impulse one day, she flew down to meet Victoria for lunch. They hadn't seen each other since the wedding, which Victoria had proudly and delightedly attended, and Deirdre was counting on her friend to bolster her morale.

"How long have you know Neil?" Deirdre asked, broaching the topic as soon as the waiter had left with their order.

"Three years," Victoria answered, cocking her head to the side. "Why do you ask?"

"Did you know him well during that time?"

"We didn't see each other often, but if I were to judge from the quality of the time we spent together, I'd say we were close." She pursed her lips. "Something's up, Dee. Spill it."

Deirdre shrugged, absently playing with the moisture on the outside of her water glass. "I don't know. It's just that everything between us happened so fast. I sometimes wonder if we rushed things."

"You have doubts about Neil?"

"No. Well, maybe once in a while. My mother said something a few weeks ago that bothered me, something about Neil—"

"Your mother," Victoria scoffed. "Your mother is a good
friend of mine, but that doesn't mean I can't see her faults.
She's one of those people who are never satisfied. You take
her too seriously, Dee. I've told you that before."

"I know. But I can't help hearing her little 'words of wisdom.'"

"You may have to hear them. You don't have to heed them."

"But it's like they niggle in the back of my mind and they
refuse to go away." She raised beseeching eyes to her friend.
"Victoria, do you think Neil is ambitious?"

"I should hope so. No one is successful if he isn't ambitious."

"Ruthlessly so? Would you call Neil ruthlessly ambitious?"

Victoria didn't have to think about that. "No. Unequivo-
cably. Neil is not a ruthless person. If anything, the opposite
is true. If he had a little more of the bastard in him, he might
not have had that problem with Wittnauer-Douglass."

"If he hadn't had that," Deirdre pointed out with a lop-
sided grin, "he'd never have run off to Maine and I'd never
have met him, so I can't be sorry about Wittnauer-Douglass."
Her grin faded. "It's just that my mother learned about all
that, and she suggested that Neil might be out for himself
when it comes to Joyce Enterprises."

"Is that what you think?"

"No. At least, I want to think that it isn't so. But he's taken
to his work with such . . . such *glee*, and there are times when
I wish he showered more of that glee on me."

"You can't have it both ways, Dee. If he's to turn Joyce Enterprises around, he's going to have to put in the hours. Take
my word for it, though. Neil Hersey has nothing but the most
upstanding intentions when it comes to your business. I don't
think there's a selfish bone in that man's body. Did he ever tell
you what he did for my niece?"

Deirdre frowned. "No. He never mentioned your niece."

"He wouldn't. That's his way."

"Well? What did he do?"

"A while ago, my niece got involved in a criminal matter. The girl was only nineteen at the time, and her mother—my sister—was frantic. They live in a small town in western Connecticut and aren't very well off, and they didn't know where to turn for help. I called Neil, knowing that criminal law wasn't his specialty but hoping that he'd be able to refer us to a capable person. Not only did he do that, but he personally involved himself in the case, and then, when the other lawyer would have given him a referral fee, he insisted that the man deduct it from the fee he charged my sister—a fee, mind you, that was on the low side, anyway, considering that my niece got away with nothing but probation. Now—" she tipped up her chin "—if Neil were only out for himself, would he have done all that for my niece?"

Deirdre felt a rush of pride in her husband. "No. And I know that he's always done charity work. It's just that the situation with us is so different. There's so much at stake for him now."

"I doubt he'd consider anything more important than your love."

Deirdre held her breath.

"Dee? You do love him, don't you?"

"Oh, yes!"

"But . . . ?"

"I'm not sure he loves me."

"Are you kidding?"

Deirdre responded defensively. "No, I'm not kidding. He's never told me he loved me. Our marriage was . . . was . . . expedient, and that was his own word."

Victoria pressed a calming hand on her arm. "Look, sweetheart, I know enough about each of your situations to realize that your getting married solved certain problems for you both. But I saw Neil at your wedding, and if that man wasn't in love, I'll turn in my matchmaker badge." She paused. "What does he say when you tell him that you love him?"

Deirdre didn't have to answer. Guilt was written all over her face.

"My Lord, Dee. Why not? You're no wilting pansy!"

"But I don't want to pressure him. Worse, I don't want to say it and not have him say it back. And anyway, when he's home there's so much else we talk about, and then we don't want to talk at all. . . ."

Victoria shot her a knowing grin. "That's more like it." She raised her eyes when the waiter approached with their plates, and waited until he'd deposited the meal and gone. "So, Neil is very busy with work, and you're feeling lonesome."

"Yes."

"Have you told him that?"

"No."

Victoria cast pleading eyes toward the ornate ceiling high overhead. "I know I shouldn't ask this, but why not?"

"Because in the first place, I don't want to sound like a complainer. When we first got to Maine, that was all I did—bitch at him, and everything else in sight. Then our relationship gelled, and I stopped griping. I liked myself a lot more then. I don't want to go back to that other way." She paused for an exaggerated breath. "And in the second place, there's nothing he can do about it."

"He can reassure you, maybe help find something to keep you busy."

Deirdre shook her head sadly. "I don't know, Victoria. I look at you and I'm envious. When you finish one thing you start another. I used to have a million and one things to do with my day, but now I can't seem to find anything that tempts me."

"You want to be with Neil. Everything else is . . . blah. So why don't you work part-time at the office?"

"That'd be tantamount to surrender. I swore I'd never work there."

"And you're so rigid that you can't reconsider, particularly knowing that working there now would be out of choice, rather than need?"

Deirdre didn't respond immediately; she sat absently nudging her cold salmon with a fork. "Put that way, I sound pretty childish."

"If the shoe fits . . ."

"I don't know, Victoria. I'm not sure that's what I want, either."

"Do me a favor, Dee, and talk with Neil? He's a patient man. Really, he is. And he's resourceful. Most important, he's your husband. He wants you to be happy." She speared a firm green bean and held it over her plate. "Will you?"

"I'll try."

"Don't try. *Do* it!"

DEIRDRE WOULD HAVE done it that night, had Neil not offered her a solution before she'd been able to utter a word. He'd come home particularly tired, and they were relaxing in the living room, sharing a glass of wine.

"I need your help, Deirdre," he announced in a businesslike tone.

"There's a problem at the office?"

He nodded. "In personnel. Art Brickner, our man there, is giving us flack about hiring people to fill in certain gaps. He wanted to bring people up from the ranks, and I agree with him in theory, except that in several of these cases there simply is no one to bring up from the ranks. Most of his resistance is to new blood, and I fall prominently in that category. Art was one of your father's original men."

"I know . . . But how can I help?"

"Work with him. Ease him through the transition. He's a good man—"

"He's stodgy."

Neil chuckled. "Yes, he's stodgy, but his instincts are good, and your presence in his office might just remind him that, contrary to what he fears, all is not going down the tubes at Joyce Enterprises."

"Oh, Neil . . . what do I know about personnel?"

"You have common sense, and a feel for the company. Art will take care of the mechanics, while you handle the, uh, the spiritual end. What do you think?"

"I think," she said, studying the features she adored so much, "that you look exhausted. You're working too hard, Neil."

Loosening his necktie, he sank deeper into the sofa. "You're right. But it has to be done." His eyes narrowed. "You look exhausted, too. Was it running down to New York to have lunch with Victoria?"

"Uh-uh. I'm tired from having too much time on my hands."

"Then helping Art could be just the thing."

"Neil—"

"You wouldn't have to work full-time, only twenty hours a week or so."

"But I—"

"You could wear whatever you wanted, since you wouldn't be in the limelight."

"But what—"

"I'd even pay you." He grinned broadly. "How does that sound?"

She sighed, stared at him in exasperation for a minute, then took his silent offer and settled under the arm he held out. "When you smile at me like that, Neil Hersey, I'm a goner. But you know that, don't you, which is why you do it! I'm a sucker. That's all. A real sucker."

"Then you will work?"

"Yes, I will work."

"And you'll tell me if it turns out to be too much?"

"It won't turn out to be too much. I'm young. I'm full of energy. I'm brimming with enthusiasm. . . ."

BUT IT DID TURN OUT to be too much—or rather, it put a strain on Deirdre that she hadn't expected. She worked from nine to two every day, and was positively drained. After a week of mornings when she couldn't seem to get going, she began coming in at ten. Even then she was dragging by the time Neil arrived home at night.

Witnessing her struggle, Neil grew more and more tense. He waited for her to come to him, to broach the subject, but she didn't. Finally, after two weeks of helplessness, he took matters into his own hands.

Arriving home early from work, he found Deirdre curled beneath an afghan on their king-size bed, sound asleep. He sat on the bed beside her, leaned down and kissed her cheek.

Her lashes fluttered, then rose. "Neil!" she whispered, pushing herself up. "I'm sorry. I never dreamed you'd be home this early!"

He pulled a bouquet of flowers—actually, three roses and an assortment of greens—from behind him. "For you."

Groggy still, she looked from him to the roses and back, smiling at last. "They're lovely. Any special occasion?"

"Mmm-hmm. Today's the day we admit that you're pregnant."

Deirdre's smile vanished, as did what little color had been on her cheeks. She lay back on the bed, closed her eyes and spoke in a very small voice. "How did you guess?"

Neil was stricken by the unhappiness he saw on Deirdre's face. He'd assumed that she'd been afraid to tell him—though he didn't know why—but apparently there was more than fear involved. He answered her quietly. "We've been married for nearly three months, and during that time you haven't had a single period."

"I'm an athlete," she pointed out. "That can do strange things to a woman's system."

"You're constantly tired. Even the slightest activity exhausts you."

"It's everything that's happened in the past few months. I'm on emotional overload."

"And the greater fullness of your breasts?" he asked, his voice deep and low. "And the slight thickening of your waist? Things that nobody else sees, I do. Come on, Deirdre. Let's face the facts. You're pregnant. Is it so awful?"

She focused tired eyes on him. "I feel so lousy right now that, yes, it's awful."

"Then you agree that it's true?"

"It's true."

"But you haven't been to a doctor."

"No."

"Why, Deirdre? Don't you want to have a baby?"

"I do!" she cried, then lowered her voice. "It's just that, on top of everything else, it's so sudden...."

"We weren't using any birth control. You had to know there was a possibility this would happen."

"How did you know I wasn't using birth control?" she countered, being contrary.

"Deirdre, I was with you constantly. I would have known."

"Not if I'd had an IUD."

"But you didn't have one, and you're pregnant now!"

"Thanks to you. If you knew I wasn't using anything, why didn't *you* use something?"

"Deirdre, I do not pack prophylactics as a matter of habit. The last thing I expected when I went up to Maine was that I'd be with a woman."

"So neither of us was prepared, and both of us knew it, and we did nothing, and look what happened."

"I don't think it's such a horrible situation, Deirdre."

"You don't?"

"Of course not."

"You don't feel that it's just another burden on your shoulders?"

"Have I ever talked of burdens?"

"No. But they're there."

"This one's a nice one. I told you I wanted children."

"'Someday,' you said."

"Then 'someday' is now. And the more I think about it, the happier I am." Scooping her up, he tucked her against him. "I know you're not feeling great, Deirdre, but once you see a doctor and he gives you vitamins, and once you pass the initial few months, you'll feel better."

To Deirdre's dismay, she began to cry. Her fingers closed around the lapel of his suit jacket, and she buried her face in his shirt.

"I'll be . . . be fat."

"You'll be beautiful."

"You'll . . . you'll be stuck with me."

"I'm not complaining."

"You're being so . . . kind."

"You're being such a ninny." He hugged her, trying his best to absorb whatever pain she was feeling. He knew she'd been through a lot, and that having a baby at a later time would probably have been better for her, but he wasn't sorry. It bound her all the closer to him.

Weeping softly, Deirdre was thinking similar thoughts. Oh, yes, she wanted the baby, but because it was Neil's, more than for any other reason. When she thought of it, having his baby made the tie between them even more permanent than marriage. It was both a reassuring and a frightening thought, because if something went wrong and Neil decided he'd had enough, a wholly innocent child would be affected.

The scent of roses by her nose interrupted her sniffles. She opened her eyes and saw Neil touch each bloom.

"One for you, one for me, one for baby. A nice bunch, don't you think?"

His sweetness brought a helpless smile to Deirdre's wet face. "A very nice bunch."

Later, she told herself, she'd watch for the thorns. For now, she was too tired to do anything but relax in Neil's arms.

9

ONCE DEIRDRE accepted the fact of her pregnancy, she was better able to cope. She saw a doctor and began a regimen of vitamins that compensated for what the baby demanded of her body. She continued working with Art Brickner, adjusting her hours to accommodate her need for sleep.

Neil seemed legitimately pleased about the baby, and that relieved her most of all. In turn, she made up her mind to do everything in her power to make their marriage work.

When she was at the office, she dressed accordingly, intent on making Neil proud. When she was at home she planned their meals and coordinated the various cleaning efforts so that the house was always immaculate should Neil decide to bring people home at the last minute. At Neil's insistence, though, they'd hired a maid to help. She resumed her visits to the health club—the doctor had okayed that—and though she didn't teach, she took part in classes. She swam. She diligently kept herself in shape—as much as a woman with a slowly growing belly could.

And she never argued with Neil. She didn't complain when he was delayed for several hours at the office and dinner was held up. She didn't say a word when he had to go away on a business trip. She didn't nag him to take time off from work to play tennis with her. She graciously attended cocktail parties and dinners, and when she and Neil were finally alone at night, she did her very best to satisfy him, both physically and emotionally.

But because she refused to give him any cause for displeasure, the frustration that had built within her had nowhere to go. She wished he didn't work so hard, but she didn't say so. She yearned for time alone with him—even their weekends revolved around business demands—but she didn't say so. She ached, positively ached to hear him say that he loved her, but she didn't say so, and he didn't tell her what she wanted to hear. She felt as if she were walking a tightrope.

The tightrope began to fray when her mother dropped in one morning. Deirdre was getting ready to leave for work.

"Have you heard his latest scheme?" Maria asked with an arrogance Deirdre found all too familiar. They were standing in the front hall; Deirdre knew enough not to invite her mother to sit, or she'd be in for an even longer siege.

"That depends on which scheme it is," Deirdre countered with confidence. "Neil's had a lot of them lately, and they're all very promising."

"This one isn't."

"Which one?"

"He's bidding on a government contract for the electronics division."

Deirdre had known that. "Is there a problem?" she asked blandly.

"We've never bid for government contracts. We've always devoted ourselves to the private sector."

"That doesn't mean we can't change now, if doing so will be good for the company."

"But will it? That's the question. Is Neil bidding for that contract because it will be good for the company or for him?"

"Aren't they one and the same?" Deirdre asked, ignoring her mother's barely veiled reference to the earlier accusation she'd made.

"Not by a long shot. You may not know it, but one of the other bidders is Wittnauer-Douglass."

Deirdre hadn't known it. She ignored the frisson of anxiety that shivered through her. "I'm sure there are many other bidders—"

"None Neil holds a grudge against."

"Neil doesn't hold a grudge against Wittnauer-Douglass," Deirdre insisted. "What happened there is done. He is very successful in what he's doing now. I think you're way off base."

"You've thought that from the start, when I told you to be careful, but this is the evidence I need."

"Evidence? What evidence?"

"Your husband is involving Joyce Enterprises in something solely for the sake of avenging himself. He would never be bidding for a government contract if it weren't for that. Think about it. Isn't it awfully suspicious that the first time we do anything of this sort, a major competitor is the very one Neil has a gripe against?"

Deirdre set her purse down on the table. "Do you know the details, Mother? Who submitted a bid first, Wittnauer-Douglass or Joyce Enterprises?"

Maria fumbled with the collar of her sable coat. "I don't know that. How could I possibly know that!"

"If it's evidence you're looking for, that'd be a place to start. If Neil submitted his bid first, without ever knowing that Wittnauer-Douglass would be a competitor, his innocence would be obvious."

"The rest of the evidence is against him."

Deirdre was losing her patience. "What evidence?"

"Deirdre," her mother said, sighing. "Think. Neil met you at a time when he needed a change of location and occupation."

"He did not need—"

"He latched onto what you had to offer, married you as quickly as possible and set about implementing his plans."

"The plans he implemented were for the resurgence of Joyce Enterprises, and he's done a remarkable job! He's done us a favor!"

"He's done himself a favor. Look at it objectively. He's at the helm of a successful corporation. He's become so well respected in the community that the two of you are in demand at all the parties that matter—"

"If you had any sense of appreciation, Mother, you'd spend your time tallying all he's done for *you*. He's married the more undesirable of your two daughters and is about to give you a grandchild. He's taken responsibility for the family business—and even gotten *me* involved in it. What more do you want?"

"I want Joyce Enterprises to remain in the black."

"And you think that bidding on a government contract will prevent that?" Deirdre asked in disbelief. "He's just bidding."

"If he wants that contract badly enough, he'll bid low enough to undercut Wittnauer-Douglass, and if he does that, he could jeopardize our financial status."

"And if he does that," Deirdre pointed out angrily, "he'll be jeopardizing the very position he's built for himself. It doesn't make sense, Mother. You're being illogical."

"It's a risk—his bidding for that contract."

"There's always a risk if the prize is worth anything. If Neil only stuck with what was safe, the business would be at a standstill."

"He's being rash. I think you should talk with him."

Deirdre had had enough. "I don't have to listen to this." She snatched up her purse, took her coat from the nearby chair and headed for the door. "You can stay if you like. I have to get to work."

Deirdre might have been fine had the conversation she'd had with her mother been the only one of its kind. But several days later, Art Brickner raised the issue, complaining that Neil had spoken with him about hiring an enlarged cadre of workers if the government contract came through. Art questioned both the logistics and the wisdom of what Neil proposed, and all Deirdre could do was to support Neil and insist that his plan was sound.

Several days after that, she was approached by one of the long-standing vice presidents of the company, who, too, had doubts as to the direction in which Joyce was headed. Again Deirdre expressed her support for Neil, sensing that what she was hearing was simply a resistance to change, but she grew increasingly uncomfortable.

She didn't tell Neil about any of the three discussions. She didn't want to anger him by suggesting that she had doubts, when, in fact, she had no qualms about the viability of winning and working through a government contract. What bothered her was the possibility that his motives weren't entirely pure, that, as her mother had suggested, he was being driven by a desire for revenge. She tried to ignore such thoughts, but they wouldn't leave her.

At the root of the matter were the doubts she had regarding their relationship. Oh, they were close. They said all the right things, did all the right things. To the outside world— and to themselves, on one level—they were a loving couple. If she recalled the original reasons for their marriage, though, as she did with increasing frequency, she couldn't help but question what it was that drove Neil. His questionable motives bothered her far more than the prospect of any contract, government or otherwise.

So she walked the tightrope. On one end was what she wanted; on the other what she thought Neil wanted. The rope frayed. It finally snapped when he arrived home unexpectedly one afternoon. She was instantly pleased, delighted by the thought of spending stolen time with him. The sight of him—ruggedly handsome, with his beard offsetting his more formal suit—never failed to excite her, as did the inevitable kiss with which he greeted her.

Threading his arm through hers, he led her into the den. When he held her back, though, the look of tension on his face told her something was amiss.

"I need a favor, Deirdre. I have to run to Washington for a meeting tonight. Do you think you could handle the dinner party on your own?"

They'd long ago invited three couples to join them at a restaurant in town. Deirdre knew the couples. They weren't her favorite people.

Her face fell. "Oh, Neil . . . do you have to go?"

"I do. It's important." He felt like a heel, but there was no way around it.

"But so sudden. You were planning to go down for the presentation tomorrow morning, anyway. Can't you have this meeting then?"

"Not if I want the presentation to be the best it can be."

"It will be. You've been working on it for weeks."

"I want that contract," he stated, then coaxed her more gently. "Come on. You can handle things at the restaurant."

"You know how I hate dinners like that."

"I know that you manage them beautifully." She'd proved it in the past weeks, and he'd been proud of her.

"With you by my side. But you won't be, which makes the whole thing that much more distasteful."

"I'm asking for your help. I can't be two places at once."

Annoyances, past and present, rose within her. She left his side, grabbed a throw pillow from the sofa and began to fluff it with a vengeance. "And you choose to be in Washington. If you wanted to be here, you could send someone else to Washington. Why can't Ben go?" Ben Tillotson was the executive Neil had brought in from the midwest.

"Ben's daughter is visiting from Seattle. He feels badly enough that he has to leave her tomorrow."

"Well, what about me? You have to leave me tomorrow, too." She dropped the first pillow and started on another.

"It's my responsibility before it's Ben's."

"Then if Ben can't make it, why don't you let Thor go?" Thor VanNess headed the electronics division. In Deirdre's mind, he'd be the perfect one to attend the meeting.

"Thor is fantastic at what he does, but he is not a diplomat, and the meeting tonight is going to involve a fair share of diplomacy."

"And you're the only diplomat at Joyce?"

Her sarcasm was a sharp prod, poking holes in Neil's patience. "Deirdre," he said, sighing, "you're making too much out of a single meeting. If you want, I can have my secretary call and cancel the dinner party, but I'd hoped that wouldn't be necessary. Believe me, I've looked for other outs. I've tried to think of someone else who can get the job done tonight in Washington, but there is no one else. It's *my responsibility*."

She tossed the second pillow on the sofa and leaned forward to straighten a small watercolor that hung on the wall. "Then you take too much on your own shoulders. I was under the assumption that delegation was critical to the smooth functioning of a corporation this size." She lowered her voice in an attempt to curb her temper. Yes, she was making too much out of a single meeting, but it had become a matter of principle. She faced him head-on. "Send someone else. Anyone else."

"I can't, Deirdre. It's as simple as that."

"No, it's not," she declared, unable to hold it in any longer. "It's not simple at all. You put your work before every other thing in our lives, which shows where *your* priorities lie."

Neil bowed his head and rubbed the back of his neck. "You're being unfair," he said quietly.

"Unfair? Or selfish? Well, maybe it's about time!" She stalked to the large ship's clock that hung on another wall, took a tool from its side, opened it and angrily began to wind it.

"Take it easy, babe. You're making a mountain out of—"

"I am not!"

"You're getting upset." His gaze fell to the tiny swell just visible in profile beneath her oversized sweater. "It's not good for you *or* the baby."

She turned to glare at him. "That's where you're wrong. It's the *best* thing for me, and therefore for the baby, because I can't pretend anymore. I'm being torn apart inside."

Neil stiffened. "What are you talking about?"

"I can't stand this, Neil. I've tried to be the perfect wife for you. I've done all the things I swore I'd never do, and I've done them without argument because I wanted to please you. I wanted to make this marriage work."

"I thought it was working. Do you mean to tell me you were faking it all?"

She scrunched up her face in frustration. "I wasn't faking it. On one level the marriage does work. But there has to be more. There has to be total communication. You discuss the business with me, but I don't know what you're really thinking or feeling. There are times when I feel totally left out of what's happening."

"You could ask more."

"You could offer more."

"Damn it, Deirdre, how do I know what you want if you don't ask?"

"Don't you know me well enough to know what I want without my having to ask?"

"No!" he exploded, angry now himself. "I thought you wanted me to make a go of your damned business, but it looks like I was wrong. I've been busting my ass in the office racking my brain, dipping into resources I didn't know I had, looking for one way, then another to make Joyce Enterprises stronger."

For an instant she was taken back. "I thought you enjoyed the work."

"I do enjoy the work, but that's because I've been successful. I've felt good knowing that I was carrying out my part of the bargain, knowing that I had the business moving again. Every bit of my satisfaction relates directly or indirectly to you."

Deirdre eyed him skeptically. "Are you sure? Isn't there a little satisfaction that relates solely to you?"

"I suppose," he answered, rubbing his bearded cheek. "If I stand back and look at what I've been able to do in a few short months, yes, I'm proud of myself. I'm a lawyer by training, not a businessman, yet I've taken on entrepreneurial tasks that two, four, six years ago I'd never have dared tackle."

"But you have now. Why?"

Neil was still for a moment, his tone almost puzzled when he spoke. "It was part of the agreement we made."

"No. Go back further." Her hand tightened around the clock tool. "Why did we make that agreement?"

"Because you needed me and I needed you."

"That's right. And I guess it's one of the things that's been eating at me. You needed a means of reestablishing yourself after what happened in Hartford. You came in here, took over the reins, and you've done more with this company than anyone else—including my father—has done in years. You've done everything I expected, and more. Why, Neil? Why so much?"

"That's an absurd question," he snapped. "If there are things to be done, I believe in doing them. Yes, I could have stopped thinking a while ago, and Joyce Enterprises still would have been in far better shape than it had been. But I've seen potential in the company. I'm trying to realize it."

Replacing the clock tool, Deirdre moved to a plant hanging by the window and began to pick dried leaves from it. "Or are you trying to prove to Wittnauer-Douglass that you can beat them at their own game?"

"What?" He tipped his head and narrowed one eye. "What are you talking about?"

"This government contract. You've told me all about your end of it, and I've been in favor of it. What you didn't tell me was that Wittnauer-Douglass is bidding for the same contract." She crushed the dried leaves in her hand. "My *mother* had to tell me that, and at the same time she leveled a pretty harsh accusation."

"Your mother's leveled accusations before, and they've proved unfounded." He was staring hard at Deirdre. When she reached toward the plant again, he bellowed, "Leave the damn plant alone, Deirdre. I want your full attention right now."

Slowly she turned to face him, but she didn't say a word, because his expression was suddenly one of fury, reminiscent of their first days in Maine, but worse.

His lips were thinned; tension radiated from the bridge of his nose. "You think that I'm going for this contract to get even with Wittnauer-Douglass!" he spat, his eyes widening. "You actually think that I'm out for revenge, that everything I've done since we've been married has been with this in mind! I don't believe you, Deirdre! Where have you *been* all these weeks?"

She grew defensive. "I didn't say I thought that. I said my mother thought that."

"But you're raising it with me now, which means that you have your own doubts."

"Yes, I have my doubts! I've stood behind you one hundred percent, defending you before my mother, before Art Brickner, before others of my father's people who've approached me with questions. I've been as strong an advocate as I can possibly be, but after a while all I can think of is that our marriage was *expedient*." She covered her face with one rigid hand and spoke into her palm. "I hate that word. God, do I hate that word."

"Then why do you use it?" he yelled back.

She dropped her hand. "Because *you* used it, and it's stuck in my mind like glue, and I try to shake it off, but it won't let go! We married for the wrong reasons, Neil, and it's about time we faced it. I can't go on this way. It's driving me nuts!"

Neil thrust a hand through his hair. "Driving *you* nuts! Do you think it's any different for me? I've tried my best to make things work, and I thought they were working. Now I find out that every one of my efforts has been in vain. I thought you trusted me, but maybe all you wanted was someone to bail you out. Now that I've done that, I'm expendable. Is that it?"

"No! I never said that!"

"Then what are you saying? What in the hell do you want?"

She was shaking—in anger, in frustration, in heartache. Clenching her fists by her sides, she cried, "I want it *all*! I don't want an expedient marriage! I never did! I want *love*, Neil! Damn it, *I want the real thing*!"

Neil was far from steady himself. Equal parts of tension, fear and anguish thrummed through his body, clouding his mind, robbing him of the thoughts, much less the words to fight her. Feeling more impotent than he'd ever felt in his life, he turned and stormed from the room.

Deirdre wrapped her arms around her middle and tried to control the wild hammering of her heart. She heard the front door slam, then, moments later, the angry rev of the Le-

Baron. It had long since faded into silence before she began to move in small, dazed steps, working her way slowly toward her favorite room, the loft above the garage.

Late-afternoon sun filtered in across the polished wood floor, splashing on bare stucco walls with a cheeriness that eluded her at the moment. Her cassette player and a pile of tapes lay in one corner. She'd often used the room for exercise, though what she'd really hoped was that one day it would be a playroom for their children.

Now all that seemed in doubt.

Carefully easing herself down onto the cushioned sill of the arched window, she tucked her knees up, pressed her forehead to them and began to cry.

Neil didn't love her. If he had, he'd have said so. She'd given him the opening; she'd told him what she wanted. And he'd left her. He didn't love her.

And their future? A big, fat question mark. In some respects they were back where they'd started when they'd first arrived on Victoria's island.

What had she wanted, really wanted then? Love. She hadn't realized it at the time, but in the weeks since, she realized that everything else would have fallen into place if she'd found love. She could teach, or not. She could work at Joyce Enterprises, or not. The one thing that held meaning was love.

NEIL DROVE AROUND for hours. He stopped at a pay phone to call the office, but he had no desire to show up there. He had no desire to go to Washington. He had no desire to bid for, much less win, that government contract he'd sought. He had no desire to do anything . . . but return to Deirdre.

That was the one thing that became eminently clear with the miles he put on his odometer. Deirdre was all that mattered in his life.

He relived their meeting in Maine, their arguments, their eventual coming to terms with each other. He reviewed the months they'd been married and all that had happened, both personally and professionally, during that time. But mostly he replayed the scene he'd had with Deirdre that day. He heard her words, pondered them, analyzed them.

And it occurred to him that he was possibly on the verge of making the biggest mistake of his life.

Stopping the car in the middle of the street, he ignored the honking of horns, made a U-turn and mentally mapped the fastest route back to the house. When he arrived, it was nearly ten o'clock. The house was every bit as dark as the night was, and for a minute he feared he was too late. Then his headlights illumined Deirdre's car, parked as unobtrusively as she'd left it beneath the huge maple tree. Pulling up behind it, he jumped from his own and ran inside.

"Deirdre?" he called, flipping lights on in each of the ground floor rooms. "Deirdre!" There was no anger in his voice, simply worry. With the irrational fear of a man in love, he conjured up every one of the dreadful things that might have happened to her during his absence. She was upset. She was pregnant. Oh, God . . .

Taking the stairs two at a time, he searched their bedroom, then the others. Only when there was still no sign of her did he stop to think. Then, praying that he'd find her there, he headed for the loft.

"Deirdre?" Fearfully he said her name as he switched on the light, then caught his breath when he saw her curled on the window seat, her head having fallen against the windowpane. In the seconds it took him to cross to her, he added even more dreadful things to his list of fears.

Lowering himself by her side, he brushed her cheek with his thumb. Dried tears streaked her skin, but her color was good and she was warm.

"Deirdre?" His voice was soft and shaky. "Wake up, sweetheart. There's something I have to tell you." He smoothed the hair from her forehead, leaned forward to kiss her wheat-hued crown, framed her face with both hands. "Deirdre?"

She took in a hiccuping breath and, frowning, raised heavy lids. Disoriented, she stared at him for a minute, then her eyes opened fully and she pushed herself up against the window frame. "You're back," she whispered.

He smiled gently. "Yes."

"What . . . what happened to Washington?"

"It's not important."

"But the contract—"

"Isn't important."

"But you wanted it—"

"Not as much as I want you." When her eyes filled with confusion and disbelief, he explained. "I've driven around for hours thinking about things, and when I went back over what you said earlier, I realized that I may have got things wrong. I was so convinced that you wanted out of the marriage, that you'd gotten tired of me and it, that I took your words one way, when they could have been taken another." His hands were cupping her head, thumbs stroking the short, smooth strands of hair behind her ears. "I may be wrong again, but I think it's worth the risk."

He took a deep breath. Once there might have been pride involved, but he'd gone well beyond that. Still, he was nervous. His words came out in a rush. "I love you, Deirdre. *That* was why I wanted to marry you in the first place. Anything else that came along with the marriage was nice, but purely secondary. Maybe I've had my guard up, because I never knew for sure why, deep down inside, you agreed to marry me. And I was afraid to ask outright, because I didn't want to know . . . if you'd married me simply because of our bargain. But what you said earlier set me to thinking. What you said, and the anguish in it, would make sense if you love me and fear that I don't love you back." His eyes grew moist, and his voice shook again. "Do you, Deirdre? Do you love me?"

Tears welled on her lower lids, and her chin quivered. "Very much," she whispered, which was all she could manage because emotion clogged her throat, making further sound impossible.

Neil closed his eyes in relief and hauled her against him. "Oh, Deirdre," he rasped, "we've been so foolish." His arms wound fully around her; hers had found their way beneath his jacket and held him every bit as tightly. "So foolish," he whispered against her hair. "We never said the words. The only words that mattered, and we never said them."

Deirdre's heart was near to bursting. "I love you . . . love you so much," she whispered brokenly, and raised her eyes to his. "We had so much going for us, and we nearly blew it."

A shudder passed through him. He took her mouth in a fierce kiss, gentling only when he reminded himself that she wasn't going to leave. "When I think of everything else I've had in my life, things I've risked, things I've lost, they seem so unimportant now. You're what matters. This is where you belong, in my arms. And I belong in yours."

"I know," she said, and buried her face against his neck. The scent of him was familiar and dear; it was an aphrodisiac in times of passion, a soothing balm in times of emotional need. She breathed deeply of it, and her face blossomed into a smile. Then the smile faded, replaced by a look of horror. "Neil!" She pushed back from his arms. "The dinner party! They'll have gone to the restaurant and we've stood them up!"

He chuckled. "Not to worry. I called my secretary and had her cancel on our behalf. We'll make it another time. Together."

Deirdre wrinkled her nose. "I don't like the Emerys. He is an arrogant bore, and she has bad breath." Neil laughed aloud, but she hadn't finished. "And Donald Lutz is always checking out the room, on the lookout for someone important to greet, while that wife of his can't take her hand off the chunky emerald ring she wears. And as for the Spellmans, they're—"

Neil put a hand over her mouth, but he was grinning. "They're important clients. Once in a while we have to sacrifice our own personal preferences for the sake of the corporation."

"Speaking of which . . ." She mumbled into his hand, then spoke more clearly, if softly when he removed it. "I don't distrust you, Neil. Everything you've done at Joyce has been good. And I *am* in favor of the government project if it comes through."

"I didn't do it because of Wittnauer-Douglass, Deirdre. I didn't even know they were bidding for the same project."

"That was what I suggested to my mother," Deirdre said, feeling faintly smug. "She's a troublemaker. Do you know that? The woman is a born troublemaker! I never realized it, because I always assumed that she was right and that everything was my fault, but she's been dead wrong about us from the start. Victoria had her pegged. My mother is one of those people who are never satisfied. It may be a little late, but I actually feel sorry for my father. No wonder he poured so much of his time and energy into the business. He was running away from her!"

Hearing her evaluation of her parents' relationship gave Deirdre a moment's pause. Her confidence wavered. "Were you doing that, Neil? Were you running away from me, spending every minute thinking about the business?"

"A good many of those minutes you thought I was thinking about the business, I was thinking about you," he said with a crooked smile. Then the smile vanished. "I wanted to please you. I felt that if I couldn't win your heart, I'd at least win your respect."

"You've had that from the start. And I admire—no, I stand in awe of—what you've done with the business." She sharpened her gaze on him. "But I meant what I said about delegating authority. I want more of your time, Neil! I want to do things with you. I want to go out to romantic little lunches every so often, or play tennis, or take off for the weekend and go . . . wherever!"

His eyes twinkled. "I think I can manage that."

"And I want to go to Washington with you tomorrow."

"No."

"Why not?"

"Because I'm not going."

She stared at him for a minute. "You're not?"

"No. Ben can handle it."

"But you're the best one for the job! You know it, and I know it."

"But there is a question of conflict of interest."

"I don't believe that! I was angry, or I'd never have even suggested it!"

"Now you're being diplomatic," he teased.

"I am not!"

He grew serious. "I thought a lot about that situation, too, while I was out driving. No, I didn't originally know that we'd be competing against Wittnauer-Douglass for that contract, but I have to admit that when I found out, there was intense satisfaction in it. I mean, we may not get the contract. The bids are sealed, and I have no way of knowing who bid what.

The contract may go to Wittnauer-Douglass, or it may go to one of the other bidders. But I did get an inordinate amount of pleasure knowing that Joyce is right up there in the Wittnauer-Douglass league."

"There's nothing wrong with that—"

"But the point is that I have already avenged myself."

"Yes, but through honest hard work and talent. Not just anyone could have done what you've done, Neil. Joyce Enterprises was marking time. You have it moving forward. If you won't take the credit, then I'll take it for you!"

Her pride in him gave him a thrill. "You will, will you?"

"Uh-huh." She thought for a minute. "But what about practicing law. That was what you really wanted to do. Don't you miss it?"

"I've been practicing law at Joyce, but with lots of other things thrown in. I do think it's time Ben and I switch places, though. I want to maintain a position of power, because I've enjoyed having a say in what we do when, but I don't need a fancy title, and I *don't* need the full burden of responsibility I've been carrying." He paused. "But what about you? You haven't been teaching, and that was what you really wanted to do. Don't you miss it?"

"No," she said firmly, then grew pensive. "Maybe I've outgrown it. Maybe the need just isn't there anymore. It filled a void in my life, but the void is gone. Being a helpmate to you is far more satisfying than teaching ever was."

He hugged her. "The things you mentioned before—things we could do together—I want to do them, too, Deirdre. We never did take a honeymoon."

"We had that before we were married."

"But I want another one. A *real* one. You know, a luxurious cottage someplace warm, champagne at sunset, hours lying on the beach in the sun, maid service and laundry service and room service."

Deirdre slanted him a mischievous grin. "What happened to the man who could do it all himself?"

"He wants to be able to concentrate solely on his wife. Is that a crime?"

"You're the lawyer. You tell me."

He never did. Rather, he kissed her with such sweet conviction that she didn't care if they broke every law in the book.

LOVE
WITH A
PERFECT STRANGER

Pamela Wallace

◆◆◆◆◆◆◆◆◆◆◆◆◆◆◆◆◆◆◆◆◆◆◆◆◆◆◆◆◆◆◆◆

An absorbing romance set amidst the breathtaking
scenery of Florence, Italy, and Ireland. Torey is a beautiful
young businesswoman in Italy to finalize a deal for her
American fashion house. While traveling she meets a
perfect stranger who will alter the course of her life.

You can order *Love With a Perfect Stranger* by
Pamela Wallace by sending $2.50 plus 75¢ for postage
and handling to:

Janet Dailey
Americana

Don't miss a single title from this great collection. The first eight titles have already been published. Complete and mail this coupon today to order books you may have missed.

Harlequin Reader Service

In U.S.A.
901 Fuhrmann Blvd.
P.O. Box 1397
Buffalo, N.Y. 14140

In Canada
P.O. Box 2800
Postal Station A
5170 Yonge Street
Willowdale, Ont. M2N 6J3

Please send me the following titles from the Janet Dailey Americana Collection. I am enclosing a check or money order for $2.75 for each book ordered, plus 75¢ for postage and handling.

_____	ALABAMA	Dangerous Masquerade
_____	ALASKA	Northern Magic
_____	ARIZONA	Sonora Sundown
_____	ARKANSAS	Valley of the Vapours
_____	CALIFORNIA	Fire and Ice
_____	COLORADO	After the Storm
_____	CONNECTICUT	Difficult Decision
_____	DELAWARE	The Matchmakers

Number of titles checked @ $2.75 each = $_____

N.Y. RESIDENTS ADD
   APPROPRIATE SALES TAX $_____

Postage and Handling $____.75____

                     TOTAL $_____

I enclose _____

(Please send check or money order. We cannot be responsible for cash sent through the mail.)

PLEASE PRINT

NAME _____

ADDRESS _____

CITY _____

STATE/PROV. _____

ALSO BY ANDREW M. GREELEY
FROM TOM DOHERTY ASSOCIATES

In honor of the men who made peace in Northern Ireland

When Irish eyes are smiling,
'Tis like a day in spring.
In the lilt of Irish laughter,
You can hear the angels sing.

When Irish eyes are happy,
All the world is bright and gay,
But when Irish eyes are smiling,
Sure, they'll steal your heart away.

— 1 —

THE REDHEAD with the green eyes continued to play with my wife's breast. She stared
at me with what I thought was undisguised
triumph. I had prior rights to that breast. The
redhead was an interloper, a latecomer, a spoilsport.

"Had enough, had you now?" my wife said to her.
"Want to go to himself, do you now?"

The myth was that this eating, defecating, sleeping
machine loved me more than her ma. She supported the
myth by stretching out her arms to me and gurgling,
"Da."

It wasn't really "da." Everyone knows that going-on-
seven-months-old children cannot pronounce words. But
Nuala Anne had decreed that the gurgle meant "da" and
there was no room for dispute.

"The child definitely likes you more than me, Dermot
Michael," my wife said triumphantly, a view which was
supposed to mitigate my unspoken anguish that the
witch had intruded into our marriage and taken my wife
away from me. Or at least destroyed my monopoly. "Ma
for food, Da for love."

The bewitching little girl snuggled contentedly into
my arms and promptly fell asleep, a characteristic she
shared with her mother. Fiona, our pure white family
wolfhound, watched me suspiciously, not at all sure that
I was capable even of the minor task of holding the little

redhead in my arms. In Fiona's eyes I was strictly number three. The intruder had taken not only my wife but my good dog away from me.

THIS IS ALL SILLY, the Adversary informed me. IT IS NOTHING MORE THAN A TYPICAL SUPERANNUATED ADOLESCENT MALE REACTION TO THE OBLIGATION OF SHARING ONE'S WIFE WITH ONE'S FIRST CHILD. ACTUALLY YOU ADORE THE LITTLE DEFECATING MACHINE.

I generally disagree with the Adversary, an inner voice which constantly criticizes me. However, I had to admit that the small creature sleeping in my arms was moderately adorable.

"She's a changeling," I replied to the Adversary. "At six months she shouldn't be trying to crawl and shouldn't be saying 'Da.' She's not altogether human. Didn't my mom say that most babies don't crawl till nine or ten months?"

AND YOU DIDN'T CRAWL TILL TWELVE MONTHS AND WALK TILL EIGHTEEN AND TALK UNTIL THREE AND ARE BARELY TOILET-TRAINED EVEN NOW.

Nuala Anne had tossed aside her robe and disclosed temporarily her spectacular naked body. I gasped inwardly. Fiona paced around anxiously, knowing that herself was dressing for her early morning run on the beach in the Indian summer sun. Breakfast for all of us, save the red-haired intruder, after her run and before my run.

A warning about my wife's name. It is definitely not Nuahla nor Nulla as in null and void. Nor is it "Null" like in "null and void" as some of my siblings call her, though not in my presence anymore. (She thinks my reaction to that nickname is "funny.") You might try "Noolah" with a touch of Galway fog in your voice or a bad cold and a long and soft emphasis on the "oo," as though you were negatively responding to an attractive invitation with a hesitant "no." I must warn you that she insists that it is impossible to pronounce it correctly unless you speak the Irish language, "and yourself with that terrible flat Chicago 'a'!"

"What was the matter with herself last night?" I asked as Nuala pulled on her running shorts.

Nelliecoyne is what is technically known as a "good baby," which means that she keeps regular hours and thus permits her parents to sleep through the night. It was unthinkable that any child of Nuala Anne McGrail, particularly a girl child, would be anything but a "good baby."

Last night, however, was another story. My wife and I are deep sleepers, particularly after a serious bout of lovemaking. Last night it had been mind-bending in its seriousness. Sometime in the depths of the early morning hours, I had heard as from a great distance an angry wail. I ignored it. Nelliecoyne was a good baby, wasn't she?

Fiona, however, was less easily persuaded by past performance, I felt her large snout nudge me.

"Go away," I told her.

Fiona thereupon barked loudly.

"What's wrong, Dermot Michael?" my wife demanded, her voice heavy with sleep.

"Your daughter is wailing."

"Is she now?"

"I'll go see what the trouble is," I said bravely.

"Ah, no. She's probably hungry and you can't feed her, can you?"

"I cannot," I said contentedly.

So Nuala bounded out of bed, and naked in the moonlight, dashed next door to the nursery, accompanied by the agitated Fiona.

Nuala always dashes. She also bounds. And slams doors.

The tyke continued to wail furiously, something had offended her sense of propriety and order. Her mother's nipple would not satisfy her.

We were spending time in my parents' home at Grand Beach in mid-October, when the place was deserted, to savor the color and the warmth of Indian summer before the arctic air imposed its winter penance on us and to celebrate the second anniversary of our marriage and the third of our chance encounter at O'Neill's Pub on College Green, just down the street from Trinity College. We would take turns each morning running on the beach, swim naked in the heated pool while Nelliecoyne would watch us under the careful supervision of good dog Fiona (who would chase squirrels for the fun of it but never run too far away), walk in the afternoon sunlight with our daughter in her traveling sack, and do our work, such as it was, in the time left over.

I would write a few desultory pages on the first novel of my new contract and Nuala Anne would practice the songs for her forthcoming disc *Nuala Anne Sings Lullabies*. She was far more serious in her work than I, but never pushed me to settle down and be as responsible as she was.

There were, however, two important reasons to escape Chicago during Indian summer—lovemaking and Nick Farmer, the "music critic" of *The Observer*, a Chicago magazine, who was grimly determined to wreck Nuala's career because he hated me. Without ever discussing it explicitly (the Irish are great at that) we both wanted to indulge ourselves in sexual abandon before winter came.

ORGY IS WHAT YOU MEAN, the Adversary sniffed puritanically.

I sleep with many different women: a shy, fragile, virginal creature, a sultry seducer, a playful child, an aggressive sexual demon, an outrageous tease, a warm and close friend. All of them are my wife. I am never sure which one I will encounter in our bedroom. I don't know whether she plays the game of being someone different every night with deliberate planning or whether it is mere random chance. I know her better than I know anyone else in the world. But I hardly know her at all.

Mind you, I'm not complaining.

As I heard her singing an Irish lullaby to our daughter, I imagined her naked in the moonlight, tenderly rocking

Nelliecoyne in her arms against the background of the silver Lake.

"The October winds lament,
Around the castle of Dromore,
Yet peace lies in her lofty halls,
My loving treasure store.
Though Autumn leaves may droop and die,
A bud of Spring are you."

I sighed happily. 'Tis good to have a wife, particularly one like mine.

Normally Nuala Anne would not cross the bedroom without clutching some kind of protection for her modesty. But when the child wailed such concerns for modesty vanished.

Slowly, reluctantly, Nelliecoyne settled down. Her wail became a mild sniffle of protest. Then the only sound was yet another lullaby. Finally, my wife snuggled into bed next to me.

" 'Tis all right, Dermot," she said. "Something upset her. Fiona is staying with her."

Good dog, Fiona.

I extended my arm around her and we both slipped back into peaceful and compliant sleep.

The next morning, as she was tying her running shoes, Nuala Anne explained why our "really good" child had disrupted the serenity of our mid-October repose.

"Och, wasn't it most likely the boat that was offshore?"

She stood up and reached for her running bra, always the last garment to be put in place, at least when I was present. Deliberate? To taunt me, to tempt me, to promise me? What did I know?

"Boat?"

"That big five-masted schooner that was a hundred yards or so offshore."

"That one?" I said as an ominous shiver began at the

base of my skull and ran down my spine. My wife is fey, you see. She *sees* things, usually from the past and, more often than not, things about which she and I must do something. Even the sight of her bare breasts, usually enough to cure me of any and all chills, didn't exorcise this shiver.

"Isn't it the one that is as long as your football fields?"

"That one?"

"You can put herself into the crib if you want, though like as not you'll want to hold her till I come back and tell yourself how much more beautiful she is than I am. . . . Come on, Fiona, girl, let's leave these slugabeds and get ourselves some *real* exercise!"

Nuala Anne and the dog thundered out of the house and bounded down the dune to the beach, two exuberant females liberated temporarily from their solemn duty to watch over Nelliecoyne and her inept and indulgent father.

Was unreal exercise what we did last night, exercise in which Nuala delighted in controlling the pace and action of our lovemaking?

I glanced out the window to watch them sprinting down the beach, a beach wider than it had ever been in my lifetime. My parents said that the March storms had swept in two mammoth sandbars that had lurked offshore for a couple of decades. There was debate in the community whether this meant greater hazard for houses on the Lake because the sandbars were better protection than sea walls. I was content with a better beach. But I've never been one with strong motivation to defer gratification.

The child stirred uneasily out of her sleep and whimpered a mild protest. I knew what that meant. So I changed her diaper, an exercise which the little monster seemed to think had been designed for amusement.

"You're a spoiled little brat," I informed her. "Your ma and your dog will spoil you altogether. It's lucky you have a stern father who will impose some discipline in your life."

THAT'S THE MOST RIDICULOUS THING I'VE EVER HEARD YOU SAY, the Adversary informed me. YOU'RE COMPLETELY WITHOUT DISCIPLINE YOURSELF AND YOU'RE GOING TO TEACH IT TO THAT POOR CHILD?

I had been joking, but if the Adversary was too ignorant to know it I was not about to tell him.

Nelliecoyne gurgled happily as I replaced her in her crib. She was not old enough yet to distinguish the various caregivers who waited on her hand and foot. We were simply "the other one" whom she had to remind periodically of her needs. Even the snow-white hound was not distinct from the rest of us, though she seemed to be particularly happy when Fiona's ridiculously massive head loomed over her.

But what did I know?

I knew one thing, however, for sure as I began to prepare the waffles and bacon for our breakfast. There were no football-field-long five-masted schooners on Lake Michigan. There probably had not been any for a century. Save for those which were on the bottom of the Lake.

We were back to our old games. Nuala Anne McGrail was having one of her "interludes" during which the past and present combined into one eerie netherworld of mystery and pain.

That was bad enough. However, I knew that my wife was fey when I married her. Now I also knew that my daughter, the placidly sleeping Nelliecoyne, was also fey.

The chill ran down my spine again. This time it didn't go away.

SHREWD WEST of Ireland peasant that she is, Nuala Anne likes to keep life under control. That's why she was studying accounting at Trinity College when I first met her three years ago at O'Neill's Pub across from St. Anne's Church, a gorgeous nineteen-year-old in whose voice one heard the bells of music floating over the bogs of Connemara, a Celtic goddess in jeans and a sweatshirt.

The course of a pregnancy, however, was something she could not control. She was angry at herself for being sick almost all the time, for "spotting" intermittently, and for two near misses at miscarriages. She considered all of these natural inevitabilities to be signs of her own moral failure as both a wife and a potential mother.

Through a long and extremely difficult labor, she apologized to me and her mother—Annie McGrail, whom we had flown over for the event—for the inconvenience she was causing us. This is very Irish behavior and there was no point in trying to fight it. Did she mean it as literally true?

What do I know?

"Sure, doesn't she half believe it all?" Annie had whispered to me.

I have never been able to comprehend what the word *half* on the lips of an Irish person means.

"Didn't I half believe it meself?"

That settled nothing, save adding confirmation to the thesis that apples don't fall very far from their trees.

However, just as Jesus had wisely observed, all these feelings of guilt and responsibility had temporarily disappeared when a worn but radiant Nuala Anne had held the intolerably tiny redhead in her arms.

"Isn't she gorgeous, Dermot Michael?"

"She is," I agreed honestly enough.

"Now," she sighed, "won't I have to work very hard to be a good mother to her?"

What happens to me in all of that, I asked myself.

I said, however, "Nuala Anne, for you being a good mother will be as natural as breathing."

"Ah, no," she sighed.

I did not try to convince her. Try as I might, I had never persuaded her that she was as wonderful a wife as a young man could possibly hope for.

"Doesn't she look like your ma?"

"Ma" in our family meant my late grandmother, the indomitable Nell Pat Malone, with whom Nuala thought she had some weird psychic link.

"She does," I admitted.

"What will we call her, Dermot love?"

Long before the child had been conceived, indeed before we were married, Nuala had informed me that our first child would be a girl and that we would name her Mary Anne, which was my grandmother's real name.

"I thought we were going to call her Mary Anne."

"That will be her name," she said patiently, as though she had two infants on her hands, "but what will we *call* her?"

"Well," I said, "we can't call her Nell Pat."

"OF COURSE we can't call her that. Your name isn't Patrick like Nell Pat's father's was."

This was said in a tone that hinted it might well be my fault that I had not been named Patrick.

" 'Tis true," I said, half apologetically.

"We could call her Nell Derm?"

"Nuala, that sounds like some kind of body lotion."

We both giggled, happy that the agony of labor was over and that we had a new life in the family, even if I had some reservations in the back basement of my brain about playing second fiddle to this tiny intruder.

"WELL, what do you think we should call her, if you know so much?"

"Well," I said, feeling like I was already an old man, "I have this fantasy of our being at a Catholic League championship game in fifteen years or so and the announcer saying, 'And for St. Ignatius College Prep at forward, five-ten and All-State, Nellie Coyne!' "

No woman in her right mind would permit a daughter to be called Nellie, just because her father wanted the child to be a basketball star.

"Five-ten, is it?"

"About her mother's height. And naturally with her mother's figure. And her red hair in a long ponytail. And a look of pure defiance on her face."

"Sure, doesn't it have a certain ring to it?"

And she began to sing Victor Herbert's "My Nellie's Blue Eyes."

Was it the name she had wanted all along? Had she communicated this to me by some weird psychic transfer?

I didn't want to think about that.

Oddly enough both families thought that Nellie was a perfect name for our little rug rat with the red hair and quickly adopted the elision Nelliecoyne. As my brother George the Priest, who knows nothing about such matters, commented, "It fits her perfectly." His boss, the little Bishop, observed more realistically, "Nelliecoyne suggests what is patent. She will be a handful, but a delightful handful."

So Nelliecoyne she was.

None of them, however, had predicted that she would be fey like her mother, that at the age of six months she would see a ghost ship, a ship that didn't exist and perhaps never existed, floating off the shore of Grand Beach. Grand Beach, by the way, is the last place on the planet one would have expected a ghost ship to appear, especially without the permission of the neo-authoritarians in the Village Council and the Michigan Department of Natural Resources.

The child remained in my arms.

"What are you up to, small girl child?" I asked her.

She continued to sleep peacefully.

Nuala Anne was a good mother, tender, gentle, but firm. Just as she was a good wife, tender, gentle, but firm. She did not let her compulsions about being inadequate interfere with her performance in either role. They impeded (or perhaps half impeded) only her self-image.

Nonetheless and paradoxically, marriage, sexual self-possession (a long time in coming), and motherhood had in fact enhanced her self-confidence. The persona of Nuala Anne, the poised woman of the world, emerged more often, though the ur-Nuala, the shy, skittish child from the Irish Gaeltacht, still lurked.

That one, I add, without going into details, is the most challenging and the most rewarding of bedmates. When the Gaeltacht lass was gently introduced to abandon, the skies fell in on us.

She needed the resources of the poised woman of the world when Nick Farmer began his "investigation" of her. By his own definition he was part of the Chicago literary establishment, a combination of Nelson Algren, Saul Bellow, and Mike Royko, a man with impeccable taste who hung out at all the right bars, knew all the right people, and shared all the right opinions.

Worse luck for us, he and I, quite by chance, published "Chicago" novels at the same time. His was, according to his friends who wrote the reviews, a "gritty, gutsy exposé of the phoniness of Chicago political life." Mine was a "trashy potboiler." Mine made the best-seller lists; his didn't go into a second printing. Farmer told people that I was a rich suburban scumbag and he would get even with me. Naturally I heard about his threats.

Farmer was, in my prejudiced opinion, an overweight, untalented, mean-spirited slob. Not good enough to become the music critic of the major media outlets in Chicago, he worked for one of the city's lesser alternative papers and a minor radio station and defined his role as "musical investigative reporter." Our least important and most sensationalist TV station gave him a few moments of airtime once a week. In both roles, he presented himself as a serious musical heavyweight, sternly upholding the highest of musical standards with righteous and crusading rigor.

He got even with me by going after Nuala. She was not part of the Chicago popular music establishment, just as I was not part of the local literary scene. She had achieved success and even a platinum disc (*Nuala Anne Goes to Church*). She was hardly a celebrity yet, but she was big enough, I guess, for a very small man to make his target.

"He's angry at her," I told my family, "because she's beautiful and Irish and a success."

"Naturally," George the Priest replied. "That's why he denounces her wonderful Celtic spirituality on the disc as 'Mystical Gobbledygook' and says that her 'pseudo-leprechaunish dialect' is a fake. The Irish are the only group in America that it is all right for his kind of person to hate."

"That's the way she talks," I protested.

"And the way you're beginning to talk."

Nick's attacks on my Nuala became feverish as her pregnancy continued. Her voice was untrained, not even pretty. Her "presence," both on the disc and on the video, was phony. Her "superstitious piety" should have been left behind in Ireland. Her success was the result of unscrupulous marketing and shameless self-promotion. She would never be a great singer or even a very good one. Once he had found his theme—"cheap

Irish-Catholic kitsch"—he pushed it unremittingly.

At our first family conference on the subject, Nuala being excused "because of her condition" (she was at "Madam's" for one of her three times a week voice lessons), it was decided by our combination of lawyers, doctors, and public relations experts that the appropriate strategy was simply to ignore Nick Farmer.

The only dissenting voice was Mae Ellen (aka behind her back as Maybelline), my brother Jeff's wife, who announced in her usual tones of absolute certainty, "He's right, she should give up the brogue and talk like an American." We ignored Maybelline as we had become accustomed to doing. I clenched my fist, however, in pent-up rage. Maybelline was on Nuala's case all the time. As in such obiter dicta, "You have a cute figure, dear, but it's the kind that a few pregnancies will wipe out. So enjoy it while you can."

Nuala Anne hates but rarely, but when she does it is passionately. "At least I'll never be as fat and sloppy as you are."

That reply shocked the family, which likes to maintain peace among its disparate members. Only my dad suppressed a grin. To give him his due, George the Priest rolled his eyes appreciatively.

For the record, my wife's mother, of whom Nuala is a clone, a woman in her early fifties, has a perfectly presentable womanly body.

Nick Farmer's next ploy was to lament the "injustice" of the attention and success of an untrained and untalented Irish-Catholic singer while better and more deserving African-American singers were ignored. In other words he played the race card. None of us thought he would get away with it until *The New York Times* featured a "report from Chicago" (a city which it views as a mixture of Kinshasa and Beirut) that reported Farmer's allegation as a serious matter and quoted a number of African-American singers as lamenting the "blatant racism" of Nuala's success. Then some of the

African-American radio stations took up the battle which enabled the *Times* to report their protest as "racial controversy grows in Chicago."

(Ever notice how many times on a single page the *Times* reports something is either growing or declining, usually without any more evidence than selective interviews?)

As Jimmy Breslin remarked, it's not that *The New York Times* newspaper is anti–Irish Catholic, it's just the way things work out.

Nuala's recording company got cold feet. Something had to be done about the "bad publicity."

"They spelled her name right, didn't they?" my sister-in-law Tracy, our "in-house" public relations expert, asked. "The people who will buy herself's records don't read *The New York Times*."

Still, it was decided that I should write a letter to the *Times* in my role as Nuala's "manager." In fact, I wasn't her manager. Nuala was her own manager. She had the good sense not to trust anything financial to me and I had the good sense not to want to manage anything.

So I drafted a letter which read, in part:

> There was a time when *The New York Times* had yet to become a racist newspaper that it would check its facts, before printing falsehoods. The allegation that Ms. McGrail has had no vocal training is untrue, indeed it is repeated in reckless disregard of the truth. For several years she has studied under a woman who is universally regarded as one of the best voice teachers in the world. Moreover, apparently your reporter and editor have forgotten your popular music critic's view that *"Nuala Anne Goes to Church* is a rare treat by a rare talent, a festival of Celtic spirituality, ancient and modern." Finally it is absurd to suggest that Ms. McGrail is the only white singer who might be in competition with African-American singers

or that she and she alone should end her vocal career to give more African Americans a chance for success. Indeed, even a cursory glance at the pop music charts would suggest that African-American women are doing very well indeed.

Mae Rosen, our "outside" media consultant, made me cut my final sentence: "Perhaps the editors of the *Times* are too obsessed with the President's sex life to treat fairly an Irish-Catholic woman from Chicago who by definition already has three strikes against her."

"Leave that to Cindy," she advised.

Cindy is my sister, Cynthia Coyne Hurley, as tough a litigator who has ever walked down LaSalle Street. She made a couple of calls to the *Times*. Their lawyers patronized her only once. After they got over the tsunami which hit them, they agreed to print my letter and to lay off Nuala.

Nuala herself was so sick that she really didn't much care. "Och, aren't you the fierce controversialist, Dermot Michael!" was her only comment on my letter.

Then Nick Farmer celebrated Nelliecoyne's birth by suggesting that it was a publicity trick timed to coincide with the recording of her third disc, *Nuala Anne Sings Lullabies*. Moreover, he accused her of intending to exploit our "poor little tot" by putting her on the cover of the record and "dragging her before the camera" for the Christmas special in which herself was supposed to sing a few of her lullabies.

The council of war decided that someone should reply.

"You do it, Dermot," Mae Rosen said. "You're so good with the media."

I pretended that I didn't want to do it.

At Grand Beach on that morning in October after I had laid out the materials for breakfast and created my very own special blueberry pancake batter (bought at the supermarket in the Karwick Plaza), I went upstairs to begin my work for the day. Then, as I sat in front of my computer and stared vacantly out at the serene blue Lake, I changed my reveries from the encounter with Nick Farmer to the subject of the five-masted schooner.

I'll think of almost anything to put off work. I'm not lazy, well not in the ordinary sense of the word. I'd finish the novel about the Irish "Troubles" in County Limerick during the 1920s in time to meet the contract deadline and keep my publisher, Tim Donegan, and my editor, Henriette Murray, happy. But daydreams and distractions, reveries and reminiscences, are, I argue, necessary for a creative writer. Naturally, I must also spend some time recalling the delights of my romps ("rides" is what she calls them) with my wife.

I had set up my laptop in the room my father uses for his library at Grand Beach. His medical books are at the house in River Forest. At the Lake he stores fiction and his beloved collection of books on the Great Lakes and Great Lakes shipwrecks. Probably my fascination with airplane wrecks off the Chicago lakefront is somehow linked with his addiction to Great Lakes stories. I glanced at the books occasionally when I was growing up and listened to him talk about the Lakes, but, sonlike, had not permitted myself to succumb to the lure of shipping on the Lakes back in the days when Chicago was the busiest port in the world. I typed a few sentences of my novel (the only work I would do on it all day), rose from my makeshift desk, and began to browse through the "Old Fella's" (as Nuala called him, respectfully, of course) books.

After I opened the first book, however, I wandered down the corridor to make sure my daughter was still breathing. Miraculously she still was sleeping the peace of a self-satisfied little angel.

I remembered George the Priest's comment shortly before Nelliecoyne had entered the world, "It will be a much more difficult adjustment than marriage, Little Bro."

I ignored George as I usually do. What did he know?

On that subject, it turned out he knew more than I thought he did.

Parent that I was, I could now put aside my adolescent rebellion against my father's obsession with the Lakes. As I paged through his books, I realized how many wonderful stories of tragedy, stupidity, and courage filled his collection.

ABOUT TIME YOU GREW UP, the Adversary sneered.

"Shut up," I told him. "I'm looking for a five-masted schooner."

THERE IT IS RIGHT IN FRONT OF YOU.

"How perceptive of you!"

The boat, a ship really, was the *Charles C. Campbell,* the only five-mast ever to sail the Lakes. She was a beautiful craft, sleek, smooth, shapely. And just a little sinister. The note under the picture said that she really was a barkentine with fore and aft sails from her four rear masts and square-rigged sails from her foremast.

So the fore and aft rigging is what makes a schooner a schooner. Fair enough.

She was also one of the last schooners built on the Lakes. She was launched in 1885. By 1890, the windjammers were losing out to the steel-hulled steamers which carried iron and wheat and lumber more efficiently than the schooners. She had spent her final years, as had many other sailing craft, as a manned barge towed by a steam-powered ship. With her consort she disappeared in the famous Indian summer storm of 1901 on Lake Huron. No one ever found a trace of the wreckage.

I had never heard of the Indian summer storm. If I remembered Dad's tales, November was the month of terrible storms.

Uneasily I glanced out at the Lake. Still smooth as glass.

"Despite her elegance," said the last sentence of the note, "the *Charles C. Campbell* was always considered somewhat sinister after her tragic collision with the wooden paddle wheel passenger ship *City of Benton Harbor* off Michigan City on a foggy night in October of 1898."

Oh, oh.

Before I could hunt for more information on the *City of Benton Harbor,* I saw my wife and my faithful hound dog racing madly down the beach. The goddess Maeve with the faithful wolfhound bitch Bran running ahead of her and then waiting for her to catch up and barking in protest that the goddess wasn't as fast as she was.

Maeve was blond, as I remember, and never did her long hair in a ponytail, and probably never ran on a beach. My own Irish deity was surely taller than the Passionate (which is what Maeve means) and her black ponytail trailed behind her like the trail of a dark comet. Also, Bran was Finn MacCool's dog and not Maeve's. But you can't expect a Yank to keep all his Irish mythology straight.

As I watched, they stopped at the foot of the dune in front of our house. Nuala Anne kicked off her shoes and socks and dove into the Lake, Fiona right behind her. They frolicked in the water and splashed each other. They were both, as Nuala would have said, out of their friggin' minds. The water was no more than fifty-eight degrees, warm for October and warmer than the Gulf Stream off Galway, but still too cold altogether.

Fiona, white fur flat from the water, beat Nuala Anne to the beach and snatched up a piece of wood. She was doubtless playing some crazy wolfhound game.

I decided that I wanted to know as little as possible about the *City of Benton Harbor.* Maybe it would all go away. So I turned away from Dad's books and paid a visit to the nursery before I went downstairs to prepare breakfast for the tribe of Danu. All the ghost ships in the Lake would please go away.

The tyke from outer space was still alive, lightly breathing in and out. She was sleeping peacefully, as well she might. She was dry and well fed and adored, so all was right with the world.

"You're a sneaky little witch," I whispered to her. "Isn't it bad enough that you've taken my wife away from me? Now you turn out to be as fey as she is. I'm not sure why we let you in the house. You do nothing but eat and shit and sleep and wail when you know there's a ghost ship around. What good are you? You're nothing but trouble and you'll always be trouble, even if you do end up as an All-State point guard."

The witch slept on, utterly unperturbed by my denunciation.

BIG DEAL, said the Adversary.

"I'm just expressing my ambivalence."

YEAH. NOW KISS HER FOREHEAD AND GO COOK BREAKFAST.

So I did kiss her tiny forehead, as I always do when I check on her to see if she is still breathing.

—3—

AS I walked down the stairs to finish my breakfast preparations I returned to my reveries about my battle with Nick Farmer.

For some reason I cannot understand, people think I'm a pushover. I'm a big blond guy whom Notre Dame wanted to play linebacker, but I didn't like football that much and didn't want to take steroids on the side. I guess I must look like a sweet but dumb innocent. Anyway, poor Nick thought he could cream me. So he was a sitting duck, a fat little sitting duck with a gravelly voice and a permanent sneer frozen on his botchy face.

"Don't you think, Dermot, that your wife is a woman without any musical talent?"

"I wouldn't be the one to judge, but Madam, her voice teacher, told her the first day she saw her that she would never be an opera star but that she had a light and lovely voice which would with practice serve well in the standards, musical comedy, and folk world. I accept that judgment. Ms. McGrail is no Dame Kiri, but she is good at what she does."

"You call a woman a dame?" he asked, befuddled. "Who is this Cleary person?"

Oh, my, it should not be this easy.

"Kiri Te Kanawa, Mr. Farmer. She's an opera singer from New Zealand who performs here at the Lyric often.

She's a Dame of the British Empire, which is kind of like being a knight. To call her Dame Kiri is a sign of respect. She is, as I'm sure you know, half Maori, which is the native tribe in New Zealand."

"And the other half?" he snapped.

"The kind of person you don't like, Mr. Farmer. Irish Catholic."

"Your wife certainly doesn't believe all that mystical mumbo jumbo about the mountain behind the mountain, does she?"

"Certainly she does. It's age-old Irish spirituality. The Irish are very sensitive to the ultimate reality which lurks behind ordinary daily reality."

"And her brogue, that's fake too, isn't it?"

"Ms. McGrail speaks Irish as her first language. She prays in it and curses in it and sings in it. She speaks English just the way everyone from her part of Ireland speaks it, English enriched by a couple of thousand years of Gaelic poetry. On her records she is careful to keep the poetry under control."

There was one outright falsehood in that response. Nuala Anne does not curse in Irish, because the language lacks curse words. Poets that they all are, however, Irish speakers have skillfully adapted all those four-letter Anglo Saxon words to their language. They mean no harm by it.

"Don't you think that all the Irish stuff is very offensive to many Americans?"

"Probably no more than hip-hop. . . . Anyway, they don't have to listen to it."

"Why are you exploiting your baby to make money?"

"I am told that you really can't sing lullabies properly unless there is a baby around to hear them. Mary Anne loves to hear her mother sing lullabies. It won't make any difference to her that there's a television camera around. Besides, we're putting all the money from the disc into a fund for her college education, except for the twenty percent that Ms. McGrail always contributes to charity."

Not that Nelliecoyne would need money for college, because she was going to be an All-American point guard, wasn't she? Even if she was fey.

"When did you get the idea of using your kid as a prop?"

Sweat was pouring down Farmer's face, messing his makeup. He had expected me to be a dumb Irish Catholic who would be both furious and tongue-tied in the face of his attack on my wife.

Bingo!

"Actually we hadn't thought all that much about it until we heard that you were suggesting it. We thought it was kind of a good idea."

His face tightened in anger.

"Your wife is docile and passive like most Irishwomen, isn't she?"

Wry laugh from D. M. Coyne.

"You don't know many Irishwomen if you think that, Mr. Farmer. Nor have you ever had to play tennis against that particular Irishwoman. You'd find it an enlightening experience."

The director, realizing that she had a fiasco on her hands, signaled us to wrap it up.

"Many people think her singing is like your fiction—exploitive kitsch."

Aha!

JUST BECAUSE HE'S ASKING FOR IT, YOU DON'T HAVE TO SAY IT.

"The hell I don't!"

"I'd rather think it's like my work which has been published in *Poetry* magazine."

ALL RIGHT, RUB IT IN!

"There are a lot of unanswered questions," Nick snarled, the journalist's final cliché.

"I'll be happy to answer them anytime," I said, with

my most genial Dermot Michael Coyne smile. "We'll be listening to you for more suggestions."

That was not altogether true, but it was a nice ending.

"I'm going to drive her off the charts," he snarled at me as the floor director led me off the stage, fearful that I might demolish him physically.

"As herself would say, that will be as may be."

The people in the control booth rolled their eyes.

"You creamed him," the director said as she led me out of the studio.

"He's a larger-than-life Chicago character," I said, piously quoting a feature article on Farmer that had appeared in *Chicago* magazine.

Nuala's only comment that evening was, "The poor frigger never had a chance."

I was inordinately proud of myself.

Great reverie. I played it over and over.

Farmer's latest ploy was to insist that someone was making threats on his life, probably, he said, Irish terrorists.

I had just organized myself, as best as I ever can do that, in the kitchen when two M1A1 tanks roared into the house. The hound rushed upstairs to check on Nelliecoyne.

"Breakfast is it?" Nuala asked, frowning darkly.

" 'Tis."

"You've made a mess of me kitchen."

"Our kitchen."

"I don't suppose you've put the lass down?"

"She isn't here, where else would she be?"

My wife leaned against the doorjamb. She was soaking wet, her green (naturally) running bra and shorts looking like they had been pasted on, her shoes over her shoulder, her bare feet red from the cold. I gulped as I usually do when I see my wife. She's tall and lithe with a woman athlete's subtle but obvious figure and the pale white skin and deep blue eyes of your standard-issue Irish goddess. Her face is that of a model you'd see on a cover of an Irish fashion magazine and her jaw has the round firmness which is required of your normal Irish matriarch. Naturally her waist measured exactly what it had on the day she had married me. She had been sternly determined that pregnancy would not affect her figure, if only to prove Maybelline wrong.

She also bluntly refused to play tennis with me while she was nursing Nelliecoyne. Nursing mothers, she said, lacked athletic mobility. I learned that this assertion was a total falsehood. Moreover, she did battle with my sister Cindy a couple of times a week. The real reason is that she had not practiced during pregnancy and I had. She would be prepared to take me on again only when she knew she could beat me more than half the time.

Unlike me, er, my wife, I am perhaps the least competitive person in the world.

I absorbed her with a dangerous blend of desire, admiration, and love.

"And you didn't change her diaper, did you?"

"Certainly I did and hadn't, to quote you, she made a fine mess of shite for herself?"

You'll note that in this dialogue I had, perforce, adjusted to the Irish rules for such a conversation.

"And you haven't looked in on her at all, at all?"

"Woman, I've looked in three times. And wasn't she sleeping peacefully, as she should?"

Sometimes I'll have to interpret my Nuala Anne for you. Not only is it necessary for a man to hear what his wife means instead of what she says (wives should do the same thing, but the same rules don't apply), in the case of an Irish spouse the problem is more difficult. They never say what they mean or mean what they say.

Herself was begging me to reassure her that her beautiful little girl child had not died while she had neglected her to take a run on the beach.

"You shouldn't look at me that way, Dermot Michael Coyne."

A tinge of flush appeared on her cheeks.

"What way?"

"Like you're more hungry for me than for your blueberry pancakes. . . ."

She lowered her eyes.

"Actually, I'll take the pancakes first. . . . But I'd be in serious trouble if I didn't look at you that way."

"You'll never learn, will you, Dermot Michael?" she said with an impish grin.

"What will I never learn?"

"That men can't win no matter what they do or say."

"I learned that long ago."

She leaned her body, now shivering a little from her unhealthy plunge in the Lake, against mine. I did not draw away from her, though she was cold and wet. I touched the firm flesh of her belly gently.

"You're a brilliant man altogether, Dermot Michael Coyne," she whispered softly as her lips touched mine.

"Brilliant" was not a comment on my intelligence. Rather it is the superlative of a generic Irish adjective indicating approval; "grand" was followed by the comparative "super" on its way to "brilliant." If she had said that I was a "grand" man altogether, my feelings would have been hurt.

On the other hand, the fire in her kiss would have canceled out the moderation of being merely "grand."

"A good run?" I asked as she drew away from me.

"Wasn't it brilliant?" she said. "And the Lake like a little child that wants to play when she touches your toes and the sky as pure as a Blue Nun's veil and the beach all creamy soft and the trees watching like statues in a cathedral and the sun peeking up to see if it likes the day and God smiling down on all of us?"

"Celtic mumbo jumbo?"

" 'Tis not at all," she said with a laugh.

"There's a lake behind the Lake?"

"Why wouldn't there be? . . . Oh, and there is something wrong with your dog. Out on the beach she wouldn't give me back a piece of wood that I had thrown into the Lake."

"Shame on her!"

"You know how she wrestles with me for the stick? Well, this time she wouldn't let me have it after I'd thrown it into the Lake twice. Didn't she even come into the house with it in her teeth?"

" 'Tis strange."

I felt an uneasy twisting in my stomach. Did I have three fey females in the house with me? One human adult, one human infant, and one pushy pure-white Irish wolfhound?

"I'll go upstairs and change. I'll be right back down, save some of the breakfast for me. And only give herself one biscuit."

Nuala dashed up the stairs. She was so very beautiful and so very wonderful and the tension around her eyes scared the living daylights out of me. But what could I do? One of the reasons you marry is to have children. You agonize when you don't have a child. Then the child comes and you adore her. But she also turns out to be a demanding monster, even if she is a good baby. And what does the mother do who has to be practically perfect at everything? She goes tense and anxious.

My reverie was interrupted by a huge mass of wet white fur dashing into the kitchen. Sure enough, Fiona crunched a piece of driftwood in her teeth. Before noticing me, however, it was necessary for her to run around the kitchen sniffing all the corners and making sure that no objectionable smell had entered the kitchen since she had left the house. Then she approached me, tail wagging furiously, and dropped the driftwood in front of me.

"Good dog, Fiona," I said.

Rearing up on her hind legs, she put her forepaws on my shoulders and nuzzled my face. I'm six feet three inches tall and when Fiona puts her forepaws on my shoulders she's still an inch or so taller than I am. An enormous mass of wet white fur.

"Good dog, Fiona," I said.

She continued to nuzzle me affectionately, as if to assure me that even though I was the third most important person in the house, she still adored me.

"That won't get you any more than one doggie biscuit," I warned her.

Whereupon she removed her forepaws from my shoulders, sank back to her normal position, and seriously shook the moisture out of her fur—in the process soaking me. This was standard procedure when Fiona came out of the water. She seemed to think that I liked the act.

"You good for nothing bitch!" I informed her.

She wagged her tail furiously, feeling that I'd paid her some kind of enormous compliment.

"Come on now," I said. "Don't tell herself but I'm going to sneak you an extra doggie biscuit because you're such a good doggie."

That comment was greeted with a bark of approval.

Surreptitiously, as if Nuala might be able to tell what I was doing, I opened the kitchen cabinet, removed a large doggie biscuit—wolfhounds only do large things—and slipped it into Fiona's open mouth. Delicately she removed the doggie biscuit from my hand and began to chomp on it.

"You'd better finish it before herself comes down," I warned her.

While Fiona disposed of the doggie biscuit I picked up the ancient piece of driftwood. It was a carving from a molding, arguably from a house but also from perhaps the dining room on a ship—ornate and elaborate. Why it had washed up on the beach this morning was an interesting question. Or maybe I was just imagining things.

I filled orange juice tumblers and poured the pancake batter on the frying pan. Nuala thundered down the stairs again and burst into the kitchen, a perfect picture of early morning vitality, in jean shorts and a dark red T-shirt which announced that she was a Galway Hooker. (A sailboat.)

"I want me tea!"

"Woman," I said, "can't you pour it yourself?"

"You're busy preparing the pancakes are you now?"

"Woman, I am. It's bad enough being the housewife around this cottage without having to make the pancakes and pour the tea at the same time—and while you're pouring it would you ever pour me a small cup of tea too?"

She poured the tea for the two of us, without polluting it with milk, a perverse Irish habit she had abandoned at my insistence.

"Hurry along with them pancakes," she ordered me. "Am I not perishing with the hunger? . . . You want a doggie biscuit, do you now, Fiona? Has himself given you one already?"

The wolfhound barked, wagged her tail, and rested a paw on Nuala's thigh. She knew what "doggie biscuit" meant and the appropriate behavior to obtain one from her mistress. Nuala did not ask me whether I had already rewarded the hound for her morning run. She knew that I had—Nuala tended to know everything I did or didn't do. But if she had asked and I had admitted my responsibility, then she would have been deprived of the pleasure of feeding her humongous pet. She reached up into the nearby cabinet, removed the box of biscuits, and said, "Say please."

Fiona whined, and then with even more delicacy than when she was accepting her prize from me, removed the cookie from my wife's fingers and retreated to the corner of the kitchen where, according to the rules, she was to remain while we ate our breakfast.

Good baby, good dog, good husband . . . sometimes even a brilliant husband!

I stacked up a half-dozen pancakes on Nuala's plate. She soaked them in maple syrup—pure Michigan maple syrup, of course, bought at the farmer's market in New Buffalo—and attacked them with vigor comparable to that of the wolfhound at suppertime. My wife displays perfect table manners in public situations when she puts on one of her public personae, of which she has many. In private, however, she consumes her food as if it might be going out of fashion.

"I want me bacon," she informed me with a mouth full of pancakes.

I brought her a paper towel loaded with crisp bacon. She jammed two pieces into her mouth.

"Aren't you a super cook!" she exclaimed. "Now eat your own breakfast, lest you perish with the hunger!"

Thereupon she poured maple syrup on her bacon. I winced—behind her back.

My wife takes nutrition seriously. Therefore, perforce, we eat healthy food. However, good Irish Catholic that she is, she is perfectly willing to grant dispensations from the rules, so long as we "don't do it too often." An Indian summer week at Grand Beach, I had argued, when proposing pancakes and bacon, was a good reason. She promptly agreed, adding for the sake of her virtue, "We mustn't do it too often."

"How's herself?" I asked, knowing that she had inspected the sleeping Nelliecoyne before she had discarded her running clothes.

"Brilliant!" she exclaimed. "Sleeping like the little angel that she is. . . . Och, Dermot, isn't she a beautiful little girl!"

"She is," I agreed solemnly, "though she does shite a lot!"

"That's what babies do, Dermot Michael Coyne!"

"So I have discovered."

"We must take very good care of her, so when she's grown up we can give her back to God as a healthy, happy adult. God only lends children to us, like me ma says."

"Somehow, I figure, Nelliecoyne will be able to take care of herself."

"It won't be me doing and meself a terrible mother altogether. Isn't she lucky to have you as her father?"

The tension around my wife's eyes deepened. My mother had consoled me with the thought that Nuala would stop worrying about her skills as a mother as soon as we had our second child. I shivered at the thought.

"Just as you're lucky to have me as a husband, and such a good cook too. . . . Have some more bacon!"

"Just one more piece. . . . Your overgrown bitch gave you that piece of wood, did she now?"

"She did." I picked the driftwood up off the floor. "It looks like a bit of fancy molding, maybe from a house or even a boat."

Nuala examined the molding carefully. If there were any psychic vibrations emanating from it, she didn't seem to notice them.

"From a boat?"

"Maybe something that was washed off in a storm."

"Boats don't sink out there, do they, Dermot Michael?"

I'd better tell her the truth.

"They do, Nuala Anne. The first ship ever built on the Great Lakes, La Salle's ship *Griffon,* disappeared maybe on Lake Huron, maybe on Lake Michigan, without a trace on her first voyage. Since then over ten thousand ships have sunk on the Great Lakes. Lake Superior, way up north, is supposed to be the most dangerous. A steel ore boat was torn in two up there not too many years ago by a couple of thirty-foot waves. However, more boats have sunk on Lake Michigan. The waves and the winds sweep down three hundred miles from the Soo in the November storms. You'll have to see one of them this year."

She glanced out of the window at the serene blue waters.

"And it looks so peaceful now. . . ."

"Those of us who have been around Michigan for all our lives know that you have to respect the Lake, Nuala. It's a lot more dangerous than Galway Bay."

She shivered. "I don't think I want to see one of them storms. I'll take your word about the Lake wanting respect."

"The bottom of the Lake is littered with wrecks," I went on, falling back on half-remembered stories from my father, "mostly from April or November storms. It's usually safe in the summer months and in the harbors. Sometimes the whole Lake is frozen for much of the winter, though some of the last ore boats were also ice-breakers."

Nuala was suddenly very solemn. However, she did not look like one of her "spells" was coming on.

"People died out there?"

"Thousands I'm afraid. Most of the traffic was freight of one sort or another, grain, iron, gravel, lumber, beer, Christmas trees; but before the railroads there were a lot of passenger ships too. Chicago was the busiest port in the world in 1870 and the fourth busiest in 1900. In those days you could look out our window here and routinely see sailing craft and steamships, some with paddle wheels, just like we see cruisers now in the summer. All that's left now are a handful of massive boats which bring iron down from Minnesota or carry gravel and sand around the various Lake ports. No passenger ships at all, though there's talk of building a few luxury cruise ships. Dad says that it was quite a business before the war."

"I'd never get on one of them," she said firmly.

"They'd be as safe as any of the Atlantic or Caribbean cruise ships, though, like Dad says, the ports aren't all that interesting."

"I'll be afraid of sailing with you in the summer," she said somberly.

"No risk in the summer, Nuala Anne, especially if you keep your ear on the weather forecasts. I wouldn't think of sailing out this time of the year, however. There were a couple of disastrous storms around the turn of the century right in the middle of Indian summer, a foot of snow in Chicago."

I admit I was piling it on. However, veteran of the hooker races in Galway Bay that she was, herself tended to think of Lake Michigan as nothing but a big pond.

Before I could continue my lesson, she and Fiona both heard a signal that was too subtle for my male ear. They both dashed for the stairs. The redhead from outer space was awake. Since she wasn't screaming, I figured there was no need for me to follow them. I finished the pancakes and the bacon and then ambled up to our temporary nursery.

Nelliecoyne was awake and smiling, content spinning the toys strung across her crib. Mother and wolfhound watched her in mute adoration.

She was, I had to admit, an absolute perfection of human offspring.

"Have you changed her diaper?" I asked.

"Give over, Dermot Michael Coyne," the child's mother protested. "You know her delicacy. If she was carrying a load of shite, wouldn't she be screaming her head off."

" 'Tis true," I admitted.

"Go along with you now and get your exercise. Won't I feed her when she gets hungry?"

"Do I have to?"

"Yes," Nuala said firmly, "I don't want a fat husband."

"Yes, ma'am," I replied docilely.

"You too, Fiona. I don't want any fat wolfhound bitches around my house."

Fat husband, I complained silently. I don't feel like running today. Why do I have to do everything the woman tells me to do?

BECAUSE YOU DON'T WANT TO PUT ON WEIGHT LIKE YOUR FRIENDS DO AFTER THEIR MARRIAGES, the Adversary informed me. WHEN YOU MARRIED HER YOU KNEW YOU WERE GOING TO HAVE TO ACT RIGHT FOR THE REST OF YOUR LIFE. DON'T BLAME ME. I WARNED YOU.

"Shut up," I told him.

It was, however, a splendid morning for a run on the beach. There was an astringent autumn smell in the air, decaying vegetation. Eliot was wrong. In Midwest America, October was the cruelest month of the year. The wolfhound and I raced each other and wrestled and played her game of rescuing sticks from the water. I absolutely refused to join her for a swim like my wife did. Then she brought me another piece of driftwood which she would not let me have.

"Good doggie," I said. "Now let me have the stick."

No way.

"Fiona!" I demanded. "Let it go!"

She wagged her huge tail but would not comply.

"I won't throw it back in . . . here, I'll throw another stick."

The bitch considered the implications, dropped the driftwood at my feet, and chased her new prey.

I picked up the piece of wood, perhaps nine inches long and three inches wide. Water and sand and time had bleached it almost white. However, at one end letters had been carved into it. I tried to read them in the bright sunlight: "bor."

As in "harbor"?

As perhaps in "Benton Harbor"?

— 4 —

A SHOCKING surprise greeted me when I opened the door of the house—a typical eighty-year-old wooden summer home on which a score or so of additions had been built and as devoid of architectural style as it was filled with disordered but soothing warmth. "A house to live in," me wife had said when she first entered it.

"Would you ever look at your daughter, Dermot Michael Coyne!"

Nuala was sitting on a white wicker rocking chair with a comfortable old red pillow. She pointed in dismay at Nelliecoyne, clad only in a diaper. The future basketball great was sitting up, grinning happily. I had made Fiona shake out the Lake water before we entered, and now she carefully picked her way over to the human child and sniffed delicately.

"She's sitting up," I said cautiously.

"She shouldn't be sitting up, should she?"

"Maybe Father George will hear her confession."

I knelt beside our redhead. She waved clumsily at Fiona, then at me. She must have known that she'd done something remarkable, but wasn't all that sure what it was.

Nuala slipped between us and drew Nelliecoyne into her arms, hugging her fiercely.

"I won't let them make you take drugs, sweetheart! Never!"

Maybelline, having noted that as a neonate our daughter was active and curious, had warned us, "The doctors say that kids that are like that usually end up hyperactive. But don't worry about it. They have drugs for it now."

"At least she won't be a tub of lard, like your kids!" Nuala had fired back, her face taut with fury.

Such ripostes had no effect at all on my sister-in-law. She seemed never to hear them, which is why the family had adopted the policy of ignoring her. "She's almost always in error," Cindy observed, "but never in doubt. Besides, she's a good soul. She means well."

I was sick of those two excuses. Maybelline was, it was argued, a good wife and a good mother even if a trifle overweight. She was involved in every good cause imaginable, from Rwandan orphans to monarch butterflies, though about all her causes she seemed to acquire only misinformation. She certainly worked hard on them, however, and Jeff seemed happy. She never thought much of me, however. "Dermot is just a good-looking oaf," she had commented when I was a teenager.

Ma, as I called my maternal grandmother, broke the family rules. "He's the smartest and best of all of them," she exploded, unfairly to my siblings it seemed to me, "and I'll not tolerate another word against him."

That had shut Maybelline up for a while. After Ma had followed Da home, she had started in on me again. Her most recent comment had been, "Face it, Dermot, your novel was just racy trash. No one with a taste for good literature could possibly approve of it."

"You've read it, have you now?" said the *bahn si* to whom I was married.

"I never read trash."

"Then you should keep your fat mouth shut about it."

The family froze and Maybelline just laughed.

"I called your mom," Nuala continued to hug our Nellie with the green eyes, "and she said that the child wasn't a changeling. She said some babies are just better coordinated than others."

She didn't seemed convinced.

"I think she is a changeling," I said with notable lack of consideration for my wife's worries. "A fairy queen from county Galway has taken her over."

"Och, Dermot, be serious," she replied as she put the green-eyed witch back on the floor, facedown. "Doesn't your mom say that she could be crawling in another couple of weeks and maybe walking in two months or so? How will we ever keep her out of trouble?"

Before I could answer that question, our little heroine rolled over and promptly sat up again. Fiona barked in approval. Nelliecoyne gurgled.

I realized I had better say something intelligent. And sensitive. So I put my arm around my wife.

"Come on, Nuala Anne, aren't we all proud of the little power forward? And herself already a great athlete like her ma? And don't we have to trust God and the angels and that overgrown wolfhound?"

Nuala laughed and said, "Isn't she ever a wonder altogether?"

Then she began to cry.

Which meant I had said the right thing.

LUCK, PURE BLIND DUMB LUCK, the Adversary remarked.

"That terrible woman was on the phone again," she said, sniffling.

"Maybelline?"

"Your man was on again last night she said."

That I knew. Cindy had called. Nick was talking about violation of the child labor laws and calling for a DCFS investigation of whether we were fit parents.

"Will they do it?"

"You can't tell what those assholes over there might do. But I'll have an injunction on them as quickly as I can walk into a courtroom. Then we'll sue Farmer and his station. I'll talk to their general counsel tomorrow and warn him."

"That'll do the trick."

"You bet."

I hadn't felt all that reassured.

"And what advice did she offer?" I asked, waiting for the inevitable explosion.

"Didn't she say that Farmer had a good point. People would say we were exploiting the poor little tyke."

"And you said?"

"I said." Nuala hesitated. "Och, Dermot, wasn't I awful?"

"I'm sure your response was appropriate."

"I told her to keep her friggin' fat face out of our friggin' business or I'd scratch her eyes out."

"And she said?"

"She said I was being terribly selfish and not being a good mother. And I told her she was a nine-fingered shite hawk and hung up. . . . Dermot Michael Coyne, put down that telephone! Bad enough that I lost my temper!"

Reluctantly I hung up.

Our child distracted us by falling back on the floor, an experience which seemed to amuse her. Then she kicked her legs and gurgled again.

"Doesn't she want to be fed again and then go to bed?" Nuala picked her up and pulled off her T-shirt. "You go upstairs, Dermot love, and change your clothes or you'll catch your death of cold."

I knew from long experience that there was no point in arguing that (a) viruses cause colds, not chills, and (b) during Indian summer there were no chills to be had. Like any dutiful Irish male I did what I was told.

Downstairs Nuala was singing as she nursed our future All-American. Before I went to our room, I peeked into my dad's study and consulted the listing in his big book under "*City of Benton Harbor.*" It had been rammed at night in October while returning to Chicago with an excursion party of Irish immigrants and their children. The *Charles C. Campbell* which rammed it pulled away without stopping to pick up survivors. The Life Guards from Michigan City had saved some of them.

Irish?

Somehow it figured.

Back in the parlor of the house, my wife, naked to the waist, was sitting on the couch and crooning softly to our sleeping sports star.

"God and Mary will take care of her, won't they, Dermot love?"

"And Brigid and Patrick too," I said fervently, "and Ma too."

"That's what she says and Nellie being named after herself too."

I avoided all questions about Nuala Anne's relationship with my late grandmother. I didn't want to know about it. But I was pretty sure that in the World of Grace (as George the Priest called it) there was not a chance that Nell Pat Malone would not watch over her namesake.

"They're all so close to us, aren't they, Dermot Michael?"

Before Patrick and his crowd came, the Irish believed that the boundaries between the living and the dead were thin and permeable. The Catholic clergy never saw any good reason to disabuse them of that notion. On this particular Indian summer day at Grand Beach, I was hardly in a position to question the belief. Too damn close, I thought to myself.

I AGREE COMPLETELY.

"The very hairs of our heads are numbered," I said, figuring it was always safe to fall back on Jesus.

"I still have a little milk left, Dermot love, if yourself feels thirsty."

This was an invitation to an occasional intensely erotic sacrament.

I sat next to my wife, who was holding the child on her lap.

"Which faucet?"

"Isn't there some in both now?"

She drew my head to her nipple and sighed as I touched it with my tongue. Her skin was soft and smooth. She smelled of milk and springtime. The precious fluid was warm and sweet. For a moment I was a little boy again. She was now crooning over me. A brief taste of heaven.

"No wonder Nelliecoyne likes it," I said, shifting to the other breast.

"I love you, Dermot," she said with a loud, West of Ireland sigh, and then murmured some magic words in Irish.

I couldn't say anything at all.

"Well," she said, reaching for her bra, "there's tea in the kitchen and some soda bread I made last night. Don't spoil your lunch."

5

"JUST KIND of curious, Dad," I said to my father, trying to sound casual. "I was telling herself some of your stories about Great Lakes shipping. I wondered if there are any wrecks around here."

"I didn't think you listened to any of those stories," he said with a laugh.

"I remember some of them," I said defensively.

I was supposed to be working on my novel. Nelliecoyne was sound asleep, watched over by Fiona, who occasionally shuffled into the study to check on me, perhaps to find out if I was really working, which I wasn't. Nuala was downstairs doing her voice exercises. Outside the window the Lake was serene under a light haze, a "curtain of gold to protect its privacy and ours," I had been told.

"You don't remember the story about the two-master which was buried under Sky High Dune?"

"I guess not."

I didn't even remember Sky High Dune.

"It was a really big dune about halfway to New Buffalo. Back in the days when I was a kid, long before the State of Michigan began to worry about the environment, a developer plowed away the top half of it and uncovered the remains of an old schooner called the *Mary Suzanne* which floundered off the beach back in the 1870s. A lot of us Grand Beach urchins walked on the deck. Most of the remnants were carted off to a museum somewhere."

"People on it?"

"She was carrying a load of Michigan timber from Sheboygan to Milwaukee. That was at the time that the timber barons were cutting down all the trees in the state. She got caught in an early winter storm. The New Buffalo papers said that the Life Guards had removed the crew of eight on their surf boats. That was before the Life Guards were combined with the Revenue Cutter Service to form the Coast Guard. They were brave men."

"How did the schooner come ashore?"

"The Lake plays games endlessly with the shore and the dunes. We try to stop it by building our sea walls but eventually it rips out our puny protections. Before the developers put up these summer homes, the dunes literally traveled as the winds and the water shaped them and reshaped them. The sandbars came in and out, the beach expanded and contracted. The wreckage probably washed in and then was covered almost immediately by the sand and forgotten."

"I never realized that. Is there much wreckage under the sand?"

"If you consider the whole Lake, probably a lot. On our particular stretch of beach, hardly any. Still you never can tell."

"Our house might be over a shipwreck?"

"Dermot," he said with a laugh, "the West of Ireland influence is finally getting to you."

Dad did not know about Nuala's psychic kinks. George the Priest was the only one that did and he had enough sense to keep his mouth shut—on that subject anyway.

"They're never at a loss for stories, that's for sure."

"How is she and my red-haired granddaughter?"

"Both flourishing. They even have a little time for me."

"To answer your question, which to tell the truth gives me a little shiver, I hardly think so. Yet our house was one of the first to be built up there. I gather from pictures from the old days, there was unspoiled dune all around. Too bad they didn't preserve some of it, but they didn't understand such things back at the turn of the century. I'm sure they leveled the dunes a bit to lay down the foundations. If they had found anything, we would have heard the legend, like the old—and false—one about U.S. 12 actually running along the lakeshore at one time."

I hadn't heard that one. Outside, the golden curtain seemed to be a bit thicker.

"So not very likely."

"But not impossible if you're thinking of making up a story. I think it would be a pretty good one."

Right! The remains of Irish immigrants buried beneath our house!

Suddenly I wanted to go home immediately.

"You don't mind if I call you and ask more questions?"

"You know how much I like to talk about the Lake."

I promised to give his love to the mother and child.

If there were remnants of the wreck anywhere around us, why hadn't Nuala noticed them before? The fey stuff was odd, however. We had driven by the site of Camp Douglas at 31st and the Lake several times before she heard the screams of the Confederate prisoners who were dying there.

When she heard them, however, it became essential that we solve the mystery of why she was hearing the cries. Nuala believed beyond doubt, beyond question, beyond discussion that when one of these incidents occurred she was supposed to discover why it was happening. It was her duty to put to rest the ghosts of the past.

As in so many other aspects of our relationship, I

didn't argue. It would not have done any good. Besides, maybe she was right.

It could be that a critical mass of the fey was required because the vibrations of the past were stirred up. What if it required two witches to stir up the dead . . . who were, I had been told, not all that far away from us.

I shivered.

I read more about the wreck of the *City of Benton Harbor* in a thoroughly scary book called *Disasters on Lake Michigan*. She was an old wooden paddle wheel built in 1860 to move Union troops around the Lake. Later she was remodeled to serve as an "elegant" passenger ship with the "most modern" cabins and conveniences of her time. She was a funny-looking craft, stubby with two big paddle wheels and a single narrow smokestack. I personally would not have ventured on such a boat from New Buffalo to Michigan City, ten miles away. But reproductions of ads from her era referred to her as "Lake Michigan's Brightest Queen." In the years after the Civil War, she carried many immigrants from Buffalo to Cleveland and Chicago in "comfort which matched that of the most splendid ocean liners" without suffering a single loss of life. In her later years she was a "much prized" craft for weekend excursions from Chicago to ports on the opposite shore of the Lake such as Holland and Saugatuck.

Then, on a moonless Sunday evening, October 16 back in 1898, she was bringing back to Chicago some three hundred members of the Chicago Chapter of the Ancient Order of Hibernians from a weekend excursion to Saugatuck. The weather had been pleasant for two weeks and there was no hint of a storm. However, several hours out of Saugatuck the wind began to howl from the north, the Lake whipped up waves, and sheets of rain beat against the wooden decks. Captain Leonard Creamer apparently decided to try to stay close to the shore and take a long route to Chicago, perhaps so he could beach the ship if the storm became too bad.

According to survivors, lightning struck the ship several times. It was unable to make much headway against waves which were now at least fifteen feet high. Then the rain turned into snow. A rare October blizzard had swept down the Lake from the Soo.

The passengers had abandoned the deck when it started to rain. However, they continued to sing and dance and drink as best they could in the crowded saloon. As a survivor later observed, "We lost a bit of the spirit of it, when someone said it was snowing. Then the saloon turned cold and suddenly we were all afraid."

The captain decided to try for Michigan City where Trail Creek provided the promise of some shelter. There was also a Life Guard Station at Michigan City which could perhaps fire a breeches buoy out to the ship to take off passengers or send out its surf boats to rescue survivors.

Although the ship was already leaking—its old oaken beams not able to stand the sudden pressures—it probably could have made it to Trail Creek. However, as Third Mate Ernest Roscoe would later report, suddenly a huge black shape loomed up out of the snow and plowed into the *Benton Harbor* just aft of her port paddle.

"It was like an earthquake. We had all our lights on. Even in the storm he should have been able to see us. I know it's harder for a schooner, especially one that big, to turn than for a steamship. He didn't seem interested in turning. Or even in coming back. He just kept on going, like a man who had stepped on a bug."

Hit-and-run driver.

Later, Hale Reed, captain of the *Campbell*, carrying "package goods," mostly whiskey and furniture from Sheboygan, brought his massive craft to the mouth of the Chicago River where a Revenue cutter tug appeared out of the snow and towed him in. The cutter had been waiting for the *Benton Harbor*, which was long overdue. Its skipper noticed that the ship's prow had been stoved in. Captain Reed didn't seem to know what had damaged it.

"Said he thought a big wave might have done it," the tug skipper later remarked at the Admiralty Court hearing. "I was a little suspicious. So I checked it out as we edged him into the dock at Wabash. I found a piece of wood which had 'Benton Harbor' painted on it hanging from the side of the prow. I asked him if he had seen an excursion boat on his way in. He said he had not."

If it had not been for the alert tug captain, Reed would have gotten away with his denial that he had rammed a ship off Michigan City and left it to sink. The author of the account in *Disasters on Lake Michigan* observed that although Hale Reed had a reputation for being an honest and upright man, it was hard to see how he could have been unaware of the impact of this crash with the *Benton Harbor*.

"Hale Reed," the author reported, "had a record of bringing his ships in on time, no matter what happened. The *Campbell* was filled with expensive cargo destined for shops in Chicago. He had promised to dock the boat on the crowded river by Monday morning. Despite the storm, he was determined to reach port on time, no matter what happened. His crew stood by him, though there were rumors that the first mate had pleaded with him to go back for survivors and several of the watchmen had whispered in the taverns along North Water Street that their captain had taken more than enough of the drink.

"The Admiralty Court conceded that the *Charles C. Campbell* had 'probably' rammed the *City of Benton Harbor*," the author of *Disasters on Lake Michigan* wrote. "However, it ruled that Captain Hale Reed was not to blame for the accident because the snowstorm had caused visibility to deteriorate. Moreover, while he should have tried to pick up survivors, it was unlikely that in the storm he would have had any success. His master's certificate was suspended for six months. The Lake Michigan Transportation and Transfer Company was held liable only for the extent of its insurance, as was the customary decision in those days. Since its insurance was negligible, that meant no money for the survivors. Those who braved Lake Michigan, even in pleasant October weather, ran their own risks."

Meanwhile, somewhere near Michigan City, perhaps just off the shore of the barren dunes which would later become Grand Beach, the *City of Benton Harbor* lay mortally wounded.

"The Lake poured in through the hole," Third Mate Roscoe reported, "and into the engine room. The old boiler exploded and the ship began to sink. I told the captain that she was going under. He ignored me and ran towards the rail. I never saw him again. I tried to sound the abandon ship horn. But it didn't work. I struggled down to the saloon and pulled open the door. A mass of screaming people tumbled out and knocked me over. It was too late to organize anything, but I yelled 'abandon ship,' grabbed a woman with a baby in her arms, and pulled them with me as the boat tilted over. I found them a large plank and put them on it. I did my best to save some of the others, but I don't know how many of them made it. The water wasn't all that cold. Perhaps in the middle fifties. But the air was below freezing and the waves were huge. Everyone was screaming. We weren't very far from shore, but we could not swim through the surf. I had three people on my plank, two boys and the woman with the baby. She lost her child when a big wave rolled over us. She wanted to die, but I wouldn't let her. Later when she found her husband alive on the shore, she thanked me."

Not many survivors were that lucky.

Ernest Roscoe and his little band were finally picked up by a surf boat from Michigan City. A young woman had seen the explosion from the shore and had rushed through the falling snow to alert the Life Guards. Typical of their routine heroism, they launched their craft into the waves with only a faint idea of where the explosion had happened and even whether there in fact had been one.

"If it were not for the alert eyes of Miss Elaine Manders and the quick courage of the Life Guards, there would have been very few survivors, save for the score or two whom the surf had deposited on the shore," the author summed up the story. "As it was, when the snow cleared the next morning, only a hundred and nine of the more than three hundred Irish Americans who had left Chicago on a hot Friday evening ever returned."

The book displayed photos of the Life Guard Station in Trail Creek, the two surf boats, and a group of very young men with very big muscles. I told myself I wouldn't ride out in one of those boats in three-foot waves.

BUT THEN, YOU'RE A COWARD.

I ignored him.

"Most of the bodies of the survivors were washed ashore along with large amounts of wreckage. Before the Michigan City Police could arrive, looters stripped the bodies. A few were arrested but later released for lack of evidence. Bodies were taken to the Michigan City morgue for identification. Twenty-three corpses were unclaimed and buried in the La Porte County potter's field. Most of the men and women who died were young, in their early and middle twenties. Every requiem mass at St. Gabriel's parish in Chicago was crowded with mourners."

No radar, no radio, no weather forecasts, no power cutters, no helicopters. How did anyone survive shipwrecks on the Lake in those days?

I closed the book, tears in my eyes. That poor woman who lost her child in the big wave certainly loved that baby as much as Nuala Anne loved Nelliecoyne. She had at least found her husband alive. How many young people had lost wives or husbands or sweethearts? I wanted to blame someone. One captain was a coward, the other a liar and a drunk. But even with the best skippers, the collision probably would have occurred anyway. The court of inquiry was perhaps right, the five-master probably couldn't have picked up many survivors. At least Hale Reed could have dropped anchor and tried. Elaine Manders and the brave and muscular young men from Trail Creek had saved many who would have otherwise drowned.

Looters, stealing from the bodies of the dead? Right out on the smooth sand at the foot of our dune? How evil could humans be?

Feeling that I may have missed something, I opened the book again, turned what I had thought was the last page of the story, and found a final paragraph:

Attempts made to find the remains of the *City of Benton Harbor* in the weeks after the wreck and then in the following spring were unsuccessful. After a brief interlude, the storm picked up fury and raged for three more days. It was assumed that the ship had been completely destroyed. The winter that year was colder than most. Long before Christmas the site of the wreck was covered with icy dunes. The *Charles C. Campbell*, reduced to the indignity of acting as a barge towed by a steamship, foundered with all hands three years later in a November storm on Lake Superior. It was an ignominious end for a graceful and tragic craft.

With no stomach for food, I went downstairs to prepare lunch. Nelliecoyne was sleeping again, the wolfhound at her side. Nuala had put aside her Irish harp and was poring over a sketch pad. I had no idea till the advent of our daughter that she could sketch. "I just draw now and then, Dermot Michael," she said, trying to hide the drawing of Nelliecoyne.

At first she wouldn't let me see it, then shyly she turned the pencil and paper drawing around. It portrayed Nellie with a goofy smile on her face. Naturally it was good. I insisted she should take art lessons. She replied that she had enough trouble with voice lessons. I argued that she should continue drawing at least while she was tied down by our daughter. To my surprise she admitted that it wasn't a bad idea, at all, at all.

"Whatcha drawing?" I asked.

"The schooner from last night, only it's not really a schooner. It's a barkentine."

"Because only the four rear masts are rigged fore and aft and the front mast is square-rigged?"

"Sure, Dermot Michael, don't you know everything?"

I didn't want to see the drawing, but she showed it to me anyway. If it wasn't the *Charles C. Campbell,* it was a dead ringer.

Oh.

IT'S CREEPY, the Adversary admitted.

"Tell me about it."

"Isn't she a lovely craft, Dermot? So sleek and graceful?"

"Looks a little sinister to me."

"Sinister?" She turned the sketch around and considered it. "I don't think so. . . . Have you ever seen her before?"

"I don't think so."

"I suppose she'd be from Chicago?"

"Maybe."

"Well," she said with a mild sigh, "we'll have to find out, won't we now?"

"I'm sure we will."

I shivered again.

"I didn't know there were ships like this on the Lake."

"Not very many," I said guardedly. " 'Tis a brilliant sketch though, considering you only saw it for a few moments."

"Thank you, Dermot love."

I escaped to the kitchen so she could not see my shivers.

6

I MADE a fusilli pasta with tomato sauce, mushrooms, and four cheeses (my own creation) for our lunch, which my bride devoured passionately ("I'm eating for two, am I not?"). She also informed me that I was the greatest husband cook in all the world. The truth is that it could have been served out of a can and she would have disposed of it with equal zest.

I didn't eat much of it, even though I was proud of my work.

We tried at lunch to feed Nelliecoyne some baby food, a process which she found amusing because it gave her an opportunity to spit the bright green-colored substance out of her mouth and throw it around. We laughed and she was very proud of herself until I said sternly, "Moire Ain Coyne, you will eat some of that food that your poor mother is trying to feed you."

She looked at me as though she were about to cry but slurped some of the stuff off the spoon Nuala held poised at her mouth.

"Aren't you the terrible stern da?" Nuala said, suppressing a giggle. "Someone has to be."

FAKER.

Nuala giggled again.

The brat licked her lips and opened them for more.

"See, Daddy is always right," my wife said with yet a third giggle.

Then the four of us went for a walk, not on the beach but in the village, to soak up the warmth and revel in the red and gold and orange embroidery of the foliage. Despite the beauty and the color of the leaves, I felt kind of somber. Mother Nature was teasing us before she turned to her favorite season in our part of the world— endless winter.

I carried the small one in the harness. Very early in her life, she refused to permit her face to be turned to- wards her parent's chest. Whichever one was carrying her must let her face out towards the wonderful world which she observed with the same wonder-filled curi- osity that Fiona displayed when she explored the myriad smells of the village.

Nuala guided Fiona on a leash, lest she terrify a stranger who didn't realize how gentle wolfhounds were—until one or the other of us gave the commands "Get 'em!" or, God forbid, "Kill 'em!" that would bring the Garda dog out of retirement.

"Isn't it glorious, Dermot Michael! Everyone getting ready for winter—the squirrels collecting their nuts, the birds flying south, the trees showing off their fancy lin- gerie before they settle in for their long winter nap, the grass putting on its autumn suit, and God bathing us with His warm sunlight and His golden haze to promise that winter won't last forever."

"You've been through one Chicago winter, Nuala Anne, you know they do last forever."

"Go 'long with you, Dermot Michael, you're in a glum mood!"

I tried to deny it.

We walked in companionable silence for a few minutes. Soon winter would sweep away the foliage and many of the old homes in the side streets of the village would be exposed to what they were: one step above resort slums.

" 'Tain't frigging proper, Dermot Michael Coyne. That a mature matron like meself should be so addicted to a man."

"At twenty-two?"

"Going on twenty-three."

"True, but still . . ."

"In a few years I'll be turning thirty."

" 'Tis different altogether."

Obviously there had been a mood change since God was promising us that winter wouldn't last forever.

"Ah?"

"Promise me." The strain was lurking again around her radiant blue eyes.

"Anything."

"I don't mean anything."

"What do you mean?"

She hesitated. . . . "Well, that you won't ever leave us?"

"Who's us?"

"Me and me daughter."

"I thought she was my daughter."

"Only when she does bad things," she said, suddenly happy again. "You know the rules, Dermot Michael Coyne. All other times she's me daughter, not yours."

"Well, I'm not going to leave either of you," I said. "Didn't I promise that when we renewed our marriage vows in the presence of my brother the priest and your friend the little Bishop just these two weeks ago?"

"Didn't you just?" she said as she leaned over and brushed my lips with hers.

She was worried about something. No amount of probing would find out. I'd have to wait till she was ready to tell me.

As we climbed over the ancient dune which was Crescent Avenue, we encountered a young matron (which is to say at least eight years older than my wife) with two small children, both walking, so not as young as our small daughter.

"Doggie!" one of them announced, pointing at Fiona.

"Big doggie!" said her older sister cautiously.

"Pretty doggie!"

Fiona perked up her ears as she always did when kids drew near.

"Is the doggie friendly?" their mother, a small and slender blonde, asked anxiously.

There was strain around her eyes too. The advent of a second child had not cured it. Maybe nothing ever cured it for a mother.

"Is the Pope Catholic?" I asked.

"She adores little children." Nuala crouched next to the doggie who was wagging her big tail furiously. "Come here, dear, Fiona wants to meet you. . . . Fiona, shake hands with the little girl . . . what's your name, dear?"

"Siobhan," said the four-year-old cautiously.

"Is it Irish you are now. . . . Well, Fiona was born in Ireland too. . . . Fiona, shake hands with Siobhan!"

The dog raised her huge paw and the child touched it gingerly.

"Good doggie," she said tentatively.

"Very good doggie," Nuala agreed.

Without waiting for instructions our outsized pooch offered her paw to the two-year-old.

"She's Brigit," her mother said.

So Nuala introduced Brigit to Fiona, who sat on her haunches to await petting.

"You can pet her, girls, if you want," she assured them.

"Gently," their mother insisted.

Very gently, they petted Fiona, who positively beamed. Siobhan put on the ground a piece of charred driftwood. I picked it up and examined it. Very, very old.

All the while our daughter was watching the whole scene with considerable interest.

"There's a baby too," the mother pointed out.

"Her name is Moire Ain, but don't we call her Nellie?"

So there was the usual scene, kids alternating between admiration for "bebe" and "doggie," mothers exchanging names, Dermot keeping his big mouth shut. The woman's name was Rita O'Dwyer. Nothing wrong with that. Her husband was Neil O'Dwyer.

"My husband is a commodity trader," she confessed. "He's coming up on Friday for the weekend."

"Sure wasn't himself a trader too. But he didn't like it much, did you, Dermot?"

No answer was required or called for.

"My husband loves it! He seems to be very good at it." She was choosing words carefully.

"I wasn't very good at it," I confessed, "only very lucky. . . . This is a very old piece of driftwood. Where did Siobhan find it?"

"On the beach by the stairs at the end of Willow Street. . . . What do you think it's from?"

Willow Street was right next to my parents' house. The spooks creeping around on this pre-Halloween day were really making a show of it.

MAYBE IT'S ONLY COINCIDENCE.

"Maybe."

"Probably a summer beach marshmallow roast," I said.

THAT'S A LIE!

"I'm supposed to say that it was a relic of a paddle wheel excursion boat which sank in a winter storm a hundred years ago today?"

"You're the young woman who sings, aren't you?"

"Is it a lullaby you want me to sing?"

"Would you ever, if it isn't too much of an imposition?"

"Would you ever" meant she was South Side Irish. We more civilized West Siders never used the Irish polite subjunctive.

So Nuala lifted Nelliecoyne off my chest, knelt on the

ground with her, and sang for the three little girls. Our daughter was so pleased that she closed her eyes. So did Fiona.

" 'Tis time to thrive, my ray of hope,
In the gardens of Dromore,
Take heed, young eaglet, the wings,
Are feathered, fit to soar.
A little rest and then the world,
Is filled with work to do.

"Sing hush a bye loo, lo loo lo lan,
Hushabye loo lo loo."

We promised to get together over the weekend.
Siobhan forgot her bit of driftwood.
"I sure wish I could get in a set of tennis with someone," I said, deliberately making trouble.
"Well, maybe Rita's husband plays. Besides, when you go back to Chicago you can play every day at the South Bank."
" 'Tis true."
"Anyway, don't we still have to do our swim?"
"I was hoping you'd remember!"
She snorted.
The haze thickened as we walked back to the house, but it was still warm, even hot. Somewhere nearby, someone was burning leaves, rather against the village regulations. I sensed impending doom all around us. Would it snow tonight?
Nuala had decreed at the beginning of our week that since there was hardly anyone around and since the wall was high and the gate was locked, we did not absolutely have to wear our swimsuits during our late afternoon swims. She dismissed my protests that this was a gross violation of modesty.
"You're having me on, Dermot Michael, and yourself

staring at me all day like I don't have any clothes on anyway."

I couldn't quite figure out whether the reason for this dispensation from proper behavior was something she enjoyed—she claimed that she had done it in Galway Bay in the middle of winter—or for my entertainment. Nuala enjoyed sexual love but this week's orgy might well be designed for the ulterior purpose of making sure I never left them.

One did not merely throw off one's clothes at the side of the pool and dive in, nothing that simple. First of all, she had to feed the brat. Then she had to put on a white bikini and a vast terry-cloth robe. Next she had to strap the child into her car seat and fasten the seat in a chair as far away from the pool as possible and still be in the pool enclosure. Finally, Fiona must be introduced into the environs and stationed next to Nelliecoyne.

Only then would Nuala toss aside her robe, dive into the pool, and aggressively swim a couple of lengths. Finally the bits of fabric would appear on the side of the pool. However, we both had to exercise vigorously before she was willing to permit what she called "foolin' around."

I didn't mind the act at all even if herself's dive and crawl were far better than mine, indeed flawless. As I have said repeatedly, I'm not competitive.

I'm only working on my own tennis game to provide me wife with some challenge.

   BULLSHIT.

"Shut up!"

While I was waiting in the parlor for the performance to progress, I flipped on the TV. I was greeted almost at once by the spokesperson for DCFS warning that her agency assumed responsibility for all children in the state of Illinois, no matter how famous or wealthy the parents might be, and that they would watch closely for any signs of exploitation by famous musical performers.

"Ms. Kenyon did not mention the name of folksinger

Nuala Anne McGrail in response to our question," the reporter insisted, "but it was clear she had in mind the charges made by this station that she would be exploiting her six-month-old daughter by singing to her in a Christmas special on another network."

"Has anyone ever lost custody of a child for doing that before, Lulu?" the anchorperson asked, obviously setting up an answer.

"No, Jennie, but there's always a first time."

"Ms. McGrail and her husband Dermot Coyne, the novelist, are presently out of town. But Buddy Marshal caught up with Mr. Coyne's brother-in-law, Thomas Hurley, as he came out of his law office late this afternoon."

"Mr. Hurley, do you think it likely that there will be a custody battle concerning Mary Anne Coyne?"

Tom, a big, handsome, Black Irish lug, laughed pleasantly.

"Only if DCFS and Channel Three and Mr. Farmer want a ton of lawsuits."

"How would you interpret Ms. Kenyon's remark then?"

"Ms. Kenyon has never seen a television camera that she hasn't wanted to talk to," he said, still grinning.

"So you don't anticipate any trouble, Mr. Hurley?"

Tom turned solemn.

"That's entirely up to your station manager and general counsel. You keep harassing my brother-in-law and his family with these absurd innuendos and we'll bury you. The complaints are already drafted."

Aha. The clan was circling the wagons. When would the government and the media ever learn that it was unwise to trifle with the Coynes?

Tom and Cindy had not even bothered to call to warn us. Small-time stuff.

In fact, Tom had seemed altogether too ready to get into a fight.

Eventually everything was arranged in good order;

Nelliecoyne, fed, reclothed, and content, slept in her car seat. Fiona rested next to her, eyes alert in case either of us needed help. The good wolfhound disdained the pool. Occasionally she would put a paw in it and sniff superciliously. It was too warm altogether. Nor did she pay any attention to our sexual high jinks which usually occurred after we had swum the prescribed laps. Fiona found human coupling uninteresting.

Nuala joined me in the pool, doffed her rags, and raced me for a couple of laps. Naturally she won.

In fact, Fiona did not seem much interested in canine coupling either. Wolfhound owners were seriously concerned about improving the gene pool, so that the wonderful pooches could live longer. Fiona had been carefully bred so that her life expectancy was now around ten years. So someone persuaded us to mate her with another snow-white hound named, appropriately, Fion. The two hounds became great friends on meeting. They bounded around the yard having a great old time with each other, like they were two pups rather than mature adults with procreative responsibilities, and herself being in heat as my wife put it.

Finally, the breeders worked the deed for them with firm but gentle skill. I will not go into the details, which I found revolting, but which Nuala, farm girl that she was, thought perfectly normal.

"Och, Dermot," she said, giggling, "no one has to do that with us, do they now?"

In due course Fiona gave birth to three snow-white pups, Fintan, Finbar, and Fionuala. We gave the first two away to delighted families and kept the bitch for ourselves because it was said that she had the makings of a show dog. However, since one wolfhound was more than enough for our family, we left her at the kennel for training.

My wife did not permit me to sentimentalize her separation from her mother or from us. "We just can't let her bond with us, Dermot Michael."

Still I liked to think that she remembered me when she greeted us warmly at the kennel.

However, wolfhounds greet everyone warmly.

We were about to turn to our romancing when Fiona barked in protest and rose from her resting position. I knew what the bark meant. The hound's sensitive nostrils were affronted by the aroma of human excrement.

"Hasn't the little brat dumped another load!" my wife protested. "Isn't that just like her and meself giving her a clean diaper.... You stay here, Dermot love.... Haven't you changed her every time today?... Fiona, you take care of Dermot till I come back...."

She vaulted out of the pool, threw her robe around her shoulders, snatched our daughter from her place of safety, and dashed into the house.

Obediently, Fiona came to the side of the pool and joined me.

"What the hell is going on, good doggie?" I asked her. "That little tyke couldn't see any ghost boat last night. There was no way she could look out the window from her crib. And what would a five-masted barkentine mean to her anyway? What does she know about collisions in Indian summer snowstorms anyway? And what does she know about 1898, she doesn't even know about 1998?"

The good doggie nuzzled me sympathetically, being very careful to stay away from the warm water.

"We do know that one baby girl died out there that night. Are her vibrations still around? Would they somehow affect a baby that happened to have a faint touch of the psychic in her makeup?"

Fiona had no answers.

I shivered once again, despite the warm water.

"I know you can't answer my questions, girl. You can distinguish a thousand different smells, but you can't quite think. Just now that makes me feel you're pretty lucky."

Nuala reappeared, clutching our daughter in her arms,

like she was a newborn babe. The child was clad in a brand-new outfit, a T-shirt and overalls, and was grinning complacently. Very gently Nuala tied her back into the chair.

"Isn't she a glorious little urchin, Dermot Michael?"

"Shits a lot."

"Go 'long with you. So did you when you were a baby."

"I never did."

She threw aside her robe, poised a moment at the edge of the pool so that I might have a full view, and then dove in. Perfect swan dive. Naturally.

She swam to me, hugged me fiercely, and began to sob. I held her in my arms till her weeping stopped.

"Sure, now," she said brightly, "isn't it time for romance?"

"Is that what they call it?"

So it was romance we had.

Later we went to the Montana restaurant in New Buffalo for supper.

"Wouldn't you be after needing a rest from all the cooking, husband mine? I'll pay."

I didn't argue.

We brought Nelliecoyne along, of course. She was dressed in Gap denim overalls, a kelly green T-shirt, and a denim pointed cap which said "Bulls!" Nuala Anne disapproved of designer clothes for children. But a sale at the Gap didn't count.

We couldn't leave the child home, of course. But we did leave Fiona, who was none too happy about it. She curled up sullenly just inside the door of the house as if to say, "It really is a dog's life I lead."

Nelliecoyne was wide awake looking for fun. We put her in the high chair and gave her bits of bread and crackers to chew on and play with. She wanted no part of them. So she started throwing them at us and at the floor. When the waitress came to take our orders and cooed over her, Nelliecoyne was as good a little girl as you could imagine. But for her regular audience her name was still trouble.

"She's a terrible little bitch altogether," Nuala said darkly. "She's doing it just to embarrass us."

"Probably."

"Well, she's your daughter, isn't she, now?"

"She is."

So I put on my stern face, shook a warning finger at her, and said, "Nelliecoyne, stop that now. NO!"

She considered me thoughtfully and then apparently decided that she better find another game.

Nuala giggled.

"I shouldn't be the only authority figure in the family," I protested.

"Och, but, Dermot love, you're so good at it."

An older couple appeared at our table. They were friends of my parents but I couldn't quite remember their name.

"And who is this gorgeous little redhead?" the man asked.

"Och, Marty, isn't she Moire Ain Coyne? We call her Nellie."

Trust Nuala to remember their names.

Our daughter smiled and gurgled and reached out her arms. Mrs. Marty picked her up.

"She's a darling child, Nuala."

"Thanks, Teresa. . . . Doesn't she have a mind of her own though?"

"Can't imagine where she got that," I said.

We chatted for a few moments.

"Kind of a spooky day out on the Lake, isn't it, Dermot?" Marty said.

"Beautiful, but just a little sinister," I said. "Like a calm before a storm."

"I don't have to tell you how quickly the storms come up, do I? I remember once when we were racing to Mackinaw. It was a summer day just like this. Almost unbearably peaceful. Then a storm cell appeared over at

Waukegan and drove the whole fleet over to this side of the Lake. The temperature fell twenty degrees, the rain was so thick that you couldn't see ten yards on either side. The wind just about tore off our sails. You could imagine that you could hear people screaming all around you."

"Oh."

Teresa had given the traitorous Nelliecoyne back to her mother. They were engaged in talk about babies, so thankfully Nuala didn't hear the conversation.

"A lot of people heard the screams or thought they did. Others didn't hear them at all. It stopped eventually."

"What were they screaming?"

"For help, I guess. I was convinced that we were losing boats all around us. Of course, we didn't lose any. . . . You know in the old days, in winter storms farther up the Lake, the watchmen said they heard men and women shouting, 'Mayday! Mayday!'"

"Really!"

"They thought there were vessels sinking all around them. Of course, there weren't any."

"Naturally not."

"Mayday is from the French *m'aidez*—help me! . . . Not that that means anything."

Well, at least we hadn't heard anyone shouting for help yet. At least I hadn't. No telling what our grinning little imp had heard last night.

That evening while we watched *Breaking the Waves* on videotape (accompanied by cries of outrage from Nuala Anne at the persecution of the Emily Watson character and cries of triumph when God vindicated her), I pondered what I had learned in the course of the day:

1) The *Charles C. Campbell* had appeared to my wife and child in the small hours of the morning, even though it had sunk with all hands in Lake Superior almost a hundred years ago.

2) Today was the hundredth anniversary of the sinking of the *City of Benton Harbor* somewhere off Michigan City when it was struggling for the Trail Creek Harbor in Michigan City. It had been rammed by the *Charles C. Campbell,* which did not stop to pick up survivors. At least two hundred Irish Americans, most of them from St. Gabriel's parish, had perished. Only a quick-witted young woman and brave Life Guards prevented the loss from being much worse.

3) Fiona, arguably also fey, had found two pieces of driftwood which were perhaps part of the wreckage of the *City of Benton Harbor.* A small child had found what was perhaps another piece of wreckage on the steps up from the dunes to Lakeview Avenue.

4) No trace of the wreck of the *City of Benton Harbor* had ever been found, perhaps because the explosion of the ship's boiler had torn the ship apart and because of the severe ice pack that winter.

5) However, the action of wind and waves had on at least one occasion covered the remains of a wrecked schooner just down the beach from us. Therefore it was possible, not likely, but possible, that some or all of the wreckage of the ship and the bodies of some of the survivors had been buried in dunes on which the early village had been built.

THAT'S STRETCHING IT, BOYO.

"I know."

But I also knew that fewer psychic vibrations than those I had listed had been enough on prior occasions to touch my wife's complex sensitivity, Neanderthal vestiges as George the Priest called them.

I did not like it at all. Moreover, what were we supposed to do about a shipwreck a hundred years old?

To the day.

"I know."

I was not so distracted that I did not enjoy the pleasures of our complicated bedtime sexual rituals, however—rituals in which I discovered which of the many possible bedmates would sleep with me that night.

The fragile Nuala, the sobbing girl in the pool, was my partner that night. Need I say, she was wonderful.

I must note that before the amusements began, herself would always kneel at the side of bed and say her night prayers. I had learned that they consisted mostly of lists of people for whom she was praying, both the living and the dead. She had said these prayers since she was a little girl, even during times at Trinity College when she had a hard time believing that God cared about humans.

When we were through, I resolved to sleep lightly because I was uncertain what might happen and I wanted to get into the nursery before my wife did.

—7—

THE TEENAGER with the red hair and the green eyes was wearing the maroon and gold uniform of St. Ignatius College Prep. She was bouncing a basketball up and down with practiced skill.

"Mom is pretty intense, isn't she?"

"Not unusually so for an Irishwoman."

"So our bond is pretty intense, huh?"

"I think I have noticed that."

"So I must be pretty intense too?"

"As the Cardinal says, arguably."

"You're not intense at all, Daddy."

"Uhm . . . well, maybe a little differently."

"No way. . . . Would it be better if I weren't so intense? Maybe I could change . . ."

"No way. You wouldn't be Nellie then. Besides, it's in your genes."

"I love Mom, like totally."

"Doesn't everyone."

"Sometimes I think we bond by fighting."

"That may be."

"But I don't want us ever to become enemies."

"For more than five minutes."

She grinned. "What do you mean?"

"I mean that you and herself stay angry at each other

for no more than five minutes. Then you conspire against
me."

"Would I do that?"

"Every day!"

"So you're not worried when Mom and I fight?"

"Only that I won't get out of the way."

"But, Daddy . . ."

Then the walls of the place where we were talking
collapsed and the cold waters of the Lake rushed in.
Somewhere there was an explosion. I was hurled out into
the water and carried by an enormous breaker onto a
beach. Nuala and Nellie were still out there. My wife
was all right but my daughter, I knew, had drowned.

I sat up with a start! I was soaking wet. Lake water?
No, perspiration.

Only a dream? No, it was too real to be a dream!

Next to me, Nuala was sleeping soundly, her naked
body glowing like polished silver in the moonlight.

Where was I?

My parents' house?

I slipped out of bed and into the room next door.
Fiona looked up at me quizzically, then closed her eyes.
Our redhead wasn't fifteen yet. She was only going on
seven months. It had been a dream. But it had seemed
so real!

As quietly as I could, I crept back into bed. I kissed
Nuala's breast as I fell back to sleep. That was at least
real. She murmured compliantly.

— 8 —

ABOUT THREE A.M. the little redhead began to wail angrily. Whatever had bothered her last night was bothering her again.

I jumped out of bed and dashed into the nursery before the wolfhound woke up and before Nuala heard the wailing. I was still soaking wet. The nursery was thick with humidity as if it were high August. The stench of dying nature permeated the air. Sure enough, in the moonlight my daughter's face was screwed up in an angry knot and she was shouting out her young lungs. So, I picked her up out of the bed, cuddled her in my arms. I decided that I had better sing a lullaby too. The only lullaby I know is the Brahms lullaby, and I have only the vaguest notion of what the words are. Still, under the circumstances, I began to sing it.

Lullaby and good night
With roses be delight
With lilies be decked
Is baby's sweet bed . . .

I hummed the next stanza. Nelliecoyne's wailing diminished somewhat but she was still one very angry little six-month, going-on-seven-month-old child.

I looked out on the Lake, illuminated as it was in the glow of the moon, once more a silver plate on which little diamonds twinkled. No boat, not that I expected there to be one.

My third time through Brahms's lullaby, the child's wailing had diminished to soft weeping. Then Nuala Anne, accompanied by a fretful Fiona, appeared, this time clad modestly in her robe. She was sleepy-eyed and smelled of sex and springtime.

"Dermot Michael Coyne," she said impatiently. "Sure, isn't your voice enough to keep the baby awake for the rest of the night? Let me have the poor little tyke!"

"You should have heard her before I started to sing," I protested as I turned Nelliecoyne over to her mother. Nuala crooned an Irish song. The baby shut her eyes.

> "Lullaby, lullaby,
> Sweet little baby,
> Don't you cry,
> I'd rock my own little child to rest,
> In a cradle of gold on the bough of a willow,
> To the shoheen ho of the wind of the west,
> And the lulla low of the soft sea billow.
> Sleep, baby dear,
> Sleep without fear,
> Mother is here beside your pillow."

"Och, isn't it that boat out there again tonight?" Nuala whispered to me. "Sure, it's a strange one, isn't it now, one of them paddle-wheeled things? And what's the name on it?"

Fiona was, thank God, not staring at the Lake. Rather she sat on her haunches, content that Nelliecoyne was no longer wailing.

"Would it be something like the *City of Benton Harbor*?"

"Sure, that's what it is. It's a strange-looking boat, I've never seen one like that before in all me life."

I was silent for the moment because there was no

paddle-wheeled steamer on the Lake, only the smooth water in the moonlight.

"You do see it, don't you, Dermot Michael?" she asked anxiously.

"Nuala, it's not there. The paddle-wheeled steamer the *City of Benton Harbor* sank in Lake Michigan one hundred years ago."

Nuala looked at the Lake, she looked at me, and then she looked at the little redhead now calm in her arms.

"Oh, Dermot Michael, whatever are we going to do?"

That was, I thought, a very good question. However, I knew that we would now have to figure out why the psychic vibrations were happening and how Nuala Anne was to bring peace to the ghosts which were haunting Grand Beach.

— 9 —

WELL, NUALA Anne, my love. I've already told you the story of the *City of Benton Harbor* and the *Charles C. Campbell.* Since I know better than to try to talk you out of one of these adventures—though I personally think we should forget the whole thing—I herewith submit background information on Lake Michigan shipping for whatever good it may do.

The Great Lakes really ought not to be here, much less contain half the fresh water in the world. If it hadn't have been for a couple of ice ages, most of the ground covered by the Great Lakes would simply be prairie land, like the prairies that stretch west of Chicago. However, the Great Lakes were created by melting glaciers which completely modified the topography of North America. Only ten thousand years ago Lake Michigan was a glacier two miles high. The Lakes are in fact a mass of intrusion of nature into the normal geography of North America. Without them, however, our fair city of Chicago would not exist.

Chicago was originally a smelly swamp on the south side of Lake Michigan. The Native Americans were generally content to travel around it though occasionally in good weather they would venture out on it in big canoes, staying *very* close to shore. That's how Father Marquette, the Jesuit priest who was the first European to visit our city, traveled back and forth. There was no skyline then, only a smelly swamp. (I must insist, however, Nuala Anne, that there were signs which said "Richard M. Daley, Mayor.") The swamp was caused by the Chicago River, which was a switch-hitter in those days, a kind of drain pipe at the bottom of Lake Michigan (not to indulge in a more scatological metaphor). When the Lake was high, it would drain into the river and the excess water would flow south to the Gulf of Mexico. When the Lake was low, the river would drain into the Lake. Chicago is only 120 feet above sea level, but it sits on a continental divide. The Des Plaines River west of the city sends its waters to the Gulf while the Chicago River itself normally aims at the Atlantic Ocean. Now we've reversed it so that it flows always to the Gulf, lest sewage discharge into the Lake and cause typhoid fever.

The "smelly" part comes apparently from wild onions which used to grow in the swamp. It was not a spot on which any of the natives wanted to spend much time. However, when Europeans swarmed into America they began to establish the patterns of travel which shaped the future of what would become the United States and also the future of that smelly swamp. The first pattern was to travel west on land and eventually in wagons and then later on in railroads and finally today in planes. The earlier modes of transportation had to get around the Great Lakes and so they turned the corner at the southern end of Lake Michigan and came to the smelly swamp. Chicago became the "breaking point"—the place where cargoes were unloaded—for grain and cattle from the west and eventually iron ore and for people and lumber from the east. The Great Lakes themselves became the second major route for traveling west. I hope all these details are not boring you—you'd never tell me if they were, would you now?

Sailing and later steam vessels carried millions of tons of freight and hundreds of thousands of passengers from places like Oswego, Buffalo, Cleveland, and Detroit to Chicago and in return carried the produce of the prairies. In 1679 La Salle built the sailing ship *Griffon,* which sailed from Lake Huron to the Soo (Sault Sainte Marie) and then returned without La Salle. It sank in a storm on September 18 of that year, the first of perhaps the thousands of ships that sank on the Great Lakes in the last three hundred years. In 1832, just at the time Chicago was becoming a city, the first lighthouse was established at the mouth of the Chicago River, a harbinger of things to come. In 1839 there was a regular line of eight ships operating from Buffalo to Chicago and the first golden cargo of wheat was carried from Chicago back to Buffalo. In 1860 Chicago was already the busiest port in the world. Indeed, forty years later it was still the fourth busiest port in the world after London, Hamburg, and New York. In 1857 there were 107 side-wheeled steamers on the Lakes, 135 power steamers, and over one thousand sailing boats. At the end of the Civil War, the shipping of lumber from Michigan to Chicago and Milwaukee began. Soon there was a steady flow of lumber west across Lake Michigan as the lumber companies cleared the state of Michigan of its finest trees. At the end of the 1860s there were almost two thousand sailing vessels on the Great Lakes, many of them on Lake Michigan. The sailing vessels were almost entirely designed to carry freight—package freight, which meant everything that wasn't bulk, and bulk freight, such as lumber and iron ore and gravel and Christmas trees and grain. From 1890 on the sailing ships began to decline on the Lake as steamships replaced them.

The Lakes imposed certain serious constraints on the big bulk carriers: they had to be narrow so they could slip through the locks at the Soo (where St. Mary's River drains Lake Superior into the other four Lakes); they had to be shallow so they could navigate the rivers which served as ports around the Lakes, and they had to be long to carry enough cargo to be profitable. So the ore boats that we used to see when we were young going by Chicago towards northern Indiana were eventually one thousand feet long. They were very strange-looking ships, but also very, very profitable.

In 1892 car ferries were introduced to carry railroad freight cars across the Lake from Muskegon, Michigan, to Sheboygan, Wisconsin, thus cutting the time passage to one-third of what it would have been if they had to go around the southern end of Lake Michigan and through Chicago.

You know, Nuala, I'm beginning to get an idea for a new novel about the Lake. Don't tell me I have to finish the present one first. I know that.

The Erie Canal connected central New York to Buffalo; the Welland Canal connected Lake Ontario and Lake Erie; the St. Lawrence Seaway connected the ocean to the Lakes; and finally the great Soo locks connected Lake Superior to Lake Huron and then Lake Michigan (which are in fact not two lakes but one since they have the same sea level and are the largest freshwater body in the world). Thus there were two continuous (though somewhat convoluted) water routes from Europe to the heart of North America—and back.

Passengers traveled for the most part on the steamships, paddle boats early on and then later power-driven boats. The shipping season was severely limited by Great Lakes weather. It began in early April and continued into early November. Between November and April, the storms were too dangerous and the Lake ice was too thick to permit shipping. This created considerable problems for the shipping companies. A lot of money could be made in a very brief time in Great Lakes shipping, a schooner for example could pay for itself within two years. But the problems with the weather and with business cycles made Great Lakes sailing a risky business for owners. Therefore, they were tempted to expand the shipping season into November and run risks of serious, even catastrophic losses. Though November first was a prudent time to stop Great Lakes shipping, most owners forced their skippers to stay out on the Lakes until middle and late November. Most of the great storms which destroyed ships were the ones of 1882, 1905, 1913 ("The Great Storm") that occurred in early November. Moreover, the *Edmund Fitzgerald,* the legendary ore boat that was torn apart by Lake Superior storms, went down on November 10, just a little too late to be out on the Lakes. The shipping business was ruthlessly capitalistic. The owners pushed the captains, the captains pushed the crews, and risks were taken with both weather and repairing ships that today would be against the law. There was some cursory inspection of ships, but safety regulations were minimal. Moreover, for most of the history of Great Lakes shipping, there was very little in the way of accurate weather forecasting and, of course, no radar, radio contact, or navigational aids like asdic which could tell a skipper where his ship was in the middle of a blinding snowstorm—and in our story where other ships were.

There were many elegant passenger ships on the Great Lakes, Nuala. Or at least people thought they were elegant. Sometimes they carried passengers from Buffalo to Chicago who were making the trip simply to get to Chicago. But some also, especially later on, in cruise ships running as regularly scheduled excursions from, let us say, Buffalo to Duluth, Minnesota, and back. In the years just before the Second World War there were two particularly large, elegant vessels—*Seeandbee* and the *City of Buffalo*—which were converted into aircraft carriers during the Second World War for training pilots from the Glenview Naval Air Station just north of Chicago. Two graceful vessels operated out of Chicago between the two wars and for a time after the Second World War, the *South American* and *North American.* Then Great Lakes excursions became unfashionable when people could just as easily sail to Alaska, or the Caribbean, or even to the Mediterranean. There is some talk now of a new era of Great Lakes excursions. Last summer a German cruise ship visited Chicago. I can understand why a cruise ship would want to come to Chicago, but why would the Germans want to visit Buffalo or Erie or Cleveland or . . . But then I'm not German!

Great Lakes shipping declined like everything else in the country during the Depression but became active again in the years after the war. In the 1960s European motor ships were coming through the St. Lawrence waterway through the Welland Canal, and docking at Navy Pier. However, these "canalers" were too small to be economical means of transportation to Midwest America. Some of them had managed to become involved in accidents on Lake Michigan and even to sink.

Eventually the Great Lakes shipping in the United States diminished to the carrying of bulk cargo via long (sometimes as long as one thousand feet) bulk carriers. Some are still out there on the Lakes, carrying sand and gravel and occasionally coal and iron ore. But I have only seen one in all my life go by Grand Beach. I hardly ever see one off the Chicago shoreline. The shipping of iron ore from the Mesabi Range in Minnesota has diminished, because the steel companies now import cheaper and richer iron ore from other countries. Where there were once thousands of vessels on the American Great Lakes now there are only forty and almost all of them self-unloading ore boats.

I've attached a picture I found in one of my dad's books on the Chicago Harbor in 1885. There are no locks and no jetties, only the mouth of the Chicago River with a tug pulling in a schooner. Notice that there is a traffic jam. Ships are crowded bow to stern on both sides of the river. The docks extended as far as 22nd Street, four miles up from the mouth of the river.

The major reasons why Chicago is hardly a port anymore is that other forms of transportation are cheaper and quicker and the limited season does not fit the needs of American industry. Some of the ore boats can operate all year round because their bows are as strong as those of icebreakers. But since the decline of the Mesabi there is not that much for them to do. I read somewhere or the other recently that there had been a slight increase in Great Lakes traffic last year. If the states and the two countries involved could get their acts together to improve the St. Lawrence waterway and the Welland Canal perhaps the story might be different. But the costs of such an improvement might be different. I said before that the two waterways from the Atlantic to the heart of America were complicated. The Erie Canal route is closed now and the St. Lawrence waterway is not very efficient because it can only accommodate ships with no larger than a twenty-six-foot draft.

So the fascinating history of Great Lakes transportation seems to have come almost to its end, though many stories remain for the nostalgia buffs of the wrecks and the ghost ships and the disasters which plagued the Lakes during the two hundred or so years when they were the most important water transportation in the world. The sinking of the *City of Benton Harbor* just off Michigan City a hundred years ago yesterday was only one of many disasters, and not even the worst.

Look out the window at Lake Michigan in the summertime. It's usually pretty calm. Sometimes there are three- or four-foot waves that challenge wind surfers and catamarans and ruin waterskiing. It's hard to believe that Lake Michigan and the other lakes are really inland seas and potentially enormous dangers to those who go out on them. Thousands of lives have been lost out there and hundreds, if not thousands, of ships sunk. Millions of dollars' worth of treasure are at the bottom of the Lake. At one time there was a suggestion that the Soo locks be closed so that the Lake could be drained and the treasure could be picked up. Needless to say the City of Chicago strongly opposed that suggestion which was, I think, more science fiction than serious proposal.

The books about Great Lakes shipping are filled with

romantic nostalgia. Yet the work of an officer, an engineer, or a watchman on a Great Lakes ship, sail or steam, was difficult, dirty, and exhausting work with danger always lurking just at the edge. You were glad when you worked no matter how miserable the pay was and how dull and routine the work usually was. Working was better than not working. There was no union to protect your income during business cycles. There was little romance or adventure, most of the time. Usually it was no more exciting than driving a truck or a railroad train.

Your wife always worried when she saw your ship put out from Erie or Chicago or wherever that she might never see you again. Brave men certainly sailed the lakes: everybody that sails on a ship is brave—and usually bored out of their minds.

It is astonishing that we have so little memory of these men and their ships in Chicago. Occasionally we see a postcard of the Christmas tree ship which sailed from Wisconsin to Chicago and was sunk during a November storm. Some of us know a little bit about the worst Great Lakes tragedy of all, the sinking of the excursion ship *Eastland* in the Chicago River.

Yet when we look out now on the empty Lake, we see only the weekend cruisers and the offshore racers and the beach boats. We are oblivious to the danger and the harshness and the tragedy of working on a Great Lakes ship not so long ago. The first shipwreck on Lake Michigan was the sinking of the schooner *Hercules* in 1818, near what is now 63rd Street. All hands were lost. Indians in the vicinity found that bears and wolves had mutilated the bodies of most of the crew.

Of all the five lakes the danger was worst on Lake Michigan. Of the fifteen worst shipping accidents on the Great Lakes, eight happened on Lake Michigan and by far the highest number of casualties also happened on Lake Michigan. The worst of all occurred on July 24, 1915, in the Chicago River. The excursion ship *Eastland* capsized for reasons that still remain mysterious. Eight hundred and forty-four people, employees and families of the Western Electric Company, who had awakened that morning eagerly expecting a delightful summer cruise, died in the muddy waters of the river before the trip had a chance to begin.

On September 8, 1860, the *Lady Elgin,* with hundreds of Irish Americans on a weekend cruise, was rammed and sunk off Winnetka by the schooner *Augusta*; three hundred people died. On November 21, 1847, the passenger ship *Phoenix* was swept by fire on Lake Michigan and approximately two hundred people died. On October 15, 1898, the excursion boat *City of Benton Harbor* was sunk in a collision during a winter storm just off Michigan City, Indiana, with perhaps two hundred lives lost.

On April 9, 1868, the *Seabird* was destroyed by fire just off Chicago with the loss of perhaps one hundred lives. On October 16, 1880, the *Alpena* foundered in lower Lake Michigan with a loss of between sixty and one hundred lives. On September 24, 1856, the *Niagara* in upper Lake Michigan at a cost of sixty-five lives. On October 22, 1929, the car ferry *Milwaukee* disappeared in the middle of Lake Michigan with fifty on board. On October 22, 1856, the *Toledo* sank off Port Washington with the loss of at least fifty lives.

Most of these major Lake Michigan disasters did not occur during the storm season, only the *Milwaukee,* the *Alpena,* the *Toledo,* and the *City of Benton Harbor* sank in winter storms. The other losses were a result of either fire or collision or, in the case of the *Eastland* disaster, an inexplicable capsizing.

Since the *City of Benton Harbor* was probably not seaworthy and was rammed in the dark by a large schooner, it cannot really be counted as a casualty of a storm because it might have made it into Trail Creek, although in the absence of a breakwater off Michigan City at that time, such a refuge was problematic. If it had not been for the *Charles C. Campbell,* the skipper could have at least beached the ship and most of the passengers' lives been saved.

The ships lost in winter storms were almost entirely freight vessels like the ore carriers *Edmund Fitzgerald* or the *Carl D. Bradley* (the latter on Lake Michigan in 1958) which carried rather small crews. Hence, while their loss was a tragedy to the families of the crews and frequently a disaster to the owners, they did not cause the major loss of life as did the sinking of the passenger ships.

Two footnotes, Nuala, about the *Eastland*; the United States Navy purchased the craft, salvaged it, and converted it into a naval training vessel USS *Wilmette*. Most people who years ago saw it moored in the Chicago harbor did not realize that it was a vessel associated with a tragedy, the worst tragedy in the history of the Lakes.

Finally, a quote from the Cleveland *Plain Dealer* of August 7, 1935:

> Chicago August 7 (AP). The United States Circuit Court of Appeals today upheld the Circuit Court ruling that the St. Joseph Steamship Company, former owners of the steamer S. S. *Eastland*, which sank in the Chicago area July 24, 1915, was not liable for the 844 deaths in the disaster. The court held that the company was liable only to the extent of the salvage value of the vessel. That the boat was seaworthy, that the operators had taken proper precautions, and that the responsibility was traced to an engineer who had neglected to fill the ballast tanks properly.

That's the way it was on the Great Lakes in those days, Nuala love. If you died in a storm or a collision or a fire or an explosion or a capsizing, no one was to blame. It was your tough luck for going out on the Great Lakes.

— 10 —

 TV clip.
Place: Daley Civic Center Plaza. Time: noon. The Richard J. Daley Building looms in the background, the Picasso sculpture is off to one side. On a raised platform is a group of people— the Mayor, members of City Council, various important people, some of them in Roman collars. A large crowd fills the plaza, larger than most that come for a noon concert. Nuala Anne, Dermot, and Nelliecoyne are in the center of the platform. Fiona is not present. Since it is still Indian summer and quite warm, Nuala is wearing a pink T-shirt dress with her long black hair tied back by a matching ribbon. Nellie, in Nuala's arms, is also wearing a pink T-shirt and her few strands of red hair are tied with a small pink ribbon. Dermot is carrying Nuala's harp case. They walk to the front of the platform, Dermot unpacks the harp case. They both remain standing in front of two chairs that have been placed there for them.

Nuala: My name is Nuala Anne McGrail and this lovely child is my daughter Nellie. I'm supposed to sing lullabies for you today and I can't sing lullabies unless I have a baby to sing them to.

Nellie smiles at the crowd, laughs, gurgles, and seems very happy.

Nuala: You can see that Nellie loves you. That's because she's Irish and the Irish love people, the more the merrier. I think this is the largest crowd that Nellie has ever seen and she seems very happy to meet you all.

Crowd applauds loudly, Nellie grins even more.

While Nuala is talking Dermot unpacks the harp.

Dermot is a tall husky blond with a dimple in his chin and a sweet, sixth-grade altar-boy smile, behind which one suspects lurks more than a touch of mischief.

Nuala: Now you needn't worry about disturbing me little tyke! (*Laughter from the crowd.*) I had to bring her along 'cause I'm nursing her. And she's just been fed and it's her naptime and she always sleeps when I sing lullabies to her, so she'll probably fall asleep and Dermot here will take good care of her. Dermot, by the way, is me first husband. He is also me only husband and he is not bad as a husband and he's pretty good as a father too. Doesn't he change herself's diapers at least twice as many times as I do!

Laughter from the crowd.

Both Dermot and Nuala sit on the chairs, Nuala holding her harp and Dermot holding the baby so Nuala can sing to her.

Nuala: Don't I think that God is always singing lullabies to us? Hasn't God brought us into the world just like mothers do? And hasn't He fallen in love with us? And don't mothers have to sing lullabies to their children? So I think when we mothers sing lullabies to our children we are imitating what God does all the time— and especially when His children are loud and noisy and cantankerous!

More laughter from the crowd.

Nuala: The first lullaby I'm going to sing is a Choctaw Indian lullaby. I had to hunt pretty hard to find it because there's not that many Choctaw Indians left in America. I'll sing it first in the original—as best as I can pronounce it! And then I will sing my own translation. You know the story about the Choctaw Indians, don't you now? Way back when more than half the people in Ireland were starving to death, the Choctaws, who were in the Great Plains of this country and knew the meaning of famine themselves, heard about us and didn't they send us some of their own hard-earned money and some food to help us through the Famine? They were the only people in the world that sent food to Ireland during the Famine and the Brits shipping grain out of the country!

In Dublin under the Milltown bridge on the Dodder River there's a restaurant called The Dropping Well and back in the famine times it was a morgue. They used to fish people out of the stream and bring them in there before they would bury them. The Irish are a strange folk, it doesn't bother us at all, at all, to have a good dinner in a place that was once a morgue. Well, anyway right out in front of the former morgue by the river, always illumined at night, is this little shrine and itself being very graceful built by the people of Ireland in gratitude to the Choctaw Indians for helping us in the Famine.

Nuala sings a lullaby in Choctaw and then an English translation.

Nuala: It's a lovely melody, isn't it? Me friend Gary Whitedeer taught it to me. The mother tells the baby to go to sleep and they'll both go to pigtown together, which meant to her dream world.

The baby has closed her eyes and is sleeping peacefully.

Nuala: See didn't I tell you that me lass would fall right to sleep on us. She's really a very good little baby, she keeps regular hours and doesn't disturb me or her da at all, at all. Of course, when she's really angry she lets us know and that in no uncertain terms. But she's an Irishwoman now, isn't she?

More laughter from the crowd.

Nuala: Me next song isn't exactly a lullaby, though it sounds like one. It's a Choctaw song too, one about leaving your native land. It brings tears to me eyes every time I sing it. And doesn't it remind me how much the Irish and the Choctaw are like one another?

"Land where brightest waters flow,
Land where loveliest forests grow,
Where warriors drew the bow,
Native land farewell.

"He who made you stream and tree,
Made the White, the Red man free,
Gave the Indians' home to be,
Mid the forest's wilds.

"Have the waters ceased to flow?
Have the forests ceased to grow?
Why do our brothers bid us go,
From our native home?

"Here in infancy we played,
Here our happy wigwams made,
Here our fathers' bones are laid,
Must we leave them all?

"White men tell us of God on high.
So pure and bright in yonder sky,
Will not then His searching eye,
See the Indians' wrong?"

Nuala: Now I'm going to sing to you an Irish lullaby. This one is called the "Connemara Cradle Song" and meself being from Connemara, isn't it the first lullaby I ever heard. When Irish mothers sang lullabies not so long ago, they knew how many dangers would threaten their children—hunger, disease, storms, English bayonets. So they sang prayers for the protection of their little ones.

"On the wings of the wind, o'er the dark,
   rolling deep,
Angels are coming to watch o'er your sleep,
Angels are coming to watch over you,
So listen to the wind coming over the sea.

"Hear the wind blow, hear the wind blow,
Lean your head over, hear the wind blow."

Nuala sings several lullabies with commentaries on each one. Each one of them is cheered loudly and Dermot grins his mischievous smile. Nellie continues to sleep.

Nuala: Just to show you that I'm not a complete Irish bigot, I'm going to sing a song from the Isle of Man in Manx Gaelic, which I'm sure youse all understand!

Laughter.

Nuala: Well, all right I'll sing it in English. It's called the "Smuggler's Lullaby." Your Manx have been known to engage in smuggling, you see—something that we Irish Gaels would never do, would we now? Well, your Brits are raiding a smuggler's house and his wife is just singing a song for her child, minding her own business, you see? Now the Brits don't understand Gaelic but her man does.

"See the excise man coming,
Sleep, my little hero,
They'll be seeking wine and whiskey,
Ah me, child of mine.
Sleep, my little hero,
Daddy's late and we must warn him,
This time we'll have nothing illegal,
The Englishmen may board us,
They'll find nothing wrong.
Let them search the boat or house,
Nothing's in the hold but herrings!"

Applause! Cheers for the brave Manx woman!

Nuala: Did you like that now? Wasn't she the clever one? Since I'm running out of time, I'm going to sing one in Welsh Gaelic, one that you all know so you sing along with me in English.

She sings in Gaelic, crowd does fine on the first stanza, struggles through the second aided by Dermot's tenor.

"Sleep, my child, and peace attend thee,
All through the night.
Guardian angels God will send thee,
All through the night.
Soft the drowsy hours are creeping,
Hill and dale in slumber steeping,
I my loving vigil keeping,
All through the night."

Nuala: Now, before I leave youse, I'm going to sing an Irish-American song, one that your purists don't like although you sing it at every wedding, including me own. I love it!

She sings it as though it is a lullaby for her daughter.

"When Irish eyes are smiling,
'Tis like a day in spring.
In the lilt of Irish laughter,
You can hear the angels sing.
"When Irish eyes are happy,
All the world is bright and gay,
But when Irish eyes are smiling,
Sure, they'll steal your heart away."

She sings it a second time. Everyone joins in. Nellie-coyne opens her eyes and smiles.

Then the fifteen-minute concert is over, Nuala and Dermot stand up. Dermot puts the harp back in its case.

Nuala takes the baby and then turns to the microphone again.

Nuala: Sure now wasn't it awful good of youse to come and listen to me singing here in the Daley Plaza. I'm glad you came and I'm delighted that your man (with a nod of her head to the Mayor) invited me and himself coming to listen too with all the terrible busy things he has to do to be Mayor. And I'm also glad that the Bishop came and my husband Dermot's brother the priest, both of whom are very fine priests let me tell you!

Laughter and applause from the audience.

Nuala: So if you want to hear these songs again—and there's no reason at all, at all why you should—won't they be out on compact disc pretty soon and you've got to imagine that I'll be singing them for Nellie because that's the only way I can sing lullabies and really mean them but I promise you it will be at her naptime like this and you'll never hear a peep from her on the recording. She will be a perfectly proper young Irishwoman with her eyes closed and her big mouth shut! Just like her ma.

More laughter.

Nuala: And if it turns out that we're going to do a Christmas special, well I'll have to bring Nellie along too because what if she should get hungry?

Laughter and applause from the crowd.

Cut to another scene.

Farmer: Well, my friends, you have seen the clips so you know what I mean. If ever there has been a disgusting display of Chicago Irish-Catholic vulgarity complete with the politicians and the clergy sitting in the back, then it was Ms. McGrail's little concert in the Daley Civic Center Plaza today. As we all know her voice isn't even pretty. She claims only to be a folksinger, but most folksingers have better trained voices than she does. Moreover the little story she told of the Choctaw Indians was a shameless exploitation of the suffering of Native Americans. The Irish mystical mumbo jumbo was what we might expect from this very untalented young woman who makes up with lies and with phony charm for her absolute lack of talent. She is no more an artist than her goofy hack novelist husband.

But the most disgusting and disgraceful thing of all was to bring that poor little seven-month-old child along to entertain the crowd. One has to wonder whether the child was drugged because she slept so peacefully. Certainly no ordinary human baby can sleep through the noise of the crowd and the awkward, uneven, and sometimes off-key singing of her mother. I hope that the Department of Children and Family Services watches the clips of this concert very carefully. They have to insist that if Ms. McGrail and her husband wish to keep custody of their child, they must stop exploiting her in public in such a shameless ambitious fashion.

The Coynes can make all the threatening phone calls to me they want, I'm not going to back off. Ms. McGrail represents all that is wrong with Chicago Irish Catholicism, its vulgarity, its phoniness, its insincerity, and its absolute lack of talent, and I'm Nick Farmer.

Close-up of Nuala, Dermot, and Nellie walking off the platform. Nellie, cradled in her mother's arms, is sleeping the sleep of a just child. A cameraman descends upon them and the young reporter jabs a microphone at Nuala.

Reporter: Ms. McGrail, don't you think that you are exploiting the little baby terribly in this concert?

Nuala: Ah! Sure doesn't the poor little tyke look like she's exploited altogether and is herself sleeping just as though she knew the angels were looking down on her and taking care of her?

11

THE YOUNG priest—with long black hair, pale white skin, flashing blue eyes, and the demon smile of an Irish operator, perhaps priest, perhaps politican, perhaps undertaker, perhaps bookmaker—welcomed us to St. Gabriel's, the parish whose people had drowned a hundred years before in the sinking of the *City of Benton Harbor*. Nuala—who solves all our mysteries (I'm only a Watson to her Holmes)—wanted to know more about the people who had died in the wreck. When she's sniffing her way through a mystery I do what she wants.

"You were wonderful yesterday at the Daley Plaza, Ms. McGrail," he said, enthusiastically shaking Nuala's hand and then mine. "And so was this cute little tyke. I'm happy that she has McGrail looks and not Coyne looks. Wouldn't it be terrible for her to grow up looking like Father Coyne?"

My brother, George the Priest, had arranged this interview with his classmate who presided over the old Canaryville parish at 45th and Wallace.

"Johnny Devlin is a smooth one," he had warned me. "Classmate of mine. Thinks he knows everything."

"Takes one to know one," I replied since herself was not around to remonstrate with me about my deplorable lack of respect for the clergy.

Nuala Ann knows very well when someone is "having her on."

"Ah well now, isn't His Reverence a grand priest and himself so holy," she replied to Johnny Devlin, "and wise and isn't me poor little tyke of a daughter lucky to have such a distinguished clergyman as her uncle?"

"In the immortal words of Sheridan Whiteside in *The Man Who Came to Dinner*," I murmured, "I may vomit!"

Nuala had done what she always does with priests. She somehow or other gets them on her side against me. Except for the little Bishop, who treats me with enormous respect, doubtless for reasons of his own.

So I tried to change the subject as Johnny Devlin led us into an office with twelve-foot ceilings and ancient but elegant oak walls, a rectory office which would only have been possible in another era of Catholic history. Built a hundred years ago, it was supposed to be a witness to the immigrant population of the majesty and wisdom of the Catholic heritage and the wisdom and power of its clergy. Surprisingly, given the age of the rectory, the furniture inside the office was new and the office was neat and clean. A computer screen blinked in the background. Here the message was that the parish might be old and the church a historic landmark, but it was still an efficient and modern operation, just like its pastor in his gray slacks, blue blazer, and white shirt with an open neck.

"So this is the great parish of the South Side Irish?" I asked. "I must say that the church looks surprisingly modern even if this rectory is something right out of the 1860s."

"When old Father Dorney, who was the pastor here, built the church, they said he was a hundred years ahead of his time and I really believe that's true." Johnny was repeating the archdiocesan line on St. Gabe's I had heard from George earlier in the day.

"He was a great man," Johnny continued. "After his funeral, the head of the cortege reached all the way to

Mount Olivet Cemetery out on 111th Street while the hearse was still waiting here in front of the church. He was on the side of the unions and the workers against management, he was on the side of black people against oppression, he was for every good cause of his time and maybe the greatest priest in the history of the diocese. Now everyone has forgotten about him. There is, Dermot, as I'm sure your brother has told you, no one deader than a dead priest."

"I seem to remember hearing that."

In fact I had heard it from George that very morning. The little Bishop, Nelliecoyne resting comfortably in his arms as he presided over breakfast, made a wry face at this bit of clerical nonsense, but ignored it.

As we were leaving the Cathedral Rectory, he observed, "It is said that there are many ghosts lurking out there in St. Gabe's."

"Do you believe in ghosts?" I asked him.

He rolled his pale blue eyes behind his Coke-bottle glasses. "In theory, of course. In practice, I am profoundly skeptical. Your worthy brother and the inestimable Johnny Devlin believe just the opposite."

"In theory they reject ghosts but in practice they believe in them?"

"Patently."

Later I asked Nuala what she thought the little Bishop meant.

"Wasn't he saying we should be skeptical about all clerical stories about ghosts and such like?"

"And your stories?"

"Och, sure, there aren't any ghosts in my stories and besides, I'm not a priest."

I had no idea what she meant. If the ships she—and presumably our "bebe"—had seen on Lake Michigan were not ghosts, what were they?

I wisely kept my comment to myself.

"Are there still some Irish people living in the parish?" Nuala asked Johnny Devlin as we sat down in comfortable chairs around a coffee table in the rectory office. "Or have they moved out?"

"Oh, as long as Irish live in Chicago there will be a few of them here in Canaryville as it's called. By the way, the name comes not from canaries singing here but from grackles which, as you folks may know, are the noisiest, ugliest, dirtiest birds in the world. One more example of Irish irony."

"Mostly Latino in the parish now, aren't there?" I asked, trying to sound well informed.

"We have four Masses on the weekend," said the priest, smiling happily. "Two are in English and two are in Spanish. Some of the old Turkey Birds come to the Spanish Masses because they say it reminds them of the Latin from the old days!"

Nuala Anne sighed loudly. "Sure aren't the Irish a terrible difficult people altogether?"

"Absolutely," the young priest said. "Could I be getting you a cup of coffee now?"

"Oh, no thanks, Father," I said quickly, too quickly. "We don't want to take up too much of your time."

"Well," Nuala said softly, "sure, couldn't I enjoy just a small cup of tea?"

Nellie, resting peacefully in her arms, sighed as if to echo her mother.

"I'll drink some of that to keep herself company."

"Any special kind of tea?" asked the young priest. "Nothing but the best for Father George's relatives!"

"Me husband drinks Earl Grey," Nuala informed him. "And I wouldn't mind a bit of Irish Breakfast tea if you have any around."

"Cream and sugar?"

"Ah, no, hasn't me husband cured me of the filthy habit of polluting me tea the way we do in Ireland?"

"Thank you, Father," I said respectfully, beating my wife to it.

"There's always hospitality here at St. Gabriel's," the

priest said with a wave of his hand. "After all, we have a tradition to keep up, don't we now?"

There had been no more incidents at Grand Beach. My daughter did not wake up screaming the final two nights we were there. We went out to supper with our new friends the O'Dwyers on Saturday and Sunday nights. Our child was a perfect little angel, save for throwing crusts of bread on the floor. Neil O'Dwyer was a nice enough fellow, though a typical commodity trader, high on aggression, energetic, and just a little crazy. Fortunately Rita kept him in line.

They had left their two children at their cottage in the care of a thirteen-year-old baby-sitter. The tension around my wife's eyes deepened at the thought that someday she would have to leave our precious little Nelliecoyne in the care of some adolescent.

I did not particularly like that idea either, though I would have to be the voice of reason reassuring Nuala that there was no reason to worry.

The Indian summer weather continued as though it were going to last forever. There were no sudden winter storms as there had been in the middle of October a hundred years ago. I had given Nuala my "brief report" on Lake Michigan shipping, she had read it with considerable interest, her face solemn as she concentrated on the text. Then she had put the papers to the side and pondered silently for several minutes.

"I'll never, never go out sailing on that Lake again at all, at all," she informed me. "It's a dangerous, brutal, murdering Lake!"

"Only if you're not respectful of it," I said. "I'm not sure that it's any more dangerous than Galway Bay."

"That's neither here nor there," she said and so the question had been settled. By next summer she would change her mind and deny vigorously that she had ever vowed to avoid the Lake. She would insist on sailing and waterskiing with us on the Lake because most of the time in the summer it looks so peaceful.

"Well," she asked me after several more minutes of pondering, "what do you think we should do about all of this?"

"I'm not sure, Nuala," I replied. "Since the, er, phenomenon has stopped, maybe there is nothing at all for us to do about it, maybe it was just an incident from the past which generated strong vibrations particularly on the hundredth anniversary of the wreck. Maybe it's something we should just forget about."

YOU'RE DREAMING, BOYO, the Adversary warned me.

"Don't you know me better than that, Dermot Michael?" she asked indignantly. "Aren't we going to have to get to the bottom of it?"

"What bottom? The bottom of Lake Michigan?"

"If I knew that, Dermot Michael Coyne," she said tersely, "wouldn't I be after telling you right now? There's a mystery out there and we're supposed to solve it. Otherwise me and me daughter wouldn't have seen the two ships."

"But first of all we have to find out what the mystery is, don't we?"

"Isn't that the truth, Dermot Michael? We not only have to solve the mystery, we have to find out what it is."

Hence our visit to St. Gabriel's rectory on a chill gray day which said firmly that we had enjoyed Indian summer quite enough, thank you.

Father Devlin returned with three pots of tea, a plate of English raisin muffins, a nice American substitute for scones, butter, and strawberry jam. Nuala did the honors of pouring the tea. The priest dipped his finger in the strawberry jam, raised an eyebrow at my wife, who nodded with a smile, and offered the finger to our uneasy little daughter. She licked his finger eagerly and smiled contentedly.

"Better get your finger out quickly," I warned, "the lass is teething."

We all laughed, the child included. She continued to

lick her lips lest she miss the smallest dab of precious sweetness.

Nuala buttered a muffin, soaked it in strawberry jam, not as good as raspberry, but still acceptable, and then placed it in my mouth, as priests did with Eucharist for those people who still want it on their tongues. She smiled at me, her smile a winsome mix of affection, love, and desire. My heart melted, my stomach became tight, my loins stirred.

"Would there be any memory in the parish," she asked cautiously, paying no attention to my abject surrender, "of a terrible shipwreck a hundred years ago on an Ancient Order of Hibernians excursion?"

The young priest frowned. "I'm not from the neighborhood, Nuala, and I haven't had time to read up on its history. I can't recall any story about a shipwreck. I do know that in those days some of the Hibernians, not all, were into things a little more violent than keeping gays and lesbians out of St. Patrick's Day parades in New York City."

"A touch of the nationalist in them?"

"The idea was that other Americans would accept us only when we had a country of our own. So Ireland had to be free before we would be respected."

"And Ireland is free," I added, "and they, whoever they are, still don't respect us."

We all laughed. So did Nelliecoyne, who thought she was part of the story. Which, come to think of it, she was.

"So some money from the people of the parish," the priest said, "undoubtedly went to the IRA or whatever they called themselves in those days."

Nuala plopped another muffin into my mouth, with the same alluring smile, which produced the same reaction. A beautiful woman and an English muffin dense with strawberry jam—who could ask for more? Well, it would be better with raspberry jam.

"That's all over now?" I asked.

He shrugged. "Pretty much. There are still some old-timers, immigrants from the 1920s or their children, who think that Gerry Adams is a traitor."

"It's easy to be a militant when the shooting is on the other side of the ocean."

"Over a hundred people from the parish died in the wreck," Nuala said softly. "Mostly young people."

"Really! Let me check our records. Everything is on microfilm now."

Nuala handed our daughter over to me and peered over the priest's shoulder as he fit the microfiches into the viewer.

"Nope, that's 1899.... Let's see.... Here we are. 1898. Two kids killed in the Spanish-American War.... Gosh, look at all these names!"

He turned the viewer knob up.

"Look at that one!" Nuala exclaimed. "Agnes Mary Elizabeth Doolan! Born March 15, 1898. Seven months old!"

Nelliecoyne had taken possession of my finger and was biting on it. The name of the child who drowned in the Lake meant nothing to her, but then, why would it?

"4615 South Emerald! That's Bob Gomez's house ... Dr. Robert Gomez, chairman of our parish finance committee and Chief of Service at Mercy Medical Center!"

"Can we learn the names of her parents?"

"Sure, if she was baptized in the parish.... Where's the Baptism records for that year? ... March 1898 ... Here she is—Father: Thomas Ignatius Doolan; Mother: Mary Louise Collins."

"Neither one of them was on the funeral list," Nuala said confidently, as if she had memorized the list. "They lost their daughter but both of them survived."

"With terrible guilt for the rest of their lives," the priest said with a heavy sigh. "Can't get away from that ... Yep, here's their marriage record. March 15, 1897. Poor little Agnes was born exactly twelve months after their marriage."

"He was twenty-seven and she was twenty-two," Nuala observed.

"A little young for Irish marriages in those days," I mused.

"He must have been well-to-do to own that big house on Emerald. Best place in the neighborhood, even today. Bob did a lot of restoration on it."

"Both baptized here in the parish," I said.

"Anything more?" Father Devlin asked gently.

Nuala seemed thousands of miles away from Canaryville.

"Nuala?"

"What terrible heartache for them all," she said, taking our seven-month-old away from me.

Nelliecoyne was upset to lose my finger.

"By now God has long since wiped away all the tears," the priest said softly.

"We have to believe that, don't we, Father?" I said as I put my finger back into the little brat's mouth.

"Dermot Michael, isn't there a teething ring in me purse?"

We thanked Father Devlin for his help. He didn't seem to want to know what we were looking for. Perhaps George the Priest had conveyed the implication that I was working on a novel.

In the Mercedes I changed the little monster's diaper, a work which required some serious contortions. Nuala was deep in thought. Or deep into something. When I was finished with the kid's mess, Nuala strapped her into the car seat, checking three times to make sure everything was attached properly.

"Let's drive by that house," I suggested.

Since Nuala didn't object, I drove over to Emerald. As I turned off 45th Street onto Emerald, the child began to wail, just as she had at Grand Beach.

4615 was a big Victorian house with a vast front porch, turrets, bow windows, and stained glass on the third floor. The paint was light blue with dark blue trim.

The lawns and bushes around it neat and trim. I reflected that it probably looked better than it had a hundred years ago.

There was not much time for reflection. Nelliecoyne went ballistic! She screamed, she cried, she shouted as if someone had stuck a pin into her.

"Dermot, let's get out of here!" Nuala begged.

We did.

The sun is going down in the deep blue sea
So close your eyes, go to sleep
I'll wrap all the milk stars around you
So dream and your dreams will come true
You can ride past the winds as a champion
   mare
O'er the moors lighter than air
You can fly to the moon as a great white swan
And back you will be before dawn.

Only when we passed the spires of Old St. Patrick's Church, looming over the Expressway like a mild and smiling angel, did Nelliecoyne calm down.

12

"YOU'RE INTERESTED in the ghosts in my house!" Dr. Roberto Gomez greeted me as I walked into his office at the Mercy Medical Center. "Well, if my grandmother is to be believed, there's a lot of them there!"

"I'm more interested in research on the history of Canaryville," I replied, wondering exactly what my father had told Gomez and how my old fellow knew that Nuala and I were out hunting ghosts.

"We are not experts in the spirits," Dr. Gomez said, waving me into a chair across the coffee table where he sat down. "My wife and I are actually skeptics on that subject, as are my kids, though I think my youngest daughter might be a little sensitive to them. Grandma, who lives with us, says the ghosts are there. Nobody argues with Grandma."

Roberto Gomez, MD, Chief of Staff at Mercy Hospital and Medical Center, was a handsome man with dark skin, neatly trimmed mustache, thick black hair, and gleaming white teeth. He looked more like an accomplished diplomat than a hotshot surgeon. He also talked a very diplomatic line.

"When your father said you've been doing research on our street, I told him I'd be happy to tell you the little I know. Your father was the best teacher I had in medical school and if it wasn't for him, I don't think I would ever have made it. And there's a hell of a lot of other people that would tell you the same thing."

"Even his children think the old fellow is special," I agreed. "It took us a long time to figure that out, however."

"We all owe him a lot and I am sure that there's a couple of dozen doctors in Chicago who would give you an interview on the strength of a phone call from Dr. Coyne."

"It's interesting, isn't it, Dr. Gomez," I said, "that you live in Canaryville instead of Beverly, or Palos or Burr Ridge or one of those places?"

He laughed easily.

"I grew up in Canaryville," he said. "I always dreamed of coming back here and raising my children. It's a wonderful neighborhood and it's always been open to people that are different. I was one of the few Mexicans in St. Gabriel's when I was growing up, but nobody ever gave me any problem. We even have some African Americans in the parish now. Canaryville is what it always was, a mixture of many different social classes, and now we have the yuppies moving in too. It's a neighborhood, and it's a real neighborhood!"

"I'm especially interested in the Irish radicals who lived in Canaryville back in the turn of the century," I said, very pointedly pushing him to the subject of our investigation.

I had driven my wife and daughter home after our encounter with the spirits on Emerald Avenue. Nuala had crooned lullabies all the way home, but they had little effect. Nelliecoyne had stopped screaming, but she was still in an angry mood. Inside our house on Southport, she rejected her mother's nipple, a rare event. I had phoned my father about Dr. Gomez. He called back a few minutes later to tell me that I could see the doctor in about a half hour.

"Go see him, Dermot Michael. This little tiger will calm down when she's a mind to."

So I had driven back to the South Side.

"Supporters of the Irish Republican Army and other such groups?" Dr. Gomez asked me.

"The way I understand it there was a family named Doolan who lived in your house back at that time who were very active in the radical wing of the Ancient Order of Hibernians. It's their story I'd particularly like to unearth."

"The Doolans lived in that house for more than a hundred years," he replied. "I bought it from one of the great-grandchildren who was moving out to Beverly because he didn't like the class of people, as he put it, who were moving into the neighborhood. He and his parents had become conservative Republicans, which I suppose is what happens to Irish revolutionaries after a couple of generations."

"Are the ghosts in your house Irish?" I asked, changing the subject ever so slightly.

"What else would they be?" The doctor laughed. "They're benign ghosts, at least that's what Grandma says, very friendly, very nice to have around. One of them seems to be a bright little girl. I have been afraid to look up the family history to see who that bright little girl might be, although old Tom Doolan was always kind of a man of mystery. People seemed to be scared of him."

"I thought you didn't believe in ghosts?"

"I don't really believe in them but you never know, do you, Dermot?"

"No," I said flatly, "you never do know."

"How would you explain these phenomena?"

"Me? I don't know—maybe psychic vibrations that remain from the past, kind of hanging around the place where these experiences were originally felt."

That was the little Bishop's very reasonable explanation of the phenomena. It was as far as I wanted to go to try and explain any of the stuff that happens to my wife.

"Well," Dr. Gomez went on, "it is certainly true that the people that lived in the house for a couple of generations were ardent Irish patriots. They raised money for the Fenians and the Irish Republican Brotherhood and the Irish Volunteers and even up to the time Ireland finally won its independence—when was it . . . 1923, something like that?"

"About that," I agreed.

"Then they all kind of lost interest in it and like I say the family just got into becoming very conservative American Republicans."

"It's a very conservative neighborhood these days, isn't it?" I asked.

"It's a hard neighborhood to figure out, Dermot, but they vote Democratic in the local elections and I suspect most of us still vote Democratic in the national elections. Many of the folks are not too happy about the few African Americans that have moved in but as one old Mick said to me, I'd sooner have them than these damn smart-assed yuppies."

"People like me?"

"No son of Doc Coyne will ever be a smart-mouth yuppie!"

Like I said, the man was a diplomat.

"The family is all scattered now?" I asked.

"I suppose so. A lot of people moved out of the neighborhood and we're into what, the fourth or fifth generation of that family."

"Is there anybody around Chicago that might have some of the documentation from the past?"

Dr. Gomez stirred uneasily. "Well, I suppose the best one would be Colleen Kavanagh, the daughter of the man I bought the house from, that is if she could find time to talk to you."

"Colleen Kavanagh?"

"She's the daughter of the last Doolan that lived in the house, the one I bought it from. Her husband is Dr. Kavanagh, who is quite famous as a neurologist out on the South Side. He's at Little Company of Mary Hospital."

"Seems to me that I've heard of the South Side. It's sort of anyplace south of Comisky Park, isn't it?"

Dr. Gomez laughed, a rich knowing laugh.

"I understand there are rivalries between the South Side Irish and the West Side Irish and if I had to choose I wouldn't. Colleen Kavanagh and her husband Patrick Kavanagh live in Beverly, for which I say God forgive them and that they could just as well have moved into Canaryville. She's a very busy woman and active in all kinds of boards and committees, Lyric Opera, Art Institute, Chicago Symphony, and doing much good around town. However, like I say, she is very, very busy."

"Somebody from Beverly that knows there's a Lyric Opera and an Art Institute and a Chicago Symphony?"

The doctor laughed again. "You are not going to get me into that argument, Dermot Coyne. I think if you call Colleen Kavanagh and ask her for an appointment she'd be happy to fit you into her schedule sometime next month. I suspect she might think any such thing as records from the past is not particularly important. She's not one of those Irish who have any sense of concern for history. If it's not good enough to be done in the present, she doesn't want to know anything about it. Still Patrick might be able to persuade her to talk to you because he's an admirer of your father too."

"Yes, I'll have to see if he's got clout," I said thoughtfully. "That house fascinates me."

"Well, it's a wonderful place to live. We've done quite a bit but maintained much of the old charm. We'd be delighted to have you and your wife, who is a wonderful singer by the way, over for dinner some night."

"That's an invitation I might take you up on."

I wondered as I said it what would happen if Nuala had one of her psychic experiences inside Roberto Gomez's house. Whatever the situation we would not bring Nellie along with us because she would certainly freak out and how would we explain that?

I thanked Dr. Gomez for his help and took my leave. In the Mercedes pulling out of the Mercy Hospital parking lot, I pondered over the whole crazy business. We were supposed to solve a mystery and we didn't even know what the mystery was. Well, I knew that would happen before I married the woman.

Nuala and I live a very low-key life financially. The Mercedes is fifteen years old. We live in an old house on Southport Avenue, a refurbished post–Civil War, two-story wooden "A" frame. Nuala buys all her clothes at marked-down prices—and with an unerring instinct about what will look good on her. We belong to a tennis club but not a golf club and we don't have a house at Grand Beach—although we use my parents' memberships in a couple of clubs for golf and we borrow their house at Grand Beach. I have money from my mistakes in the commodity markets and make something off my novels and Nuala makes a lot off her songs, but most of that we either stash away or invest in our children's future.

A lot of people are nervous that I don't seem to do much work and it looks like Nuala is supporting the family. We're both frugal, Nuala by disposition and background and myself because spending a lot of money or spending it conspicuously is just too exhausting for me to bother with it.

I had scarcely turned on the ignition when the phone rang. It was Nuala in tears.

"Oh, Dermot love, haven't I done a terrible thing. Won't you be angry at me for ever and ever! Am I not just the most awful woman in all the world!"

All this must be translated as saying, "I expect you, Dermot Michael Coyne, to agree with everything I've done."

"Maybelline call again?"

"So isn't she just the most horrible woman and didn't I tell her that I never want to speak to her again and if she ever called me I'd hang up and she just laughed and laughed and laughed and said I couldn't give up my curiosity to hang up on her!"

"What did she have to say this time?"

"Didn't she say that our poor little Nellie was almost an alcoholic!"

"What!" I said.

"She said that the Irish habit of giving kids a little bit of whiskey to calm them down was pernicious because recent studies had shown that children who are given alcohol for such purposes are much more likely to be alcoholics when they grow up!"

"Maybelline and her studies!"

"Dermot, that isn't true, is it?"

"I never knew Maybelline to have a study right and I'm sure, Nuala, she's got this one wrong too."

"Well, that's what I told her and I said I didn't want to ever talk to her again and she just laughed and hung up on me!"

"What's this business about giving Nellie whiskey to keep her quiet?"

"Dermot Michael, I never did it, I never did it. I never even think of it. My mother never did it and I'd never do it either!"

"I know that, Nuala. I'm absolutely sure you wouldn't do it. But what made her think you did?"

"Didn't your man put it in his column this week!"

"Farmer!"

"Sure, he said it was the way all the Irish kept their kids quiet at night and that's why there is so much Irish alcoholism. We're not a heavy drinking people, are we, Dermot Michael?"

"Ireland has the lowest per capita alcohol consumption in Europe. Nuala, you know that."

"Well, what am I going to do?" She was sobbing again.

"About Farmer?"

"No, Dermot Michael, about your poor sister-in-law. I was so terribly rude to her!"

"You do exactly what you said, every time she calls you hang up on her."

"Dermot love, I could never do that!"

"Of course you could."

Nuala was a very courteous young woman, she couldn't hang up on anybody. Unless she was told to.

"Nuala Anne, that's an order and you can blame me. The next time she tries to harass us about Nelliecoyne you tell her that I've told you that you should hang up on her and that you always do what I say."

Nuala's sobs turned into a giggle.

"Don't I always do what you tell me to do, Dermot Michael?"

"Well, you certainly do it when it suits your own plans as it does this time. You just tell her to go away and we don't want to have anything to do with her. Tell her that's what I've told you to say, which indeed is what I've just done."

"Haven't you now, Dermot Michael!"

Now laughing instead of crying, Nuala hung up. I turned off South Park onto the Stevenson absolutely furious. Something had to be done about this terrible woman. I simply could not permit her to harass my wife and my child the way she seemed bent on doing. I punched in the old fellow's number.

"Dr. Coyne."

The usual calm, cheerful, reassuring voice.

"Dermot," I said firmly.

"Did you have a nice interview with Dr. Gomez, Dermot?"

"Very nice, Dad. He was very helpful. And now it would appear that I have to talk for a while to a Colleen Kavanagh."

"Patrick Kavanagh's wife?"

"The very same."

"I'm not sure, Dermot," he said cautiously, "whether

I have that kind of clout. With Patrick certainly, but with Colleen? She's so busy doing so many good things I don't know whether she has time to talk to anybody, even to her husband."

That was about as close to uncharitableness as my father or my mother ever came.

"Well, see what you can do. I really have to see her soon."

"I'll try," he said dubiously.

"And one more thing, Dad, something has to be done about Maybelline. She is harassing Nuala constantly. I don't like it and I want it to stop."

"Dermot," he said with a sigh, "she's done that to everybody else and we just got used to it. The woman has a good heart and she means well. Jeff loves her and she's wonderful with her children."

It was surely true that my brother loved her. The kids, however, were creeps, but perhaps not incorrigible creeps.

"Dad, she doesn't have a good heart and she doesn't mean well. She's a mean, vicious bitch and I am not going to tolerate her messing in my family life."

"Dermot," he said reprovingly, "we've been through this with all the others and there's just no way to stop her. She's awfully good to Jeff and we have to support him."

"Dad, he's a psychiatrist, he should recognize the syndrome that he's dealing with."

"Psychiatrists can't deal with their own problems, Dermot, any more than surgeons can operate on themselves."

That was a wise statement, it was also irrelevant to the topic under discussion.

"Look, Dad, let me be blunt. Either the family finds some way to get Maybelline off Nuala's back or we're going to secede and I'll have nothing to do with her or anyone else in the family."

"Dermot!" Dad gasped.

Well he might gasp. His youngest son was a sweet, gentle young man who almost never lost his temper. Now he had lost it completely.

"It's just this simple, Dad. If the family has to choose between Maybelline and Nuala—and I'm saying it does—and it chooses Maybelline, then Nuala is out of the picture and so is her daughter and her husband. My mind is made up and I'm not prepared to compromise!"

The Adversary intervened.

YOU'RE OUT OF YOUR MIND, DERMOT. WHY IN THE WORLD ARE YOU CREATING A FAMILY CRISIS LIKE THAT? YOU DON'T HAVE THE GUTS TO STICK IT OUT.

I ignored the Adversary as I was doing, it seemed, with increasing frequency these days. "Dad, I'm sorry to create a crisis but I'm not going to put up with that woman. She damn well better leave my wife alone."

"Well," my father sighed sadly, "I'll have to talk to your mother and see what we can do about it. But, Dermot, this is a terrible thing to do to the family."

"Dad, Maybelline is doing terrible things to Nuala and it has to stop."

After we had hung up I thought about what the family would do next. Dad would call Mom and Mom would be more flustered and disturbed than he was, and then Mom would call Cindy, and Cindy would be assigned to call me to calm me down. Well, I'd make it clear to Cindy beforehand that I wasn't in a mood to be calmed down. So I pushed her number on the telephone as I worked my way north on the Dan Ryan. "Cynthia Hurley," she said brightly as though she were a switchboard operator at a very prestigious Loop law firm instead of a senior partner.

"Dermot," I said grimly.

"Oh, hi, Dermot, look, I don't think we should worry about Farmer. He's crazy, everybody knows he's crazy. He's like that guy who writes for the *Trib*, a professional hater. If we react to him we are just going to give him more publicity, he's going to wither on the vine of his own viciousness. The TV people are already uneasy about him. Just let him run his course and I don't think he's going to do us any harm."

That was sound legal advice but as it would turn out, however, it would not be that easy. Not at all, at all, as my wife would have said.

"I'm not talking about Nick Farmer," I said tersely. "I'm talking about that bitch Maybelline."

"Dermot!" Cynthia said in surprise. "What terrible language to use about your poor sister-in-law!"

"Poor sister-in-law be damned, Cindy, she's a bitch. She's making my wife's life miserable and I'm not going to tolerate it."

"Dermot!"

"I want to make my position clear to you, Cindy, and to everybody else in the family. Either you folks get Maybelline out of our hair or I'm going to get Nuala out of the family. You can make your choice, it's Maybelline or Nuala. You can't have both."

"Dermot Michael Coyne, that's an outrageous statement. There's no way we can negotiate a compromise at all. You can't possibly take such a position. Moreover, I don't think you'd stick to such a position for long."

For a moment I seethed silently and then I said in the coldest tone of voice I could produce, "Cindy, listen very carefully to what I say. Unless Maybelline leaves Nuala alone we are going to secede from the family. I don't want to do that and Nuala doesn't want to either, but I don't want her sobbing every day when Maybelline makes one of her sickeningly vicious phone calls. Is that clear?"

Cindy hesitated.

"Dermot, she makes those phone calls to everyone."

"She may make them to everyone, Cindy. She's not going to make them to Nuala anymore. And Nuala and I aren't coming to any family gatherings where that woman is present. And don't look for room for negotiation because this isn't a legal matter. It's a matter of

protecting my wife and my daughter and I am not prepared to negotiate that."

Again Cindy was silent. Good lawyer that she was,
she was always looking for room for settlement. I had
presented her with the kind of issue in which there didn't
seem to be any room for settlement.

"Dermot, I'm going to have to think this over. But
it's a very, very serious matter."

"Of course it's a serious matter. My wife's peace of
mind is a serious matter. Nuala is a very fragile and
vulnerable young woman, as you know, a shy, proud
creature from the West of Ireland despite all the other
masks she wears. Maybelline is trying to break her heart
and I'm not going to let her do it."

"I'll have to think about it, Dermot, but I don't like
ultimatums."

I drove by the Old St. Patrick's Church towering over
the Expressway with the Loop towers standing respectfully behind it. Church! One more phone call to make.
I pushed in another number.

"Holy Name Cathedral Rectory!" a teenage womanly
voice announced cheerfully.

"Hi, Megan, it's Dermot."

"Oh, Mr. Coyne, how are you? How's Nuala? How's
that gorgeous little daughter of yours?"

Megan was one of the porter persons who, with great
charm and marvelous efficiency, managed access to the
Cathedral Rectory after school hours. There were actually four Megans who worked at the rectory—an
African-American Megan, a Korean-American Megan, a
Latino-American Megan, and an Irish-American Megan.
I couldn't distinguish among their voices but it was still
safe to say hi to Megan. All the Megans, however, insisted on calling me Mr. Coyne and my wife Nuala. That
was because I was real old and Nuala was still almost a
teenager like themselves. Five years make that much difference?

"Do you want to talk to Father George? He's in and

I'll buzz him, but he's terribly busy, Mr. Coyne, so don't take too much of his time."

"Yes, Megan."

Busy indeed!

"George Coyne," my brother the priest announced with brief, brisk efficiency.

"George, Dermot."

"You sound upset, Dermot," he replied.

"Not bad, George."

"I know you pretty well, Little Brother. Maybelline is it?"

Cindy could not have got to him so soon. George had guessed.

"She is a vicious, insensitive, nasty bitch."

"I quite agree."

"Something has to be done to stop her."

"You're absolutely right."

"I will not have her reducing my wife to tears every day."

"If I were in your position, I wouldn't either."

"Nor will I tolerate her saying nasty things about my daughter."

"How could anybody say nasty things about such a sweet little redhead."

"George, I'm serious. Unless the family can shut her up, Nuala and I are going to secede."

"Bravo! I'll secede with you."

"George, I am perfectly serious."

"Dermot, you're not listening to me. I've been telling you, or trying to tell you, that I'm on your side. For her own good Maybelline has to be stopped, but even if it doesn't help her, it's going to help not only Nuala but all the rest of us. She's getting worse every year."

"Are you saying you're on my side?"

George the Priest sighed loudly. "That's exactly what I'm saying, Dermot. Am I the first one you've talked to?"

"No, I talked to Dad first."

"That was inept."

"I guess so. There's no way he could deal with the problem."

"Then who did you call?"

"Cindy."

"Much wiser. She's the one who's going to have to drag the family into a solution on the subject of Maybelline. She'll want to come up with a negotiated settlement. We're not going to accept a negotiated settlement, Dermot. We're going to precipitate a full-scale family crisis and they're going to have to do something finally with their Maybelline problem. They've done nobody any favors by letting her get away with her little terrorist attacks on people."

Terrorist—that's what she was.

"So what do we do?"

"What you mean is what do you and I and Nuala do?"

So George had dealt himself into the conflict. I felt that somehow or the other, he had edged off the top of the mountain.

"Exactly."

"We'll wait and see what happens, Little Brother. We'll let them worry about it for a while. Cindy will almost certainly be on the phone in a few minutes. I'll tell her that I'm on your side. That will really make the crisis serious."

"OK."

"Don't worry about it, Little Brother, we're going to win this one. And we're going to win it not because you and I are involved, they can do without us, but the family worships Nuala and they've already fallen in love with your daughter. They'll do anything to keep those two women in the fold."

I hadn't thought about it in those terms. But then I wouldn't think about it in those terms. Now all I had to do was to cool this crisis that I had created and which George was abetting.

It would, I suddenly realized, reduce Nuala to tears

again. She wouldn't want to create problems in the family. Well, she hadn't.

TRY TELLING THAT TO HER.

When I turned off the Kennedy Expressway at Fullerton, rain was falling, a light rain at first but the kind of Chicago rain that you know is a harbinger of a major rainstorm, maybe even a thunderstorm. I drove east on Fullerton a few blocks and then turned south on Southport, the street on which we lived. Despite the rain it was like driving through a Gothic cathedral. The huge old trees still clung to most of their orange and red and gold leaves. Even without sunlight there was an air of reverence about the street. One sensed that holiness lurked just around the corner.

The homes on Southport were larger and more solid than the homes in Canaryville, a sometime dwelling place for different ethnic immigrants than Canaryville—Swedes, Germans, and Poles. Our own house was the rare wooden house in the street. Over 125 years old, it was in the area west of DePaul University, where Lincoln Park West petered out as it approached the Chicago River. The huge Polish Church of St. Josephat, across the street from us, presided over the block with aloof Slavic charm.

"Our house," Nuala always boasted, "is the prettiest house on the block, even if it is the oldest."

She could have added that it had the best electricity and plumbing on the street too. However, in its soft gray paint with white and blue trim, it was indeed the most attractive home on the street.

I pulled up to our parking place with a sigh of relief. I had been away from my wife and daughter for several hours and I missed them.

—13—

NO ONE heard me come in. Four females, one canine and three human, were playing on the floor. The canine wore her usual white coat, the three humans were wearing the standard issue of jeans and sweatshirts, my daughter a red and black Chicago Bulls shirt, just like her mother's. Nessa's proclaimed that she was from DePaul University.

None of them paid any attention to me. The focus of attention rather was my daughter's attempts, sometimes more successful than others, to sit up. They laughed, herself included when she succeeded, and they laughed again, herself once more, when she failed. Only Fiona took notice of the return of the man of the house and then only perfunctorily. She ambled over to me for a quick pat on her huge head and then returned to the game.

"Oh, Mr. Coyne," Nessa exclaimed finally, "isn't your daughter the most darlin' baby in all the world, totally brilliant!"

Nessa, a graduate student in education at DePaul, was a combination mother's helper and baby-sitter. Like Nuala she was from County Galway and spoke Irish. A cute and very vivacious little blonde, she was studying for her Ph.D. in some kind of remedial education. She and

Nuala always referred to it, as was proper in Irish English, as her P. Haitch D.

She was on retainer in her role because Nuala had insisted that the "poor child" (three years older than my wife) needed the money and she'd never earn enough money if she came only when we needed help or a babysitter. She was, I thought, worth all we paid her and more because she was a sounding board for my wife of the same gender and background. They had become thick as thieves and were constantly, I suspected, plotting against me.

Moreover, Nessa always insisted that I was either "Mr. Coyne" or "Sir."

" 'Tis because you're so solid and reliable," Nuala reassured me.

I doubted that.

"Nuala and I were just having some fun with your daughter, sir," Nessa said. "I think she's the happiest baby in all the world!"

"She apparently inherited that from her mother," I said with just a touch of irony in my voice.

I told everybody that I was an old man and Nuala was an only child.

My daughter rolled over and sat up as if to say, "See, I showed you what I could do."

Then she fell back on the floor, rolled over again, and tried desperately to crawl.

"She's going to make it, Dermot Michael, one of these days you're going to come home and your daughter is going to crawl across the floor to you, and then won't you have a grand feeling altogether!"

"The happiest baby in all the world."

"Isn't she now?"

Nobody asked me to sit down but I did. Moreover, I picked up my daughter and held her on my lap, a position in which she seemed quite content to lie.

"Nuala, would you ever like to visit a bar tonight for an hour or so?"

"The one down the street?" she asked.

"No, on 44th Street. It's called Michael's Bar and Tap."

"Why would I ever want to go there, Dermot Michael?" she asked suspiciously.

"I gather it's a bar where some of the old-time Irish revolutionaries gather at night. Perhaps we could pick up some of the folklore about our friends, the Doolans."

"Go on, Nuala," Nessa said. "It'd be good for you to get away for a couple of hours. It'd be good for your daughter too."

"You just want to play with her by yourself," Nuala said, somewhat petulantly.

"Give over," Nessa said with a laugh, "you need a night out and don't give me any new excuses."

"Well, maybe you're right."

"After I make a dish of pasta for supper," I said.

"I could bring over my homework and finish it off. Nelliecoyne won't be nearly as much a distraction as that amadon Seamus Lynch."

Seamus was an alleged boyfriend about whom we heard occasionally but never saw.

"I don't know." Nuala, eyes downcast, hesitated.

"Sure, won't it be good to get away for a little while?"

"If you think it would be all right, Dermot Michael?"

"I do indeed."

The tension around her eyes broke my heart.

"Well . . ."

" 'Tis all settled then. I'll come over right after supper."

"I'll ask Mr. Forest to pick you up."

"You don't have to do that, sir."

"Yes, I do."

Mr. Forest was our own personal taxi driver.

Fiona joined me and my daughter and rested her large muzzle on my knee.

My wife came over and kissed me on the forehead.

"All right, Dermot Michael, I'll go to your bar on 44th

Street but only for an hour, no more than that, do you understand?"

"An hour and a half," I said.

YOU AND YOUR BROTHER ARE BOTH ASSHOLES, THERE'S NOTHING IN THE WORLD NUALA CAN'T HANDLE. SHE CAN TAKE CARE OF THAT CRAZY SISTER-IN-LAW OF YOURS WITHOUT YOU GUYS CREATING A FAMILY CRISIS.

"She's a fragile child."

BULLSHIT, DERMOT MICHAEL. SHE CAN BE ANYBODY SHE WANTS TO BE. SHE CAN DEAL WITH THAT WOMAN WITHOUT ANY OF YOUR HELP.

The Adversary is usually wrong, but he represents a dimension in myself or I wouldn't be hearing him. This time I was afraid he was right.

While I prepared our lasagna, I explained to my wife what I had learned from Dr. Gomez.

"I don't ever want to go into that house, Dermot Michael," she said firmly.

"I don't know that we'll ever have to."

"That will be as may be," she said ominously.

After we had disposed of the pasta and washed the dishes and Mr. Forest had brought Nessa back, Nuala and I departed for Canaryville. My wife was very tense at the prospect of leaving our child alone—that meant alone with Nessa. Nuala fed her properly, indeed tried to force more of her milk on the child than she wanted. Then, by using a torture instrument that I despised called a breast pump, we obtained a bottle of mother's milk and put it in the refrigerator. Finally my wife secreted in her purse a small portable phone so she could call home immediately without having to wait for me to dial the number on the car phone. So, prepared for all eventualities, off we went with the tension around Nuala's eyes as grim as I had ever seen it.

By now the rain was pouring, so she put a trench coat on over her Chicago Bulls jersey. The two of us looked like a pair of yuppies who might very well not be wel-

comed in Michael's Bar and Tap. So we'd have to play
the game of being good yuppies. We had hardly turned
off Fullerton and onto the Kennedy Expressway when
Nuala pulled out her phone and, like E.T., called home.
She babbled in Irish for some minutes, sighed, and
closed the phone and returned it to her purse.

"Well, the little brat is sound asleep, Dermot," she
said. "She doesn't seem to miss her mother and father
at all."

"That's the way kids are."

She sighed in agreement.

Then after a long pause she shook her head and said,
"Dermot Michael, you know something strange happened in front of that house on Emerald today."

"Oh?"

"I mean, why did our Nellie feel so angry?"

"I don't know. Did you sense anything there?"

"Only vague and distant emotions, Dermot. Conflict,
tension, anger, terrible anger, and then it all kind of
turned off, if you take my meaning."

"What was so strange about Nelliecoyne's anger—I
mean strange even granted that she's fey on both sides
of her family?"

"Well, it was just like the one at the Lake, wasn't it
now?"

"It was."

"I thought the anger was at the death of poor little
Agnes Mary Elizabeth Doolan, didn't you?"

"You mean at the Lake?"

"Yes, because the poor little tyke probably drowned
right opposite your parents' house?"

"Probably."

"But then why would Nellie go into a rage at 4615
Emerald? Agnes Doolan wasn't there, Dermot, don't you
see? I mean, she died on the Lake. So there would be
no memory of her being at the house. Her mother's pain
and her father's pain would be but not Agnes's."

I couldn't help myself—I shivered.

"Nuala, that's scary!"

"It's always scary, Dermot, but this one is more than just scary, it's odd."

As far as I was concerned the whole business was odd but I didn't think it wise to say that.

"And we don't even know the mystery we're supposed to solve, do we?" she went on.

"The only mystery we know about is the mystery of why Nelliecoyne grew angry those two nights at Grand Beach and even more angry when we passed the Doolan house this morning. And of course the mystery why both of you saw the ships that have been underneath the waters of Lake Michigan for one hundred years."

"Well, didn't the schooner survive a little longer?"

"That's true."

My conversation trailed off. Nuala made one more phone call and reported to me that the child was still asleep. I expressed some surprise at such good behavior.

"Isn't she the best baby in all the world?"

"You'll get no disagreement with me on that, Nuala dear."

Then she changed the subject abruptly.

"I'm worried about Nessa."

"Uh?"

I suspected that this was one of those times when it is the husband's role to listen very carefully, not to what his wife is saying, but to what she means. It was a knack that I was in the process of developing. I'd improved at it but I doubted I'd ever be adequate to the challenge.

"Well, isn't her young man Seamus the problem now?"

"Is she living with Seamus?"

"Dermot Michael Coyne, that's none of our business. But, no, she's not living with him. I won't go so far as to say that she doesn't sleep with him, however."

I waited for a further explanation of that. But none was forthcoming, so I asked, "Is she in love?"

"Oh, Dermot, she's in love with him all right, but isn't that the problem now?"

"She shouldn't be in love with him?"

"Don't be an eejit, Dermot Michael Coyne, of course she should be in love with him. Isn't she a wonderful girl and he a wonderful fella?"

"Indeed."

"The problem is that she is not in love with a painter, I mean a house painter, not one of your artist type painters."

"Ah," I said.

"Do you understand now, Dermot Michael?" she asked with a great show of patience.

I tried.

"Herself doesn't know whether she should marry somebody who has much less education than she has?"

"Haven't I been saying that all along? I wouldn't say she's a snob exactly. Because she's not, she's a very nice young woman. And she's very much in love. But she wonders about the social class difference between them. Isn't that a terrible thing to worry about, Dermot Michael Coyne?"

"It never bothered you to fall in love with a rich man's son!"

Nuala thought that was hilariously funny.

"And himself rich too. But only because he'd been lucky. You know, Dermot, I don't believe at all, at all in this social class stuff. Yet she has a very good point. It would be more of a point if Seamus wasn't so eager to read books and go to art museums and concerts and even operas. To tell you the truth, even though he doesn't have a Ph.D. and will never have one, he still has better taste than she does."

"Are they going to stay in Chicago?"

"Och, there's not a chance of that. They're both in love with the County Galway and doesn't he have to go back and take over his family's construction company? He's going to end up a rich man."

"And himself with no education other than from high school?"

"So that's the problem. Don't you see?"

"I do indeed."

But I didn't see what we were supposed to do about it.

"Well now, don't you think we ought to do something about it?"

Nuala Anne felt we'd better do something about it so that meant I ought to think we might do something about it.

"Like what?"

"Dermot Michael Coyne, don't be an eejit! Shouldn't we invite them both over for dinner one night so you and I can get to know Seamus better?"

"So we can judge whether he really is right for her?"

"You're still talking like an eejit, Dermot Michael Coyne!"

"I am?"

"We know he's good enough for her, we've just got to confirm that, Dermot, don't you see?"

Finally, yes indeed, I did see. Nuala was merely asking whether it would be all right to invite Seamus and Nessa over for supper one night.

"Won't I make my Hungarian goulash for them!"

"Ah, Dermot Michael Coyne, you're the most wonderful husband in all the world!"

I had to agree that I was.

After yet another call home as we turned off the Expressway at 43rd Street, Nuala began to relax a little bit.

"You know, Dermot Michael, the child doesn't seem to mind us going out at all, at all."

"As long as she has a full stomach and a dry diaper and Fiona and Nessa to adore her, why does she need us?"

Nuala giggled and slapped me very lightly on the arm as she might slap Fiona, if the wondrous canine had misbehaved slightly.

As bright and lively as Canaryville had seemed earlier in the day, it was now dark and strange. Most neighborhoods in Chicago look mysterious on rainy autumn nights with sheets of rain falling against the windshield of the car and the soggy tree branches hovering over our heads.

We managed to find a parking place near Michael's Bar and Tap and made a dash for the door. When we entered the bar, a dim and dingy place whose walls were lined with pictures of unfamiliar politicians and athletes, all conversation suddenly stopped and every eye in the tavern turned towards us. The room smelled of stale beer, indeed beer that had been stale for decades, maybe a century. My wife and I were the youngest people in the bar by a good thirty-five years.

We took off our raincoats, sat at a small, unstable table near the doorway, and began to chat softly. The bartender wandered over and asked us what we'd like to drink. Nuala ordered a diet cola—no alcohol in her mother's milk—and I asked for a pint of Guinness. The bartender nodded.

"You're newcomers around here, aren't you?"

"I guess so," I said as once more every eye in the place turned towards us.

"Me husband is a writer," Nuala said with her thickest Galaway accent. "And isn't he doing research on all the Chicago neighborhoods? And weren't we here in Canaryville this morning? And didn't we think it was one of the nicest places we'd ever seen—mind you outside of County Galway? And didn't I say to him why don't we come here tonight and find a nice cozy bar and see what the insides of the bars in Canaryville are like?"

"So you're not exactly yuppies?" said the bartender, beginning to warm to us.

"My husband used to work at the commodity exchanges and wasn't he a complete failure there, but like most Irishmen he's a grand storyteller and doesn't he write wonderful stories?"

Suspecting this was a cue for me, I said, "And doesn't herself sing beautiful songs?"

The man's eyes narrowed on us. "Aren't you the woman that sings on the television? Of course you are, what's your name again? Ah, I know, you're Nuala Anne!"

My wife blushed becomingly. "Well, it's wonderful altogether that you recognize a poor child from the Gaeltacht in County Galway and yourself wearing a Chicago Bulls jacket on this cold, rainy night!"

No direct answer to the question, of course, that would indicate a lack of good manners, in County Galway— for cold, rainy nights are even more frequent there than in Chicago.

"Well," said the bartender, "we wouldn't dream of asking you to sing a song for us. Just a minute and I'll get your drinks."

Herself looked happy, knowing full well that once she turned on that kind of charm she was utterly irresistible. I knew it too because she turned it on me once in a bar on the street of Trinity College and periodically turned it on again. Like when she had given me the English muffin covered with strawberry jam earlier in the day.

The bartender brought back my pint of Guinness and her diet cola.

"Would you ever mind if I sing one of my husband's favorite Irish songs? It was the first one he ever heard me singing in a pub in Dublin and the poor man never had a chance after that!"

There was applause, discreet and quiet applause, because this was a discreet and quiet bar.

So Nuala, her eyes filled with love, sang for us all "Molly Malone."

And after enthusiastic applause she sang a couple of lullabies. And then reached for the phone to call home again. It turned out that her daughter astonishingly was still sound asleep.

An elderly couple in their late seventies, tall, handsome people with silver hair and red faces, asked if they could join us. We said we'd be delighted. They were sweet old folks who had to show us pictures of their children, grandchildren, and their one little great-granddaughter. And of course, Nuala pulled out a whole wallet full of pictures of our Nellie. Both our new friends insisted that she was the most beautiful baby they'd ever seen. This was not a falsehood, though maybe a rhetorical exaggeration.

She was, however, one very pretty little girl, even if she had hardly any hair and was fey on both sides of her family.

"You folks are here from Galway are you?" asked the woman.

"Your man is from County Cook. I'm from away out in Connemara," Nuala said. "You've heard of the town of Carraroe."

"Well, we've never been back to Ireland," the man said. "Our parents emigrated you see, they came over after the Troubles and we were born here. Our parents could never go back and didn't want to go back and of course we didn't want to go back either and still don't."

"Ah?" I said casually.

"You see," the man said, going a deep red, "we don't approve of the puppet Free State government in Dublin."

"It's run by a pack of traitors," the woman joined in. "Traitors like Michael Collins, and then after him didn't Eamon De Valera sell us out? And all those other fellows even up to the crowd that's there now."

"But it looks like it's all over," I said, "with the Good Friday Accord and all."

"Gerry Adams," said the man bitterly, "is the worst traitor of them all. That Good Friday agreement put the whole of Ireland once more on the cross of suffering and injustice. How could they possibly have given up a legitimate claim for the six counties under colonial occupation?"

"It'll be another fifty years," the woman said, her lips

thin with anger, "before there's a chance to unite all Ireland as God intended it to be united."

"The Republic is one and indivisible," her husband insisted loudly. "But nobody seems to realize that anymore even up in the occupied territories. It will take a lot more suffering and a lot more violence before the people in Ireland on both sides of the border can come to their senses."

Nuala nodded sympathetically though she thought the IRA were a bunch of eejits and disapproved of terrorists.

"This parish has always supported Irish freedom, hasn't it now?" she said so softly that I had to lean towards her to catch the words. "I can understand why that is, there were so many people leaving Ireland because of the oppression."

Almost every emigrant who came in the 1920s claimed to have a price on their head. Fortunately our new friends didn't make that claim.

"There has always been a lot of support for Ireland in this neighborhood, all the way back to the time of the Fenians," the man said, his voice becoming a little bit calmer. "Most of that died out a long time ago but there's still some of it around. There are still some true Irish patriots in the neighborhood, not very many but more than most people think."

I wouldn't have thought there were many Americans who would be that involved emotionally in a war of terrorism four thousand miles away in a country they had never visited.

Nuala smiled her most demure and charming smile. "It used to be said back in Galway that a long time ago back in the time of the Fenians, even before the Irish Volunteers, there was a lot of money from Chicago coming to support the cause of a free Ireland."

"Aye," said the old man, "there certainly was. The Ancient Order of Hibernians, which are now just a pale imitation of what they used to be, were deeply involved in raising money right here in this neighborhood for the cause of Ireland."

"If it hadn't been for American money, the lads would have never won all the battles against the Brits after the Easter Rising," his wife said bitterly. "Then the Free Staters lost it all for us."

"They collected a lot of money in St. Gabriel's parish," her husband sighed sadly. "It's a shame that our money and many lives were wasted when the Free State government in Dublin sold us out."

"Wasn't there a man named Thomas Doolan that was involved back in those times?" Nuala asked. "I seem to remember hearing his name now and again even out in Carraroe where I lived."

That wasn't altogether true, in fact it wasn't true at all, at all. Nuala had never heard of Thomas Doolan until this morning. But she heard of him during the day in St. Gabriel's rectory and that was probably enough to make her statement reasonably true. I was amazed at how hard she was pressing the angry couple without seeming to press them at all. I kept my mouth shut.

"He was a strange fella, that Tom Doolan," the man said slowly, "himself all puffed up because he was a lawyer and a judge and had a lot of money, most of which he inherited from his own father. He certainly talked a good revolutionary line. But I'm not sure that he was serious. There were a lot of strange rumors about him, let me tell you."

"And his wife," the woman went on. "She was a stuck-up one, so pretty and so proud of herself and so filled with piety and holiness. But there was something a little wrong with her too."

"How awful," Nuala said sympathetically. "For people to pretend to be supporters of Ireland and still to be put up as an example for the rest of us."

"Now mind you, they were never turned out," the man went on, "they were too important and too influential and too rich for the supporters of Ireland to ignore. But a lot of the folks in my parents' generation said that we should never trust them. And so we never did."

"Old Tom Doolan died in 1947," the woman said abruptly, "right after my man came back from the Pacific. I don't quite remember when his wife died. I could never stand the woman."

"It was a few years later," her husband added. "They were both buried with all kinds of ceremony and every crooked Irish politician in Chicago at their wakes and funerals, and the Bishop himself preaching the sermon. It was enough to make one sick to one's stomach because there was something terribly wrong with them."

"Something about money I suppose?" Nuala said.

"It's always about money, isn't it?" the man replied. "But let's not talk about them anymore, let's talk more about the music and your writing and when your next record is coming out."

They were gentle, thoughtful, kindly old people who had a good life in America, who loved their children and their grandchildren greatly, even if some of the grandchildren had moved out to Beverly or even to Burr Ridge or even, God forgive them for it, to the North Side.

Nuala made yet another call home, babbled in Irish, and then said with a happy smile on her face, "Isn't the little girl still sound asleep?"

"Would you ever then sing one more song for us before you go home to her?" the woman asked.

The bartender brought me another glass of Guinness and Nuala another diet cola and she sang several more songs including the granddaddy of all Irish patriotic songs, "The Wearing of the Green."

Later in the car with the rain beating so fiercely against our windows it was hard to see more than three or four car lengths ahead of us, Nuala said, "Weren't they a lovely couple now, Dermot Michael?"

"Are you being ironic?"

"I'm never ironic, Dermot. You know that. They don't believe any of that revolutionary rhetoric and they wouldn't dare to imitate the real revolutionaries. It's just the slogans they learned when they were kids and they can't give them up. Deep down in their hearts they're as happy as anybody about the Good Friday Accord but they're sure it's not going to last."

"Ah," I said. They had seemed like strident, bitter people to me. Nuala Anne, however, was a better judge of people than I was. "We did learn something, however, didn't we now? We learned that the Doolans were leaders in the faction supporting the Fenians and the IRB and the Irish Volunteers and probably the IRA after the Easter Rising. We don't really know which side they were on during the civil war."

"Och, sure we do, Dermot Michael, they were on the side of Michael Collins and the government in Dublin. They were sensible people and they realized that the Brits had given the Irish just about all they could get away with. I don't think that the Doolans were idiots."

I might well have asked how she knew that. But one didn't ask Nuala how she knew things, I just assumed that she did.

"Well, we're making progress of a sort, we know that some kind of a problem is tied up with money?"

"As her man said, isn't it always money . . . I wonder if the cruise a hundred years ago was about money?"

"A benefit for the rebels?"

"It might have been, Dermot Michael."

We were quiet for a few minutes as I concentrated on navigating from the Dan Ryan into the Kennedy Expressway.

"Nuala, do you remember when you gave me the English muffin today in the rectory?"

"Dermot Michael Coyne, I gave you two English muffins!"

"And you did so with all the reverence of a priest putting a host on somebody's tongue."

"That is a pretty big host if you ask my opinion!"

"I have a pretty big mouth."

"Ah, there's that too, isn't it now?"

"And you smiled at me."

"Did I now?"

"And the smile was a mixture of love and affection and desire?"

"Dermot Michael Coyne," she protested, "would I ever look at you with desire inside a rectory with a holy priest around?"

"Nuala Anne McGrail, you would and you did and the priest never noticed."

"I knew he'd never notice. But you certainly noticed and you looked back at me like you wanted to fuck me then and there."

"And you liked that?"

"Of course I did."

"Sex and Eucharist," I said hesitantly, "an odd combination, isn't it?"

"Isn't it just like the little Bishop says, both are about the union of bodies in intimate love? And doesn't each of them remind us of the other?"

Her hand crept to my thigh.

"The little Bishop said that?"

"Didn't he say exactly that?"

Her fingers slipped up and down my leg and then over to more sensitive parts of my anatomy. I gasped audibly and she laughed, an amused seducer.

Thus encouraged, I thought it was safe to tell Nuala in some detail about the family crisis that I had created that afternoon. She listened silently as we crept northward on the rain-drenched expressway system with lightning crackling across the sky.

"Is that all you said?"

" 'Tis," I replied.

"Well, now, aren't you and His Reverence a pair of friggin' eejits!"

Rarely, if ever, had I heard George the Priest called an eejit or indeed anything unfavorable by my wife.

"Something had to be done about it, Nuala," I said.

"I'm afraid it wasn't a very Irish way. I know you prefer things to be indirect, but I don't know how to break out of a family neurosis on Maybelline without being direct."

"Hm," she snorted derisively. "Well, I suppose that's the most I can expect from a man whether he be Irish or American or a combination of both!"

"Nuala, I have the right to defend my wife and children from that she terrorist."

"You only have one child, Dermot Michael Coyne. And your wife can take care of herself and the child without any help from you."

Her fingers abandoned my loins.

"Nuala Anne!"

She sighed loudly. "Well, Dermot, I shouldn't have said that and I'm sorry. Our little girl and I DO need your protection. But not against Maybelline—I can handle that woman all by meself."

"She had you in tears this morning, didn't she?"

"Well, no, it was afternoon, wasn't it?"

I had learned very early in our relationship that one did not correct a woman when she insisted that one was inaccurate in a minor and irrelevant detail.

"Well, all right, this afternoon."

"That was different," she said dismissively. "From now on I can take care of her all by myself."

"Nuala, I don't doubt that for a moment. Still, I think I have to stand up to the family and to Maybelline. It's not that you can't take care of her. It's not your job to stop her. It's mine."

She thought about that for a minute. "Give over, Dermot Michael," she insisted. "You didn't have to make such a mess of taking care of her, now did you?"

"I don't know how you'd break through our collective neurosis other than by confrontation."

"I'm not a psychologist like you or His Reverence, but it would seem to me that's the last way to break through it!"

She was still angry at me and maybe she had reason to be. Still, something had to be done about Maybelline.

"I'm not sure it could be done any other way. The family has let this problem go on for so long and I don't see any other solution."

"Well, she's your problem, Dermot Michael Coyne, and His Reverence's and Cindy's and everybody else in the family's. And I suppose that youse have to do something about it. And you brought it upon yourselves by letting that poor unhappy woman take out her unhappiness on all of you. So, sure you have to stand up to her. I think you have to do it a lot more delicately and discreetly. But then, what do I know?"

"You know more about human nature, Nuala Anne, than anybody I've ever met."

Nuala opened her purse and took out the phone to make yet another call. She and Nessa exchanged the usual conversation in Irish. Nuala clicked the phone shut and put it in her purse with a sigh. "The little one is still sound asleep, which is what she ought to be doing, and it shows she has a lot better sense than her mother."

"In my observation her mother always shows sense," I said cautiously.

"No I don't, Dermot Michael, not at all, at all. I'm a worse eejit than you and His Reverence put together and I'm sorry for acting like one."

Her hand returned to my thigh.

"Oh?" I said, wondering what would come next.

"I like to pretend that I'm utterly self-sufficient and don't need anyone to take care of me. Of course, that's silly and I should have given that up when I married you, shouldn't I now?"

"Well, if you say so."

"I do say so. I knew you'd take care of me all the time, which is not to say that you don't need me to take care of you all the time, I hope that's clear, isn't it now?"

I imitated her sigh and said, "Sure, 'tis."

She had long since stopped objecting to my sigh and my use of the word 'tis.

"And I do appreciate you and His Reverence trying to protect me from that poor unhappy woman. And I need your help. But still, Dermot Michael, I think I can pretty much take care of her myself. Now before you say I didn't this morning, that was this morning and now is now. Isn't it?"

I sighed again and repeated, " 'Tis."

I had no idea what the difference was, save that there would be a dramatic change of personae the next time Maybelline made one of her terrorist phone calls.

"All right, that's settled now. I'll fend the woman off when she calls me and you and His Reverence can worry about how you straighten things out in the family. Mind you, I'm not incapable of offering some advice now and then."

"I hardly thought you would be incapable, Nuala."

"Good." She squeezed my knee again. "So now we'd better think about our shower tonight, mind you after Mr. Forest takes Nessa home."

"How could I not want to think about that?"

Nuala loved joint hot showers. She said they were inexpensive entertainment and a lot more interesting than watching the telly. Naturally I agreed.

Her fingers found the most vulnerable part of me and played gently.

I decided to risk the delights of a shower by asking her one more question, "And what happens if Maybelline goes after you at some other family gathering?"

"Och, Dermot Michael, she won't do it a second time, will she now?"

"I'm delighted to hear that."

"No, she won't go after me a second time at all, at all."

"I'd love to be there to see it."

"Oh, come on, Dermot Michael, you'll probably be there but afterward I'll feel terrible for hurting the poor unhappy woman. Just the same, like you say, it has to be done."

In the space of twelve hours on the subject of Maybelline my wife had changed from the fragile girl from Connemara into a sophisticated, tough-minded woman of the world. The latter was not as authentic as the former but it was authentic enough.

The lightning continued to crackle above us and thunder exploded as though it were following us down Southport Avenue. I turned off the ignition and crushed my wife into my arms, kissing her, caressing her, fondling her.

"I'd like to fuck you out here with the thunder crashing all around us."

For a moment she seemed afraid that I meant it.

"Dermot Michael," she said weakly, "not that it wouldn't be interesting, but we're not courting now and we don't have to make love in the front seat of a car, not mind you that we ever did. . . . And Nessa . . ."

"I'll get you some other time," I said in mock resignation. "But someday, woman, when you're teasing me, I'll just pull over to the side of the road and teach you a lesson or two."

She giggled.

"Won't I be waiting for that?"

YOU CAN'T MAKE LOVE IN THE FRONT SEAT OF A MERCEDES, the Adversary rebuked me.

"Someday I'll show you differently."

Despite our raincoats we both rushed for the door. While I fumbled with the keys, Nessa opened it inside and announced, "Come in quick! Glory be to God! Wasn't I crying every moment since your last call, Nuala Ann. It's such a terrible, terrible night out. No one should be out tonight on the streets of the city. You'd never know when lightning is going to strike one of these trees and knock it right over on top of your pretty car."

Nessa was patently an Irish matriarch in training. She

might not go to church—Nuala told me she didn't—but she still had the Irishwoman's inclination to see grave danger in almost every possible situation and to turn to prayer against the danger. As though to confirm her fears, lightning sizzled right above us and almost instantly there was a mighty boom of thunder.

"Come on in, come on in," she ordered us. "You'll catch your death of cold in the rain and it sounded to me like that lightning had our names on it and ourselves in a wooden house as well."

I tried vainly to explain that the house was grounded so as to resist even a direct hit of lightning and completely fireproof. It did no good, both Nessa and Nuala cited the Chicago fire as evidence that fires happened in this city and worried that the next time it might spread farther west on Fullerton Avenue than it had the last time.

I didn't tell them that the Chicago fire was in October.

Our little princess with the few strands of red hair was still sound asleep. Our wolfhound slept next to the crib in her standard guard dog position. She opened one eye somewhat contemptuously, I thought, as we came in, wondering where we'd been all night. Nelliecoyne was sound asleep and breathing, as far as I could see, normally.

Mr. Forest's cab pulled up and I escorted Nessa to the street under a big umbrella that informed the world that Chicago was a city that worked. As Nessa went out the door, I glanced back at my wife and noted that she was removing her sweatshirt.

Mr. Forest took Nessa home and Nuala and I settled in for our evening entertainment. Of course, we set up a monitor in the nursery and its counterpart in the bathroom right next to the shower so there was no danger that we would miss the slightest cry. Indeed a couple of times during our entertainments—about which I won't tell you in any detail except to remark that they were spectacular—Nuala had opened the shower door and listened to the monitor. At one time she even dashed into the nursery to make sure that the child wasn't crying. I can imagine Fiona's distress at a soaking wet human standing over her.

After the entertainments were over and I languished in bed Nuala, having donned a satin and lace gown with a matching robe (open of course!), was brushing her long black hair and looking very, very thoughtful as she carefully counted each stroke. Sometimes I was asked to brush her hair for her, at other times not. Tonight was one of those nights when she decided to do it herself. She'd shared enough of herself with me during our romp in the shower.

Fiona wandered into our bedroom from her post in the nursery and rolled over on her back for the night routine of belly scratching.

"No, I don't like it, Dermot Michael. I don't like it at all, at all. But I'm afraid we're going to have to take up your man's invitation."

"What don't you like? And which man and what invitation?"

She stopped brushing a moment to look at me in astonishment.

"Dr. Gomez's invitation, who else? That house is a scary place and I don't want to go into it, but still I think we'd better, don't you?"

"If you say so, Nuala, we will certainly do it. Do we bring herself?"

"Och, Dermot Michael, I wouldn't think of that. She'd carry on something terrible. And there would be too many questions we'd have to answer. No, it would be much better not to let Nelliecoyne near St. Gabriel's parish until we've solved the mystery."

"A mystery that the exact nature of which we don't know."

"I want to know a lot more about it, Dermot." She finished counting and put her hairbrush back on the table. "We know it's about money, we know it's about

Irish revolutionaries. We know that it's something about which rumors circulated for the rest of their lives. And we know that it was somehow connected to what happened over in Michigan City. The more I know about it, Dermot Michael, the less I like it."

She climbed into bed next to me and snuggled up close. She reached for the bed lamp and flicked it off. "No, Dermot Michael, I don't like it one bit. But we're going to have to figure it out, aren't we?"

"If you say so, Nuala Anne," I murmured sleepily.

There was no answer to that, because my bride was already asleep.

Later in the night, or more likely early in the morning, we engaged in some activities which were to a certain extent a reprise of what happened in the shower. Our amusements might have gone on much longer had not Nelliecoyne exploded with another cry of outrage followed by terrified wailing. This time Nuala and I, both of us in what the newspapers call an advanced state of undress, charged into her nursery before Fiona could come drag us out of bed. Nuala snatched the little girl up in her arms and began singing her lovely lullabies once more. The wolfhound paced back and forth nervously in the nursery. She disapproved of this whole business of Nelliecoyne wailing in the middle of the night and of the child's human parents who were responsible for the disturbance.

I opened the drape on the window and looked out on Southport Avenue. The rain had stopped but the wet street glistened a shiny black, in the pale glow of the tree-shrouded streetlight. As far as I could see there was nothing outside. Nuala joined me at the window and looked out nervously and shook her head.

"No, Dermot Michael, there's nothing out there. No ships sailing down Southport Avenue. Nothing sinister at all, at all."

"What do you think happened?"

"Maybe she had a dream that recalled the morning at

the Lake. If we needed any more motivation to get to the bottom of this mystery, Dermot Michael Coyne, we have it now! Our little tyke wants us to."

There were some weaknesses in that reasoning, but I had enough sense not to dispute my wife.

— 14 —

THE GHOSTS were gone the next morning. I decided that I would pretend that nothing had happened. It was not a morning for ghosts.

The day dawned sunny and cold, a clear blue sky, the temperature in the upper fifties, an acrid smell of real autumn—rotting leaves—in the air. It was autumn, it was time for autumn, so we may as well make our peace with it. After our morning exercise and breakfast, Nuala settled down to do her voice exercises and I went to my study and began to pound away on my computer. Is there any explanation why the writing demon (as distinct of course from the Adversary, who is someone else altogether) takes possession of me? I know of none. But for some reason or other, he did that morning. Still singing, Nuala stuck her head into the office. "Would you look at him," she exclaimed. "Isn't he acting just like he was a professional novelist?"

"Woman, you're a terrible distraction altogether! Can't you see that I'm hard at work!"

"Far be it from me, Dermot Michael Coyne, to distract a great writer when he's hard at work."

But she did distract me by leaning against me and pressing my head against her breasts.

"Sure," she went on, "won't a little bit of affection increase your productivity?"

"If there's much more of it," I said, "won't I be dragging you off to the shower again?"

"Och, wasn't I thinking to myself, Dermot Michael, that the next time we should use the bath instead of the shower? That will be more relaxing and yourself putting in a big bath just for that purpose."

"Away with you, woman," I ordered, not expecting her to go away at all. Then the phone rang. It was my father. He did not mention the ultimatum that I'd delivered yesterday.

"I talked to Dr. Kavanagh a couple of times, Dermot," he began uneasily. "At first his wife absolutely refused to see you. She doesn't think there could possibly be any interesting history in Canaryville. She's much more interested in late medieval England and its tapestries."

"Is she now?"

Dad laughed. "You know, you're beginning to sound more and more like that gorgeous young woman to whom you're married."

"Ah, isn't she a very influential person now? This Colleen Kavanagh person won't see us because she's not interested in Chicago history."

"I picked up a few markers from her husband and he tried again. She'll see you next Tuesday from eleven-thirty to eleven forty-five at her house on Hopkins Place in Beverly. You will only have fifteen minutes and not a second more. She also told her husband to tell me to tell you that she didn't think she had any useful documents about Canaryville. She said she didn't imagine that her father would have saved anything because he despised the neighborhood. The few times that she's driven through it she thought it was tacky."

"Tacky was the word she used?"

"It's the word her husband used—I presume he didn't make it up."

"I guess we'll just have to wait. Thanks much."

"Tacky is it?" Nuala said, an ominous look in her eyes.

This Colleen Kavanagh ought to beware. It's unlikely that she would encounter a shy child from Galway and much more likely that she will be seeing the serious determined woman of the world—the woman who would take care of Maybelline. And the woman who was adamant in her resistance to directors who try to make her sing songs that she didn't want to sing when she was doing her recording. Nuala could be as stubborn when she wanted to as anybody I've ever known. Rarely, thank God, was she stubborn with me.

"You remember, Dermot, that we were supposed to take poor Fiona up to the kennels this afternoon."

"I had forgotten it completely." Once a month we would take our dog up to Lake County to the kennel that raised wolfhounds. They worried that the new popularity of the dogs might weaken the bloodlines of the species which the professional wolfhound breeders were trying to enhance. So they maintained a lofty standard of what the wolfhound breed was.

Fiona loved to run with the other dogs. They don't recognize their mates or children I was told. I wasn't altogether sure I believed that. Wolfhounds are quite capable of deceiving us to protect their privacy.

"I'll let you work till noontime," Nuala said, "but then we'll have to go up to Lake County."

"Nelliecoyne?"

"Sure, Dermot Michael, we can't leave her all alone, can we now?"

You idiot. Why did you bother to ask?

So we drove up to Lake Country and watched Fiona romp through the fresh pastures with the rest of her club. Some of them, including her daughter Fionulla and her sometime mate Finn, were as snow white as she was. They played, tumbled, and raced one another and had a glorious afternoon altogether. Our daughter, dressed in an orange and blue Chicago Bears sweatsuit, must have thought she was in paradise because there were so many dogs and some of them looked exactly like her own beloved Fiona.

As much as Fiona liked playing with her friends—dogs like to be with other dogs—she was not about to let us leave without her. As soon as we turned towards the car, she came charging up, jumped over the fence which was supposed to restrain the huge beasts—and dashed to the door of our car where she waited wagging her tail expectantly. Nuala embraced her. "We wouldn't go without you. We love you too much to leave you up here with all your friends but we'll come back next month."

I wondered about the separation anxieties which would occur when we left for Ireland at Christmastime. Nuala's parents would meet their new granddaughter and Nelliecoyne would get her first sight of the land of her ancestors. Dogs, I told myself, are not like humans. They don't like to see us going away but they enjoy themselves until we come back and then go crazy with joy when they see us again. As I reflected on this it occurred to me that it was a sensible way to deal with the uncertainties and the problems of life.

Cindy called as soon as we got back into the house.

"Dermot, where have you been all day?"

"We took Fiona up to Wolfhound Park in Lake County."

"If you decide to do something like that again when we have a situation on our hands, please leave word on your answering machine where you can be found. I called you in the car too but you must have been out cavorting around Lake County with your dog and her friends."

"Guilty as charged," I said, with a touch of asperity. We really didn't have a "situation." Only Nick Farmer.

"What's Farmer done now?"

"Farmer has lost his job at the television station. They received too many complaints from listeners about his anti-Irish bias. It plays in the taverns where he hangs out, places like Billygoat's and the Old Town Alehouse. Those folks seem to forget that there's an awful lot of Irish Catholics in the city."

"The way I heard it, we run it."

"More or less. Anyway, he's telling his friends that you got him fired. He's talking the usual junk that he won't be censored and he won't be intimidated and he'll keep on speaking out against the misuse of art."

"He doesn't have an original line," I said.

"No, Dermot, he doesn't. He's a terribly insecure and inept man who is trying desperately to make a name for himself, probably for the last time since he's already in his early forties. It looks to me like his plans have backfired. I'm calling to warn you and Nuala that if anybody in the media calls to discuss his complaints about you, you just refer them to me and make no comment. Indeed, as Nuala would say, you make no comment at all, at all. Got it?"

"Anything you say, Counselor."

After Cindy hung up I wondered who my sister thought she was to tell me I should or should not talk to the media. No one was going to tell me when I should talk or when I shouldn't talk.

AREN'T YOU BECOMING THE FEISTY ONE WITH YOUR FAMILY? I WONDER HOW LONG IT WILL LAST.

I explained to Nuala the gist of the message.

"That poor unhappy man," she said. "We really have to pray for him when we say our prayers tonight, Dermot."

"Is that before or after the bathtub?"

"Nobody ever said we were going to use the bathtub tonight, did they now?"

She was having me on.

The next day I continued the work on my book and Nuala put Nellie in her arms and went down for her singing lesson with Madam in the Fine Arts Building on South Michigan Avenue. Mr. Forest drove her down and then picked her up an hour later to bring her back. I busied myself in the afternoon with preparing the Hungarian goulash for our two possibly star-crossed Irish lovers who were coming to supper that night. Nuala wasted no time when she was involved in the matchmaking game.

"How did the lesson with Madam go?"

"Och, Dermot Michael, she says I'm getting terribly sloppy, that I'm not practicing hard enough or long enough, and I'll never get better, much less be a great singer, unless I put more time in practicing."

"And you said?"

"Didn't I say that I was a mother with a little daughter around the house?"

"To which Madam replied?"

"Madam replied by saying that such a lovely little girl could take care of herself enough while her mother practiced her singing, and that she would probably enjoy the singing a lot better if it was better done."

"Did she now?"

"It's one more judgment that I'm not good at anything, Dermot Michael. I'm not a very good mother or a very good wife or a very good singer."

Sometimes when Nuala says things like that she doesn't mean them, but today she meant them and the lines of tension around her eyes grew tighter.

"Nuala, I can't complain at all about the wife part and I haven't heard Nelliecoyne complain much about the mother part. As far as I can tell all Madam said was that you have to practice more carefully."

In answer, Nuala threw her arms around me and hugged me and cried again.

She had done a lot more crying, it seemed to me, since the advent of Nelliecoyne.

While I was preparing the Hungarian goulash for our supper that night, I had another idea, in fact the first good idea since Grand Beach. I washed my hands and picked up the phone to call the Michigan City Public Library. Yes, of course, there were several newspapers in the city in 1898, of which the largest was the *Michigan City News*. Yes, that year was on microfiche. Yes, the records went back more than a hundred years. Yes, I could come up any time I wanted to look at them.

If Seamus wasn't the right young man for our Nessa (as we called her now), would she ever find the right one? Of medium height, slender, with sandy hair and freckled face, he was quiet at first, doubtless thinking that we were "gentry." When Nuala talked to him in Irish, however, he relaxed and smiled—a warm, wonderfully absorbing smile. His wit was deft and understated, as the best of Irish wit is. Moreover, his admiration for our daughter was unfeigned—as it had to be.

He examined our house with attention to minute details.

"Aye, they did a grand job, didn't they, and themselves putting up these homes in a short time?"

"This one took a little more time because it has two floors and because it was to be the first home of a lawyer who had returned from the Civil War and his young wife. Still, these houses were sturdily built. The construction people were an unsung proto School of Chicago Architecture."

"Ah," he said as he rubbed one of the walls, almost affectionately, "it's a shame to let a place like this just deteriorate, isn't it now, Mr. Coyne? Doesn't it take a lot of money to fix it up?"

"Nuala and I wanted a home that would be close to a church and a school with easy access to downtown. This seemed to be a real neighborhood with a wide variety of people, not as elegant perhaps as my home neighborhood out in River Forest, but much more interesting."

"And the outside staircase is because of the mud?"

"Right. People would enter on the second floor because there was so much mud on the ground. Chicago was still a swamp in those days. Later when they raised the street level, the first-floor entrance was right at ground level and the backyard, where Fiona runs, is a couple of feet below street level. We use the stairs now only as a kind of porch or balcony."

Fiona had decided promptly that she liked Seamus and rolled over on her back to have her belly scratched.

"And your wife keeps her canogi stick in the parlor, does she now?"

"She claims it's her good luck sign. I won't let her have it in the bedroom."

Canogi is a woman's version of the Irish game of hurling, a dangerous form of field hockey in which several dozen young men (or women) are equipped with clubs and permitted, nay urged, to beat each other up. Nuala's team won the Galway championship when she was fourteen. Wherever she went, the stick, longer than a hockey stick with a twist on the end, went with her, just in case there was a chance for "the odd game."

She thought it was very funny that I had banned it from the bedroom because, "Sure, I'd never hit you with it, Dermot Michael." Nonetheless she had conveyed it to the parlor, decorated in all respects other than the television as it might have been in 1880.

I showed Seamus around the second floor while Nuala and Nessa gossiped in the kitchen.

"You've furnished the house in the fashion of the times, haven't you?" he said as we walked through the master bedroom.

"More or less, so long as it didn't cost too much."

"They wouldn't have a bathtub like that in the 1870s, would they?" he said, gesturing at the deep and wide tub in which my wife and I periodically frolicked.

"We have to adjust to the customs of the times," I said, feeling my face grow warm.

"Ah, you're a lucky man," he said.

It was a rather forward comment from one so reserved. I felt my face grow warmer.

"I wouldn't deny it," I agreed.

Although Seamus had no formal education after he

had left secondary school, he was a very intelligent young man. In the booming Ireland of the present, he would indeed become a wealthy man. He was in every respect a good catch, even if I was Mr. Coyne and my wife was Nuala Anne.

He and our Nessa were very much in love although they rarely spoke to each other during the course of the evening. However, they certainly were not sleeping together. Looks of longing were on their faces that would be more discreet if they had become "partners."

"What do you think, Dermot Michael?" Nuala asked me later in the bath as she rubbed her big toe up and down my chest.

"What do I think about frolicking in the bathtub with a naked woman? I think it's wonderful."

"Don't be an eejit. I meant about Seamus and Nessa."

She reached for the monitor on the washstand next to the tub and listened to it carefully to make sure there was no noise coming from the nursery.

"Oh, are you talking about Seamus and Nessa? I didn't know that was the subject of conversation."

I reached down and tickled her.

"Don't change the subject, Dermot Michael!"

"I thought they were well matched. He's a very intelligent, serious young man and has a fine future. Perhaps a little too serious but that's not necessarily a fault in an Irish male."

"I never married one like that."

"Come to think of it, I've never heard anyone say I was too serious."

I continued to tickle her. She squealed and squirmed and giggled.

"He's a nice guy, she's a wonderful young woman, and they're deeply in love. All this class stuff is nonsense!"

"That's what I hoped you'd say, Dermot. But still . . ."

"The way Ireland is building these days he'll make more money in the construction business than he would ever make teaching at University College Galway. My advice to Nessa would be to grab him while the grabbing is good."

YOU'RE JUST SAYING WHAT SHE WANTS YOU TO SAY.

"Don't I have a mind of my own?"

NO.

"So, you agree with me on that, do you now?"

"Have I ever been known to disagree with you, Mrs. Coyne?"

"Mrs. Coyne is your mother. I'm Nuala, OK?"

"That's right. . . . Hey, I almost forgot. I'm taking a ride up to Michigan City tomorrow morning. I'll be back in time for your singing lesson and then to get ready for the opera tomorrow night."

"I don't want to go to the opera, Dermot Michael. It would be terrible, wouldn't it now, to leave that poor child alone and ourselves over in luxury at the Lyric Opera listening to a bunch of Italians caterwauling all around the stage!"

"Nonetheless, you agreed that we're going to go to the opera. Nessa is all signed up to baby-sit and you can use your magical little telephone between each act."

"They won't let me use it during the opera!"

"Nuala Anne, don't be ridiculous!"

"All right, I'll do what I'm told but I won't enjoy it a single moment worrying about our daughter."

I wasn't sure whether she meant it or not. So before she could continue on that subject, I embraced her and pushed our two bodies together, chest against chest.

"You didn't say why you were going up to Michigan City?" she gasped.

"Oh, I was distracted by this naked woman that's cavorting around in the bathtub with me."

"Whom you're abusing something terrible!"

"Right!" I turned my attention to the most secret wonders of her body. She threw back her head and groaned.

"I called the library up there and asked whether they had copies of newspapers from one hundred years ago.

It turns out that they put them on microfilm back in the early nineties. They did a series of stories on the events of 1898, including the sinking of the *City of Benton Harbor*. I'll take a look at the records. Maybe I'll find something that we've missed."

"Aren't you the greatest detective in all the world!" she moaned.

"What you really mean is that I'm not a half-bad Dr. Watson."

She was in no condition to answer.

I stopped thinking about the mysteries we hadn't solved and concentrated on making the most of the mystery with which I was at the moment involved.

Later I was assigned to brush her hair. She wore a wrap, open of course, but this time without a gown.

INSATIABLE.

"You've noticed."

DON'T YOU THINK SHE'S DOING IT TO MAKE UP FOR THE INTRUSION OF THE CHILD INTO YOUR LIFE?

"So what if she is!"

The next day was clear and cold like the previous one, only much colder. Indeed the temperature when I got up in the morning about seven o'clock to go out to Michigan City was twenty-four degrees. When winter comes to the Midwest, it comes quickly, though not normally so quickly as it did on that October night of 1898.

The people at the Michigan City Library could not have been more helpful. They put me in a room with a viewer and microfiches that contained all the stories in 1898 and 1899 about the sinking of the *City of Benton Harbor* seven miles up the beach from Michigan City.

The journalistic media had advanced greatly in their technological skills in one hundred years. But the obsession with tragedy and heartache had not changed. The *News* contrasted the suffering and the tragedy of the disaster with the courage of the Life Guards in their surf boats and of the young woman who braved the storm to ride her bicycle into Michigan City to alert the Life

Guards. Down the same road I presumed that now runs through Long Beach on the edge of the Lake.

The horror stories told by the survivors were heart-breaking. Those young men and women who had lost a lover, sweetheart, partner or spouse, or a child, were lac-erated by agony which would last all their lives.

"I want to die. I want to go back and throw myself into the Lake."

"What's the point in going on in life if I've lost the woman I love? The Hibernians are guilty of a terrible crime."

The Hibernians? Why blame them? They were cer-tainly not responsible for the ramming of the ship by a five-masted schooner in the midst of the storm. Nor for the poor maintenance of the ship itself. What was going on?

"I'll always blame the Hibernians for the shipwreck. If they weren't so eager to raise money they wouldn't have organized a cruise this late in the year."

"Thank God my wife and kids are still alive but it is not the Hibernians' fault they survived."

"Nobody in their right mind wants to go on an autumn cruise even if the weather is nice, nobody but your money-hungry AOH."

Oddly, none of these complaints against the Hiberni-ans had appeared in any of the books in my father's library at Grand Beach. The people who wrote the books were probably not interested in Irish revolutionary or-ganizations.

The rescue workers had found a little girl baby on the beach the next morning nearly dead from shock and ex-posure. They rushed her to the hospital in Michigan City and kept her alive. Nobody knew who she was or who her parents were. It was assumed that her parents died in the wreck. Several weeks later her name came up in a subsequent edition of the *News*. She was the daughter of a Mr. and Mrs. Hill from Detroit who had drowned.

She had recovered from the trauma at the Lake. There were no known relatives.

Odd. What was that all about? How many people boarded the ship on the Michigan side at Saugatuck before it struggled back to Chicago? I pulled out of my briefcase a copy of the burials at St. Gabriel's which Father Devlin had printed out for us. Mr. and Mrs. Hill were not among the names of the people who were buried from the parish. They were probably buried in a potter's field in Michigan City. And their little girl? What had happened to her?

There are a few calm days in November before the winter storms. The southeast corner of the Lake usually turns to ice in late November or early December. Vast ice dunes appear offshore, created by the prevailing wind driving waves up against the beach. Salvage operations could not start normally until March or April, if then. An expert on salvage in Michigan City said that he very much doubted there would be anything to salvage because the ship had for all practical purposes broken its back. Only driftwood and small remnants of people's possessions were still out there.

Driftwood? Would there still be bits of driftwood around one hundred years after the wreck?

In the summer of 1899, there were, according to the news stories, major attempts at salvage. Salvage barges anchored off the Michigan/Indiana border searched for the relics of the *City of Benton Harbor*. The paper carried faded pictures of the barges taken from the beach, three of them strung out about one hundred yards offshore, with divers in old-fashioned diving gear going up and coming down. It didn't look from the pictures like they'd found very much.

Then came the show stopper.

"Thomas Doolan of Chicago, a survivor of the wreck, was supervising the salvage work. He told the press, 'Many of us lost loved ones in the wreck. I myself lost a little girl. They found her body and we buried her in

Mount Olivet Cemetery. We hope that maybe we'll find something else out there under the waters of the Lake that will help us to remember her.' "

Bullshit!

What the hell was going on?!

Whatever Tom Doolan was looking for, he must not have found it. The final article from the summer of 1899 about the salvage operation said it had been discontinued because remnants of the wreck had already been covered by large sandbars.

Or maybe he had found what he was looking for. Or didn't find what he hoped he would not find.

As the elderly man said in Michael's Bar and Tap, "It's always money, isn't it?"

It cost a lot of money to mount a salvage operation even for somebody who had a lot of money. What could have been worth poking around on the bottom of Lake Michigan if it wasn't money?

We were, I thought, beginning to get at not a solution to the mystery but a definition of it.

I printed out copies of the relevant articles for Nuala.

On the way back to Chicago I stopped at the Chicago Historical Society and bought books by Louise Wade and Thomas Jablonski about Packingtown, as the area around the Union Stockyards was called. Perhaps they would contain something about the Hibernians and their activities in and at the end of the last century. I would read the books the next day, I promised myself. But the next day was a lot busier than we were expecting it would be.

Nuala was nursing our daughter when I returned, humming softly to her. Fiona was out in the yard running around and barking at falling leaves.

"If you're real good, Dermot Michael, I think there might be a tiny drop left for you."

"I'll be real good."

"Didn't your sister call me while you were away?"

"Which sister?"

"Wasn't it Cindy?"

"About Maybelline?"

"What else would she call me about?"

My temper flared. I jumped out of the chair and clutched my fists.

"Why the hell is she trying to go behind my back?"

"Will you sit down and stop acting like a shite hawk? Didn't I tell her that five or six times?"

I sat down.

"What did you tell her?"

"I told her that she should talk to you instead of me. Finally she heard what I was saying and apologized."

"Well . . ."

"She asked me if I thought Maybelline was a problem."

"And you said?"

"I said she was a terrorist, that no one should have to put up with her, that I could take care of myself and would in the future. Didn't I say she was Cindy's problem, not mine?"

"Wow," I said softly.

"She agreed, though I don't think she wanted to."

"Well done!"

"What else did you expect?"

There were indeed a few drops of milk left. I was offered some despite my poor performance on the subject of Cindy's phone call. There was enough milk to make me wish I were a baby again.

Nelliecoyne was consigned to her crib and promptly went to sleep.

"Poor little darlin' is not feeling all that well," her mother murmured. "Probably more teeth."

"She seems in a good mood."

"Some of the time."

I gave her the printouts. She read them carefully. Then, as is her custom in such matters, she read them again.

"I don't like it, Dermot Michael," she said as she put the sheets of paper aside.

"I don't either. But I think we have a clearer idea of the mystery, at least the lay of the land."

"I'll have to think about that."

So that evening it came time to go to the opera. While Nuala continued to insist that she did not want to go, she spent an inordinate amount of time preparing herself for the evening. Finally, all the preparations were in order.

Nuala had nursed Nelliecoyne and put her down. The kid's mood was fickle. She was both a bundle of energy who had expended much of her waking hours trying desperately to crawl and at the same time a sullen little brat who seemed to blame us for her discomfort. She cried in protest when we came close to her.

Nessa had arrived with her homework. A bottle of mother's milk was in the fridge. Nuala, dressed in a long black gown with a very high neck and very little back, a thigh-high slit, and a silver belt, was totally gorgeous, as Nessa and I repeated to her at least a dozen times. She had piled her long black hair up on the top of her head and tied it with a matching silver ribbon. She was indeed a perfect picture of a very elegant aristocratic young woman going off to town to weep at the sad story of Violeta.

She put her little telephone in her purse. "Dermot Michael, do you think they might possibly make an exception and let me use this phone while the singing is going on?"

"To quote something you might say to me, Nuala Anne, 'If you think that, you're out of your friggin' mind!' "

She smiled wryly.

"I didn't suppose they would. I really do have to get used to this separation anxiety, don't I, Dermot?" Tears sprang to her eyes. "What will I ever do when the poor little kid goes off to university!?"

"We'll burn that bridge when we come to it. . . . Most likely sigh with relief."

Mr. Forest's cab pulled up outside and we set off for the opera. Nuala had donned a white cloak. I was wearing a cashmere topcoat that my wife had insisted on buying for me.

We called home twice from the cab and once sitting inside the Lyric before the music started. With a great show of reluctance, Nuala put the phone in my jacket pocket.

"Would you ever protect me from temptation, Dermot love?"

Despite herself, Nuala relaxed, took my hand in hers, and hummed very softly the opening lines of the "Drinking Song."

We were sitting next to a Ted and Florence Genovese, a couple from River Forest about my parents' age. They were quite dazzled by Nuala and impressed, naturally, by our wallet of pictures of Nuala's daughter. We invited them up to the Green Room for a drink between acts. They had white wine, I drank my Baileys, and Nuala was content with iced tea. She made only two calls home during intermission between the second and third acts, which was better than the three she had made between the first and the second acts.

Flo Genovese whispered in my ear, "Dermot, don't worry about her. Every mother is like that with her first child. She'll get over it."

"I'm not so sure I'd bet on that!"

Flo and Ted both laughed.

After the final act and the curtain call—Nuala would never let me leave anytime before the curtain calls were finished—the moment we entered the lobby, she grabbed the phone from my jacket pocket. Nuala was dismayed, horrified after the exchange of Irish banter.

"You know what she's doing, Dermot Michael?"

"Nessa?"

"No, not poor Nessa. I mean your daughter!"

"She's my daughter so she must be doing something terrible."

"She's awake and she's playing and she refuses to go to sleep."

"Playing at this hour of the night! Nelliecoyne doesn't do that!"

"She's doing it now and I don't think it's Nessa's fault. I think she knows we're out and she's just having a good time without us."

"Sounds like her."

"Ah," she sighed, "Dermot, we're going to have a terrible, terrible time with that young woman."

"I always said she took after her mother!"

"Amadon," she said, tapping my arm in reproof as I helped her into Mr. Forest's taxi.

On our way back to Southport Avenue, two more phone calls confirmed that indeed Nellie absolutely refused to go to bed and was having a great old time playing with Nessa and the ever cooperative Fiona.

Mr. Forest remained outside the house as Nuala and I went in. He would finish the day by taking Nessa back to her apartment. West Lincoln Park is a safe neighborhood but nobody in their right mind would let a young woman walk any street in Chicago at eleven-thirty at night by herself.

Nessa was at the door as I reached for the lock.

"You'll never believe what she's doing!"

"Is it something awful?"

"You gotta see it for yourself!"

She opened the door wide and there on the far side of the room with Fiona in attendance, my daughter Mary Anne Coyne, aka Moire Ain Coyne, aka Nelliecoyne, began to crawl across the living-room floor towards us, an enormous grin on her face. Nuala moved as if to run to pick her up, then stopped and hung back.

"Let her show off!" I said.

So unsteadily but persistently, Nellie dragged herself across the floor in our direction, determined to complete her navigation of the room. When she got to Nuala's feet, her mother snapped her up into her arms and burst into tears.

"Nellie, darling," she said, "aren't you the grandest little baby in all the world! So clever, so determined, so happy! Aren't we the lucky ones to have someone like you?"

"I maintained that all along," Nessa informed us.

"Isn't going on eight months a little young to be crawling?" I asked.

"Don't be silly, Dermot Michael! It's early but not too early! Besides, we have a very gifted daughter, as you certainly ought to be able to see for yourself!"

"What you're saying is that your daughter is very gifted!"

"Didn't I just say that very thing?"

And then she began to cry and rock her daughter back and forth. Nellie cuddled in her arms and waited for the lullaby.

"O winds of the night, may your fury be crossed,
May no one that's dear to our island be lost,
Blow the winds lightly, calm be the foam,
Shine the light brightly to guide them back home.

"Hear the wind blow, hear the wind blow,
Lean your head over, hear the wind blow."

I walked Nessa down to the car and gave her two tickets for a performance of *Traviata* next week.

"Oh, Mr. Coyne, sir, you don't have to do that!"

"Yes, I do, Nessa, because tomorrow morning Nuala will have asked me if I'd got anything for you, especially since you were here with us to celebrate our daughter's creeping crawl. If I hadn't I'd be in deep trouble. Now take this envelope with the opera tickets and go on home."

"Yes, Mr. Coyne."

"Nessa?"

"Yes, sir?"

"If you let that young man get away, you're the worst eejit in the whole West of Ireland."

She giggled happily and climbed into the cab.

In the house my wife continued to weep, tears of sadness and joy, tears of fear and hope. Nelliecoyne fell asleep. Nuala put her in the crib. Then the two of us retired to our own bed, utterly exhausted. She turned off the light and cuddled in my arms. I understood that sex would be inappropriate that night. Anyway I'd had more than enough in the last couple of weeks. Then suddenly Nuala sat up in bed. "Oh, I am a terrible eejit altogether, Dermot Michael! Why didn't you tell me?"

"What didn't I tell you?"

"You didn't tell me to call me poor ma and tell her that her granddaughter was crawling and herself not eight months old."

She grabbed our bedside phone and punched in the numbers that would connect her with the lovely little town on the shore of Galway Bay three thousand miles away. I figured that it was about eight o'clock in the morning in Carraroe and her ma would be wide awake.

Nuala laughed and cried and shouted in Irish, but mostly laughed. She had to talk to her da too. Finally she said good-bye and hung up. Off went the light and she curled up in my arms and wept some more.

"You know what me ma said?"

"No, Nuala, what did your ma say?"

"Didn't she say I was crawling at the same age meself. So isn't Nelliecoyne perfectly normal?"

"Somehow the logic of that thought escapes me."

"Go to sleep, Dermot Michael Coyne, you're a terrible gobshite."

I did go to sleep with no expectations at all of the trouble we'd encounter the next morning.

—15—

THE DAY started at three-thirty in the morning when Fiona appeared at our bedside barking loudly.

"What's the matter, girl?" I asked. She barked more loudly and then charged off back to the nursery. I followed after her and discovered that our world's champion crawler was crying her eyes out, not screaming angrily as she had done at Grand Beach or on Emerald Avenue, but rather crying steadily and consistently.

"Huh?" I said not too intelligently.

Nuala bounded into the nursery and got the baby. "Glory be to God, Dermot, the child must be sick!"

"You don't think it's the teeth?"

"Not with the way she's crying—oh! what are we going to do?"

I put my hand on Nellie's forehead. It was quite warm.

"Nuala, I think she might have a fever!"

"A fever!" she shouted. "How could she ever get a fever!"

She ran to the bathroom and came back with a baby thermometer which confirmed that our little princess did indeed have a fever of 102.

Nuala wailed more loudly than her daughter. And the wolfhound, clearly distressed at the proceedings, barked anxiously.

"We might call a doctor."

"Wherever are we going to find a doctor at this time of night, Dermot Michael?"

"I'll call her pediatrician."

After some panicky stumbling around we got the man's answering service.

Nuala kind of lost it. She was moaning in Irish, prayers or curses or arguably both.

Then I had an idea.

"I think there's a pretty good chance we'll find a doctor at the end of my parents' telephone line." I picked up the phone and punched in a code number for Dr. Patrick Coyne.

"Hello," my mom said sleepily. "This is Dr. Coyne's house."

"Mom, this is Dermot, we are looking for a doctor."

"A doctor?" she said in some surprise.

"My father, your husband. Our little daughter has a fever and her mother is terribly upset."

"Dermot, remember it's that way with the first child."

She handed her phone over to my dad and I gave ours to Nuala. I slipped into the nursery where, naturally, there was another phone and picked it up.

"It's 102," my wife moaned. "She's terrible sick, Dr. Coyne. Should we bring her over to the hospital?"

"You could probably give her better treatment than she'd receive in some of the emergency rooms around your part of the city."

"Whatever should we do!"

"I tell you what, Nuala, why don't you touch her ears and see how she reacts?"

"Do you think she's losing her hearing?"

My father suppressed a laugh, "No, but I suspect she probably has an ear infection. There's a lot of those going around just now."

That is the most frequent opinion doctors give. There is always something going around.

"I just touched her left ear," Nuala said cautiously. "And she didn't cry any worse."

"All right," my father said, "now try touching the other ear."

Nelliecoyne's wail shook the whole house. Fiona howled in protest.

"I heard that on the phone line," Dad observed. "Dermot, is that Osco pharmacy down at Webster Place open twenty-four hours?"

"It is, Dad," I said. "You call in a prescription and I'll go down and get it."

"That'll do it. It's an antibiotic that we use for children with ear infections. It works very effectively but sometimes it takes a day or two. Keep taking her temperature, see that she gets a lot of liquid. And call me later in the day or tomorrow whichever day today is."

Through her tears Nuala thanked my father from the bottom of her heart.

I wondered what would happen when the little girl really got sick.

I trotted down to the Osco, picked up the prescription that they had ready, trotted back, and gave the precious, lifesaving bottle to my wife, who carefully spooned two teaspoonfuls of it into Nelliecoyne's mouth.

Our daughter wanted no part of it. She waved the spoon off and spit the liquid out.

"Dermot, she won't take it! Whatever are we going to do!"

"Give me the bottle, Nuala," I said confidently. "They make this stuff sweet so babies like it once they get the first taste of it."

I bent over the kid with the spoon in my hand.

"Now listen here, young woman, you are going to take this stuff because it's going to make you better. I'll put up with none of your foolishness, do you hear?"

Nelliecoyne, surprised at the tone of my voice, looked up at me, her mouth open. I immediately poured the two spoonfuls into her mouth.

"Now swallow!"

She discovered that the liquid didn't taste bad at all and decided to do what I told her.

"See," I said to my wife, "your daughter knows who she has to really listen to in this house!"

"Och, Dermot Michael, she just got a taste of how sweet it is! Look at her licking her lips! She wants more!"

"She won't get more for three more hours."

We also gave her two teaspoons of the liquid aspirin which was waiting for me when I picked up the prescription. That also must have tasted sweet because Nelliecoyne managed a faint smile.

"There's no point in both of us losing a night's sleep," I said. "You and Fiona stay here for a couple of hours, I'll go back to bed. I'll spell the two of you about five o'clock."

I slept quickly enough, confident that Dr. Coyne knew what he was talking about.

When I awakened at a quarter to five, the child was sleeping restlessly.

"She seems better, Dermot Michael," Nuala informed me anxiously.

"She's at least not wailing. Fiona seems to think she's better because she has gone to sleep too. Now you take a nap. I'll wake you if there's any sign of her fever going back up."

Nuala hadn't taken the child's temperature for fear that it would be higher. So I took it and discovered that it was down under a hundred. I reflected briefly on how hard it must have been for parents of children in the days before antibiotics and children's aspirin.

Nuala woke up in an hour, checked out the child's temperature, which was now down to ninety-nine, and decided that it was now time to feed her.

"Best let her sleep for a while. Why don't you do your run and go to Mass. Then we'll see if she's hungry."

Nuala did as I suggested. I had established myself as

an expert when dealing with sick little girls.

So as the sun popped up over the edge of the sky, something it was doing later each day now, much to my dismay, Nuala and Fiona departed for their sunrise run. Out of deference to the laws of the City of Chicago, Fiona was attached to a long leash. She didn't like it, but sensible canine that she was, she adapted herself to it, most of the time running at Nuala's speed.

I began to make breakfast—Mueslix, blueberries, orange juice, dry toast, and a strong pot of tea. Without milk, sugar, or lemon.

After I had set the table, I walked into the parlor and I looked out the window. My wife and my wolfhound were running back in our direction, two elegant and confident females. They paused at the door of St. Josephat's Church while Nuala debated whether it would be better for her to go into Mass and pray for Nelliecoyne or to dash into the house. Faith won. She chose the church. The wolfhound accompanied her as she always did.

The pastor of the parish and Nuala had not exactly hit it off. He could not figure her out and she thought he was a "gobshite." Nor did he like our snow-white wolfhound sitting at the back of his church during the first morning Mass. However, Fiona was very well behaved in church, curling up next to Nuala's pew and falling asleep. The priest knew that he would get absolutely nowhere by trying to forbid Nuala to take the dog into the church.

The phone rang.

"Dermot Michael Coyne."

"Cindy."

My sister was in her lawyer mode.

"Ah, Cindy, you heard about Nelliecoyne's sickness. She seems to be recovering."

"No, Dermot, I didn't hear about it. I'm glad she is getting better but I'm calling because . . . have you heard the news this morning?"

I confessed that I had not.

"Your good friend Nick Farmer was shot last night coming out of some bar in Evanston."

"That's too bad. Did he survive?"

"Apparently he did. They're saying at Evanston Hospital that he is in serious but stable condition. That means that he will live."

"I'll be a good Christian and say I'm glad of that."

"The problem, Dermot, is that he claims that you and Nuala are the ones that shot him."

"What!"

"Apparently when the patrons in the bar poured out to see what had happened he was screaming that the two of you were responsible. I suspect the Evanston Police will try to question you. Do you have an alibi?"

"Alibi?" I asked, astonished that I needed one.

"Dermot," Cindy said efficiently, "where were you and Nuala last night?"

"We went to the opera."

"*La Traviata,* wasn't it?"

"Yeah, it was superb."

"That's almost three and a half hours?"

"Something like that, it started at seven-thirty and we were out by eleven and home here by eleven-thirty."

Cindy sighed with relief.

"I suppose you saw people there that you know?"

"Sure, Ted and Flo Genovese sat right next to us. As a matter of fact, they joined us between the acts for a drink in the Green Room. Or the Graham Room as I guess we must call it now. They can testify to our presence at the Lyric Opera for the entire length of the performance. Mr. Forest picked us up and drove us home. We were back home I suppose a little before eleven-thirty."

"That's all we need, Dermot. Farmer was shot coming out of the bar at about ten o'clock. The Evanston Police will probably come after you. They'll figure they're under pressure to look like they're doing something because Farmer is a media figure, however lowly. You

don't talk to them unless I'm present and unless somebody from the Chicago Police Department is present,
and unless Mike Casey is present. Got it?"

Mike Casey presided over Reliable Security, a firm
which I employed periodically to protect Nuala and myself from the real crazies, like renegade Irish revolutionaries. He was the former Acting Superintendent of the
Chicago Police Department, an author of a standard text-
book on criminal investigation procedures, and now a
famous artist.

"I got it, Cindy. Do you think they'll show up, without
Chicago cops?"

"Sure they will, the media are going to be all over
there. They'll want to look like they're acting swiftly.
Don't trust them."

"OK, I'll keep you informed."

I heard a lot of noise outside and walked from the
kitchen into the parlor and glanced outside. It looked like
every television channel in Chicago had camped on
Southport Avenue with trucks, minicameras, and cars
halfway to Webster. This we did not need, especially on
a day when our little girl was sick.

Then as I watched, Nuala emerged from St. Josephat's. She stopped in dismay when she saw the crowd
around her house. Fiona strained at her leash. She didn't
like the crowd of people in front of her house.

Deftly Nuala walked across the street weaving her
way among cameramen and reporters, the wolfhound
now on a very short leash.

I ran to the door and threw it open. "There she is,"
someone shouted. The cameramen wheeled and journalists with their microphones in their hands rushed towards
Nuala. This, I said to myself, was going to be very interesting.

Fiona barked, an angry bark that indicated she was
not yet ready to start a fight. Several reporters, noting
the dog's size, hesitated, but one bold woman jammed
her microphone at Nuala's mouth and shouted, "Did you

really shoot Nick Farmer last night, Nuala?"

That was too much for the dog. Her admonitory bark turned into a menacing growl followed by the wolf-hound's favorite sound effect: a howl that suggested thousands of years of angry wolfhound bitches fighting off threats to somebody who was in their charge. The reporter retreated quickly. Our Fiona would have snatched the mike from her hand.

"No, Fiona, no," Nuala informed the wolfhound. "It's all right."

Fiona wasn't so sure. She went through the motions of struggling against the leash as if to chase the fright-ened young journalist.

"You'd better stay away from me," Nuala warned the members of the media, crusaders for the people's right to know in thirty-second sound bites. "Fiona is a very gentle dog. She likes people a lot but not when they seem to be threatening me. If you don't back off I can't promise you what she may do. She was a police guard dog in Ireland before we adopted her and she has some very strong instincts about what to do to people who seem to be attacking her friends."

That was a remarkably contained speech, I thought, from a woman who had a sick daughter in the house and now found herself surrounded by half-wits.

Calmly and confidently and not pulling on the leash, she walked in the door to the house. I slammed it shut.

"Dermot Michael, whatever in the holy hell is going on? Why are all them gobshites out there?"

"Somebody took a shot at Nick Farmer last night. Cindy called me when you were in church. Farmer is blaming us for it. We are not to say anything to the Evanston Police until Cindy, a Chicago cop, probably John Culhane, and Mike Casey are here with us."

"But, Dermot, we didn't shoot the poor man!"

"He claimed we did. It's one more way for him to get publicity, perhaps a chance for him to get his television slot back."

"Whatever shall we do?"

"First thing we'll do is eat our breakfast, then we'll see if your troublesome daughter is well enough to have something to eat, and then we'll wait for the Evanston cops to show up. Maybe I'll get some time to write my report on Louise Wade's and Thomas Jablonski's books."

Nuala was nursing Nelliecoyne when the Evanston cops showed up. I opened the door cautiously, my hand firmly gripping Fiona's collar.

"Yes?" I said tentatively.

"I'm Lieutenant Knox of the Evanston Police," the taller cop said.

The shorter and fat one added, "And I'm Sergeant McKechnie. We're both in Evanston Homicide."

"Kind of out of your jurisdiction, aren't you?"

Fiona growled, a long plaintive and threatening growl.

"Is that dog dangerous?" Lieutenant Knox asked nervously.

"Sometimes. It depends on who she is growling at. She's a retired police dog from Ireland. She took a very early retirement. Now what can I do for you gentlemen?"

"We are here to ask you some questions regarding the shooting of a Mr. Nicholas Farmer on Chicago Avenue in Evanston last night."

"How interesting."

"Mr. Farmer asserts that you and your wife were the perpetrators of the shooting."

There must have been an especially sinister tone in his voice because Fiona's growl got louder and her strain against my hand more vigorous. She wouldn't break away unless I let her and she wouldn't leap on either of these two jerks unless I told her to do so. But the growl caused them both to back off a foot or two.

"I find it interesting that you are here outside of your own jurisdiction, as far as I can tell, without the presence of a Chicago police officer."

"It would be better for all concerned if we got to the

bottom of this allegation of Mr. Farmer's quickly."

"I'm sure my lawyer wouldn't agree. Her name is Cynthia Hurley. You call her and she'll make arrangements for you to interview us at a time of her and our convenience."

Their faces both grew hard, like the cops on TV.

"You may regret this, Mr. Coyne," the sergeant said. "Regret it a lot."

"Good day, gentlemen, we will see you later when you follow the standards of appropriate police procedure in this kind of matter."

I closed the door firmly in their faces, an action which was followed by one of Fiona's loudest howls of protest. That would teach the Evanston cops a lesson.

Behind me Nuala was standing, holding a softly whining Nelliecoyne.

"Och, Dermot Michael, weren't you wonderful now!"

"I thought Fiona was more wonderful than I was. Did herself have anything to eat?"

"At first she wasn't interested but then she started to think 'oh milk again' and then, Dermot Michael, to tell you the truth, she's got something of her appetite back. What time is it? Oh, God, it's time for me to give her the medicine and hadn't I forgotten that altogether?"

So Nelliecoyne was given her medicine and put back in bed. After considerable unhappy protest, she decided maybe it would be a good thing to have a nap to make up for the sleep she had lost the night before.

I had one of my more insidious ideas. I opened the front door of the house and walked out to face the assembled media, a challenge which after a number of incidents I rather enjoy. I'm not very bright, but I'm brighter than they are.

"Dermot, do you and your wife have an alibi?" one of the half-wits demanded.

"An alibi?"

"Where were you last night when poor Nick Farmer was shot?"

"Is this gathering in honor of Nick Farmer?"

"He made certain allegations as he was taken off to the hospital."

"Allegations indeed?"

"Where were you last night at ten o'clock, Dermot?"

"I refused to answer that question to the police because they weren't following proper procedures. They should have come with a Chicago policeman since this neighborhood is out of their jurisdiction. I told them that they should talk to my attorney and find a Chicago cop to accompany them. When an appropriate time is agreed on, we'll be happy to answer their questions."

"Were you anywhere near Evanston last night?"

The young man must have thought he was Sam Donaldson.

"Only if the Lyric Opera of Chicago has been moved to Evanston."

"You were at the opera?"

"Indeed we were—from seven o'clock till eleven-thirty. And, yes, there were people there who could identify us, indeed the people we sat next to joined us in the Graham Room during intermissions. Any more questions?"

"What about Nick Farmer's allegations?"

I shrugged. "They are probably actionable, though I don't think we'll take any action."

I turned on my heel and, supremely satisfied with myself, walked back into the house.

Nuala had been standing close to the door listening to my performance.

"Sure, Dermot Michael, weren't you wonderful with them gobshites! We have our denial and our alibi on the record before them nine-fingered shite-hawk Evanston cops come back!"

"Piece of cake," I said as though I were an old hand in fending off the media.

"Dermot, isn't it terrible cold outside this morning? And them poor folks up so early? And doesn't it look

like they have no coffee or tea or anything to eat? Why
don't I make them some soda bread and some coffee
and tea?"

That I thought would be a wonderful idea—ashes on
their heads. It would also provide me with a chance to
consume some of her world-class soda bread.

A half hour later, as the media folks shivered in the
premature November cold, Nuala and I walked out with
trays filled with soda bread. We returned to the house
and came out again, this time with coffee and tea and
paper cups. Nuala, against my strong advice, supplied
butter and jam for the soda bread.

"Sure, they're only Yanks. They don't know you
should never put jam on soda bread!"

Our visitors were astonished. They thanked us with
something which, for media half-wits, came close to
shamed faces.

"Isn't it what we should be giving to folks whose jobs
get them up so early on a cold morning?" Nuala said,
complacent in her virtue.

" 'Tis," I perforce agreed.

Generally reporters are not much into looking sheepish. However, when we arrived with their breakfasts they
did look a little sheepish. Their mildly hangdog expressions were replaced by visages of pure delight when
their teeth sank into Nuala Anne's soda bread, warm
soda bread with butter and an extra layer of strawberry
jam. Naturally, she put a piece into my mouth with her
now expected alluring Eucharistic Minister smile.

We had left the door ajar when we came out with
their breakfasts and who should parade out after us in
all her canine glory but Fiona the wolfhound. She surveyed the crowd of media people, and having decided
they couldn't be hostile or we wouldn't be feeding them,
she ambled out to walk in her domain. At first they were
frightened of her—who wouldn't be frightened of such
a massive dog? They quickly discovered that all she
wanted to do was be friends. So they patted her affec-

tionately as she wandered about accepting their admiration and veneration.

"What would have happened," the young woman who had poked the microphone at Nuala asked me, "if I hadn't pulled back the mike when your dog growled at me?"

"If you were lucky she would have just taken the mike," I said.

"And if I wasn't lucky?"

"Then she might have taken your hand."

The young woman recoiled in horror. At that same moment Fiona chose to nudge her in a request for affection. The woman reached down and patted the dog's huge head.

Actually, I don't think Fiona would have chewed the woman's hand unless she'd been told to. Nonetheless, it is not wise to mess around with Irish wolfhounds, especially when they have been trained as police dogs.

The pastor of St. Josephat's emerged from his rectory to survey the scene. Fiona walked over to greet him. He did his best to ignore her, which is difficult when Fiona is determined that she wants to make friends with you.

"There always seems to be a lot of media activity around here, Mr. Coyne," he said. "We've had more since you moved in than we had in all the years before you arrived."

"Father," I said, "it must be nice to see a picture of your church on television."

He had a number of good reasons for not liking us. We went to Mass on Sunday at Old St. Patrick's because Nuala sang in the choir. We had a close relationship with the Cathedral, where my brother was on the staff and our friend the little Bishop presided. We were notoriously good friends with Cardinal Sean Cronin. However, we did contribute substantially to St. Josephat's and it would be most unlikely that our children would be barred from the school.

With a sniff of disapproval, he turned around and

walked back into the rectory, the lord of the manor dismayed by the disorder in front of his castle.

The TV mob departed later in the morning. Their news directors must have decided that there was no more good footage on Southport Avenue.

—16—

AFTER THE media people left, disaster overtook our family. Nuala became ill.

This was an absolutely unique event, because, save for morning sickness, Nuala protested that she had never been sick a day in her life. This day she, however, was really sick. She had caught whatever bug was affecting our daughter and was promptly laid low by it.

"I feel dizzy, Dermot Michael," she said as we returned to the house with the remnants of our take-out breakfasts. "I feel like I'm gonna collapse."

She did just that in my arms. I helped her lie down on the couch in our parlor and felt her forehead. It wasn't as warm as the child's had been the night before but it was still warmer than it should be.

"I'm very much afraid that my daughter has infected you," I concluded.

"Then we'll just have to give her away to somebody who has more immunities than I do!"

"Do you want me to call the doctor?"

"Oh, please do, Dermot Michael, before I perish with the bug, sure, I'm not long for this world!"

When Nuala was sick, even with morning sickness, she also became very funny. There would be a lot of laughing in the next couple of days. I didn't care, I wanted my healthy Nuala back.

I called her internist and her OB doctor. Neither of them was available. Naturally. So I called my father.

"Couldn't find her real doctors, huh, Dermot?"

"Yup."

"I figured I'd hear from you this morning. That's the way these family epidemics start. One of the kids gets it, then the other kids get it, then the mother gets it, and then finally the father gets it."

"You'd better order prescriptions or whatever for me too."

"It's something they never warn you about when you decide to have children. You just have to take it for granted that you are going to be sick about half the time. I'll call the prescriptions in to your local Osco."

So I trotted down to the drugstore again, collected two bottles of each, and brought them back to the house. Nuala had not stirred from the couch on which she had collapsed. Fiona, anxious about the mysterious behavior of her mistress, stood next to her, feeling perhaps it would be more useful to watch her this morning than to watch the child.

"How is Nelliecoyne doing, girl?" I asked the dog.

At the word *Nelliecoyne* she bounded up the stairs, at about the same speed Nuala would bound, and with the same amount of noise, to check on the baby.

"Are you awake, Nuala Anne?"

"I'm not awake, Dermot Michael. Haven't I died and gone to heaven? Promise you'll take good care of me daughter and me dog."

"I brought the medicine."

" 'Tis too late altogether for medicine. I'm not long for this world."

I made her take medicine just the same.

"Nuala, you'd better come upstairs and go to bed. You're not doing yourself or anybody else any good down here. You have to get as much rest as you can."

"Dermot Michael, would you ever make me a hot toddy with Irish whiskey and lemonade?"

I helped her up and led her to the stairs.

"Nuala, there is no medical evidence that such concoctions can heal viral infections."

"Och, sure, Dermot Michael, I know that. But it kills the pain. You don't notice how sick you really are!"

So I walked her upstairs and put her to bed.

"I should be nursing your baby, shouldn't I, and meself on me last legs?"

"When she wakes up, I'll bring her in."

"She is responsible for it all. Why didn't they warn me that babies do this kind of thing to you!"

"Weren't you after doing it to your own ma?"

"Och, Dermot," she confessed, "I did indeed. 'Tis a wonder the poor woman didn't throw me out into the bog!"

"I don't think there is any danger of us taking Nelliecoyne over to the Chicago River and dumping her in."

"You know, Dermot Michael, at a time like this, that doesn't seem to me to be a half-bad idea! Now would you ever please go off and make me a hot toddy."

I was leaving the bedroom when she shouted after me, "Dermot, unless I'm delirious, more so than usual, didn't your sister Cindy call and say that the police were going to be here at two o'clock this afternoon?"

"Two o'clock this afternoon. We'll get it over with and settle back to healing whatever ails you."

I glanced in the nursery. Our daughter was awake and not in a particularly happy mood but she didn't seem to be hungry.

"All that will have to happen, Fiona girl," I said to our wolfhound, "is for you to get sick. I'd be taking care of all three of you!"

So I made a hot toddy—which broke all of Nuala's rules about what she should drink when she was nursing—and brought it up to her.

"Hadn't I better feed the little monster before I drink this, Dermot?"

So I went to the nursery, picked up Nellie, who was

not happy at my disturbing her, and carried her into the bedroom. She drank her late morning's milk, however, with her accustomed vigor.

"She seems to be on the mend, Nuala," I observed.

"I hope she's happy that she's getting better and her mother all but half dead. I don't care about what this kid will do for her next feeding. Maybe she'll have to go hungry and, sure, won't that serve her right!"

"Drink your hot toddy, woman, and go to sleep."

Before she went to sleep she muttered, "Dermot Michael, what will I ever do when them constables come?"

"What you'll do, Nuala Anne, is get up and answer their questions and go right back to bed."

Cindy and Mike Casey appeared promptly at two o'clock.

"I saw on the twelve o'clock news that you'd got your alibi out on the record, Dermot," my sister said. "That was very clever."

Cindy, a slender, blond, good-looking woman in her early forties, had to go into the nursery and investigate Nellie's condition. Fiona, who adored Cindy, insisted on licking her face before she went up the stairs.

"Is your little girl sick, Fiona?" she said, hugging the dog. "She'll be well in a little while."

Mike Casey, a tall, slim man, just turned seventy, sat down in one of our Victorian chairs and accepted my offer of a cup of tea. He was impeccably dressed in a blue Italian suit which set off his silver hair and his lean, handsome face. He looked like the late Basil Rathbone playing Sherlock Holmes in the old movies.

"A lot of cops will try to do what those two guys tried to do this morning, Dermot," he said. "They know they shouldn't but they always hope they can get away with it."

"They might have, if Cindy hadn't called us. They don't have a thing on us. We have the perfect excuse."

"Still, they'll want to come and question you if only to give the impression that they're seriously searching for the would-be assassin, if there is a would-be assassin. It should only take a couple of minutes."

Our doorbell rang. I opened it and the two Evanston cops stood there, both doing their best to look stern and responsible.

"You have time for us now, Mr. Coyne?"

"The lawyers are both here but we'll have to wait for a representative of the Chicago Police Department."

"May we come in?"

I looked back at Cindy, who had just come down the stairs from the nursery. She nodded.

"You may," I said.

Cindy began the conversation by remarking on the elementary professional standards that cops are supposed to follow when they go out of their jurisdiction. The two cops said nothing in response. What could they say? They knew the rules. Their boss had told them to forget the rules.

I introduced Mike as Mr. Casey, so they didn't know that they were facing one of the most influential cops in America.

A blue and white Chicago police car rolled up to the door. John Culhane, Area Six Commander, emerged briskly. I opened our door and let him in.

"Dermot Coyne," he said with a big grin, "what are you and that beautiful wife getting yourself into now? We haven't had any trouble from you for almost a year. I was beginning to wonder if you'd moved back to Ireland."

"Hi, Superintendent," John said to Mike Casey. "Nice to see you again. You're looking as fit and happy as ever."

"So do you, my friend. Glad to see you're still working out every day."

"There are days I don't work out. Like when I get involved with this dangerous duo."

John was about fifty, trim, muscular, good-looking, with rimless glasses and sandy hair closely trimmed, very much the ex-Marine that he was. And one of the finest cops in Chicago.

He turned to the two Evaston policemen who were standing awkwardly.

"Lieutenant Knox," said the tall cop.

"Sergeant McKechnie," said the short one nervously.

"It would have been better if you'd called us first," John said, as he declined their handshakes.

"It's a murder investigation," said Knox. "We thought that it might be appropriate to question the Coynes because of our haste to resolve the problem. Sorry to have offended you."

"Attempted murder," Cindy corrected him.

"Next time, call," John said tersely.

"I suppose we can begin our discussion," Cindy took charge of the gathering. "You might as well ask your questions, Lieutenant Knox."

"Now, Mr. Coyne, we are here to ask if you know anything about the shooting last night of the music critic, Mr. Nicholas Farmer."

"Lieutenant," Cindy interrupted, "I can't imagine a more amateurish way of beginning an interview. I instruct my clients to ignore the question."

Nessa was in the nursery with Nellie. Fiona was out in the yard chasing falling leaves and barking at them. Nuala sat in the old rocking chair, perhaps in the same place Laetitia Walsh often occupied back in the nineteenth century. She was wearing jeans and her beloved Marquette University sweatshirt and looking very, very pale.

"Next question, Lieutenant," Cindy demanded.

"Mr. Coyne, would you account for your movements last night, say between seven o'clock and eleven o'clock?"

"I would be happy to."

Casting myself as the hero in one of my novels, I recited our story and provided the names of Flo and Ted Genovese, Peter Forest, and Nessa O'Toole.

"What are their phone numbers?" McKechnie asked as he jotted rapidly in his notebook.

"You don't expect, do you, Lieutenant, to get that kind of information from my client?" Cindy scoffed. "Do your police work and find out the phone numbers for yourself."

"Mrs. Coyne, you carried a handheld telephone with you at the opera last night, did you not?"

Nuala stared blankly out in space.

"Mrs. Coyne?" he said again.

"Nuala Anne," I said, "he means you."

"Och, are you talking to me now?" Nuala Anne stirred a bit in the rocker. "Don't I always think of Dermot's mother when someone says that name? What were you asking?"

"You are reported as having a handheld telephone in the opera last night."

Big deal discovery. Someone had called that in to him after seeing me on the noon news. Were we supposed to be frightened?

"Sure, but I only used it during the intermissions!" Nuala strongly protested. "I didn't break any laws, I didn't disturb the concert with the phone!"

I couldn't tell whether she was serious or whether she was just having them on. Probably both.

"May I ask who you were calling that often on your portable phone?"

"Is eight times often, Lieutenant?" I asked.

"We will return to that, Mr. Coyne."

"Why can't Mrs. Coyne use her telephone at intermissions during an opera?" Cindy cut in. "Are you implying that she might have been in touch with someone involved in the shooting of Mr. Farmer?"

"We have to investigate every possibility, Counselor."

"Anyway, it was nine phone calls, Dermot, not eight."

Wrong again!

"And who were those phone calls to?"

"Wasn't I calling our baby-sitter to see how our little

girl was doing while we were at the opera?"

"Nine times?"

"That's enough, Officer," Cindy said impersonally. "It is no business of yours how many times Mrs. Coyne checks on her daughter's health."

"It does seem to be a lot of phone calls."

"Do you have children, Officer?"

He ignored the cross-exam.

"Would you tell us your phone numbers, both here and on your portable phone, so that we could check that out, Mrs. Coyne?"

"She certainly will not, Officer," Cindy exploded. "Do your own police work and find out the numbers yourself. When you check the records, I'm sure you will discover that all of Mrs. Coyne's phone calls were indeed to this house."

The lieutenant squirmed. He wasn't getting anyplace and didn't have any idea where he wanted to go.

"Mr. Coyne, are you acquainted with any persons involved in organized crime?"

"Officer, do you really have to think I'm such an incompetent attorney that I would permit you to ask such a question? What do you mean by 'involved with' and what do you mean by 'organized crime' and what do you mean by 'acquainted with'?"

"I'll try to be clear."

"Mr. Coyne, do you know any Mafia hit men?"

"We call them Outfit here in the big city," John Culhane murmured.

"One more question like that, Officer, and I'll terminate this interview," Cindy said with icy menace in her voice.

"Counselor, the injured man alleges that Mr. and Mrs. Coyne were involved in the attempt on his life. They have supplied us with information that would lead us to suspect that they were not physically present at the time of the shooting . . ."

"Leads you to suspect," Cindy snorted. "Officer, you have got to be kidding!"

"Therefore we must pursue other possibilities. Mr. Farmer must certainly have reasons to suspect your clients' involvement or he would not have made the accusation."

"Officer, I'm not going to take that issue seriously."

"I will change the question, Counselor. Mr. Coyne, do you know of any reasons why Mr. Farmer would make these allegations against you?"

"None whatever."

"Yet he has made these allegations?"

"Instead of asking Mr. Coyne for Mr. Farmer's reasons, Lieutenant, you might ask Mr. Farmer. If he doesn't have any evidence, then he may be guilty of defamation."

"Mr. Farmer insists that your clients are responsible for his dismissal from his television job."

"He better have something more than an allegation like that, Officer. Dermot, you may answer that if you want."

"The implied question being whether we tried to get Nicholas Farmer fired from his television slot?"

"Yes, something like that."

"We did not," I replied, trying to suppress my grin.

"He thinks you did."

"He thinks wrong."

"Do you know anything about the attempt on Mr. Farmer's life?"

I was becoming more angry than I should have.

"All that I know I've heard on television. It makes no sense to me at all. I have no idea who might have wounded him last night or why they might."

"And if I could add a word," Cindy interjected, "you would be much better advised to spend your time trying to find out who the people were that drove up in the car and fired the actual shot at Mr. Farmer."

"Shots, Counselor."

"From what distance?" Mike Casey joined the conversation for the first time.

Lieutenant Knox glared at him.

"Who the hell are you anyway?"

Mike ignored him.

Knox gritted his teeth and answered the question.

"Maybe ten feet. The car pulled up right along the curb."

"And how many shots?"

"Three."

Mike sighed, "Lieutenant Knox, have you ever had any experience investigating possible contract killings?"

Knox shifted uneasily.

"We don't have many such in Evanston, sir."

"Let me tell you two things about Outfit contract killers. They don't miss. And they don't fire shots recklessly. If this was indeed an Outfit hit, it was very unprofessional. The hit man will wait a long time for another contract."

"I see," said the lieutenant, not altogether sure whether he should take Mike seriously.

"Were other people standing around?" Mike continued.

"Farmer was standing outside with three friends, a man and two women."

"The car, a late-model Saab according to the press, simply pulled up and apparently someone fired three shots?"

"That is what the witnesses say."

"It has none of the marks at all of a contract killing," Mike Casey said, shaking his head and sitting back on his chair. "It was an amateur job, almost as amateur as this investigation is. Besides, the Outfit doesn't drive Saabs."

"What did you say your name was, sir?" Sergeant McKechnie asked. "So we can have your full name for our records."

"Michael Patrick Vincent Casey." Mike gave his name slowly with emphasis on each word.

Sergeant McKechnie looked up from his notes, pencil in hand. "The man who wrote the book?"

"Indeed, Sergeant, the man who wrote the book. I would recommend to you that you might reread it sometime soon."

"Och," my wife spoke up. "Things are never what they seem, are they now?"

"What do you mean, Nuala dear?" Cindy asked.

"Isn't it clear what happened? Things never are what they seem to most people."

"And why is that?" Lieutenant Knox asked, baffled by the pale oracle.

"The shots weren't supposed to hit poor Mr. Farmer. The shots were supposed to miss him. The man with the gun made a mistake. It's a lucky thing that he didn't kill poor Mr. Farmer or somebody else who was standing nearby. The story is not about an assassination or an attempted assassination. This story is a fake assassination that was bungled. Isn't it clear as the nose on all your faces that the whole thing was a fake? Then go into the hospital room and ask Mr. Farmer why he tried to fake his own assassination and he'll break down and admit it."

John Culhane glanced at Mike Casey. Mike smiled back.

"Any time she wants to stop singing she can have a job at Reliable Security."

"Not if the Chicago P.D. gets there first."

Nuala was staring blankly off into space.

"You're all out of your friggin' minds," she said.

Cindy intervened.

"I think I'm going to call this interview to an end. It is a pointless waste of time for the Coynes and for the rest of us. I'm going to notify the ethics board at the Evanston Police Department that this was an utterly unprofessional interview."

"And I will call your Chief of Police and tell him that he shouldn't have sent boys to do a man's job," Mike Casey added.

The two cops left quietly.

"They should follow up on Nuala's suggestion," I said.

"They will," John Culhane replied. "It's too good an idea to pass up."

Mike Casey stood up to leave with the Commander.

"Your guys, John, could clean this up in no time. Nuala is absolutely right that it smells of a fake. All they have to do is find out who Nick Farmer knows that might agree to a trick like this."

"Why were they so dumb?" Nuala asked as John and Mike were leaving the house.

Mike turned and smiled gently.

"When you are as old as I am, Nuala Anne, you'll realize that there are a lot of dumb people around."

"Is it over, Dermot Michael?" Nuala asked. "I must go back to my bed and prepare for the end with one last hot toddy . . . would you ever bring me one, please?"

"You certainly helped to solve another problem," Cindy said softly.

"Which problem?"

"Maybelline."

"What!" I cried in disbelief.

"Apparently she called here to harass Nuala about something."

"Terrorize."

"I grant you the word. And Nuala told her off."

"Twice," my darling wife, obsessed with precision even in her sickness, corrected Cindy. "I was terrible altogether."

"And very effective. She was hysterical when your brother came home and asked him whether he thought she might need psychiatric help."

"Impossible!"

"Impossible, Dermot, but true. So I guess you and

George are not going to have to secede from the family."

"They never would," Nuala remarked.

"It's too early to predict what's going to happen but it's a beginning. She called all the women in the family and told them that she's going to try to straighten out her life."

"I'll be damned," I said in astonishment.

"No you won't, Dermot Michael, I'll be up there right next to St. Peter's computer defending you against all the charges just like Cindy defended us this afternoon."

SEE, said the Adversary. WHAT DID I TELL YOU? THAT ONE CAN TAKE CARE OF HERSELF.

IT WAS fun to minister to Nuala while she was sick. I didn't enjoy the sickness and I didn't enjoy her dependency but I did enjoy the opportunity to be nice to her. I enjoyed bringing her hot soup and her pot of tea and her hot whiskey toddy.

"Sure, Dermot Michael Coyne, aren't you spoiling me rotten altogether!"

"What else can I do when my poor wife is at death's door?"

"I know that and I enjoy your attention, but I'm not sure I deserve it!"

"Spoken like a true Irishwoman."

"Besides, you'll turn me into a terrible alcoholic with all this whiskey toddy you're giving me."

"You're the one that's demanding it, woman."

"Sure, it doesn't make my cold any better but, as I said, Dermot Michael, doesn't it help to kill the pain?"

My daughter had recovered from the infection she'd brought to the house and was her usual happy self though she hadn't yet tried to repeat her crawling feat. Fiona kept a close eye on her while I was being nice to Nuala.

My wife was so "destroyed" by her cold that she wasn't able to sing at Old Saint Patrick's on Sunday or to walk across the street to Mass. Nonetheless, she insisted that I attend and bring the baby along because didn't she have to get in the habit of going to church on Sunday?

Nessa was absolutely banned from the house for fear she too would be infected. "The poor young woman has to study for her Ph.D. exam. She can't afford to be sick."

My wife looked pale and haggard, utterly exhausted by the nasty virus which had taken possession of her. I suspected myself that all the strain and tension of motherhood had also caught up with her and she was in no position to resist any wandering bug.

Nick Farmer had been restored to his job but apparently warned to lay off us because the Lyric Opera was now his target, though it seemed to go beyond his popular music venue. He appeared on camera ostentatiously wrapped up with a bandage around his arm looking like a returned war veteran, probably trying to win sympathy. He was a desperate, desperate man.

I heard from George the Priest that Maybelline had regressed from her decision to see a therapist. She had come back from her first treatment wailing that there was nothing wrong with her and called all the women in the family, except my wife, to tell them that it was a waste of time. However, a number of people responded that she should stick at it because it might help her to relax a little. Whether she would respond positively to this advice still was in doubt.

I tried to find more information about Canaryville and the wreck and the Town of Lake. I phoned the Chicago Historical Society but they didn't seem to have much information other than the standard literature. So I sat down when I wasn't waiting on Nuala and keeping an eye on Nellie to write a report on Louise Wade's fine book *Chicago's Pride* and Thomas Jablonski's book *Pride in the Jungle*.

Picture hell, Nuala Anne. Then you will know what the Stockyards and the neighborhood around them were like a hundred years ago.

The sky is dark and filled with clouds of dirt and dust, fires burn fiercely. An unbearable stench permeates the air. Drunken men stagger out of the long rows of taverns. Garbage lies everywhere. The streets are seas of mud. The sewage system doesn't work, water is available only intermittently. Nearby streams are filled with offal and pieces, large and small, of dead animals. The people who live there are shabby, dull, discouraged, overwhelmed. As you ride through the area dismayed by the stench and misery and suffering, you think it would be good if the whole area could be obliterated from the face of the earth.

For the people living on the inside of the environs of the Union Stockyards it was another matter. The Union Stockyards and the neighborhoods surrounding them were sites from which they were wrestling for a better living than they would have dreamed possible before they migrated to America, the first step on the ladder to success and affluence in America. The dark gloom of the malodorous streets to them was not hell but perhaps an antechamber to heaven, purgatory at worst.

The most infuriating thing, Nuala, about reading the literature on "Packingtown," as they called it, is the snobbery of the University of Chicago graduate students who snooped around it looking down their long elite noses at the masses of immigrants. The same for Upton Sinclair, whose novel, *The Jungle,* was a marvelous example of elite left-wing snobbery.

Consider this particular passage, from a certain Charles Bushnell who was writing his doctoral dissertation at the university: "With our cities growing much more rapidly than our country districts, many hordes of population, of diverse languages, customs, and habits, are being crowded annually into congested city wards where life becomes a wild, saddened, sickening, inhuman, and infinitely tragic struggle; not only a menace to those finer dreams of noble, joyous and beautiful national life but a threat to the very essentials of common and decent civilization itself."

Another outsider said that "Packingtown begins to seem like a world in itself. You feel that there is a great mass of humanity, the kind that is hardest to manage, the easiest to inflame, the slowest to understand."

The University of Chicago do-gooders swarmed all over the neighborhood. They saw the externals but did not really understand what was happening. Many of them thought that it would be wonderful if the whole residential district could be swept away with its muddy streets, its poor lighting, its inadequate water supply, its dubious sewage, its irregular garbage removal, its dirt, its filth, and its foreigners.

Especially the foreigners.

Yet they missed the fact that by the turn of the century more than half of the people in the area around the Union Stockyards owned their own homes and that they and their elected representatives were struggling to improve the water, the lighting, the garbage disposal, the sewage, and the streets. Moreover, through the years they would convert the neighborhoods into decent, comfortable, and attractive places to live. The story of the preservation of "Packingtown" is part of the great American secret of immigrants who survived and succeeded in American life. Moreover, if the Union Stockyards were dirty, smelly, ugly, horrible places, the workers still earned more money than people in the steel mills or other industrial jobs, worked more regular hours, and had better chances for promotion. The "Yards" were an appalling place to work but also a good place to work if you were first- or second-generation American struggling to find your way in the world.

There were a number of immigrant communities that circled the Yards. On the north from the Canal to 31st Street was Bridgeport, the village where the Irish canal workers had lived. Just south of them was the German village of Hamburg running from 31st Street to 39th

Street. When the Irish migrated in great numbers through Bridgeport they pretty much took over Hamburg, though there were always a lot of German immigrants in the area. From 39th Street, the border of Chicago until just before the time of our story, to 47th Street was Canaryville, which was also called North East Corners and was supposed to be "a notorious hangout of Irish toughs."

From 49th Street to 55th was Englewood, the neighborhood to which some of the more successful immigrants moved. Englewood's pride and joy was Cook County Normal School. (They now call it Chicago State University.) Englewood looked down on its neighbors to the north. West of Canaryville (part of which was also called "Car Shops" because there were so many railroad yards and repair facilities along the east end of the district) was New City, the major German immigrant settlement neighborhood, which engaged in constant political infighting with the Irish. The Germans usually lost—because the Irish were too tricky for them. West of New City, the section around Ashland and back up to 39th Street, was a neighborhood called "Stockyards" or eventually "Back o' the Yards." Here the immigrants after the Irish and the Germans settled—Bohemians, Poles, Lithuanians, and eventually some Italians. So the Yards were surrounded by diverse communities which often fought with one another and which also often united, sometimes in labor unions, to resist the imperialism of the meat packers.

Religiously the center of Canaryville was St. Gabriel's. While other parishes were cut off from it, like St. Rose of Lima and Visitation, and there were Lithuanian and German and Polish parishes, Maurice Dorney, the pastor of St. Gabriel's, was the towering religious figure of the district.

There were several strikes in the late part of the nineteenth century at the Yards. They were not, however, as violent as the railroad strikes would be later on. The packers were robber barons, but they were more generous with their workers than many of the other barons. They could afford to be because meat packing was an enormously successful industry. It went through a revolution in technology every ten years as assembly line and mass production techniques were applied to the slaughter—a horrible scene that I would not want to witness. I wonder how the men that worked there could go home at night and sleep. Apparently they became inured to the savagery of the whole business and slept soundly. Perhaps they dreamed of the prosperity and respectability for which they were striving and which the Canaryville Irish had come reasonably close to achieving. Some of them, of course, like the Doolans, had already arrived.

I pondered as I read the books why the Doolans hadn't moved south to Englewood where there were more homes like the kind in which they lived on Emerald Avenue and where they could have been free of the aggravations of Canaryville. Perhaps they thought that they would rather be closer to their Irish friends and, if Tom was involved in politics, constituents. Moreover, Canaryville was itself a hotbed of Irish nationalism of which Father Dorney himself was one of the leaders—the Clan'a Gael, the Ancient Order of Hibernians, and the Irish Rifles. After one of the strikes (which the unions lost, mostly because of the stupidity of Terence Powderly, the head of the Knights of Labor), the various ethnic groups established their own militias in case it was necessary to fight a war against the Pinkerton agents who had killed a couple of Irish workers during the strike. The state passed a law forbidding these rifle companies from putting bayonets on their guns but they still wore uniforms and drilled with their rifles, much to the dismay of the more affluent people living nearby in Hyde Park and Englewood.

Politics, Irish nationalism, and the Church were all tied up in one twisted tangle. As Mr. Dooley, about whom I've told you, said to his close friend Hennessey,

"Did you ever see a man who wanted a free Ireland the day after tomorrow that didn't run for Alderman sooner or later?"

Ashland and Halsted had been paved with large granite blocks. The side streets were mud, thick mud, much of the year. When the Doolans came down the steps of their house to step aboard their carriage and eventually their Stanley Steamer—I imagine they must have had one—they would wear boots and tread very carefully. In their fine clothes they were in constant danger of being spattered with the thick mud that was a reminder that Chicago was built on a swamp.

We must picture the Canaryville Irish, Nuala, living in a world of mud, terrible odors, darkness at night, and unruly people even if they were struggling up America's economic ladder. The unruly people carried rifles when they drilled in front of St. Gabriel's Church. Moreover, both Ashland and Halsted were little more than long rows of saloons. There was no rule against drinking on the job, so there was a steady stream of men across the two streets at all hours of the day to fetch buckets of beer to bring back into the Yards.

One can imagine that young Tom carried a gun and marched in the Irish Rifles and perhaps he belonged to the Clan or the Land League as well as the Ancient Order of Hibernians. Canaryville then was not merely a center for Irish nationalism at the time of our mystery, it was a contentious and on occasion dangerous hotbed of Irish nationalist politics.

The homes must have some memories of conflicts within families. Perhaps the Doolans, father and son, were split on the issue. Perhaps husband and wife disagreed. However, it's hard to imagine that both of them did not respect Father Dorney. I can't suppress some images of that zealous, fierce, magnanimous parish priest meeting the two of them when they came back from Michigan City and sobbing with them over the death of their little girl.

That's about it, Nuala, make of this whatever you can.

Nuala was sitting up in a robe in the parlor when I gave her my report. As usual she read it twice and put it aside, her face locked in a deep frown—and looking very attractive despite its unnatural pallor.

"A grand bunch of friggin' eejits, weren't they, Dermot Michael?"

"They were, Nuala Anne."

"What brave people too, to work in such a horrible place and themselves owning their own homes and improving their neighborhood and their life."

"They were that too."

"And they'd already begun to go to college?"

"Not all of them surely but enough of them to pass the national average. By the turn of the century the Irish, including Canaryville Irish, had already become successful Americans, and being Irish they didn't care who they told about it."

"And themselves taking over the City of Chicago. Sure, that shouldn't have surprised anyone, should it?"

"Not anyone who knows the Irish."

"Is that where your man is from?"

"The clan hails from Hamburg. It's all in the Eleventh Ward now."

"That just goes to show you, doesn't it?"

I agreed that it did, though I wasn't sure what it showed us.

"Does this report of mine throw any light on our problem?" I then asked.

"Dermot Michael, it suggests there must have still been a lot of conflicts going on in 1898, perhaps not openly but still strongly felt. Our kind of people, as I don't have to tell you, have long, long memories."

Nuala pondered my report again and put it aside on my part of the bed.

"Things are never what they seem, are they, Dermot Michael?"

"You've been saying that a lot lately."

"There seems to be a story here. Maybe your Ancient Order of Hibernians is split. It's late October, not exactly a time for an excursion, but the weather is wonderful and the Hibernians are trying to raise money for the Cause. So they charter this old ship to go across the Lake. Everybody is looking forward to a grand time. Some folk say, 'Isn't it too late?' but they are overruled and the boat goes off. Unbeknown to them, however, there is going to be a rendezvous between a man, maybe named Hill, who somehow represents the revolutionaries in Ireland, and young Tom Doolan. Mary Louise Collins Doolan does not want to go but he insists, everybody else is bringing their wives and, if they have any, their children. It will be a pleasant weekend, no great trouble for anyone. A man from Detroit gets on the ship in Saugatuck, perhaps your man Hill. The ship heads back for Chicago. Whatever mysterious exchange is supposed to happen takes place between him and Tom Doolan. Then the ship is rammed and sunk. Doolan and his wife escape. Their poor little girl dies. The man from Detroit and his wife, whatever their real name might have been, also die. People blame Doolan for organizing a cruise at the wrong time of the year. He has to live with that guilt for the rest of his life. He can never forgive himself for all the deaths, including the death of his daughter. His wife refuses to forgive him. Their marriage is blighted, their love is destroyed, their lives are ruined. Still, Doolan, an Irish patriot no matter what, comes back the next summer and tries to find whatever it was that went down with the ship. Apparently he fails. End of the story. Doesn't that seem likely, Dermot Michael?"

"That's what I thought."

Nuala Anne sighed.

"Sure, it looks plausible, doesn't it? A bunch of eejits—and Irish eejits at that—doing eejit things and risking the lives of their wives and children. But we don't know if any of that's true, it's all something that we pieced together from a few clues. And, to tell you the truth, it doesn't fit. Who needs a cruise boat to exchange something from Ireland? And if it's money going to Ireland, then why couldn't it have been given to the man in Chicago? And if it's something coming from Ireland, wouldn't it have been a lot simpler in 1898 to take one of your trains around the south side of the Lake? Why risk a dubious excursion at the wrong time of the year?"

"Yet something strange happened, something besides a random accident, an unexpected collision in the dark. You're right: every incident in the story could somehow point in the opposite direction."

"And the biggest question of all, Dermot Michael, is why are we involved?"

"Because you and Nelliecoyne saw the ships on the Lake and herself went crazy when we drove by the house in which the Doolans once lived!"

"These things always happen to me for some kind of purpose, Dermot. Why wouldn't the same thing be true for poor little Nelliecoyne? There is something from the past that we're supposed to straighten out. But what could it be? We can't bring little Agnes Mary Elizabeth Doolan back to life, can we? Even if she hadn't drowned in Lake Michigan, she'd now probably be dead."

"Or a hundred years old."

"Something needs to be straightened out," my wife announced firmly. "And ourselves not knowing what the mystery is."

"Let's hope this Ms. Colleen Doolan Kavanagh is able to give us a few more pieces next week."

"Dermot Michael," she sighed, lying back on her pillow, "I wouldn't count on that very much if I were you. Now would you ever bring me another one of your brilliant hot toddies?"

—18—

MONDAY WAS not exactly a brilliant day. The two women in my life were recovering, my wife much more slowly than my daughter. Nuala spent half the day in bed with a touch of fever. I began to wonder whether we had to really take her to see a doctor. I called my father, however, and he assured me that what Nuala had, had been going around a lot lately.

Naturally.

Things started out badly in the morning when I decided that I ought to take the wolfhound for her morning run, since Nuala now had missed two days. For some reason Fiona was in a contentious mood. She objected to my putting the flexi-leash on her collar, she objected to going outside, though it was a nice enough if bitter cold morning. Then, when we were outside, sensing that the situation might be different with me, she ran faster than I did, tugged on her leash, almost pulled me over, and generally misbehaved like a very bad dog. In the struggle for dominance between her and me, I emerged at best a close second. A squad car came by as we were running down Webster and the cop rolled down the window to warn me that I should be very careful to keep that dangerous-looking dog on the leash. He added that it looked to him that she was about to break free.

I thanked him politely. Fiona barked loudly at him as

if to tell him he had absolutely no business at all, at all, interfering with her morning run.

Back on Southport I decided that perhaps I ought to replace Nuala at Mass too. So I walked into church just as the pastor was beginning the liturgy, and ordered Fiona to sit down next to the last pew. She absolutely refused to do so and continued to strain on the leash as though she wanted to dash up to the altar and smother the priest with affection. Finally I tapped her on the nose and said, "Fiona, you are a very bad dog today—stop it, and stop it now!"

She yiped in protest. The priest winced as though somebody had stuck a knife in his back. I felt that it would be nice if temporarily the ground opened and swallowed me up.

"Fiona," I said ominously, "bad dog."

She looked surprised and then guilty and curled up at my feet in a solid, sullen knot.

"Miserable bitch," I whispered to her.

We went back to the house and I let her out in the yard where she could continue her recreation of chasing what was left of the leaves falling from the tree.

Nuala was making breakfast, pale and tired and discouraged.

"Dermot Michael Coyne, I'm never going to get better. Why don't you just take me to the home for the incurables and leave me there for the rest of my life."

"We don't have homes for incurables anymore, Nuala, and Ireland doesn't either."

She poured me my morning shot of Earl Grey tea.

"Maybe they could start one for me because I'm not ever going to get better, not ever, ever, ever, at all, at all, at all!"

"Your dog was misbehaving this morning," I told her.

She sank into a chair across the kitchen table from me and brushed her disorderly hair away from her face.

"Kind of pushed you as far as she could to see what she could get away with?"

"That seems a fair description of it."

"Och, the poor thing, she must miss me on her morning runs."

That was one explanation.

Finally, we let the wolfhound back into the house. She sort of sulked by me, avoiding my accusing stare. Nuala went back up to bed and I went into the nursery to investigate Nellie. She glared at me too, not at all ready to be pleasant on a day on which the blue sky now was rapidly turning gray and the wind suggested that it was getting colder and colder.

It was time for a diaper change. So I put her on the diaper table and wiped her off. That improved her disposition considerably. She waved her arms, kicked her legs, and gurgled.

I folded the smelly diaper and stuck it in the diaper genie. I noted that I had better empty the genie before Nuala was well enough to inspect it. I lifted my laughing daughter off the table and put her on the floor for a moment so I could remove the bag inside the can. She rolled over and tried to sit up, but failed in her attempts. Still weak from the infection I thought. The phone rang, Nuala picked it up in the bedroom. Very cautiously Fiona thrust herself into the bedroom and nuzzled me. I patted her on the head very briefly.

"We're not making peace yet, girl. You were a bad dog in church this morning."

She hung her massive head in shame.

Why do dogs show shame so easily?

"Dermot Michael," Nuala cried from the bedroom.

"Coming."

I walked out of the door of the nursery, which was only a few feet down the corridor from the bedroom. I'd walked maybe half those feet when suddenly Fiona went berserk, barking like she were the hound of heaven.

"What's the matter with you now?" I demanded and then I looked at my feet. Scooting around me at full speed was a going-on-eight-months-old baby, crawling straight for the staircase. I snatched her up and carried her back to the bedroom and put her in the crib. Her dignity had been badly violated. She shouted in protest.

"Shut up, you little brat," I told her. "Before this day is over I'm going to get a gate put at the top of that stairway so you won't ever risk your life doing a crazy thing like that again."

Fiona nuzzled me as I turned to go to Nuala's room.

"Yes, Fiona, you're a very good dog. We're good friends now. Don't ever let Nelliecoyne do that again."

As I went into Nuala's room I thought to myself that it might be a good idea for me to get the hell out of the house and go back to working in the Board of Trade, a far more peaceful place. Thank God my wife had not caught me in that moment of carelessness.

"What's the matter with herself?" she demanded as I entered the bedroom, a warning frown on her face.

"She tried to crawl out of the bedroom and Fiona and I stopped her. She was most upset when I put her back in the crib."

"Och, Dermot Michael, won't that child be the death of all of us!"

"We're going to have to keep a pretty close eye on her from now on. I guess she's discovering the world and has found out that it's a very big place."

"And doesn't she want to know everything about it? Och, Dermot Michael, what a shame it is that I'm never going to recover to be able to take care of her."

I sat down in the chair next to the bed and felt her forehead, still a touch of fever.

"I hope you get better soon, Nuala Anne."

"So you can get back into the habit of fucking me?"

"Nuala!"

"Don't tell me you're not thinking about it now because I know you are!"

"The thought had occurred to me."

She sighed loudly.

"I guess we'll just have to make up for lost time, if I ever do recover, which I know I won't."

"I suppose I could manage that."

"I just had a call from poor Nessa," Nuala changed the subject. "Hasn't the little eejit broken up with her Seamus?"

"Why did she do that?"

"She had him out with some of her fancy friends from the University last night and they had some big argument and he disagreed with all the rest of them and embarrassed her something terrible."

"How did he do that?"

"Faith, Dermot Michael, I don't know. They were arguing about the Church and all of them were your kind of fallen away Catholics who felt the Church was terrible, and your poor man had the radical notion that people are the Church and it's crazy to leave it."

"That's what the little Bishop says, isn't it?"

"Sure is," she said, sighing. "But these friends of hers like to stand on the outside and criticize."

"So she was ashamed of him?"

"Didn't she say that very thing? She said he was a nice young man and he was going to make a lot of money when he went back to Galway. They had different interests and they would have different kinds of friends and she simply couldn't trust him in a room with a bunch of intellectuals."

"How many intellectuals do they have at DePaul?"

"I don't know, Dermot. Most of them are probably pretend intellectuals instead of real intellectuals like your man the little Bishop. But your pretend intellectuals are worse than your real intellectuals."

The next blow came in midmorning when we had a call from a very officious woman who informed us that she was Ms. Kavanagh's administrative assistant. Ms. Kavanagh, she said superciliously, had an emergency board meeting and would not be able to see us on Tuesday morning. She was rescheduling our conversation for

Thursday morning at the same time. I hardly had a chance to say "thank you" to her for the message.

Then at noontime Cindy called to report on Maybelline.

"She went ballistic after her first session with the new psychiatrist this morning, Dermot. She screamed and ranted and insisted there was nothing wrong with her and she was never going to go into the psychiatrist's office again, that all psychiatrists were charlatans."

"Her husband is a psychiatrist, isn't he?"

"I'm afraid that Maybelline has been on the edge for a long time. The rest of us simply haven't noticed because she doesn't seem very different than in years gone by. Maybe she's been right on the edge as long as we've known her. Her confrontation with Nuala might have pushed her over the edge. I'm not sure whether that's good or bad, but it's going to be hell on her husband and probably on the rest of us."

"Oh, great!"

I told Nuala only a little about that phone call.

She felt better as the day went on and found enough strength to get out of bed and put on her jeans and her Bulls sweatshirt and walk downstairs into the television room.

I joined her.

"Is it because of your Stockyards, Dermot Michael, that they call the basketball team the Bulls?"

" 'Tis, though the Yards are gone."

"I keep learning about this strange city. . . . Strange and wonderful. . . . I should really be practicing me songs, shouldn't I, Dermot? And doing the voice exercises? Won't Madam be furious at me when she finds out that I have missed three whole days of exercises?"

"You can tell Madam that you were sick, can't you?"

"Madam's pupils are not permitted to get sick, Dermot Michael, you ought to know that."

She did work up enough energy towards suppertime

to sing a little bit. When Nelliecoyne heard her, she cried in protest.

"Would you ever bring her downstairs, Dermot Michael?"

Our daughter was standing up and hanging on the side of the crib when I entered the bedroom. She scowled at me and shook the crib angrily. I better let her mother discover this new trick for herself.

I removed her from the crib and brought her down to the television room so she could rest contentedly in her mother's arms while the singing went on.

Nuala turned on the five o'clock news to see if Nick Farmer would appear. He was only supposed to have one slot a week but now that he had made himself into a celebrity, perhaps they would give him more.

The lead story on the news was about Nick Farmer.

"Chicago journalism," the artificial blonde began solemnly, "has lost one of its most vivid and controversial commentators. Nicholas Herman Farmer's dead body was found late today in an alley in the Uptown neighborhood. According to Area Six Commander John Culhane, he probably died last night and his body was only discovered behind a clump of bushes late this morning."

The camera cut to John Culhane at his usual station behind a podium in Area Six headquarters.

"We have no report on the cause of death yet. Mr. Farmer does not seem to be a victim of foul play. We are investigating further."

Then there was a shot of a covered body being brought into Ravenswood Hospital.

"Farmer had a distinguished career in Chicago journalism," the blonde went on. "He had worked for the *Chicago Tribune*, the *Chicago Sun-Times, Chicago Magazine*, WMAQ Radio, *The Reader*, and a number of other journals. Most recently, he had also been a commentator on this station. He also contributed many articles to culture reviews. His voice was always clear, firm, and honest. Jody Clough, station manager of Channel

Three, said in a statement this afternoon, 'Nick Farmer was the last of an old breed of Chicago journalists. A man of total integrity and gutsy honesty. We will miss him, we will not see his like again.' "

"Bullshit."

"Dermot Michael Coyne!" Nuala said in shock. "The poor man is dead!"

"Indeed he is."

"Funeral details are not confirmed yet," the anchorperson continued. "Mr. Farmer is survived by his wife Martha and two teenage children."

"I never knew that the man had a wife and kids," Nuala said. "Poor dear people!"

The phone rang. I picked it up.

"Dermot Michael Coyne!"

"John Joseph Culhane here, Dermot. You've seen the five o'clock news?"

"Yeah, quite by chance we turned it on."

"I wanted to get to you before it broke. We haven't told them yet that Farmer was almost certainly murdered. He was given a huge overdose of heroin while his hands and feet were bound. After he was dead, his killers dumped the body in an alley behind Ashland Avenue and just north of Wilson in Uptown. The irony is that someone came forward in Evanston this morning and admitted that the assassination last week was, just as Nuala thought, fake. Farmer was hoping to get enough publicity so that somebody would give him a slot on television again. Evanston didn't call us until the news broke this afternoon that this time he was really dead. I'll try to keep you informed. By the way, there's a wake tomorrow afternoon and evening up on Clark Street and the funeral Mass at St. Gregory's on Wednesday morning."

"St. Gregory's?"

"Yeah, Dermot, I guess the poor man was one of us."

There was mystery aplenty in the world.

"Dermot Michael," my wife said to me, "you look

stricken! Aren't you at least as pale as I am?"

"He was murdered, Nuala, it wasn't a heart attack, it wasn't a stroke, it was a massive overdose of heroin administered hours before his body was thrown into the alley in Uptown. The wake is tomorrow afternoon and evening and the Mass is at St. Gregory's Church up in Summerdale on Wednesday morning."

"Dermot Michael," she said firmly, "we're going to have to go, aren't we? The poor man was a Catholic, it is the only thing for us to do."

Catholics, especially Irish Catholics, have a dangerous habit of being ready to forgive everything at the time of death—however temporary that forgiveness is.

"Nuala, he tried to destroy your career, he tried to frame us for attempted murder, he was a mean, nasty, vicious man. I don't see why we should pay any attention to his death other than to breathe a sigh of relief."

"Dermot! You should be ashamed of yourself! The poor man is dead. We have to go up there and offer our sympathies to his wife and children! We are Catholics after all, are we not, Dermot Michael?"

"I guess so."

"Besides, now we have another mystery to solve, don't we?"

"Why is this our mystery, Nuala? Can't we leave it to John Culhane and Area Six?"

"It's our mystery, Dermot, because if it isn't solved there's always going to be a suspicion that somehow or the other we did it."

"Culhane doesn't believe that for a moment. The Chicago Police Department isn't going to put us on its list of suspects."

"It isn't the Chicago Police Department that we have to worry about, Dermot, it's public opinion. The poor man attacked us on television. He said that we were making threats against him. Someone wounded him in front of a bar. Then he turns up dead. Though they'll never have any proof that we were involved—because of course we weren't—the suspicion will still linger. I don't want our poor little Nelliecoyne growing up with that kind of suspicion around her family."

"Now that you put it that way, Nuala, I can see your point. We do indeed have two mysteries."

"And both of them, Dermot, are mysteries in which we really don't know what the mystery is and a mystery in which what things seem to be is probably not what they are at all."

"We have a pretty clear idea of what happened to Nicholas Farmer, don't we? He was a mean, nasty man who made a lot of enemies and his enemies finally caught up with him."

"That's what it looks like, Dermot, but we should know by now that often things aren't what they look like."

The following afternoon Nuala announced that she was well enough to go to the wake. Irishwoman that she was, she would pull herself out of bed with a 103 fever to make it to a wake.

"What does His Reverence's book say about St. Gregory's, Dermot Michael?"

There was no point in denying that I had looked the parish up in George the Priest's two-volume history of Chicago parishes.

"It was a German national parish founded in 1904, two decades after St. Gabe's. Germans were a major component of the population of Chicago, more of them, in fact, than there were Irish. They were moving up from the near North Side to a district which people tend to call Lakeview or Edgewater but which, across Clark Street, is really Summerdale, because once there were summer homes up there. The Germans built lovely churches while, with the exception of Father Dorney, the Irish put up school buildings and used the auditoriums as churches. They also were much more serious about church music and liturgy than we were. The day the parish was founded, they chose eight men to be their choir."

"Not wild men from the bogs, were they now?"

"More civilized and more literate than we were, but not nearly as clever when it came to politics."

At the wake we met Nick Farmer's estranged wife, Martha. She was a tall, attractive, and somewhat haggard but extremely pleasant woman in her early forties. She introduced us to her son and daughter, two somber but presentable teenagers who both attended St. Gregory's High School.

"It was so very nice of you to come," she said sweetly. "Poor Nicholas was a deeply troubled man but he had so many good qualities and so much talent. Though we haven't been together for many years, I still will miss him. Every once in a while he would feel terribly guilty about what he had done and would try to patch together our marriage. It never worked. His ambition was too strong and the sense that his great talent had been frustrated always burdened him."

"How very sad," Nuala said sympathetically.

"I know that he gave you a very hard time, Ms. McGrail. I don't think there was any personal animosity in it. He had a hot temper but it cooled down very quickly. His vitriolic attacks on people were sudden bursts of anger which he knew called attention to himself and his work. He meant no harm by it."

He may not have meant any harm by it, I thought to myself, but he surely did a lot of harm.

"Och," Nuala said, "we weren't thinking about that at all, at all. We just feel sorry for the poor man and for all your own sufferings."

Martha nodded solemnly. "It's very strange. I received a letter from him just yesterday, it must have been mailed right before he died. There was no hint in it that he expected to die. He pleaded for my forgiveness more strongly than he had ever pleaded before. Of course I forgave him, I had always forgiven him. I'm only sorry

I didn't have a chance to tell him that one last time."

"He asked for forgiveness?" Nuala whispered.

"Forgiveness, Ms. McGrail. Here, let me read the paragraph."

She opened her purse and removed a much worn sheet of paper.

" 'Martha, I have been a rotten husband and a rotten father and I'm not much of a music critic either. I don't know what's happened to my life. I'm terribly sorry for having let you down so many times. I hope you will forgive me. I know that it is impossible for us ever to get together again. How did you and the kids put up with me at the times we were together? I'm a slob, a phony, a faker, and also a burnt-out case. I always will be that. On this day, when I feel a little guilt for the bad things I've done to people, I want to tell you how sorry I am.' "

Tears poured down the woman's cheeks. Behind her, her daughter was weeping too and her son was struggling with his emotions.

"Daddy was not a bad man," the daughter said. "Things simply never seemed to go right for him."

Nuala was crying too when we left the funeral hone.

John Culhane greeted us as we emerged.

"I saw the ancient Mercedes," he said, "and I thought I would stop to have a word with you."

"It's all so terrible," Nuala said, dabbing her eyes with a tissue. "The poor dead man, the poor woman, the poor kids."

"You see it every day in police work," John replied. "Wasted lives. This man was apparently talented and he didn't have the character to use his abilities."

Too simple, I thought.

"Who might have killed him?" I asked. "What kind of enemies did he have?"

These are the kind of bread-and-butter questions that I am permitted to ask. It's only the questions about ul-

timate meetings and stories that Nuala bothers herself
with.

"A long, long list of enemies, Dermot. Lots of people
disliked him. He had very few friends. The crowd he
hung out with in the bar on Chicago Avenue up in Evanston were celebrity worshipers, would-be intellectuals
and would-be liberals who cluster around Northwestern
University like vultures. In Chicago he hung out at the
Old Town Alehouse which, as you know, is a dingy
place for dingy journalists. I'm not sure that he had
friends there. He has offended just about every editor
and news director in Chicago and most of the journalists
too. There won't be a very big crowd here at his wake."

"What did he do to offend editors and other journalists?"

"What didn't he do! He stole other people's work, he
faked scoops, he plagiarized, he betrayed confidences,
he attacked the innocent, he took advantage of young
reporters. He didn't destroy people but it wasn't for want
of trying. He seemed to think that he could succeed only
if other people failed. For him all other Chicago media
people were miserable fakes. He might have been right,
but you can't be too obvious about your contempt for
your colleagues. He was smart and charming when he
wanted to be and had a way with words. However, he
usually destroyed himself before he achieved any real
success."

"That's pretty sad."

"Yeah, and he drank too much and he was always
overweight and he pumped all kinds of chemicals into
his system."

"How did he get the job at Channel Three?"

"Doug Jurgens, the news director there, was an old
friend. Went to high school with him. Figured he owed
him a couple of favors. There weren't very many markers out there for Farmer to pick up."

As we angled over to Lake Shore Drive, Nuala said,

"Dermot Michael, don't you think it's time you check with your friends out on the West Side?"

"I hadn't thought of that at all."

When Lieutenant Knox asked the question about contacts with people who are involved in organized crime I completely forgot that Nuala Anne and I both knew the top leader of the Outfit. I had gone to grammar school with his grandson. He was terrified of Nuala because he realized that she was one of the dark ones.

"I could find out whether this was an outside job."

"And maybe find out who did it."

"As you know, that has to be an indirect approach. I'll see what I can do as soon as we get home."

"We're really going to have to go to the funeral mass tomorrow, aren't we, Dermot Michael?"

Did I have any choice? No.

"Certainly."

"And to the cemetery afterward. There is bound to be only a handful of people there."

"I quite agree."

I agreed, mind you, but I would never have thought of doing it myself.

Nuala flipped open her tiny phone and called Nessa. She shook her head after the usual brisk exchange in Irish.

"I think, Dermot Michael, that we better get gates at the top and the bottom of the stairs. This little monster is trouble."

"Seamus?"

"Not a thing."

Later, when Nuala was nursing Nellie after we returned to the house, she informed me, "That young woman is not only an eejit, she's a fookin' onchuck!"

"Nuala, I thought you'd given up such language!"

"Give over, Dermot Michael, sometimes only that type of language expresses the reality of things."

"I suppose it does."

"She didn't say anything to you about Seamus?"

"If she wouldn't say anything to you, she wouldn't say it to me."

"You're right, Dermot Michael, as always you're right."

As always, huh?

"In two days," Nuala predicted, "she'll be missing him and then it might be too late, poor little thing."

I wondered how often I was poor little Dermot when she was talking to Nessa.

I called my friend out on the West Side to see what he could do for me.

"My friend out on the West Side" didn't necessarily mean that the man in question lived on the West Side, though in fact in this case he did. Or that he was necessarily a friend. It merely meant that he was "connected" with the Outfit and sometimes acted as a go-between.

"Hey! Dermot my friend, how are you? It's been a while since I have seen you!"

"Hey! I don't get downtown too much these days. I stay home and I work on my stories."

"I don't blame you, Dermot. There's nothing much going on downtown."

We chatted for a few moments for the sake of professional courtesy.

"I wonder if we could find out something from some friends of friends of yours?"

Instantly he became uneasy.

"Dermot, I'll be happy to talk to some of my friends to see if their friends can provide anything for you."

"There was a certain business operation in Uptown the other night. I've been wondering if you could learn from any of your friends whether it was a legitimate business operation."

"Gotcha, Dermot."

"Sounds like something crazies out in South Chicago might try."

I meant the Latino drug gangs who made the Outfit

in its present elderly manifestations look benign.

"I'll see what I can do. I'll be back to you, Dermot, as soon as I can talk to some of my friends who have friends."

I was asking whether the mob was involved in putting down Farmer. It didn't sound like the kind of thing they would go after. He was far too small a target for the cautious old men who now ran it. Some hits went down without authorization, which they knew about but did not stop because it was not worth their effort to do so. Rarely did the Outfit use anything so crude as heroin overdoses. I wanted to be able to exclude them from our considerations and perhaps open the possibility that they might be our allies.

There was only a small group of people at the funeral mass the next day at St. Gregory's, a delicately beautiful church of the sort the Germans tended to build in Chicago. The Catholic funeral liturgy, done properly as it would be in a church whose origins were German, is an extraordinary experience. Restrained sadness and serene joy invade the souls of the participants. The service dulls the pain and lifts the spirit.

Hope is not a bad idea.

The elderly priest who had known Farmer as a student in high school thirty years before talked about his earnestness and enthusiasms and especially about the hungers in his heart.

"Nicholas hungered for the infinite," the priest concluded, "we all hunger for the infinite. His hunger was stronger than that of most of us. I don't think he came very close to the infinite during his life, though on occasion he seemed to know what he was seeking. Now he has it all and we rejoice he's gone home to the peace and love for which he was always hungering."

Several pews in front of us his wife was crying. Naturally Nuala Anne was crying next to me.

Then we rode up to All Saints Cemetery on the edge of the city. The same elderly priest said the prayers at the graveside and offered his sympathy to the family. Nuala and I shook hands with the widow and her children. Nuala and Martha embraced.

A strikingly handsome man, with a shock of iron gray hair and big sad eyes, one of a dozen or so mourners around the graveside, extended his hand to me.

"Dermot Coyne?"

"That's me."

"I'm Rog Conrad. I went to St. Gregory's with Nicholas. It was very graceful of you and your wife to come to the funeral. Not many people cared about him."

"My wife insisted."

"I would like to buy you both lunch, as a sign of my gratitude."

"Sure . . . Nuala, this is Rog Conrad. He wants to buy us lunch."

"Sure, we never turn down a free meal, do we, Dermot Michael?" Nuala said, turning on all her charm.

Nuala's eyes flickered at me as we turned to walk to our cars. The flicker meant, "We ought to talk to this man."

I was improving at the art of reading her signals.

He was a freelance writer, a sometime reporter for *The Wall Street Journal* who had specialized in business scandals. He had written several books on the subject and was, he seemed to hint, very successful at that trade. I vaguely remembered reviews of a prizewinner about American oil companies in Africa.

He took us to an elegant restaurant in downtown Evanston—rich green wall hangings, daylight filtering in through skylights, crisp white linen tablecloths, shining silverware, attentive waiters, and a fascinating menu. In French.

Big deal.

Nuala made another phone call home. Apparently reassured by Nessa, she continued to charm our host.

"This is a brilliant restaurant altogether, Mr. Conrad," she said. "Isn't it, Dermot Michael?"

I agreed that it was.

"I owe you two something for being so generous to Nicholas. He didn't deserve it, but it was still good of you to be concerned about him and especially his family."

"Your man must have been terribly unhappy."

Sure, wasn't she on the case and wasn't I therefore advised to keep my mouth shut?

"And himself with a very nice wife and two beautiful children," Nuala continued.

"He had lots of talent, as Father Reinhard said at Mass. As a high school kid he was magic. Pure charisma. Enormously popular. What he lacked, I think, was patience. He had to have instant success. When he left college to go to work for the City News Bureau, an apprenticeship for many of us in those days, he charged in with supreme confidence that he was better than anyone else in the shop. Naturally, the veterans—guys a couple of years older than he was—found ways to make him look ridiculous. He was furious. He set out to get even with them and he did, but he made a lot of enemies."

"Poor man."

"Nick was too brash, too ambitious. He wasn't able to keep his mouth shut, you see, and wait for the next time. And there would have been next times. Then later on he had to pick on younger guys just as older guys picked on him. He couldn't help himself. When he wasn't stirring up trouble against the boss, whoever the boss might be, he was feuding with his colleagues."

We were served a mild red wine. Nuala ordered tournedos Rossini. So did I.

"I don't want to get involved with this," Conrad continued. "I don't want to dig into his life and his past to get a story. There are enough stories going around as it is. I know you two are close to Culhane and I think you might want to pass something on to him."

Aha, now we get down to business.

"I'm sure John would be happy if we passed something useful on to him," Nuala said easily.

"Nick was working on a big story. A really big story. Or so he told me. He was always on to something big. This time he was more excited than usual. It'll knock your socks off, Rog, he said several times."

"Were any of his other stories really big?"

"Some weren't, but some were. He'd always blow it."

"Did it have anything to do with the music industry?" Nuala asked as she destroyed altogether an oil and vinegar salad.

"It might have. I think so. He was very vague about it. Nick was always vague about his top stories because he was afraid someone was trying to steal them. A couple of times his stories were stolen. Other times he tried to steal stories himself. I suspect that it was music. It was the beat he had chosen for himself."

"Any idea what kind of music?"

"Gangsta Rap."

"Bad business," I said, tasting the wine and then tasting it again.

"Did he seem to think his investigation was dangerous?" Nuala asked, sipping delicately from her glass.

"Things were always dangerous for Nick. To hear him tell it, he never moved onto something that was safe. It was always a big story that people were trying to prevent him from telling. Danger, even if it was imaginary danger, turned him on."

"How horrible!"

"Yes, indeed, Ms. McGrail."

"That's me mother. I'm Nuala or, if someone is wanting to say something special to me, Nuala Anne."

Conrad, who did not seem much into smiling, smiled.

"All right, Nuala Anne. When we were all back in St. Gregory's twenty-five years ago, he didn't seem crazy. Ambitious, yes, a little ruthless, yes. But lots of fun. He was the leader of our little group who ran the school paper, a bunch of kids who wanted to grow up and be like Woodward and Bernstein. He was a charmer too. Martha Grimm was the prettiest girl in the class. She fell totally in love with him and never really stopped loving him."

"She's free now though," Nuala said.

"Free indeed but really not free and she might never be."

"Poor woman," Nuala said with the barest hint of a flicker of an eye in my direction.

"I don't really know what he was working on. He certainly had lots of contacts around the city. And a nose for dirt. Sometimes he made up the dirt as he did about you folks. . . . He trusted me more than anyone else, but not by any means one hundred percent. I think he was a little scared. He made me promise to try to take care of Martha and the kids if anything happened to him. He had never done that before."

"And would they be needing someone to take care of them?"

He shrugged indifferently.

"She doesn't need anyone to take care of her or the kids, at least not financially. And I'm happily married so that's not a route I'd be inclined to go."

There was a faint hint in his voice that at one time he might have been inclined to go that route. Was Nick an old rival who had won in the contest for Martha?

"Tell us more about that darlin' little parish. Did you all go through school there?"

My wife was up to something. I didn't know exactly what she was up to but she was up to it.

"From first grade to high school senior year."

His eyes clouded over and a quick spasm of pain raced across his face.

"And you all wanted to be journalists, did you now?"

She attacked the beef with a savagery that astonished me. Yep, she was getting better.

"Everything was clear during the time after the Watergate crisis. We wanted to make money, become famous, and perhaps improve the world. Since the North-western Journalism school was up here in Evanston, we figured we would go there and become the Pulitzer Prize winners of our generation. Martha, Nicholas, Johnny Quinn, Doug Jurgens, Robin Cleary, and I. Nick dropped out after his sophomore year because he said they had nothing more to teach him. Johnny and Robin married each other and gave up on journalism. Johnny is an investment banker downtown and she has her own PR firm. Very power people. Martha heads up a small but well-respected market research firm. Doug is news director at Channel Three. Only Nicholas and I stayed in reporting."

The facts in his narrative did not seem to justify the deep sadness with which he told the story.

"Ah, sure, don't we all have great dreams when we're young and we settle down and accept whatever happens."

"You and Dermot seem to have done all right in your professional careers, Nuala Anne."

"I never thought I was going to be a singer and Dermot never thought he was going to be a writer. I was going to be an accountant and he was going to be a commodity trader. And we were both going to be huge successes. Dermot was a failure as a trader, but made a lot of money at the exchange by mistake and got out while he could. And I had a good job at Arthur Anderson, but I liked singing better. So our dreams didn't come true and ourselves being lucky that they didn't."

I didn't like Nuala's comment that I had failed in my chosen career. Still, it was the absolute truth, wasn't it now? I had no idea what she was talking about. Neither, I suspected, did Rog Conrad.

"I've made it, I guess," he said. "I've become the kind of journalist I wanted to be back in the days at St. Gregory. Sometimes I think it's better if your dreams don't come true. Today I wish we were all juniors again, just taking over the school paper."

"Isn't that the truth about dreams?"

"I never feel safe in Evanston," I said to my wife as we drove home in the rain. "It's where they started Prohibition."

"It's no wonder I was uneasy the whole time . . . what a terrible thing to do!"

"It was indeed. I expected any moment that someone from the Women's Christian Temperance Union would come in and take the wine away from us."

There was a silence, then Nuala said, "Dermot Michael, whatever did you make of that man?"

"I'm not sure, Nuala. I remembered who he was during lunch. He's a very famous writer. His book on Nigeria will probably win the nonfiction Pulitzer this year. The reviews were ecstatic. He managed to break through the protection around the military government and find out how they live. He reported in detail the corrupt relationship between the government and the oil companies. Somehow he was present at a number of embarrassing conversations in which the oil people bought off government leaders and later defended their actions to him on the grounds that America had to have oil and that's the way business is done in the third world. Vivid, searing, scary stuff."

"Doesn't seem like the kind of man who could do that, does he?"

"His earlier books were pretty good too. Some people say he's the best journalist in America. . . . What did you make of him?"

That was the question I was supposed to ask.

"Dermot," she said thoughtfully, "he's an awful nice fellow and very charming and he's always been in love with Martha and he can't wait to get rid of his own wife and pursue her, but he doesn't have the courage or the passion to do it. And he really never liked poor Nicholas, especially since he stole Martha. Yet he came to the funeral. And himself trying to throw dust in our eyes, which I found most unusual, didn't you now, Dermot?"

"Oh, yes, most unusual," I said, not having noticed any dust at all. "Why would he want to throw dust in our eyes?"

"Now isn't that the real question. Why would he tell us so much that he didn't need to tell us without any good reason?"

"Because he had a good reason."

"I think, Dermot, someday before the week is over we're gonna have to pay a visit to Martha Farmer. Did they really think that journalism would be exciting when all it means is standing around outside a house on South-port Avenue on a cold morning waiting for something to happen, and knowing all along that nothing was going to happen?"

We turned off Sheridan Road and onto Lake Shore Drive. The skyline of Chicago loomed in front of us, a silver etching against the dark gray sky.

"Maybe he knew a little bit about your detective record and wanted to steer you down a wrong track."

"Isn't it clear that he wanted to do that? He didn't need us to pass on a hint to your man."

"Didn't he take a risk by talking to us?"

"He was afraid of us, Dermot Michael."

"Oh."

"Don't we now have two mysteries in which we don't know what the mystery is?"

"In this mystery isn't the puzzle who killed Nick Farmer?"

"No, Dermot Michael. It's what happened to those poor people when they were back at St. Gregory's High School."

—19—

WE ONLY consumed ten minutes of Colleen Kavanagh's precious fifteen minutes of time. She took an instant dislike to Nuala, which reduced my ordinarily feisty wife to silence. Moreover, she didn't have much to tell us and gave the impression that if she did she wouldn't have told it to us.

On Thursday morning we drove out to Beverly, which Nuala thought was a darling neighborhood but not as darling as River Forest. As we drove through the valleys and the hills and the curving streets with gracious old homes, I told her stories about the neighborhood as a onetime hideout for cattle rustlers.

"You're having me on, Dermot Michael. This grand little neighborhood isn't the wild west."

She particularly liked the dazzling modern parish church.

"You have to admit, Dermot, that it's almost as lovely as Old St. Pat's."

Forest Preserve woods on three sides shield the massive Kavanagh house at 2020 Hopkins Place from the rest of the world. We were admitted into the house by a supercilious maid who looked down her nose at us. Apparently she did not realize that West Side Irish are more refined and more sensitive than refugees from the Yards.

We were conducted into a small sitting room and told that Mrs. Kavanagh would be with us as soon as was convenient.

Promptly at eleven forty-five we were shown into her office; a large, flawlessly neat room overlooking a carefully tended backyard in which the rosebushes were already covered for winter protection.

Mrs. Kavanagh did not stand to greet us but at least she asked us to sit down. She was a slender woman in her middle forties who would have been attractive, perhaps, if she ever smiled. In our ten minutes in her office she didn't begin to smile. Moreover, her eyes were hostile and her tone of voice contemptuous. She was obviously a very important person and we weren't important at all.

I introduced myself and Nuala as my wife.

Some women don't like Nuala on sight—her beauty is too perfect and too patently durable to be tolerable to women who are prone to envy about physical appearances. I don't know whether Nuala has ever understood or recognized this envy, but it was impossible to avoid Colleen Kavanagh's antipathy.

"You don't have any children yet, do you?" was the first question she fired.

Nuala's technique when she encounters hostile women has always been to revert to the simple pleasant lass from the wilds of Connemara who needs mothering and protection. In that role she does need protection, but it is by no means her only role.

"Oh, indeed I do, Mrs. Kavanagh," she said, beaming proudly, and pulled the wallet with Nelliecoyne's pictures out of her purse.

Colleen Kavanagh barely glanced at the pictures.

"Yes, very pretty, I'm sure."

"Thank you, ma'am," said Nuala, putting the wallet back into the purse.

"Now let's get down to business. I have two board meetings this afternoon and I must be punctual for both of them. I believe you are interested in the house our family used to occupy on Emerald Avenue?"

"We are," I said.

"I must confess I'm not much concerned about history. The experience of our family living in such a terrible neighborhood was something that I have no reason to be proud of. I do not want to remember it. While I am perfectly prepared to accept the notion that the immigrants had to struggle to escape poverty, it does seem to me that the very fact that the community remains is proof that there is very little in the way of work ethic or ambition among the Irish in this city."

"Yes, ma'am," Nuala said, cutting off effectively the outburst of temper she anticipated from me.

I was about to comment on the fact that Chicago's Mayor was from that neighborhood, more or less.

"You are particularly interested in my great-grandparents, the Doolans, who lived there at the turn of the century?"

"Yes, ma'am," Nuala said.

"I can't understand why anybody would be interested in them. My great-grandfather was not a particularly attractive man, a cheap lawyer and politician, and deeply involved in the violence of Irish nationalism from what I understand. We don't have much in the way of documents."

She reached into a folder on her desk and pulled out some photographs and a number of papers.

"Here is the family of Mr. and Mrs. Thomas Doolan in 1916. You can see they have five children—two daughters and three sons. The second oldest"—she pointed at a young man who was in his early teens—"is my grandfather. For reasons that escape me, when his parents died in the time after the Second World War, he moved into the house and raised my father there. They had lived on the North Shore before that time and you can imagine what a shock it was to my father as a young lad to move into the Stockyards area."

"Yes, ma'am."

"Do you keep in contact with your cousins, who are also descendants of the Doolans?" I asked cautiously.

"Generally I don't find it convenient to do so," she said. "There is just so much time in life and I have enough obligations with my own family and my brother's family not to want to extend the boundaries of intimacy any further."

"Do you know where they live?"

"Vaguely." She waved her hand negligently. "I believe we send Christmas cards to them but I have very little other contact with them. Only a few of them still live in the Chicago area."

"What about the descendants of this child, the pretty daughter?" Nuala asked.

"Oh, my dear, do you consider her pretty? I'm afraid I wouldn't think so. I don't really remember what her name was."

"Ellen," Nuala said, turning over the picture to read the names on the back.

"I do know that one of her grandchildren does live in a western suburb, Oak Brook perhaps. Her name I believe is Ellen Hegarty. Her husband is some sort of commodity broker. They may have better records than we have. I encounter her occasionally at important Chicago civic functions and generally find that the two of us have nothing in common."

This woman, I said to myself, is a classic snob. She knows something about her predecessors, enough to be ashamed of them. Still she's only a generation removed from the Yards and acts like she might be a first cousin of the Queen of England. Her husband is a respectable doctor with a nice income, but they are not exactly aristocrats. Certainly no more than the Coyne clan.

"Hegarty," I said. "Perhaps we'll look her up."

"Tell me, ma'am, do you have any recollections of the house itself? Didn't you live there before your father sold it?"

Colleen Kavanagh lost her composure. She shuddered briefly; I watched her fingers tremble slightly and saw the enormous struggle on her face not to show any emotion.

"I . . . I try to think of it as little as possible," she said. "It was a horrid house; old, dirty, decrepit, dismal, discouraging."

Nuala's eyes became wide, an expression of quite believable but to me phony Irish surprise.

"It sounds like you found the house frightening, Ms. Kavanagh?" she said.

"Frightening! Well, dear, I wouldn't go so far as to say that. It was simply unpleasant and I was very happy when we moved out."

We took the pictures and the clippings and departed with as much dignity as we could muster under the circumstances.

"Bitch with a capital B," I observed in the driveway.

"Dermot Michael! We must be charitable, mustn't we now? She's a very insecure and unhappy woman and all her activity isn't able to fill up the hollow inside of her. And herself a dark one like me."

"A dark one?"

"Didn't she feel the vibrations in the house!"

"Dr. Gomez says that his grandmother finds the vibrations pleasant."

"His grandmother isn't Colleen Doolan Kavanagh. Canaryville isn't what she's trying to forget. It's that terrible, terrible house! I don't want to do it but I'm afraid we are going to have to dine there with your friend, Dr. Gomez."

Nuala flipped open her little telephone and pushed the magic button to give her almost instant contact with her daughter. She talked for a few quick moments with the virtuous Nessa and then stopped. She closed the phone with a gesture of impatience.

"The little bitch really is just not going to grow up!"

"My daughter?"

If the child were a bitch she certainly couldn't be Nuala's daughter!

"Of course not, Dermot Michael Coyne, what in the world is the matter with you? No, I meant Nessa, she still doesn't want to talk to me about herself and Seamus. We have got to put a stop to that, do you understand, we have to put a stop to it!"

"Oh. And how are we going to do that?"

"I have a scheme in my head and I might have to activate that scheme pretty soon."

"And what is the scheme?"

"Och, I won't be telling you that, Dermot Michael, till it's clearer in my mind than it is now. I think you'll love it, no, I know you'll love it!"

"Oh. . . . Would it be too much to ask how our daughter is doing?"

"You mean Nelliecoyne? Why, she's doing fine, how else would she be doing, Dermot? She's playing with Nessa and with the dog and crawling all around the floor and drinking milk out of the bottle I left in the fridge and slurping up carrot baby food. What else would she be doing?"

So all right, what do I know!

In the car Nuala flipped through the pictures and documents while I steered us down 87th Street.

"Dermot, they are a fine-looking bunch of kids. Five of them. That means that whatever happened between Mary Louise and Tom Doolan they at least didn't stop sleeping with one another."

"Did people do that in those days?"

"How should I be knowing? I wasn't there, was I now? Sure wouldn't losing a child that way break up lots of marriages. The woman might just have moved into another bedroom and stayed there for a half a year or so. Still, she doesn't look like the kind that would do that. In fact, she looks very pretty and very sweet and very nice. Also, despite that terrible corset thing she's wearing, she was a very sexy woman. Tom Doolan was lucky to have a wife like her . . . and, Dermot Michael, don't you be looking at the picture . . . you're driving the car. Let us just get out of this terrible neighborhood and back home where we belong!"

I obeyed. Naturally.

However, the blond woman certainly did look sexy.

"Now, let's see," she went on, "there's five kids and on the back here they have written their names: Ellen, Tom, named after his father I suppose, John, Joseph, and Mary Louise. None of your Tiffanys or your Taylors or your Traceys or any of them other weird names, are there now?"

"Should you ever want to burden one of our children with a name like that, Nuala Anne, I'd be the one sleeping in another room!"

She found that very funny. My wife, still a little pale, was her feisty self again.

"So the woman we have to look for now would be the granddaughter of Miss Ellen. Did you know anybody named Hegarty when you were working on the Board of Trade?"

"I think so, Nuala," I said. "A very nice guy, good-looking, friendly, and as smart as they come. Crazy, like they all are. I wouldn't be surprised that he is able to afford a new home in Oak Brook these days."

"Not as successful as your lucky traders or your young novelists, is he now?"

"I mean not everybody marries a successful singer either."

"Somebody in your family must know them. You'll have to give them a ring and find out what they can tell us."

"Yes, ma'am."

"Dermot, will you ever drive north on the Lake Shore Drive instead of on this terrible Dan Ryan thing?"

"Sure, why do you want the Drive today?"

"It's such a wonderful day with the wind blowing and the waves dancing along the shore. Doesn't it take me back to Galway when I watch the waves dancing on the shore!"

So I turned off the Ryan onto the Stevenson and then onto Lake Shore Drive heading north by McCormick Place. Sure enough, the Lake was raging and dancing all along the shore with ranks of whitecaps radiant under the bright sun attacking like an army besieging a city.

"Does it really remind you of Galway Bay?" I asked.

"Oh, Dermot, not really. Galway Bay never gets that angry and besides it doesn't wash up such big waves into Galway City either, does it now?"

"I guess not."

"Isn't it a beautiful lake, Dermot Michael? It's hard to imagine it is as dangerous as you say it is and them terrible stories about the ships sinking."

"Let me tell you a story, Nuala, one I haven't told you before. Sometimes I tell it to people who are new to Lake Michigan so they'll be careful when they go swimming in it. I never told it to you because you're a very careful swimmer."

"It sounds like a scary story, Dermot Michael."

"No, it's a tragic story. Many years ago when I was a kid, I mean a little kid like eleven or twelve, one of the families down the beach imported an Irish seminarian to kind of baby-sit for their two boys during the summer. They figured that a young male would be a much better role model for their two sons, who were effeminate punks as I remember them. The young man turned out to be a fine lad. It was his first time out of Ireland and he was excited by the trip and excited by the United States and Lake Michigan and Grand Beach. He sang songs and told stories and all the little kids my age at Grand Beach fell in love with him. One day, when the Lake was really bad and the surf was washing, and the kids shouldn't have been swimming, the lifeguard wasn't there, we dove into the Lake anyhow. One of the boys he was in charge of went out too far and he was caught in the undertow. The seminarian couldn't swim but tried to save him. He grabbed him and shoved him towards the shore where someone else who could swim grabbed the lad. The current caught the seminarian, pulled him under, and sent him out into the Lake. He disappeared like he'd never been there. The fire alarms went off, the police cars pulled up, and the Coast Guard came by in their search boat. No sign of the poor seminarian at all. Three days later I was walking down the beach by myself feeling very sad for this lad: he was such a nice young man and he sang such wonderful songs and he seemed so happy. And I came upon his body, purple and twisted and lying lifeless on the shore."

"Glory to God!" said Nuala, grabbing my arm as though to protect me from the sight.

"I was scared. I'd never seen a dead body before. It was horrible. Once he'd been so alive and so vigorous and so happy and filled with so many plans for the priesthood. He wanted to be a missionary in Africa. And now he was this lifeless thing, like an old, rotten dead fish on the beach. I ran back to the house and told my father. He and my mother came down to the beach. I trailed after them, hoping that my father, who was such a wonderful doctor, could revive him. It was too late, several days too late. Lake Michigan had claimed one more life."

"Dermot, what a horrible thing to happen to a little boy!"

"No more horrible than a lot of things that have happened to many twelve-year-olds through the centuries, Nuala. Maybe we twelve-year-olds on Grand Beach had been protected too much from the sight of death. I'll never forget that twisted, purple face that had once been so vibrant and so handsome. I can't figure out why God let it happen. He would have made a wonderful priest. He would have done good things for many people. He would have been a credit to the Church and Ireland. Instead he died in a foreign country, thousands of miles from his family and friends. As I remember the story the people who had recruited him were not all that interested in paying the money to send his body back to Ireland. It was said they wouldn't call the undertaker. My father and mother took charge of it."

"A lot of death all around us these days, isn't there, Dermot Michael?"

"Indeed, Nuala, it's sad and scary. But we all must die, I guess. And there are no good ways to die."

"No, Dermot Michael, there are not, although some are worse than others."

We were silent for a minute as we drove by Grant Park with the skyscrapers standing watch behind the park. We continued north along the Gold Coast and Lincoln Park.

"It makes me feel more sorry," Nuala said, "for poor Mr. Farmer and his family."

"It makes me feel sorry, Nuala, for everybody. Those that die and those who mourn the ones who die."

"You know, Dermot Michael," she said as we turned off the Drive at Fullerton, "there's something wrong with this picture."

"Something wrong with it, Nuala?"

"This picture of Tom and Mary Louise Doolan and their five children—there's something wrong with it altogether and I'm not quite sure what it is. If I can figure out what's wrong with it, then a lot of the pieces of our puzzle might fit together."

I concentrated on the Fullerton traffic.

"We drink our water from that Lake, don't we, Dermot?"

"Life and death, Nuala? Like Baptism . . . I'm really sounding like a philosopher this afternoon, am I not?"

"Sure, Dermot, aren't you talking like a storyteller?"

Fullerton was designed for carriages. With cars parked on either side and other cars constantly moving in and out of the Lincoln Park neighborhood, it is permanent rush hour. I like the Drive better than the Expressway, but I try to avoid the intersection of Fullerton and Sheridan Road as though it were a permanent crime site.

We pulled up to our parking spot in front of the house. Inside the wolfhound was barking, apparently welcoming us home. This was a new trick. Perhaps she had decided to appease my anger of the other morning.

I opened the front door and walked in and there was the barking wolfhound and Nessa and our daughter pulling herself up on the coffee table with a grin of pure delight on her tiny face.

"Isn't she the terrible one altogether?" Nessa said approvingly. "She's been doing that all morning and she just won't give up." Whereupon Nellie fell back on her rear end with a bump. She looked startled and then grinned and began attacking the coffee table once more.

"Och, haven't I warned you, Dermot Michael, this one's going to be the death of us!"

"She'll never give you a moment's peace, that's for sure," Nessa agreed.

Nessa sped off immediately before either one of us could talk about Seamus and their sometime relationship.

"Isn't she a sneak?" Nuala asked me. "She knows if she gives us a chance we will tell her what an eejit she really is!"

By the telephone there was a note that Nessa had scrawled.

"A Mrs. Martha Farmer called. Unless she hears from you she'll come by to visit you about seven o'clock."

"Look at this, Nuala!"

Nuala read the note and shook her head.

"Dermot, we're getting deeper and deeper into the mystery."

"Isn't that what you want?"

"There's just a little bit too much mystery going on now, if you take me meaning."

The phone rang—it was John Culhane.

"Dermot, the word is out that the assassination up in Evanston was faked. It's probably going to be on television this evening. Maybe some of them will come by to see if you have any comment. We now have the fascinating puzzle of why a man should fake his own assassination and then a couple of days later actually be assassinated. I don't see any connection between the two of them except coincidence. See what your wife thinks and let me know."

"Is your man asking me questions?" Nuala said as she began to nurse our daughter. "Isn't he the Commander of detectives in Area Six? Does he expect me to be solving his mysteries for him?"

It had been several days since I had fondled that lovely breast. I wanted it.

"In a word, Nuala Anne, yes!"

"If they ask me and I guess he did, I think there is a close connection between the fake assassination and the real one and that it goes back a long time and I have no idea what it is."

"Uh-huh."

"That woman is coming this evening to tell us something more about poor Mr. Farmer. There's too many people wanting to whisper in our ears about poor Nicholas Farmer."

"Should I call him back and tell him that?"

Nuala pondered it.

"Not today, Dermot Michael, we're going to have to wait awhile to see what happens . . . and I wish I could figure out what's wrong with this picture!"

We looked over the picture and the few newspaper clippings that came with it. They were death notices for both Mary Louise Collins Doolan and for Thomas Patrick Doolan. He had served as a colonel in the United States Army in the First World War. One of his sons, John Doolan, was killed in the Second World War. Their family history looked like a history of Irish Catholics in the twentieth century—eager to serve in defense of America because America had done so much for them.

A later generation would be much less patriotic and much more cynical.

"So it all looks like ordinary family stuff, doesn't it?" my wife asked me. "How bright and hardworking men and women make the most of the opportunities in America. It is a wonder, isn't it, that they didn't have a house at Grand Beach, just like your folks. . . . Oh, Dermot, what an eejit I am! They wouldn't want to rent a house at Grand Beach, not Tom and Mary Louise anyway. And if they told their children any of the story, then they wouldn't want a house there either."

"Maybe they spent their summers at South Shore Country Club, which was right along the Lake a couple of miles farther south."

"Isn't that the place that you told me that the people that were members sold it to the city instead of letting black and Jewish people join?"

"The very same."

"I wonder how the Doolans would have voted."

It was a fair question. There were strong racist tendencies in some of the South Side Irish. Were the Doolans the kind who would give in or the kind that would resist? That was probably irrelevant to our attempts to solve the mystery.

The phone rang again—this time it was Mrs. Kavanagh's assistant. Mrs. Kavanagh had discovered, quite by chance, another document similar to the ones she had given us. She only glanced at it but it seemed to be a family diary. She saw no reason to withhold the diary from us. When we were finished with the materials we could pass them on to the Chicago Historical Society. She could not understand why anybody would be interested in a story of a family who lived in St. Gabriel's one hundred years ago. Could I send a messenger to pick it up?

I explained her message to my wife, whose daughter was now sound asleep in her arms.

"Dermot Michael, would you ever call the messenger

service and have them pick it up for us. We should have it in a couple of hours."

Nuala finally tossed the picture aside. "Dermot, give a call to your brothers and sisters and find out where them Hegarty folks live. Your wife and your daughter are going to have themselves a nice little nap."

"I'll see to it, Nuala."

— 20 —

BEFORE I could make my phone calls, my friend from the West Side called me.

"Hey, Dermot!"

"Hey!" I responded.

This is the proper password when dealing with friends from the West Side.

"I looked into that business matter you asked me about. My friends and their friends were very interested in what you were interested in. They wanted to tell you the truth because they didn't want anybody to misunderstand. They had nothing to do with that business arrangement. They hoped that the people who did were not successful in it."

"Uh-huh."

"They said it was a foreign firm that was involved."

"Foreign?"

"Yeah, hired Eastern European, Dermot. You know what they're like."

"No respect?"

"And no ethics."

"A Russian firm?"

"Naw, Balkan. Located up there in Lakeview. Not very ethical businesspeople, though they have a wide range of interests."

"Indeed!"

"My friends think they're dangerous. They firmly believe that the Chicago Police Department ought to do something about them."

"I can only agree with them."

"Yeah, Dermot, it's been nice talking to you. Stay in touch. I'll deliver your message back to my friends to pass to their friends."

Anybody tapping the phone would hardly suspect that he was telling me that the hit that went down on Nick Farmer came from a Balkan Mafia-style gang located in Lakeview just across Clark Street from Summerdale. Nor would a listener suspect that the wise guys out on the West Side didn't like the Balkan gangs. They wanted me to pass on the word to John Culhane. What a marvelous Chicago way of doing things!

I called John promptly.

"John, I have information that the group responsible for the Nick Farmer business is a Balkan gang up at Lakeview."

"Really! They're mean, mean guys. The sort of thing they might do. I don't suppose you have any evidence?"

"Not a bit. But I thought the hint might be of some help to you."

"So, you just talked to friends about it?"

"Me have friends? John, don't be ridiculous!"

He laughed.

He too understood that the word had come through a chain of friends for me to pass on to him to go after the Balkan mob in Lakeview. The Outfit leaders didn't like "foreign" groups imitating the style that was theirs when they were young.

I then called Mike Casey.

"Mike, I think you'd better put some of your people around us again."

"What!"

"I don't want to go into detail. I don't think we're in any real danger. But I don't want to take any chances."

"Twenty-four hours?"

"Yeah, for a few days anyhow."

I then called the messenger service to pick up the package waiting for us at 2020 Hopkins Place.

This was a lot of work for me, a busy day, all these phone calls. Not much time for writing novels, was there?

The final call was to Liam Hegarty at his office at the Board of Trade.

"Dermot Coyne! I haven't heard from you for ages. How does it feel to be a famous novelist married to a famous singer!"

"Being married to a famous singer is wonderful!"

"I can believe that!"

"Liam, I have a strange question for you. I'd like to meet with your wife someday to talk about her great-grandparents."

"Ellen's great-grandparents?"

"Yeah, her great-grandparents the Doolans who lived in St. Gabriel's."

"That's before her family became civilized and moved to the West Side. I'm sure Ellen would like nothing more than to talk to you about her grandmother who was also an Ellen as was her mother. They were quite a bunch of people. Hey, how about lunch at the Trader's Inn tomorrow? Ellen works down here too. She thinks she is a better trader than I am."

"She's Irish, isn't she?"

He laughed, "You know all about it, huh, Dermot?"

"Maybe I'll bring my own wife around."

"Hey, we'd really like to meet her!"

I decided that I had done everything I was supposed to do. Maybe it was time for me to take a nap too.

The phone wouldn't leave me alone. This time it was Cindy.

"Maybelline is in a psychiatric hospital, Dermot. It's supposed to be a secret, so I can't tell anyone where she is. The doctors have given her tranquilizers to calm her down. It should only be a week or so and she'll be at least able to get back to the family and settle down to serious therapy."

"Wow!"

"This hospitalization, Dermot, comes as a tremendous shock. And we shouldn't be surprised, should we? We knew there was something hyper about her, we just didn't know how deep it went. Poor woman, she's now at least got a chance to straighten out her life if she wants to."

"I sure hope she does."

I hung up the phone and there was something like a shout from upstairs. It was a baby shout so it had to be my daughter instead of my wife. The wolfhound, whose belly I had been scratching, rolled over and jumped up and charged the stairs in two or three bounds. I followed her almost as quickly.

Nellie was standing up in her bed hanging on to the rails of the crib and shouting. She wasn't crying, she wasn't wailing, she was shouting. Almost like a gorilla pounding on his chest. She swayed back and forth, and then began to throw her toys out of the bed, probably at me.

I took her off the rail of the crib. She kept right on shouting. An exuberant little brat.

I picked her up, she squirmed. That was unusual, normally in somebody's arms Nellie settled back. But this time she squirmed. She was having too much fun demonstrating in the crib. She didn't want out of the crib yet. She wanted to raise a little hell.

"Shush, Nellie, isn't your mother trying to get a nap and herself worn out from her virus?"

Her diaper was undisturbed and she didn't seem particularly hungry. All she wanted was to make noise. And throw things.

"I'm going to leave you in here," I told her. "You can shout your heart out and that's fine, it's good exercise for your lungs. But I don't want you waking up your mother so I'm gonna close the door. Okay?"

Her next shout did not at any rate indicate disapproval of my plan. So I tiptoed out of the room and closed the door. The wolfhound showed no intention of accompanying me. I started downstairs. I hesitated and opened the door to Nuala's room to see how she was doing.

"Is it you, Dermot Michael?"

" 'Tis."

"What took you so long and meself up here waiting for you?"

"Were you expecting me, woman?"

"Wasn't I now?"

How could I refuse an invitation like that? My rival in the nursery could shout all she wanted. Now I had my woman to myself.

Later, after our exertions, I was half-asleep and pondering the mystery of love between a man and a woman. We were at the age in our marriage where the wonder was supposed to be wearing off. For me the love between myself and my wife seemed to grow each time we were together. My desire for her, after a session of love, was almost unbearable. The intensity of our romance was entirely her doing. She was determined that our romance would never fade. I was one very lucky guy.

"Dermot Michael!" my wife shrieked, "I know what's wrong with the picture!"

I rolled over. She was sitting straight up in bed, one arm and a hand covering, ineffectively, her bare breasts.

"What's wrong with the picture, Nuala?"

"Ellen, the oldest daughter!"

"What's wrong with her?"

"In the death notice when she died in 1975 it said that she was seventy-seven years old. Dermot Michael, what happens if you subtract seventy-seven from seventy-five?"

I calculated quickly.

"You get minus two!"

She pounded on the bed.

"Not if you die in 1975. You get 1898!"

"So?"

"So, Dermot Michael, Ellen Doolan could not have been born in 1898."

"Why not?"

"Because that was the year that Agnes Mary Elizabeth was born and later died. They couldn't have had another daughter the same age, unless they were twins, and if you remember the records at St. Gabriel's there weren't any twins."

I tried to think about it but the excitement of our nap had temporarily dulled what passes through my Dr. Watson mind.

"So, Nuala, what does that mean?"

"I don't know what it means yet, Dermot. But it means somehow or the other they acquired a baby to replace Agnes Mary Elizabeth. They integrated her into the family, perhaps didn't tell her of her origins. And she became a regular member of the family, the oldest child. Don't you see, she was a replacement child in the strict sense of that word. How many families would do something like that?"

"Families that are trying to forget something."

"At least that, at least that." She pulled the sheet over and snuggled down next to me.

"I don't see how that solves things for us."

"It doesn't solve anything at all, at all, Dermot. But I have a hunch that it's going to solve everything."

After supper Martha Grimm Farmer appeared at our front door. She was dressed in black, a neatly tailored suit with a long skirt. Properly made up as a career woman should be, she seemed much less haggard than she had at the wake. Yet there was an expression of deep sorrow in her gray eyes.

"I'm sorry to disturb you after you being so kind and coming to Nicholas's wake and funeral. I heard that Roger Conrad has talked with you. I don't know what lies he might have told you. I wanted to clarify things a little."

I invited her in. She declined a drink but accepted a cup of tea. Fiona rumbled downstairs from the nursery, sniffed Martha approvingly, and then curled up at her feet.

"She's a pretty fierce watchdog, isn't she?" she said with a smile.

"Mostly she's just a good dog and responds positively to that title. Still, she checks everyone out. You are obviously a person approved so she adopts you as one of her friends."

"Rog Conrad is a very nice man. I've always been fond of him. Though he does some strange things every once in a while. My late husband was too predictable. Roger is just the opposite, too unpredictable. I don't know why he told you those stories about Nicholas working on some big scoop."

"He wasn't working at a big scoop?" Nuala asked her.

"He was always working at a big scoop, Nuala. It was an obsession with him. He was going to win the Pulitzer Prize eventually no matter how many people he had to ruin. For some reason he always undercut himself. I have no idea what this particular story was supposed to be about but I'm sure the same thing would have happened. It just isn't important."

"However," Nuala said gently, "it may be what led to his murder."

"I don't want revenge. I hope the police find out who they are and why they killed him. That won't bring Nicholas back to us. I don't think he told anybody about the story, if there was one. Not even Doug Jurgens at Channel Three who went to school with us."

I had forgotten that he was part of the group that had gone to St. Gregory's.

"And not Johnny Quinn or Robin Cleary, his wife, either?"

"We never see them. Rog's trouble is that he lives in

the past. Although he's been very successful and made a lot of money, he thinks that the best days of his life were at the newspaper at St. Gregory's High School. I don't think those were such happy days at all. Roger is covering over the unhappiness and rivalry with nostalgia."

"He seems to have been fond of your late husband?" Nuala murmured.

"We all were," she sighed. "I don't know when Roger turned melancholy. It was probably after the marriage, but I don't blame the marriage. His wife is a lovely woman. He has no grounds for complaint against her."

"It's also very sad," Nuala said, leaving the way open for Martha to tell us more.

"Very, very sad. Nicholas was such a wonderful young man. Everybody adored him. He got away with everything. The priests and the nuns and most of the kids loved him. I suppose he had too many successes too early. That was the way it was in those days. Investigative reporters were the folk heroes. I thought they were snoops and that's why I went into market research instead of reporting. I suppose that market research is a kind of snooping too but it doesn't try to destroy individual people. I'm afraid Nicholas believed that a good journalist was somebody who destroyed famous people. Like he tried to destroy you two, which was really crazy of him. . . . He was so desperate to get back on television."

"Poor man."

"It was a shame that Nicholas had to grow up. He thought that the whole world would be like our high school in that little room where we edited the newspaper. When he found out that it wasn't, he was disillusioned, shattered, and furious. I fell in love with him when we were juniors. I joined the newspaper staff so I could be with him more. I never did fall out of love, despite all the terrible things that happened later, because I remembered who he had been. At first, I didn't notice the change in him after he dropped out of college. I didn't notice when we were courting and after we were married. It was only after he was fired from the *Tribune* that I began to realize that he wasn't the same old sweet, gentle Nick. He was a raging, bitterly angry man. He drank too much, smoked too much, ate too much, and fought too much. After a while, much as I loved him, it was impossible to have him in the same house, especially with the kids."

"St. Gregory's must have been a very nice place to grow up," Nuala said softly.

"It was really quite wonderful, it's kind of a small neighborhood, actually called Summerdale to distinguish it from Lakeview, squeezed between Rosehill Cemetery on the west and Clark Street on the east. Twenty-five years ago it was still very German. Not all the people were German like Nicholas and I were. There were a lot of us around and Germans kind of set the tone of the parish—music, drama, celebrations of national events. We managed to protect it from you Irish. Mind you, the Irish didn't seem to object. They liked the neighborhood too and were willing to concede that it wasn't theirs, at least until they became a majority. Which they never did. We all got along very well together."

"And you still live there?"

"I do and I still love it. The neighborhood's changed, we still have the Germans and the Irish and we also have Filipinos and Palestinians and Koreans and some Albanians. Yet Summerdale's still a nice, quiet, friendly place and kids in the high school, like my son and daughter, get along with each other just fine."

"Even the people from the Balkans?" I asked.

Nuala Ann looked at me surprised. I hadn't had the chance to tell her what was said to me; that folks from the Balkans were now part of our story.

"I think there's only one or two Balkan children in our school. Most of them are passionately loyal to the Orthodox Church. Some of them are Catholic like the ones at St. Gregory's. My kids tell me they're more Balkan than they are Catholic."

"Och, sure," Nuala sighed, "no one would ever say that of us Irish now, would they!" We all laughed.

"Do I hear a baby crying?" Martha asked. The wolfhound stood up and listened and then fell back again.

"What you hear is a baby shouting," I replied. "Our daughter is going through a shouting phase. As far as we can figure out, it's for the pure fun of it. When she's unhappy and needs her diaper changed or wants something to eat or is sick, then she cries. When she's feeling bored she shouts. If you were to go up to her nursery now she'd keep on shouting. We trust Fiona. When there's something wrong with Nellie she knows it before we do."

"I'd like to see her before I go home if you don't mind."

"Nuala Anne McGrail not want to show off her redhaired, green-eyed daughter?" I asked.

Nuala laughed and bounded up the stairs.

"All of you have known one another since first grade?" I continued the discussion.

"I don't think so. Nick and I were baptized in the parish. Rog joined us in second grade. I think the others came later."

"I was surprised to learn that Doug Jurgens, the news director of Channel Three, was part of your group."

"He was and he wasn't. He was more of a loner than the rest of us. He moved in, I think, in seventh grade and never quite fit. He was a runner-up to Nick for salutatorian. They never got along too well as you might imagine. Nick was the hero of the school and Doug was an outsider."

An astonishing reversal in positions through the years. The outcast becomes a news director and the leader at school a down-at-the-heels reporter looking for one more chance.

"He really didn't owe Nick anything. It was awfully

good of him to give Nick a chance on Channel Three. And Nick was quite good at first like he always was. Then he became angry again. At your wife. I have no idea why. I suspect there was some anger against the Irish from his days in high school, though I don't know whether that was the reason. I was horrified when I heard his first commentary. Maybe just before he died he really lost his mind."

"You were the valedictorian, of course?"

"Doesn't do me much good as a single mother wondering how she can pay for two college educations."

Nuala, who never bounded with Nelliecoyne in her arms, walked carefully back down the stairs, wolfhound in tow, with Nelliecoyne in her arms. Our daughter was still screaming and loving it. Fiona walked down the stairs like she were a queen-empress, proud of this screaming little redhead.

Nuala put Nellie on the floor and she promptly crawled over to the coffee table, reached up for it, pulled herself erect, and then flopped back onto her rear end much to her delight.

"What a beautiful little girl!" Martha Farmer exclaimed. "And very determined and very athletic. I bet she's a handful, a delightful handful."

"Och," said Nuala, "isn't she crawling already and won't she be walking in another month and you know what happens to people like that?"

"No," said Martha seriously, "I don't know what happens to people like that."

"They grow up to be total harridans altogether!"

"Nuala knows that from experience because her daughter is simply a clone, despite her red hair which she inherited from my side of the family."

We returned to the subject of Nick Farmer.

"And he had a nice family, did he now?" Nuala asked.

"I suppose that's how all the trouble began. No, he did not have a nice family. His father was a machinist and a sullen, angry man. Nick quit college because his father refused to help with the tuition. He hadn't gone to college. So he saw no reason why Nick should. It was time, he said, that Nick got out and earned his own money in payback to his parents for all he owed them."

"This was back in the 1950s?" I asked in surprise.

"Not exactly, this was growing up, that's when Nick was born. It was the 1970s when he was growing up and his dad made him quit college. He was a very domineering man and resentful. He avoided his neighbors and intimidated his wife completely. Nicholas hated him but he was also afraid of him and desperately wanted his respect."

"Which of course he never received."

"Not as far as I ever saw. His father was awful at our wedding. He didn't talk to me or my family but kept to himself at the ceremony and the banquet. I don't know why. I don't know what I ever did to him. He hated the Irish but we weren't Irish."

"Different social class, was it now?"

"He was born in Germany, and came over here as a prisoner of war. After the war he returned. Though he liked America better than Germany, he complained a lot about America too."

"He thought your family was too rich for his son?" I asked.

"I suppose so, but we weren't really that rich. My father owned a couple of restaurants that were quite successful and one absolutely wonderful bakery. There were no doctors or lawyers in our family."

"What was it like between your family and his family growing up with part of the German heritage but still cautious about asserting it after the two wars?" I continued.

"From what my grandfather said it was terrible during the First World War and the years after that. He stopped speaking German except occasionally at home. I know a little bit of German because my own mother and father spoke it sometimes. It's been useful in dealing with European clients. It wasn't something you wanted to reveal to people in the fifties and the sixties. By the time we were at high school in the seventies it didn't make any difference anymore. Still, probably there was a lot more German-related culture that we could have preserved but were afraid to. It's never been a problem for me or any of the other people I know. I didn't think it was a problem for Nicholas either. Maybe I was wrong. I was so wrong about so many things."

She removed a tissue from her purse and dabbed at her eyes.

"You think we should pay no attention to Roger?" Nuala asked, leading Martha back to her alleged reason for the visit.

"I can't understand why he told you those things. I don't know what good it will do."

"And then," Nuala said, "didn't he have to go and tell you he told us those things to make you worry?"

"As a matter of fact he did just that. As I said before, Rog was always a very strange man."

I shook hands with her. Nuala embraced her and promised they would get together soon. I doubted they would unless we were still pursuing a solution to the mystery.

Fiona escorted her to the door.

"Wasn't that an interesting conversation?"

"Nuala, what the hell is going on with these Germans from St. Gregory's?"

"Dermot Michael, they know something they don't want anyone else to know. They're trying to cover it up by pretending there's nothing to know. It's twisted all around altogether. You'd think they were Irish."

"So where does that leave us?"

"We know now for sure that Rog Conrad and Nicholas Farmer were rivals for Martha and Nicholas won. Roger has always thought that he was the better and would have made a better husband—which he probably would have."

"Does she know that Roger is still in love with her?"

"Of course she knows, Dermot Michael, women always know things like that!"

"Do you think his wife knows it?"

"I would be surprised if she didn't. She's probably worried now Nick is dead that Roger will drop her and go after Martha."

"Do you think he will?"

"Not until he's sure that Martha would accept him. There's not a chance in the world that would happen!"

"And you think that his death is somehow or the other connected with rivalry from the past?"

"I do, Dermot Michael, otherwise why would his wife and his alleged close friend come and talk to us about it. Aren't they trying to throw us off the scent?"

"Yet the things they told us would have put us on the scent."

"Sure, Dermot Michael, they'd put us on a scent all right, but I'm thinking it's the wrong scent. And what was this about your men from the Balkans?"

"Our friends on the West Side tell us that it was a Balkan gang from Lakeview that was responsible for Nick's death. I passed it on to John Culhane."

"Isn't that the neighborhood right next to St. Gregory's?"

" 'Tis."

"Oh, my, Dermot Michael, the mystery gets thicker and thicker, doesn't it now?"

"It sure does, Nuala Ann, it sure does."

Now our determined daughter was trying to pull herself up next to the wolfhound. She clung to the dog's thick white hair and pulled. It didn't seem to bother Fiona. Nelliecoyne stood upright hanging onto the dog and once more fell back to the ground. This time her feelings were hurt. She began to cry in protest. Fiona backed off in surprise. What had she done to her little charge?

"Don't worry, Fiona," Nuala said, reassuring the huge

dog with a hug as she picked up the baby from the floor. "It's not your fault. Our little terror here has suddenly discovered she's tired and wants to go to bed immediately. Dermot Michael, I'm going to put her down and then I'll come back and we can talk more about it."

It was then that the messenger arrived with the diary from Colleen Kavanagh.

— 21 —

the widow that is also close to the city from the front.
It seems just right. Our time there will be wonderful.
Thank you for this, for coming to me. I had enough
guilt Patrick without . . . without having to put the cross
on with denouncing and watch his . . . his . . . .
I'm so glad that the picture arrived with the light
. . . .

— 21 —

Christmas Day, 1896.

I have thrown away all my old diaries and am beginning to keep a new one. It is settled that I am going to become a married woman right after Easter next year. March 15, 1897.

I don't want to become a married woman; I'm too young to marry. I don't know what wife means or what marriage means. I want to learn more of both. Perhaps my father should not have sent me to Cook County Normal School. I didn't learn much there but I did learn how much I don't know.

I don't want to marry Tom Doolan. I don't want to marry anybody but particularly I don't want to marry him. I don't hate him. I don't even dislike him. He's a nice enough man in a solemn, pretentious way. I am not in love with him and I will never be in love with him. I'm in love with Timmy Millan. Pa will never let me marry Timmy, a common laborer in the Yards.

My brothers told me I'm a spoiled little girl and maybe I am. Maybe Dad spoiled me deliberately so I could be used to win him social respectability. He actually insists I must marry Tom Doolan who, after his father's recent death, is the richest man in the parish. It will be a great achievement for a skilled meat cutter to marry his daughter off to what he thinks is wealth.

I would rebel if I could. But how do I rebel against the family? Dad has made up his mind. My brothers, who don't like me, think it's a wonderful idea and that Tom Doolan will force some sense into my head. My mother never disagrees with anything my father wants. So regardless of what I think I'll marry Tom Doolan on the Saturday after Easter next year.

I don't even know that Timmy Millan would want to marry me. He has a wonderful smile and he laughs a lot when we're together. But that doesn't mean he's in love the way I'm in love.

I'm so miserable I don't think anybody really loves me, my parents and my brothers not at all. Timmy I'm not sure about. Tom Doolan wants me but that's not the same as love.

I remember the first day he took me riding. He wanted to show me the big ditch they are building to reverse the flow of the Chicago River so it will not empty sewage into Lake Michigan anymore. He is on the committee responsible for the canal. His sister died in the last cholera epidemic.

It is a very big ditch. I did my best to seem completely uninterested in it. Then we rode back. He wanted to show me how thick Bubbly Creek is with refuse from the Yards, so thick that birds walk on it.

"That stuff goes into Lake Michigan when there's too much rain," he said as he lifted me off my horse. "We're going to stop that with the Sanitary District Canal."

The smell of the creek was disagreeable, even for someone who has grown up next to the Yards. It was even more disagreeable to find myself in his arms for even a moment. He is a strong, powerful man. He held me like I was his plaything. I escaped as quickly as I could without losing my dignity.

Everybody in the family is so proud of this huge diamond ring I'm wearing. I feel that it's more like a chain around my neck. Tom Doolan was very nice and polite, courteous, respectful, the perfect gentleman in his fab-

ulous suit and shirt and waistcoat. I don't know what
goes on inside his head, if anything. He is supposed to
be a brilliant lawyer. But that would be said about the
richest man in the parish anyway. But what he thinks
about life, about God, about marriage, about a wife—I
don't know any of these things and have a terrible feeling that I will never find out.

It is not a merry Christmas at all.

Wednesday, January 13, 1897.

I don't know why I'm keeping this diary. I don't make
entries in it very often and I'm certain I'm not going to
let anyone else read it. Maybe I'm keeping a diary so
that years from now when I'm old and terribly unhappy
I can look back and see how the unhappiness started.

We have already begun preparations for the marriage. Nobody cares what I think or what I want. Mother
is completely in charge and she and Mrs. Doolan are
fighting constantly—all very politely of course—but
when they talk to one another their voices are filled with
nastiness. My fiancé, my future husband, God help me,
is very distant, reserved, and self-contained. He doesn't
argue with his mother or my mother, he doesn't support
me against them, he simply stays out of it. Maybe that's
the only thing he can do, but I wish I could say that he
was on my side. Will he ever be on my side in the course
of the marriage? Thank God his mother doesn't go to
the house and has her apartment downtown at the Palmer House. If I had to live in the same house as that
nasty, mean woman I think I'd die.

I might die anyway. Sleeping in the same bed with a
big, dark, hairy man like Tom Doolan. There's probably
going to be even worse than that.

Father Dorney is very nice. I think he understands
what's going on. But he wouldn't dream of interfering.
Yet he tells me every day, every time I see him, what a

wonderful man Tom is and how I should give myself a chance to get to know him.

The last time he said it I snapped at him, "I have a whole lifetime to get to know him."

"Ah, no, my dear," he said. "Many people are married for fifty years and never get to know one another. Getting to know someone else takes work and patience. And sensitivity to the fact that the other might be hurting even worse than you are."

I don't know what he meant by that. It sounded very wise, but then he's never been married, has he? And it doesn't seem to me that in that sort of hard work where you get to know the other one there is room for love.

Tuesday, February 16, 1897.

We decided that we are going to spend our wedding night at the Palmer House and then go to Los Angeles for our honeymoon. Tom had talked about taking a trip to Europe. But both his mother and my mother opposed that. They want to keep a close eye on us, very close, or perhaps I should say a close eye on me because they agree that I am an irresponsible scatterbrain and that my moods as I approach the happiest day of my life are a sign that I have a lot of growing up to do.

How do they know it's going to be the happiest day of my life? I don't feel happy now and I am not looking forward to the "happy" day. I think it's going to be an ugly day. I will be displayed for everybody to see as a beautiful virginal bride being given over by her father to her husband. They'll admire my good looks, whisper behind my back that I'm still childish, and think to themselves that I'm getting what I deserve.

I'll want to scream at them, scream, scream, scream, scream at my parents that I hate them, scream at Mrs. Doolan that she's a mean, old harpy, scream at Tom thinking he can buy me and that I don't love him and that I never will love him.

Will I do that? Probably not. I don't have the courage to do that. But I would love to.

I don't mind going to California, I've never been there—in fact I've never been west of Lyons Township. Or east of Lake Michigan. I would like to travel to Europe. Tom whispers in my ear that we will after we are married. I wonder it that's true.

He's telling people that we've decided on Los Angeles. Perhaps to keep our family, our two mothers, out of the picture because they want us to go somewhere else, Niagara Falls. Everybody goes to Niagara Falls, and I don't like the idea of spending my wedding night in the same hotel where my mother-in-law has her suite. I will certainly have the feeling that she's peering through the keyhole to see what we're doing. As if I had any idea what we'd be doing!

Monday, March 1, 1897.

I'm absolutely furious.

My mother decided it was time to tell me about what men and women do after they're married. She made it sound perfectly hideous. Maybe it is. It certainly doesn't sound like fun. She seemed to think that I was somehow to blame because I didn't know the details. Who else is there to teach me the details except her? And she waited until it was too late or almost too late. I'm not as ignorant as she thinks I am. We did have a course in biology at Normal School and I understand how babies are made and where they come from—which is more than a lot of girls here in the parish do. I know what Tom will do to me in bed. I have no idea what I will feel when he does it. I expect it will be painful and hurt. My mother told me that it was something that women have to put up with in order to have children and raise a family. I don't know whether I want to have children and I told her so.

She slapped my face and told me that I was a shameless hussy.

I don't understand why what I had said was shameless but it was probably a little rude.

She warned me that like most men my new husband would want to take off my clothes or have me take off my clothes. She said I ought not to let him do that. It is vulgar, disgusting, and totally unworthy of a Christian mother. She said I ought to be firm about that at the beginning of the marriage. No nudity, never. She said we should make love with the gaslight out in our room. And then she said but the man usually wants the lights on but that's because the man is a savage brute when it comes to lovemaking.

I'm tempted to walk into the hotel room with the lights on and undress immediately. That would show my mother how seriously I take her instructions. Of course, I would have to tell her I was going to do that or tell her afterward. No, it will be more fun to tell her beforehand just to see her reaction.

Maybe a woman must let her husband do whatever he wants to her in bed. Maybe it's disgusting and brutal and has nothing to do with love. I can't imagine what it would be like to undress in front of Tom Doolan. I wonder if he thinks I will. I wonder if he will try to make me do it. He'd better not, nobody makes me do anything.

Would you listen to that! My family is making me marry a man that I don't love and I said nobody's going to make me do anything.

March 7, 1897.

It's only one week plus one day 'til my wedding. I am the most miserable person in the world, I don't want to marry, I don't want to marry Tom Doolan. I just want to be left alone.

I saw Timmy Millan at Mass this morning. He was shy and sad and he admired my diamond ring and *wished me all possible happiness. I thanked him quite politely. I was tempted to tell him that I would never be happy and that the only one I wanted to marry was him. But that would have been foolish.*

Oh, Timmy, Timmy, Timmy! How much I love you.

March 10, 1897.

Tom Doolan kissed me good night, the first time ever. It was a very mild kiss. Nothing exciting but he certainly didn't force himself on me either.

"I will always treasure and respect you, Mary Louise," he said softly. "I'll treat you with reverence as if we are equals. We'll be partners, I won't be the boss and neither will you."

"Irishwomen are always the bosses!" I snapped at him.

He doesn't laugh much and when he does it's not for long. But he laughed.

"I think we're going to have a great time together, Mary Louise," he said.

"Incidentally," he said, helping me out of his Stanley Steamer, "why was your mother so furious with you this afternoon?"

I was tempted not to tell him and then I thought what difference would it make. Maybe he would like to hear it.

"My mother has been giving me instructions lately about what men and women do to one another in marriage."

"Swell," he said grimly.

"She told me that you would be a brute like all men and that you would want to make love with the lights on and that you would want to see me naked and she said I should draw the line and never permit that because it was savage and unchristian and just giving in to a man's brutal instincts."

"Oh?" He smiled that small little smile of his under

his thin mustache. "That sounds like a very interesting preparation for marriage."

"It sounded horrid to me. If that's what marriage is like I don't see why men and women marry. I told my mother that and she said they marry in order that they could have babies. And I said if that's why women marry that's not why men marry. Men marry because they want to possess us."

"I do want to possess you, Mary Louise, but not that way," Tom said, a light blush appearing on his face under the gaslight in front of his house.

"Well, Thomas Doolan, I don't know and I don't care. I didn't have much choice about this marriage as you know. It's all up to you anyway. It always has been."

"I'm sorry to hear that you feel you're being forced into the marriage, Mary Louise," he went on almost as solemnly as Father Dorney himself was when preaching at the noon Mass on Sunday, "I thought the arrangements were acceptable to you. I would be happy to cancel the wedding if it be your wish."

I suppose he thought he was being generous. He knows very well that my life won't be worth living if I try to cancel now.

"Too late, Tom. It was always too late."

He sighed. "If that is your wish."

"Tom, my wishes don't count! Haven't you seen enough of that as they prepared for the wedding?"

"Mary Louise, I am ashamed of myself for not defending you against my mother and your mother. I really am. I should have, I knew I should have, but I guess I was afraid of them all."

"I don't believe you're afraid of anything. You have too much money and too much power to fear anyone!"

"Would that were true, Mary Louise. Right now I'm just a little bit afraid of you."

"Well, maybe you should be."

"So you and your mother were arguing earlier about her premarital instructions which you found useless?"

He was talking just like a lawyer now.

"Yes, that's about it."

"And you said something outrageous?"

"You're learning a lot about me tonight, Thomas Doolan, though I'm not learning anything about you and probably never will. Yes, when people try to back me into a corner I say outrageous things. I will say outrageous things to you whether you like it or not."

"So I've been warned."

"They warned you that I am a spoiled little brat and that it is going to be up to you to make me grow up."

"Yes, Mary Louise, that's about what I've been told by both my mother and your mother."

"And you believe them?"

"I don't believe a single word they say, Mary Louise."

That comment took my breath away. "Really?"

"No, I don't believe a word of it. If you act childishly sometimes it's because they've forced you into a situation where you really would have to fall down and be dead for them or act childishly. I don't think you're childish."

He loves me and I didn't even like him. But he seemed to be a nicer man than I had expected.

"So what did you say to your mother that so infuriated her?"

"I probably shouldn't tell you."

In the back of my head, however, a voice was whispering you want to tell him.

"It is your decision."

I suspected that I would hear those words many times in the course of our marriage.

"Well, what I told her was that despite all the things she'd warned me against I would walk into our room at the Palmer House and immediately take off all my clothes!"

Thomas was startled. His eyes popped open and his mouth fell.

"Did you really?" *he said in astonishment.*

"Yes, I did really and I'm glad I said it."

"Mary Louise, I certainly will not hold you to that."

"I don't care whether you hold me to it or not, I'll hold myself to it. If you like me naked, fine. If you don't like me then that's your problem. It's too late when we are married."

"I have no doubt at all," he said, putting his hand on my shoulder rather nervously, "that I will be overwhelmed by your beauty. . . . I must confess, Mary Louise, that the vision of that moment in the hotel room is going to haunt me every moment till then."

"Good enough for you. If you're a brute like my mother tells me that all men are, it serves you right."

"I don't think I'm a brute, Mary Louise, and I'll never be brutal to you."

My face gets very hot even as I write about this exchange. It was absolutely improper between a bride-to-be and her groom. It was probably sinful. My mother had told me that it was sinful even to think of such things and not to say them. I don't care. I'm going to do it just to see what happens. And then the first time I see her I will tell her I did it and will say it was wonderful, whether it was or not.

I'll show them all.

What do I think about my future husband after that conversation?

I think about what a friend of my father's whispered in my ear the night of our engagement party.

"Sure," he said, "there's a lot worse around than Tom Doolan."

March 14, 1897.

Tomorrow is my wedding day and I am the most lonely, most miserable, most discouraged woman in all of the world. I don't want to marry him, absolutely do not want to marry him. He is a good man, I know that. He is even a nice man. I suspect he's truly a gentleman *as well as intelligent. But it's not something I want to do. He offered last week to cancel it. I should have accepted that offer. No matter how furious my family would have been I would at least have been free. After tomorrow I will be bound to him until death do us part and I don't want that. I don't hate him but I hate the thought of being his wife and his being my husband. Dear God in heaven, if you exist, and tonight I'm not sure you do, please don't let this happen tomorrow. Please let Father Dorney announce to the whole congregation that on his own authority he is canceling the wedding. What if I went up to him before Mass and said, "Father Dorney, I don't want to marry Thomas Doolan." He would laugh like he always does and then he would look in my eyes and he would say, "You mean that, Mary Louise, don't you?" and I would be crying and I would say, "Yes, Father Dorney, I do mean it. Please, please don't make me marry him."*

If I said those things Father Dorney would cancel the marriage. He's canceled other marriages when the same thing happened. I would be so humiliated, so ashamed everybody would stare at me next day at Mass and for the rest of my life. I would be humiliated, my parents would be humiliated, my rejected husband would be humiliated. Am I willing to pay that price for my freedom? I don't even have to answer the question. So tomorrow I will bind myself to Thomas Patrick Doolan.

March 22, 1897.

We are in Los Angeles. It is a lovely place, all sand and ocean and flowers. The train ride out was very interesting too. We had our own stateroom and it was very comfortable but not as comfortable as having your own bed. I enjoyed looking out the windows at the prairies and the mountains and the forests and deserts. How much fun it would be to see more about it. Thomas Doolan remarked that I seemed to be a good traveler. That

I didn't complain much and I enjoyed it. "We will travel anywhere in the world, Mary Louise, anywhere you want."

"I'll hold you to that," I said.

Our first night on the train he offered to take the upper berth.

"Don't be ridiculous, Thomas Doolan. After all, we are husband and wife. There is little point in having a husband if you don't have him in bed with you."

He blushed. I love to make him blush. It is so easy to do. He is really quite delightful when he is embarrassed.

We are getting along reasonably well. He seems quite satisfied with me, which surprises me.

I am surprised to discover that it is amusing to be in the company of a man. I hated the very sight of my brothers because they were so crude and mean. My husband is neither crude nor mean. His male presence is pleasant, so different from that of both my brothers and other women.

He is very strong. He delights in lifting me off the ground and carrying me. Though I should be offended by his presumption, I rather enjoy it.

He also watches me very carefully, studying me as though I were a horse whose purchase he was considering or a law case he was working on. I fear I will lose all my secrets to him, that I will be quite transparent. That should worry me, but somehow it does not.

I still don't love him and I know I never will love him but I do like him. It is hard to find fault with him except that he is so solemn and so ponderous and so courteous.

And so intent on understanding every detail of me.

I suppose many brides on their honeymoon would agree with what my mother said—that husbands are brutes. Thomas Doolan is not a brute, he is, I hesitate to use the word, sweet. Solemnly sweet, ponderously sweet, but still sweet. There is so much reserve in him, so much hidden behind the courtesy. I don't think I will ever, ever come to know him. However, as the man said at my engagement party, there are a lot worse.

There are deep, deep fires within him. I do not understand those fires. Oddly, I do not dislike what little I see of them.

He has said certain things to me on our honeymoon which are either very filthy or very beautiful. Perhaps both. I am not troubled by them. I would not dare write them down, though it excites me even to think about them. I will not forget them. Not ever.

I did live up to my commitment when we walked into the Palmer House by the way. I guess he must have liked me. At least he didn't send me back.

"Mary Louise," he gasped, "you are so very, very beautiful."

That quite melted my heart.

My mother was completely and totally wrong about what happens between men and women in their bedrooms. I won't say that I'm accomplished at it and I probably will never be. But still it's nice.

Monday, May 3, 1897.

We're back home in Chicago now and in Thomas Doolan's house. I keep calling it "your house" and he insists that it is our house. It's not our house at all, it's really his mother's house in which she's letting me move with him until he gets tired of me.

That really isn't fair. He will never get tired of me. He said that today and somehow I believe him. He should get tired of me. I'm an ill-tempered, spoiled, diabolical bitch.

I've never written that word before. That's what I am, I'm a bitch.

I'll have to tell him that to see if he's shocked. Sometimes I think I do shock him. Well, too bad for him.

That's what I am just the same.

He wants me to redecorate the house. There were painters here today and I was making suggestions. Tom of course agreed with all my suggestions. Then his mother stormed into the house in fury because she'd seen the decorator's wagon in front.

"Don't you dare do anything to this house!" she snarled at me.

She was just like my own mother when she was mad at me. I wished the ground would open up and swallow my humiliation.

"Ma," said Thomas. "This is now our house, my house and my wife's. I have asked her to make plans for redecoration. Ah, I believe she has excellent taste. I have authorized her to go ahead with the decoration. I would be very pleased if you would not interfere."

I could hardly believe my ears. It was all solemn and polite and courteous, but he'd drawn the line between me and his mother.

She burst into tears and stormed out of the house.

"I dreaded that happening," he said to me.

I searched for a compliment.

"You did it very well, Thomas."

He glanced at me. "It's one of the few times in my life I've stood up to her. I suspect I will have to do that many times in the years ahead."

He was all so solemn and reasonable and lawyerlike. Not a hint of temper.

"Don't you have a temper at all, Thomas Doolan?"

He smiled his attractive little smile. "And if I do, Mary Louise Collins, you will never be the object of it, that I promise."

What could I say? So I said, "Thank you" and hugged him.

My own mother came over a couple of hours later and demanded to know what I thought I was doing to the house. "Who do you think you are?" she shouted at me. "What will people say?"

"They'll think I'm Mrs. Thomas Patrick Doolan," I said firmly. "If they don't like the way I decorate our house, then that is most unfortunate."

*She continued shouting at me and I continued to ig-
nore her. Tom came in from his office over in the
Exchange Building on Halsted Street for lunch about
that time.*

He looked solemnly at my mother.

*"Mrs. Collins, I respect and revere you as the mother
of my wife. Nonetheless, I cannot in this house tolerate
anyone abusing my wife. I will thank you never to shout
that way at her again." Then Ma stormed out of the
house.*

*"Well, Thomas Patrick Doolan," I said, "that wasn't
bad for a beginning."*

*He laughed again, lightly and softly like he always
laughs.*

*"If I wasn't so crazy in love with you, Mary Louise,
I would never have dared to take on either one of those
dragons."*

*I said something about him being a wonderful St.
George.*

*He is a strange man. Fires burn beneath his courteous
exterior. Frightening fires.*

June 20, 1897.

*I'm certain that I am pregnant. I have been sick the
last couple of mornings and seem to have all the other
signs of pregnancy. It was to be expected that I would
have a child. That's what happens to people when
they're married and they sleep in the same bed at night.
They have children. I don't want to have a child. I am
too young to have a child. I don't want to be saddled
with the responsibility of a squalling little brat. Like
everything else in my life it was not up to me. I suppose
the baby will come sometime next March just around the
anniversary of our wedding. My mother and father will
be delighted, my brothers will laugh at me and say that
I'm now going to find out how difficult life is. Mrs. Doolan will drool over her grandchild and want to take com-*

plete charge of her. My husband will smile his thin quiet little smile and, I think, be very pleased.

You can never tell what's going on inside his head. I suppose I should give up trying to find out. I know what goes on in his body when he looks at me. And I have to be content with that.

I do hope I'm not too much of a failure as a mother. We will have an extra maid to help us he has told me. That's not what I'm worried about.

I haven't informed him yet. He'll be very happy. Somehow or the other I want to hold it back for a while, keep my secret to myself like he keeps all his secrets to himself.

Tuesday, February 8, 1898.

I only have to wait another month the doctor says. I wish the baby would come tomorrow. I hate her, hate her, hate her, hate her! She's turned my body into a balloon. She's made me sick most of the time, she makes me awkward. I've fallen in the mud twice. I'm ashamed to go out for fear I will stumble and fall in the mud again. I hate her.

My husband says to me that it might not even be a girl. I tell him I know it's going to be a girl and I hate her. He smiles at me that same maddening little smile of his and says the day she comes you'll adore her.

"That's irrelevant!" I shout at him.

He has been very patient with me through this pregnancy. He's always patient. I wish sometimes he would shout at me or lose his temper or say something terrible. Then I wouldn't feel so guilty for being such a terrible person myself.

I do hope the baby that comes is healthy. I also hope that I survive at least long enough to get to know her. There was a time when I thought I would sooner die than be married. Sometimes I still feel that way. Yet I might almost say that I'd be happy if I wasn't so huge.

February 16, 1898.

Tom came home from his office in the Exchange Building today and collapsed into the big easy chair in our parlor.

"What's the matter, Thomas? You look like something terrible has happened."

"There's going to be a war, Mary Louise!"

"In Ireland?"

"No, with Spain. In Cuba and probably the Philippines and Puerto Rico. We will take over their whole empire. God knows we could do a better job at it than they do. However, I don't want to see our country ever become an empire like England."

"Why is there going to be a war?"

He sighed deeply. "They blew up the battleship Maine in Havana harbor last night! Hundreds of American sailors died!"

"God rest them all!" I said, making the sign of the cross.

"Yes indeed. God rest them all!"

"Who blew it up?"

"Nobody knows who blew it up. The Spaniards probably but I don't know how you ever prove something like that. That madman Theodore Roosevelt and the yellow journalists Hearst and Pulitzer will be determined to get us into a war. A lot of young Americans of our age are going to die needlessly."

"We can't let them blow up our ships and kill our sailors, can we, Thomas?"

"I suspect we could probably negotiate our way out of it somehow if we were of a mind to. Unfortunately, the American people are not of the mind to negotiate. The Civil War ended thirty-three years ago. Most people have forgotten what a terrible bloody mess it was. Our country seems to wait a generation before it gets into wars, until we've forgotten the horrors of the last one."

I went over to the chair and sat on the floor next to him with my arms around his legs.

"You didn't used to think this way about the war, did you, Thomas? You have a commission in the Irish Rifles. You belong to the Clan'a Gael and the Ancient Order of Hibernians. You support revolution in Ireland, don't you?"

"Yes, to all of those questions, Mary Louise. Yet, since I became a husband and almost a father I began to wonder about those things. I will resign my commission in the Rifles, that's certain. As to the Clan and the Hibernians, well, I can't leave as long as Father Dorney is under pressure. However, I'm not so sure that I'm going to give any more money for killing in Ireland. There has got to be some better way."

"Will the English ever give the Irish their freedom unless they take it?"

"I don't know, Mary Louise, I just don't know. Maybe not. Probably not. Maybe there has to be more bloodshed over there before Ireland emerges as the free nation that can take its place alongside the other nations of the world. Still, I personally don't think I will spend any more money on killing. I don't want blood on my hands, even if it is English blood."

"You won't be going to war, will you?" I asked, suddenly terrified at the prospect.

He patted my hand reassuringly. "You don't have to worry about that, Mary Louise. It's going to be a short war. There are many young fellows from Canaryville who know nothing about the last war and will be eager to sign up and run off for adventure and excitement. And all they will find, I'm afraid, is disease and death."

I ought not to have been surprised. Since I know very, very little about this man whom I married, and since he has disclosed almost none of himself to me, there is no way I can predict how he will react when something happens in the world outside our home. If I'd been asked beforehand what I thought he would do if the Spaniards blew up one of our ships, I would have said that he would be for marching not on Havana but on Madrid.

I hope my baby comes soon.

March 15, 1898.

Agnes Mary Elizabeth was born on our first wedding anniversary. That means we are going to have to have two parties on that day for the rest of our lives. I am very tired and very sore but very happy. She is an adorable little girl, looks more like her father than she does like me, and seems to be healthy in every way. Thomas Doolan was delighted.

July 13, 1898.

I have been sobbing all day, Timmy Millan, the love of my life, who dashed off to fight in Cuba the day the Maine blew up, died on San Juan Hill, not from a Spanish bullet but from disease. What a terrible end for such a young life! He was bright and quick and charming. Unlike my husband, he made me laugh. Now I will never see him again. Somehow I know I let him down. I shouldn't have married my husband, I should have waited for Timmy. I should have defied my parents. I didn't and now he is dead. If I had married him or even told him that I would marry him eventually, he would not have run off to Cuba, so it's all my fault.

My husband said to me when he found me in tears, "I am told that Timothy Millan died in Cuba."

I nodded.

"I am very sorry, Mary Louise. Very sorry."

He must know that I loved Timmy.

I don't want to go to the funeral mass. My husband says that he will go; whether I attend, he says, is my decision. I wonder what Father Dorney will say.

July 21, 1898.

My little Agnes is becoming so cute, she's not four months old and has a personality all of her own. She is a good baby. She sleeps at night. She makes very little fuss. As one of the maids said, "She's a pleasure to have in the house."

I don't know whether I'm a good mother or not. I spend a lot of time with her and take care of her. It's not right that the maids should act like a mother and so I try to be a good mother. Thomas says he thinks I'm a good mother. He would say that anyway.

The war with the Spaniards is over, Cuba is free and we've got the Philippine Islands and Puerto Rico. Thousands of Spaniards are dead and thousands of Americans, including the love of my life Timmy Millan. I don't know whether Thomas understands how much I was in love with Timmy and still am. If he does he says nothing. I wonder what he thinks. That's something I guess I will never know even about Timmy or about anyone else.

I do know, however, he absolutely adores our little Agnes.

October 11, 1898.

The fool Hibernians are having a cruise across the lake to Saugatuck on the weekend. I've never been to Saugatuck. I hear it's very nice. I don't want to go on a silly boat ride even if the weather is nice. Thomas says that we have to go because the Hibernians are raising money to help the people that are starving in Ireland.

"I don't believe it's for starving people," I said angrily. "I believe it's for more guns to kill policemen and English soldiers."

"I don't think so, Mary Louise. It looks like some sort of home rule is going to go through, if not this year or

next year, certainly in the very early years of the next century. And then Ireland will be partially free and able to work its way peacefully to full freedom. The English know they can't hang on to Ireland much longer. The Land League wars have made it possible for Irish farmers to own their own land at least for all practical purposes. The country is prosperous now. I don't think anyone wants a war."

"Then why do we have to go on the cruise? I don't want to take my baby out on that lake!"

"Because I'm still one of the leaders of the Hibernians. Though I'm not as active as I used to be, I owe it to Father Dorney to support the cause of Irish freedom. I owe it to my friends who belong to the Hibernians. My father was their leader for a long time."

"I remember," I said sadly. Sometimes Thomas seems to feel that his father—a nasty old man—is still alive and still watching him. If his father could hear the things Thomas says about war these days he would be horrified. I understand that Thomas must go on the excursion. I'm only sorry that my baby and I have to go with him.

He told me that it was my decision, as he always does. Perhaps I will decide not to go.

October 18, 1898.

I wish I were dead.
Really dead. I should kill myself. There is nothing more to live for.

October 21, 1898.

Father Dorney came over this morning to try to calm me down. I'm still hysterical. I tear at my clothes, I pull at my hair, I scream, I shout, I am a disgrace to my husband and to my family and to my parish and to my church. It was my fault poor Agnes died. If I only held on a little longer she would still be alive. I didn't, I *didn't have the strength or courage to keep her in my arms. I've never had the strength or courage to do anything right.*

October 31, 1898.

Father Dorney was back again today. Thank God that he doesn't say what most everyone else says, I must accept it, that I should pull myself together and get on with my life. I murdered my little daughter and I don't want to go on with life.

I'm not speaking to Thomas. I haven't spoken to him since the shipwreck. When I saw him on the beach still alive and I knew that our daughter was dead, I hit him in the face, I punched him in the stomach, I tore at his clothes, I screamed curses at him. He did not respond because he knew that he was responsible. If he had not made us go on the cruise our daughter would still be alive.

Tuesday, November 1, 1898.

I dream about it every night. I'm in the salon of the old ship, the band is playing. Thomas and I are dancing. He has become a very good dancer since he knows that I like to dance. Everybody is having a wonderful time. I have enjoyed the cruise. I loved Saugatuck. I'm all ready to cross the Atlantic. Someone comes round and says there is a terrible snowstorm outside. I don't believe him. There can't be a snowstorm in October, not even on Lake Michigan. The boat rocks more in the waves. Someone else says we're going to be a couple of hours late getting back into Chicago. That worries me for a little while. Thomas and I are having too much fun and our daughter is sleeping comfortably in our cabin. Every five minutes I go down to make sure she is all right.

Then there is a terrible noise as though we have been hit by a gigantic rock, the ship trembles and shakes, tilts over in both directions and then stops. People are screaming. I break away from Thomas and run to get the child. I don't know what happens next. I don't know what happens to him. I find her in our cabin and snatch her up. Then there is this awful explosion and fire bursting out of all sides of the ship. The wind is howling, the snow is beating against my skin and blinding my eyes, I'm screaming, I think Agnes is screaming too. There is so much screaming around us. Then the ship seems to fall out from under us and I'm in the water with my baby. The water is cold and the wind continues to howl, the waves wash over me, my clothes are dragging me down, I know I'm going to die. Then a man grabs my arm and pulls me to a piece of wood. Hang on to this he tells me. We are not far offshore.

The waves are bigger and I'm shivering all over. I know I'm going to die, I only hope that Agnes survives. I cling to her for dear life, I must not let her go no matter how weak I am or how cold my body is or how I'm shivering I must hold on to her. And then a big wave comes and it washes over us. The water flies into my mouth and my nose and down my throat into my lungs and stomach and I can't breathe, I cough and shout and scream, hang on for dear life to the piece of driftwood, and then finally I can breathe again. Only Agnes is no longer in my arms!

Another big wave sweeps over us and I no longer want to live. I let go of the little platform we were hanging on. The man grabs me and won't let me drown. Then amazingly we feel the sand of the beach beneath our feet and another big wave hits us and washes us up on the shore. I sit there for hours and hours and hours in the cold, wet and sick and in the depths of despair. I want so much to die.

Then it's morning, the sun comes out, the storm is gone, it even feels a little warm. I struggle to my feet and see Thomas coming towards me down the beach. He has Agnes in his arms, she is still alive, and we are both happy.

When I wake up from the dream, I think for many minutes it is really true, that our baby is still alive. Then I know better, she is dead and I am dead myself.

I might just as well be dead.

Tuesday, December 13, 1898.

I tell Thomas I want no Christmas tree, no candles, no plum pudding and no decorations, nothing. I don't want to celebrate Christmas this year or ever again, Christmas is a trick, a deception, I want no part of it.

He looks at me sadly and says what he so often says, "It's your decision, my dear."

How disgusted with me he must be, I'm acting like a woman who has no faith, a woman who does not believe in God, a woman who is a hypocrite every time she walks into church to pray. Maybe I'll get over it, maybe this terrible ache will go away. Maybe I'll be something like myself again. I can't imagine that happening. It would be better for me and for Thomas and for everybody else if I were dead.

Then I relent a little.

"Thomas, that doesn't mean you shouldn't celebrate Christmas."

"If you're not going to celebrate it, my dear, then neither am I."

At least I am talking to him again. I have not forgiven him, however. It's his fault he killed my daughter and he killed me.

Wednesday, December 21, 1898.

Father Dorney came over again today to see me. I'm astonished that the man pays any attention to me. He knows that I don't believe in anything. He knows that I hate God, he knows that I don't listen to his kind words.

Yet he keeps coming, time after time after time. He promises me that he is going to bring a little present over on Christmas Day. I tell him not to bother, I don't believe in Christmas anymore. He just laughs and says, he'll come with his present anyway.

Sunday, Christmas Day, December 25.

I can't believe Father Dorney would be so heartless and cruel. I told him I never wanted to see him again, I slapped his face and ordered him out of my house. He was shocked. I don't think anyone has ever hit him since he was ordained a priest. He deserved to be hit for what he tried to do to me. I think Thomas was really angry at me, more angry than he has ever been. He did not, however, speak a word of anger.

Father Dorney brought over a baby girl for us. It was a survivor of the wreck. No one had claimed it. It has neither mother nor father. He wanted us to raise it.

"I don't even know whether she's Catholic," he said to me, kindness radiating from his flashing blue eyes. "So I baptized her conditionally and called her Ellen, which was my mother's name. It's a form of St. Helena, who was the mother of St. Augustine."

"What am I supposed to do with it?" I said.

"Well, I thought you and Tom might take care of her and see that she gets a decent Catholic upbringing."

I looked at the child, I thought she was terribly ugly. Why did she live, and my beautiful Agnes die?

"I don't want a child!" I shouted hysterically. "I hate this little thing. I want my Agnes, if I can't have her back I don't want a baby to take her place."

"Now, my dear," Thomas said with his usual polite gentleness, "this little girl isn't supposed to be a substitute for Agnes. There will never be a substitute for Agnes. This is a child who needs a home and a family. Father is asking us to take care of her."

"Father can take her back to his rectory and raise her there! I don't want her in my house!"

The little girl began to cry, probably because of my sobbing. I didn't change my mind, I knew what they were doing. They were trying to cheer me up by giving me another daughter, I didn't want another daughter, I didn't want a son, I wanted no more children.

"Maybe, Mary Louise," Father said carefully, "just maybe God wants you to help this little child have a decent life."

"God be damned!" I shouted at him. "Why didn't God want my little girl to grow up. Why has he sent me this ugly replacement for her!"

Thomas took a deep breath. "It's Christmastime, my dear, we can't turn this child away. Why don't you let me take her into the house. I'll be responsible for her. The maids will take care of her, you won't have to have anything to do with her."

"No!" I screamed. "I absolutely forbid that thing to come into my house."

Thomas turned to Father Dorney. "We'll take care of her, Father," he said, "leave her with me."

"If you take her into this house, I'll leave you!" I shouted.

Father Dorney hesitated, the child still in his arms.

"Thomas, maybe now isn't the time."

"It's Christmastime, Father. It's the time when we must give a home to somebody for whom there is no room in the inn. I'll be responsible for her."

He took the child out of Father Dorney's arms. I stormed upstairs to the guest bedroom in which I had been sleeping. I will kill that child before New Year's Day.

Monday, January 2, 1899.

The last year of the century. I don't know what that means to me. It was a cruel century. I hate it, I hate everything.

I have not killed Ellen. One night I went down to her nursery with a knife in my hand, I was going to slit her throat. When Thomas woke up in the morning he'd find his new love dead in her bed covered with her own blood.

I didn't do it and I suppose I'm glad of that. I'm not talking to Thomas, I'll never talk to him again unless he gets rid of this obnoxious and ugly child. He's trying to win me back by giving me a new baby to worry about and to love. He doesn't understand that I'm not capable of love anymore.

After Nuala had read the red leather notebook for a second time she handed it back to me.

"Where is the rest of it, Dermot Michael?"

"There is no rest of it, Nuala. This was all that came in the envelope."

"That terrible woman is keeping it from us!"

"Probably, but I don't know how we are going to get it away from her."

"It's such a terrible sad story, isn't it?"

Nuala had sobbed through the diary.

"That poor, poor mother."

"And the poor father too."

"The poor dear man. She was probably a very lovely young woman but so immature. Still, if I lost our Nellie that way I'd be every bit as bad, maybe even worse."

"We still don't know how the story ended."

Nuala Anne dabbed at her eyes.

"We do know a lot of things, Dermot." She reached for the picture of the Doolan kids that was on her desk. "We know they had four more children and we know that Ellen was raised as one of them, perhaps not even realizing that she was a kind of foster child. There is nothing in this picture, now is there, that suggests that she's something of an outcast? So most likely Mary Louise did fall in love with her. And if she wasn't the substitute for little Agnes, she was a wonderful girl child to have around the house."

"You just want to put a happy ending on the story, Nuala."

"Well, I think the story has to have a happy ending, Dermot Michael. Don't you, girl?"

She scratched the wolfhound's belly. Upstairs there was no sound at all from the nursery, an exhausted Nellie was sleeping soundly, neither wailing nor shouting.

"We know more than we knew before," Nuala went on. "We know that Thomas Doolan was no longer a fervent nationalist. We know that he didn't want to go on the cruise either. He did it out of a sense of duty. We know that he felt terrible guilt for what happened."

"And we know that he was an extremely patient man."

"Sure, didn't he love her something terrible, Dermot Michael, and himself so shy and reserved."

"Shy?"

"Certainly the poor man was shy! She must have terrified him from the very beginning and herself not knowing it at all, at all."

"No one will say that about your husband!"

"Not twice if I'm around!"

"Do you think the little girl was the child of the couple from Detroit that drowned?"

"She had to be, didn't she, Dermot Michael?"

"We still don't know what might have gone on between Thomas and the man from Detroit. We don't know what he went over to the dunes in midsummer after the wreck to search for. We don't know why you saw the ships out there last month and why Nellie went ballistic. We don't even know why she did the same thing when we drove by the house on South Emerald. So it doesn't seem that we're much closer to solving anything."

"We don't know the whole answer, Dermot. Let's hope that this Hegarty person has the rest of her greatgrandmother's diary."

THE NEXT morning Mr. Forest picked us up promptly at nine-thirty. Nessa was in residence again keeping an eye on our daughter while Nuala and I set out for a couple of hours of exploration. My wife continued to carry the telephone with her and used it every half hour on the half hour.

"Well," she said as we settled down in the back of Mr. Forest's taxi. "At least we've got one problem a little better under control."

"I'm glad to hear that, Nuala Anne."

"Don't you want to know which problem it is?"

"Well, I guess I do if you want to tell me."

"Dermot Michael Coyne, you're just being deliberately difficult!"

"Who me?"

"Haven't we got the beginning now on solving the Nessa problem?"

"Do we now?"

"Yes, we do. Aren't she and Seamus coming over for dinner tomorrow night?"

"Was that wise?"

"They both know that the other is coming, so that might give them one more chance."

"Are we supposed to talk them into a reconciliation?"

"Dermot Michael Coyne, don't be an eejit all the time.

Who is going to try to talk anybody into anything? Oh, no, that's not what I have in mind at all, at all."

"Well, what do you have in mind?"

"Won't the little Bishop be here?"

"You invited the little Bishop to dinner, with Nessa and Seamus?"

"Well, you and me too!"

I thought about it for a moment.

"Nuala Anne, that's just brilliant. The little Bishop won't talk a bit about reconciliation but when he's finished they will be reconciled!"

"Och, haven't you caught on now, Dermot Michael," she said, inordinately pleased with herself. "I told you I was working on something."

Our first stop at ten o'clock was at the John Hancock Center where I had once lived and where I still kept the apartment and watched it appreciate each month. Sometimes Nuala and I used its swimming pool when, for one reason or another, we didn't want to go to the West Bank Club. I would have felt guilty about having a second home in the city if it wasn't earning me at least as much as common stock was earning.

We were not, however, going to the apartment. We were headed rather for the offices that front on the forty-third floor of CTC, Channel Three Chicago. We had an appointment with Doug Jurgens, who was the news director of Channel Three.

He looked like news directors are supposed to look, lean, distracted, nervous, and frightened. His edgy, dark-brown eyes jumped nervously under his high forehead. His hairline had receded pretty far, his stomach had projected farther than it should, and he chewed gum even more vigorously than Michael Jordan.

"Come right in," he said with an attempt at geniality. "It's nice to meet you."

"To begin with, Mr. Jurgens," my wife said, "I'm not here to complain about those terrible things that poor

Mr. Farmer said about me and me music. I believe that we should let the dead bury the dead."

Jurgens looked baffled. He'd heard the quote somewhere but he wasn't quite sure where it was from. Probably would have his researchers dig it up after we left.

"Well, I'm glad to hear that," he said with a sigh of relief. "I'm ready to apologize to you personally for what Nick said. He claimed he had evidence to back up any words but of course he didn't have any evidence."

"You still put him back on after he arranged his own assassination?"

"I did, and I shouldn't have. We were flooded with protests. He would have been off the following week anyway."

"You figured you owed him something because you worked on the school paper with him?"

"I really wasn't part of their crowd," Doug Jurgens said with a thoughtful frown. "We only moved into the neighborhood when I was going into my sophomore year in high school. Since St. Gregory's is right down the street and the tuition was cheap, my parents sent me there. It wasn't a bad place. I'm sure I got as good an education as I would have if I'd gone to Loyola or St. Ignatius. It's kind of hard to break into the crowd in a new school at that age, particularly a small school where everyone knows everyone else, I didn't feel much like an outcast. Since I wanted to go into broadcast journalism, I lobbied pretty heavily to get on the school newspaper. I had no idea why Johnny Quinn didn't want me. Perhaps because he thought there were too many Germans as it was. Nick seemed to side with him until Martha took my side. Then he seemed happy to have me on board. I can't say that I ever became as friendly with him as the others. I did admire him. He was an awfully gifted young man."

"Martha ran the show?" I asked.

"Dermot Michael," my wife interjected, "of course she did!"

"You're right, Ms. McGrail. Martha was a special kind of woman. Everybody in the school was in love with her, including me and, unless I'm mistaken, a couple of the priests."

"Sure, why wouldn't they be in love with her?"

"She was beautiful and fragile and smart and gentle and very determined. Absolutely irresistible!"

"And Nicholas Farmer won?" I asked.

"That's right," he said sadly. "That didn't surprise anybody then because he seemed far and away the best bet of the lot. No way you could foresee what would happen to him. . . . Hey, are you two investigating the question of who killed him?"

"We're kind of interested, as you well might imagine, Doug," I said as smoothly as I could. "We were accused of the first assassination attempt which he plotted himself. Though the cops don't think that we're behind the assassination attempt that worked, it's still something that's going to float around out there and perhaps embarrass our children unless we put it to rest now."

"Good idea," he said. "If you figure it out could we have an exclusive on it?"

"And why wouldn't we be giving you the exclusive? Sure, you were a friend of his and resent his killing even if you weren't such a close friend."

There was, I thought, a lapse of logic in that response.

"Roger Conrad has been talking to you, hasn't he?"

"Didn't he take us off to lunch after the funeral?"

"I don't know exactly what motivates Roger. He is an extremely successful journalist, makes tons of money. Somehow or the other there is always a little something uneasy about him. I'm not quite sure what it is, but he certainly likes to stir up trouble. . . . I think he's never really accepted defeat in the contest for Martha. Rog certainly doesn't like to lose."

"And you think he still wants her?"

"Yeah, I suspect he does. I don't see that he has much hope, however. Martha is a pretty straight-laced Catholic. She'd never have an affair with a divorced man, much less a married one. You never can tell what goes on in Roger's head . . . I suspect there's a trace of depression in him. He takes pills of some sort."

"Not enough in love to kill Nick, however?"

"No." Doug Jurgens considered his words carefully. "I don't think so. Somehow I can't imagine Rog being involved in murder. Even his journalism is a bit soft. He's won prizes, but somehow the hard edge is missing. It's the color of his style and his ability to pry out the inside story that makes him a success. Maybe I resent that because I'm in television and we have only enough time for the hard edge. We don't have the leisure of a long article in the *Journal* or a book. Rog saw both sides of every question. He understood the oil companies and the Nigerian military. I can't see somebody who saw both sides of every question putting out a contract on poor Nick."

"Was Nick working on a big story for Channel Three?"

Doug Jurgens's eyes narrowed and he shifted position in his chair.

"I don't suppose there is any reason not to talk about it now. Yeah, he claimed that he had found something really big, prize-winning stuff. Nick always wanted prizes. It would knock my socks off, could blow the Chicago business community out of the water. It really was something terrific. Or so he said. He promised us if we gave him another shot at television exposure he'd give it to us."

"Did you believe him?" I asked.

"Not really. We'd all heard this many times before from Nick. I figured there was nothing much to lose. He always gets attention when he goes on the camera. He loses it after a couple of weeks. In the initial period he would boost our ratings at a small cost. Nicholas came cheap. And maybe, just maybe, you think, he's finally latched on to something big. Maybe it wasn't too late for him to turn his life around."

"Something with a flavor of the old days of St. Gregory's in it?"

A mask descended on Doug Jurgens's face.

"You guys have found out more than I thought you would find out. To tell you the truth, Nick hinted at that. I don't know what he meant. He was always trying to settle a grudge. There was no reason for a grudge against any of us who went to school with him because he was certainly a hero at school. Yet everyone who was in that newsroom in the old days is a success, except Nick. I'm a news director. Martha heads a successful market research firm. Robin is one of the best PR consultants in town. Johnny is a big investment banker down at First Cook County. Roger is a world-famous business reporter. Nick is still scrounging. I think that would stir up some resentment now, wouldn't you?"

"Was he trying to destroy someone?" I asked.

"That's what investigative reporters do, Mr. Coyne. They destroy people."

We thanked Doug Jurgens for being helpful and took our leave.

Nuala Anne called home, spoke a few minutes in Irish, and reported to me that our daughter was still shouting and still throwing herself up and then falling on her rear end. She showed no signs of giving up.

"You know what standing up means?"

"Woman, I do. It means that she's fixing to walk. Then we'll have our work cut out for us."

"We will, won't we, Dermot Michael. But sure won't it be fine to see her walking around."

There, I thought to myself, speaks the mother of her first child. On second thought, however, my wife would be as delighted when our fifth or sixth child started to walk.

It was a brisk autumn day and we had some time so we strolled down Michigan Avenue and then turned on

Monroe Street to walk over to the Trader's Inn.

"Well, Dermot Michael, that was interesting now, wasn't it?"

"Wasn't it now, Nuala Anne?"

"Your man knows more than he is saying."

"So do they all—Roger Conrad, Martha Grimm Farmer. I'm sure if we talked to Robin Cleary and Johnny Quinn they'll all tell us a lot but they won't tell us anything we really need to know."

"They're all trying to put us on the wrong scent, Dermot Michael."

"And what's the right scent, Nuala Anne?"

"The right scent, unless I'm wrong altogether—and you know, Dermot, that I'm never wrong altogether—someone was involved in something that revealed a character trait back in the years when they were at high school together. Your man found out something about one of them. He remembered what happened in high school and that confirmed his suspicions. Whatever it was, there's a link between the present and past—but isn't there always?"

"And in this one there's more hints floating around in that neo-Neanderthal vestige of yours."

The little Bishop had once said that "arguably" psychic sensitivity was a throwback to an earlier stage of evolution in our species when, much more poorly equipped with voice boxes, humans had developed an ability to communicate by reading psychic vibrations. The fact that it is now agreed that we are not descended from Neanderthals did not bother the little Bishop.

"We are patently descended from an earlier species," he said, eyes flicking rapidly behind his Coke-bottle rimless glasses, "who would not have as sophisticated speech abilities as we have. Certainly the evolutionary process at that time would have selected the people who were psychically sensitive. Obviously that change persists in our species even today, and is probably a lot more common than we realize."

Who was I to disagree?

At one-thirty in the afternoon, Trader's Inn, around the corner from the world's largest commodity exchange, attracts milling throngs of high-powered and noisy traders eager for a bite to eat and a couple of drinks to calm their jagged nerves. The atmosphere is of a men's locker room—obscenity and forced geniality—and the maturity of a children's playground.

The Hegartys were two of a kind. A couple of years older than I am, medium size, outspoken, energetic, jumpy, charming, and, like all good traders, just a little crazy. Ellen was a redhead like my grandmother and like my daughter—pretty, opinionated, and very much in charge of the family. Liam was your typical black Irishman. Dark hair, dark skin, dark mustache, and deep, deep blue eyes that didn't miss a thing. They would either make a fortune together or go broke together. Kill each other perhaps, but as the saying goes, they would never divorce.

"So you are interested in my grandmother," Ellen asked as soon as we found ourselves a table and ordered beer and ham and cheese sandwiches.

"We're really interested in your great-grandmother. They both were remarkable women it seems," I responded.

"My grandmother Ellen was an astonishing woman," Ellen Hegarty said enthusiastically. "She was an Ellen and my mother is Ellen and I'm Ellen too. Everybody in the family simply adored her. I only knew her for the first eleven or twelve years of my life, but she made an enormous impression on me. She was handsome and intelligent and vigorous and determined and funny and just plain wonderful. Any family party where Ellen showed up was bound to be a success."

"Did she ever talk," Nuala asked, "about what it was like growing up in St. Gabriel's back at the turn of the century?"

Ellen Hegarty talked in rapid, enthusiastic, convulsive paragraphs.

"Did she ever! Grandma Ellen couldn't talk enough about that subject. It sounds like an incredible place. Like Bubbly Creek, a branch of a fork on the south branch of the Chicago River which carried so much waste that they said it would compare to the waste from a city of one million people. It bubbled because there was so much crap and corruption that you could walk on it. One story was that a bubble once consumed a whole boat. I don't think that's true but Grandmother loved to tell the story. And stories about the Dumps over on Damen Avenue, where poor people used to come and collect Christmas trees after the season was over so they could save them for the next Christmas and clothes and furniture and all kinds of other things, and the infant mortality rate in the houses around the Dumps was ten times above the city average."

"Your grandmother didn't live there, did she?"

"Oh no, she lived on Emerald Avenue in St. Gabe's when, as she liked to say, the shanty Irish were about to become the lace curtain Irish. Her parents, Tommy and Mary Louise Doolan, were lace curtain. However, they had very strong social concerns. They were involved in cleaning up the Dumps and filling in part of Bubbly Creek and trying to diminish the smoke and the fire and the noise in the Yards. Her father was a lawyer whose practice involved the Yards. He was so good at it, however, that he was able to talk a lot of the packers into cleaning things up. A really forceful and remarkable man. Ellen worshiped him and her mother too. I suppose that's why she was the woman she was. She was powerfully loved as a kid and she powerfully loved other human beings throughout her life. I hope a little bit of it is passed on to her grandchildren."

"You may have noticed," her husband joined in, "there is a lot of the old lady in my wife."

"Why, Liam, such a nice compliment!"

"Don't husbands reserve their compliments now," Nuala Anne observed, "for when there are guests around to be impressed with the gentlemen they are!"

We laughed, Liam and I uneasily.

"You wouldn't be seeing much of your cousin out on the South Side, would you now, Ellen?"

"As little as possible, she was so embarrassed by the fact that she'd spent a little bit of time Back of the Yards that she's never recovered from it. She is the worst snob I have ever met, an absolutely insufferable snob. She has wormed herself into key positions on a number of important boards and now she's wearing out her welcome. It won't be long now before she gets dumped on some new and unsuspecting boards."

This was a surprisingly bitter outburst for a young woman who seemed to have a sanguine personality.

"You'll have to excuse my wife on the subject of our cousin Colleen," Liam explained. "Colleen drives her up the wall. She thinks she is not only superior to her ancestors who lived Back of the Yards, but she is also superior to all us West Siders who live in civilized places like River Forest and Oak Brook."

"Och, sure, how could anyone make that mistake!"

We all laughed again. Ellen Hegarty relaxed a bit.

"What made you ask about Cousin Colleen?"

"She gave us a diary in a red leather notebook which Mary Louise Collins Doolan began to keep on the day of her engagement. It ends in 1899. And we need to know more about what happened after that."

"You have read her notebook?" Ellen asked.

"We have," Nuala replied. "Would you ever have some of the later editions of it?"

"Yes, as a matter of fact I think I do. There is a lot of Great-grandmother's things up in our attic, in a chest in which Grandmother put them. She told me many times that someday the historians would come looking for it. I haven't looked through it much. But there is at least one of the red leather books up there. I glanced at it, and it seemed to be in Great-grandmother Mary Louise's script. I was too busy to explore."

"I should think that the Chicago Historical Society would be very interested indeed in it now," I said. "Your great-grandparents and your grandparents were obviously important people in the development of the City of Chicago. Those records and other relics could just be priceless information."

"Tax deductible?" Liam asked brightly.

"Liam!" his wife warned him. "You shouldn't say things like that. It's all right to think them but you shouldn't say them. You can never tell who has a wire on for the feds in this place."

It seemed obvious that Ellen had only the vaguest notion of life in Chicago at the end of the last century—about what I knew before those two ghosts ships appeared off Grand Beach.

"St. Gabe's wasn't exactly in Back o' the Yards," I said. "Back o' the Yards, strictly speaking, is the south and west of what used to be the Union Stockyards while St. Gabe's is east of it. It was an older community and more established than the others. The Irish who lived there fought their way into the middle class, before the other immigrants made it. It wasn't exactly a comfortable place to live, there were open sewers and muddy streets and hunger and poverty and disease, even when your great-grandparents were living at 47th and Emerald."

"Was the stench as bad as they say it was?"

"Some people fainted when they smelled it for the first time on a hot day. The South Side Irish used to say that's what put the color in our cheeks. It didn't do that, but it did put money in their pocketbooks and purses as they struggled out of the mud and the filth into the American dream, such as it is."

"Are the Irish still out there?" Liam asked. "There are a bunch of traders from a place they call Canaryville. Is that the neighborhood?"

"It was meant to be an insult because grackles used to live there. As the Irish have been known to do, they turned it into a compliment and the whole neighborhood proudly became Canaryville."

"These guys are really proud of their neighborhood," Liam agreed, "and they're pretty rough customers."

"Would you ever let us look at that diary? Me husband belongs to the Chicago Historical Society and they might be very interested in having it. And aren't we fascinated altogether by their story. We'll give it back to you and the volume we have."

"Fair enough," Ellen Hegarty agreed briskly to the trade. "I'd like to read them together if I get time from this job and from kids around the house. Maybe we'll have some more of those red leather notebooks in the chest."

While we were sitting at the table eating a scoop of chocolate ice cream, an enormous man with silver hair and a red face and a huge belly blundered into the dining room. He was about my height—six-three—and probably outweighed me by a hundred pounds, almost all of it in fat. His face was pushed into a furious scowl, one I suspected was his usual facial expression. He was trailed by a sleek, well-decorated, well-dressed woman in a black leather suit with a miniskirt. She glared at the crowd with a hungry feline face, a cat ready to pounce. A gorilla and a panther.

"Who's that guy?" I asked Liam Hegarty.

"Oh, that's Johnny Quinn, he's a real jerk. He messes around in some of the money markets, mostly Eurodollars. He's a vice president of some sort or the other at First Cook County, one of their allegedly smart investment guys. I hear he's in real trouble with the funds that he's managing and that the feds are all over him. He always looks that angry."

"The woman is his wife," Ellen told us, "Robin Cleary. Poison."

Johnny Quinn and Robin Cleary. Fancy that!

They headed right to our table as I thought they might. How did they know we were here? Doug Jurgens call them?

"You, you're Coyne?"

Johnny Quinn shoved my arm.

"That's my name, Dermot Michael Coyne at your service."

"Listen, you fucking bastard," he bellowed, grabbing my shoulders and shaking me. "You fuck off! You've got no right to fuck around in my life and my past. Leave me and my wife alone or I'll fucking kill you, you hear me?"

"Like you killed Nick Farmer?"

He shoved me again. "Keep those fucking ideas to yourself, you hear? I don't need somebody like you fucking around in my life."

"I can understand that with the FBI investigating your financial dealings."

"Dermot!" Nuala barked. She didn't want a fight. Women never do, well almost never.

Neither did I, at least not one that I started. Johnny Quinn was going to have to floor me before I fought back. Then I'd have a hundred witnesses saying that I fought in self-defense.

"Mr. Quinn," I said pleasantly, "my wife is a sensitive young woman from the County Galway. I don't appreciate hearing that kind of language in her presence."

Nuala laughed. So did the Hegartys.

Quinn pulled me out of my chair and shook me. That was a mistake, because now he saw that I was as tall as he was and much more solid.

"You take your hands off me, sir, or I will land one punch to your fat belly and you will explode like the balloon of flesh that you are."

"Dermot Michael!" my wife shouted.

"Don't worry, Nuala, I don't beat up on fat men or little children, especially when they are combined in one moronic person."

He backed off, apparently intimidated by my size and demeanor. I was astonished. I don't intimidate very many people. I noted in the back of my head that Johnny Quinn was easy to intimidate.

"If you do anything to our reputation we'll sue!" Robin Cleary hissed.

"Go ahead and sue," I replied. "My lawyers will be better than your lawyers. However, I have no reason to want to do anything to your reputation. I'm trying to find out who killed Nick Farmer so that lingering suspicion won't be held against me and my family."

"Don't confuse us with that crazy bunch. They are no good, they are fakers," she snarled. "They've always been fakers. They were faking things back at St. Gregory's. That's why Johnny and I broke away from them. We can't stand fakers."

I almost said that it takes one to know one. However, the warning light in my wife's eyes silenced me.

They turned on their heels, the leopard and the gorilla, and strolled out of Trader's Inn. Now wasn't that interesting?

"Isn't Ellen a darlin' little thing, Dermot Michael?" my wife asked as we walked back up the Magnificent Mile. "And didn't she love her grandmother something terrible? And her having all them wonderful things in the chest in her attic. Isn't it surprising that she's never looked at them?

"I wonder if Ellen Doolan ever realized that she was not a Doolan child? Maybe we ought to try to keep that a secret."

"You can depend on it, Nuala, that Ellen and Liam will never go up there to take a look at the notebook. They are too busy with their family and their careers and other important things. She will never read her great-grandmother's diaries!"

"Not very likely. We Chicagoans really don't care much about our past. We would rather not think about what our ancestors went through."

"Maybe that's because you only had a couple of generations of history and ourselves a couple of thousand years!"

"Probably. . . . You think they know that Ellen was a foster child? Do you think that Ellen knew? Do you think she read her mother's diaries after her mother was dead?"

My wife hesitated.

"I think she probably did and that it didn't bother her at all. . . . And what would you be thinking about your friends Johnny Quinn and Robin Cleary?"

"I think they have a lot to hide."

"Wasn't I thinking the same thing! And they making fools out of themselves in public!"

"They would have been perfect targets for Nick Farmer—rich, successful, and Irish."

"I wonder," she murmured as she slipped into the deep silence in which she communicates with . . . well, with whatever she communicates with.

— 23 —

"THE POPES are not, by and large, an attractive lot," the little Bishop commented as he destroyed altogether my fettuccine Alfredo.

Nessa and Seamus looked up in surprise.

"They tell us the Pope is the Vicar of Christ, don't they?" Nessa demanded. "Doesn't God choose each one of them."

The Bishop looked in some surprise at his empty wineglass but waived aside my proffered bottle of Niersteiner.

"Then God has chosen murderers, simonists, blasphemers, womanizers, adulators, fornicators, liars, thieves, poisoners, spendthrifts, drunks, gluttons, incompetents, men who have kept slaves and harems, men who have committed incest, men who have drunk toasts to the devil, men who have bought and sold ecclesiastical office, men who wasted money and lives, men whose only desire was to enhance their own power and the wealth of their families, vicious men, mean men, arrogant men, cruel men."

"All of them?"

"Oh, no"—the Bishop waved his hand—"as Eamon Duffy says in his book and TV series, *Saints and Sinners*, there were a lot of good men in between. Even a few wise administrators. Not all the sinners were bad administrators and not all the saints were good administrators. Occasionally there has been a saint who was also a good administrator. On the average, the Popes have been a good deal better than your typical European emperor or monarch of the last two millennia. My point is that if the Lord wanted perfect men sitting on the throne of the Fisherman, he would not have turned the job over to human beings."

"They never told us that in school," Seamus said thoughtfully. "They never told us that there was so much evil in the Church."

"A mistake for which we are paying." The Bishop shook his head sadly. "No thanks, Dermot. Your fettuccine would do honor to Alfredo himself. However, two helpings is quite sufficient. . . . From Peter on down, Popes have been flawed humans. At least Peter had the grace to apologize, which most of the others have not. So we have some Catholics, all too many I fear, who worship the Pope and not God. There is no room in the Catholic heritage for personality worship."

"So why stay in the Church, me lord?" Seamus asked.

"Because it is the only Church we have and because we do not make the mistake of equating the virtue or the wisdom of our leaders with the wisdom and grace of the heritage which embraces us. Why do you stay in, Seamus?"

"Well"—he hesitated, trying to put his thoughts together—"because of the Mass and the parish back home and the parish priest and my family and Christmas and Easter and First Communions and May Crownings and the angels and the saints and Mary especially and the Souls in Purgatory and because the Church tries to take care of the poor and the hungry, though often it makes a mess of it, much as I am doing now."

"I don't think you're making a mess of it at all, at all," Nessa said fervently.

"You'd answer the question the same way, Nessa?" the Bishop asked.

"Yes, me lord."

"Call me Blackie. . . . Now with the two of you agreeing about the Church, don't we have the voice of the faithful?" he sighed contentedly, feeling that his work was done.

Which it probably was.

"What I like about the Church," Nessa said, "is that it always forgives you."

"Hadn't it better." Nuala could contain herself no longer. "Isn't that what your man preached when he was here with us?"

"It never lets us go, even when we try to get away," Seamus agreed.

"Once a Catholic, always a Catholic," I permitted myself to intrude.

"It can't let you go, you see," the Bishop said, attacking my cherry cobbler. "Because you are the Church, not just we poor priests and bishops. All of you. We need bishops and priests to have a church. And we need lay folk to have a church. Neither can make it without the other. We've always had a grand bunch of laity from Ireland. . . . Yes, Dermot, a little more whipped cream won't hurt."

Thus we had done the job on our young friends, older than either me wife or meself, without a word being said about their silly quarrel.

Nuala beamed triumphantly.

The second volume of Mary Louise's diary arrived right after our guests left.

— 24 —

March 15, 1899.

Today is the anniversary of my marriage and the birth of my daughter. I am no longer hysterical. I have not been hysterical for a month and a half. I suppose that is good, I am acting mature. I haven't forgiven anyone, neither myself nor my husband, nor the Hibernians, nor Father Dorney, nor God. The estrangement between my husband and myself is complete. It will be so for the rest of our lives. I hope my own life is not a long one. It would be better if he were free. The little girl continues to live in what he once called my house, adored by the servants and spoiled by my husband. I no longer become furious at the sight of her. I continue to avoid her on all possible occasions. She's a very seductive little person, winning everybody over with her smiles and her beauty. She will not, however, win me. I do not want a substitute child, in fact I do not want any children. I feel oppressed by her presence in the house. I no longer scream at her. She is not to be blamed for what happened to my own daughter and for what other people have done to me by bringing her into the house.

April 15, 1899.

My husband has decided that he must have a birthday party for his daughter Ellen. We have no idea of when she was born. It seems likely that she is a few weeks younger than my beloved Agnes. Therefore he has chosen April 15 for her birthday, a month to the day after Agnes's birthday. Which is cruel. I suppose he didn't realize the coincidence. I absolutely refused to come to the party. Why should I? She's not my daughter, I don't want her in my house.

July 4, 1899.

It is unbearably hot here in Canaryville. My husband has taken his daughter and some of the servants to a new house he has bought at Lake Geneva. I am sure it is hot there too. As he says, there is not the smell and the smoke of the stockyards and life is more informal. I hope they have a delightful time. I will not miss them. I refused to go to Lake Geneva because I thought it would be inappropriate, as inappropriate as taking off my black mourning clothes, which I never intend to do.

August 30, 1899.

My husband has gone back to Michigan City again for the second time searching for whatever it is he's been searching for. I now realize that there was something more involved in that cruise to Saugatuck than just an autumn weekend. He did something there on the trip or obtained something that was extremely important. I wonder if he organized the trip behind the scenes so that whatever exchange took place in Saugatuck or on the Lake coming back could occur. He is spending a lot of money searching for something in the sand and the dunes along the lakeshore. Though he has the money to spend, he has never been reckless or foolhardy with money. To be fair to him, however, he's always been generous to me. I want nothing from him now, however.

If I knew what the mystery was behind the clues it would not bring Agnes back nor would it change my attitude towards my husband. He did not need to insist that his wife and child accompany him on the voyage. Therefore, he was responsible for her death and my loss. I am responsible too. I didn't hold her tightly enough while we were floating on the waters after the ship went down. I wouldn't have had to hold her tightly if he had not made us come on the trip.

Am I being fair to him?

Why should I worry about fairness, has God been fair to me!

However, when he asked me if I wanted to go on the trip to Saugatuck and I argued against it at that time of the year he did tell me it was my decision. He always tells me things are my decision.

I hate him for that. Why does he shift so much responsibility to me? Why am I the one who has to make the decisions? It is not fair.

October 3, 1899.

The child is irresistible. I do not like her, I do not want her in my house. I do not accept her as a member of my family. Nonetheless, when she walks over to me with her funny little walk and looks up at me with her wondrous blue eyes and calls me "Mummy" I cannot help myself. I pick her up and hold her in my arms. My embrace is not too affectionate. I do not want her to think she has been accepted. Nonetheless she curls in my arms very contentedly. Since I'm going to have to live with her for many years to come, I must at least be civil to her. I must pretend that she is welcome. I don't know what this pretense will do to her or to me or to my husband. One must do the best in the circumstances in which one finds oneself.

December 1, 1899.

Our poor little Ellen is terribly sick. Somehow she has caught pneumonia. She has a high fever, her doctor is not optimistic. I am weeping all the time. As much as I do not want her in the house, I also do not want to lose her. My husband is terribly distraught. He blames himself for taking her out to make snowballs last week. My feeling is that if you are going to catch pneumonia you can get it anywhere. At least it's not diphtheria or typhoid fever. The doctor says the crisis will come in a day or two. I pray to God he grants the poor little child health and long life. She is not responsible for anything. Rather she is a victim just like I am.

December 3, 1899.

Our poor Ellen is in crisis now. She may be dead by morning. Or she may have surmounted the fever. The doctor does not think she will survive, she is too young and too frail. I have never thought of her as frail. Perhaps that is because I only notice her smile.

We have suffered so many losses, I pray to God that this will not be one more.

December 7, 1899.

Ellen is still alive. The doctor says that she is recovering. Although she will be weak for some time, she certainly will be able to celebrate Christmas.

I had forbidden her father even to think of Christmas. What can I do now? I suppose they have to have Christmas. It doesn't mean that I have to be part of it.

When I go into the room to see her, she holds out her arms to me and repeats over and over again, "Mummy, Mummy, Mummy." I must restrain my heart lest I fall in love with her.

December 25, 1899.

Christmas Day. We went to Mass at St. Gabriel's and wished everyone merry Christmas. People told me how well I looked. They admired my smart new gray dress. Perhaps they wanted to tell me that it was time that I gave up my mourning clothes and went on with life. It is so easy to say that one should go on with life. Those that say it have not had the life torn out of their hearts.

Christmas was pleasant at our home. My mother and father and my husband's mother came to dinner. They were very cautious with me. Perhaps my hysteria on past occasions warned them away from my temper. I hope so. I hope they are cautious with me for the rest of my life.

They also seemed to have been enchanted by Ellen who is, I must say, a very skillful enchantress. Nobody says a word about our poor lost Agnes.

Will I mourn forever? How can I not mourn forever?

Father Dorney said this morning to me it was good to see me looking so well and now that we're about to start a new century I should consider smiling again.

"What do I have to smile about?"

I snapped at him. I tell myself that I have not forgiven him for being part of the plot that brought that child into our house.

"You have to smile, Mary Louise," he said to me, with a laugh, "because it's in your very nature to smile. You have the best smile in St. Gabriel's. You will not be able to deprive us of it much longer."

What a terrible thing to say!

Nobody ever told me before I had the best smile in St. Gabriel's.

I asked my husband after our mothers had gone home whether he thought Father Dorney was right.

"Father Dorney is always right," he said. "Everyone knows you have the best smile in the parish."

This upsets me. Now suddenly I find yet another ob-

ligation imposed on me. My freedom has been taken away from me so often. Now they are trying to deprive me of my freedom not to smile.

January 2, 1900.

I returned to our marriage bed last night.

It was an impulsive act. I realize now that it was ir-rational, that I should not have done it. In the moment, after the celebration of the beginning of a new century that my husband had organized, I seem to have lost con-trol of myself. Perhaps I had consumed too much cham-pagne. Maybe I wanted to be in bed with a man. Without searching for a reason or understanding what I was do-ing I simply walked into the room in my nightdress. He was, much to my surprise, very happy to see me. He asked no questions, he offered no recriminations, he did not mention the beginning of the new century or suggest a new beginning in our marriage.

He simply said, "Mary Louise, you are so very, very beautiful."

I have enough vanity left to be influenced by such a remark. In fact, for the second time in our life together those words quite melted my heart.

I thought my heart would never melt again.

Recklessly, shamelessly, I threw aside my gown.

Today I am filled with remorse and mortification. I have been false to poor Agnes's memory. I should not have permitted a renewal of our marriage. Indeed, I am firmly determined not to share the same bed with him tonight.

Despite that statement of determination I know that I will. Perhaps it is the only sensible thing. A man and a woman living in the same house can hardly avoid one another indefinitely. Even if there is no love and very little affection, even if rage and grief clutch at my heart, it is absurd to pretend that we are not husband and wife.

Later.

I am anxious, frightened, and curious.

At noon, Tom came home from his office for dinner as he often does. It is bitter cold outside and the snow is falling. Yet another blizzard which makes the lives of the poor even more miserable.

We said very little over the dinner table.

As he rose to return to the office, he said, quite softly, "Is it your intention to share my bed again tonight, my dear?"

I was flustered by the candor of the question, especially in the dining room where the servants might have heard it.

"I think it was the champagne last night," I said grudgingly.

His face was grim, his fist clenched white, his eyes burning brightly.

"It is your decision, my dear. However, I must warn you that if you make the decision to join me again, I shall never again permit you to leave."

All I could say before he was gone was a meek, "Oh."

I spent some of my time this afternoon making sure that the servants had warm clothes and blankets. They looked at me strangely. It has been a long time since I showed any concern for them. They surely know that my husband and I slept in the same bed last night.

It is the fire that was in his eyes which terrifies and intrigues me. What will he do to me?

January 3, 1900.

Last night I put aside the book I was reading and unsteadily climbed the stairs. Tom, whose eyes were more fiery at supper than at dinner, followed, a large and foreboding male presence behind me. I imagined his fingers tearing at my clothes, his hands digging into my body. No, I would not tolerate disgusting male passion.

My heart beat wildly. My limbs were unsteady.

"I shall sleep in my own room," I said, trying to sound confident.

"It is your decision, my dear."

I do not have to say, however, that I turned into the room with our marriage bed. He chuckled softly.

I will not describe what happened, save to say that now I know the fires which burn within him. They consumed me last night, utterly and completely. I was but a piece of straw riding on those waves of fire.

"I trust I did not hurt you or frighten you, Mary Louise?" *he asked weakly much later in the night, as we lay exhausted and covered with perspiration, despite the blizzard outside.*

"Don't be absurd," *I said, with as much dignity as I could muster.* "You never would hurt me. You didn't give me time to be frightened. . . . And, Thomas Patrick Doolan, you need not be concerned about my departing from this bed ever again."

"I am happy to hear that."

"I have one question."

"Ah?"

"Do you propose that we engage in this kind of behavior every night?"

He chuckled.

"Not every night, Mary Louise, but often enough."

After that we slept in each other's arms. I was certain that I was loved with a love that, like God's, would never end.

We are, I believe, now fully married. Perhaps one must overcome tragedy with passion to be fully married.

I try to adapt myself to being happy. I refuse to give way for the euphoria that is building up inside of me. I do not see how I can resist. I learn much about human nature. We get over our grief. They are still part of us, but we get over them and we do go on with life. People who told me that I should get on with my life appeared heartless and insensitive. However, they were right. I am

*now in the process of getting on with my life. As much
as I hate it, happiness seems to be lurking for me just
around the corner of 46th and Emerald. I cannot escape
from it much longer. Nor can I escape from him. Amazingly, I do not want to.*

April 15, 1900.

*It is our darling child's second birthday. She smeared
the birthday cake all over herself and then all over me
and her father. She is a very pleasing child. And also
very smart. She's talking in whole sentences now and
humming along when we sing. She is convinced that I
am her mother. I wonder if we ever should tell her any
different. We don't know, we will never know who her
mother and father were. She is in every respect now our
child. And so I must begin to think of myself as her
mother. This is no longer difficult. As a matter of fact it
is easy, I do it without thinking. Our Ellen has captured
my heart. In the process and despite my resistance she
has put its broken pieces back together again. I will
always love her for that and for everything else that she
is and will become. I will love her because, though I
didn't want her in the first place, she is now my daughter.*

July 4, 1900.
Lake Geneva, Wisconsin.

*Our entire family is here this year for the summer
months. Tom has been able to arrange the responsibilities of his law practice so that he need only spend three
days a week in Chicago. He rides back and forth on the
train to Williams Bay. It is a splendid place. I love to
be here and I know I'll miss it when I go home. I think
I'm pregnant again though this time it does not seem
that I will be quite so sick. I haven't told Thomas because I want to be sure. I never wanted to have another*

*child, the heartache of losing a child was too horrible.
Then, whether I wanted it or not, another child was included into my life. Now that I may give birth to yet
another child I find that I am delighted. It was a terrible
risk to have a child. We Doolans cannot help ourselves.
We want children just the same. I pray to God that I
will be a good mother for this new child as I am trying
to be a good mother for our dear little Ellen. I have even
got into the habit of thanking God every day for Ellen,
not as a substitute for Agnes but as a great blessing in
my life.*

*My mother and father and my mother-in-law were
here with us several days last week. It was intolerable.
They complained about the inconvenience, about the
house, about the cooking, about the servants, about
everything they could see. I completely ignored them. My
husband, poor man, simply nodded politely. He would
whisper into my ear later, "Don't pay any attention to
them, we're not going to change a thing."*

"They resent my happiness," I said bitterly.

*He guided my arm to him, "As always, my dear, I
believe you are right."*

*I still have my quick tongue. I told the two of them
one afternoon as I was strolling along the lakeside that
Tom and I swam almost every night, Indian style, in the
lake. Of course we don't do that. They were horrified.
They both told me I was an evil sinful woman, that I had
no modesty, that I was a disgrace, and that I would
corrupt my children with such behavior.*

*God forgive me for it, but I was delighted by their
reaction. Perhaps they will not come here again.*

*Now I will have to tell Tom what I said. Perhaps the
prospect would interest him.*

I confess it certainly interests me.

July 18, 1900.

"You told them what!" Tom exploded in surprise and
dismay.

"I told them that we swim Indian style in the lake almost every night. I said it just to make them angry, they are always picking at me and our marriage. I thought that would keep them away for a while."

Tom's face was red but he was not angry. I had embarrassed him—which I love to do.

"Mary Louise," he said, "you are an astonishing woman."

"If you say so."

"Oh," he said, "I say so. I would love to have been there to see the expressions on their faces."

"The expression just now on your face is interesting too," I said. "I have embarrassed you again. You know how much I like that."

"Well," he said cautiously, "what time tonight?"

I took a very deep breath and said, "Oh, Tommy, would eleven o'clock do?"

May 30, 1907.
Galway, Ireland, The Great Southern Hotel.

We have just crossed the country by train. Our hotel, a sumptuous and elegant place, is above the train station. We are taking a day off to rest from our trip. I thought it might be time to reflect. I have decided to jot down a few more thoughts in this old red leather notebook.

So long it has been since I kept this diary and so many things happened. Tom and Johnny are our two new and wonderful boy children. Our Ellen, now nine years old, has appointed herself an assistant mother to help me take care of these little hellions. She's got them charmed too. I wonder if there is anyone who is immune to Ellen's charm, the priests, the sisters of the school, the people on the streets, the servants, everyone is delighted by her.

As naturally so am I.

Sometimes, not very often but sometimes, I wonder

what her parents were like. The charm has to be natural, she was born with it. In the family we've helped her to grow and develop. Her charm was there the first night that poor Father Dorney brought her into our house.

I cannot believe how terrible I was that year. Tom has often said that we won't discuss that interlude in our life. What was there to discuss? I was a fool, something I often am, and he's been an extraordinarily patient husband.

He's still a mystery, still impossible to figure out, still big and handsome and aloof and reserved. What goes on inside his soul escapes me completely. I want to know who he really is. I wanted to know that when we married but one way or the other it didn't seem to be necessary. Now that we have been married for ten years and are taking a second honeymoon here in Europe, I tell myself that I must find out who he is. I cannot live with this man towards whom my affections are so intense and still be a stranger. I must ask him on this trip to Ireland who and what he really is.

Thomas and I have discovered that both our families had come from the poorest part of the poorest county in Ireland. My family is from Ballyhaunis and his from Castlebar. The poverty of people there is just unbelievable. Even the poorest foreigners in Canaryville have proper places to live instead of the stone and thatched cottages. And even the poorest people in St. Gabriel's have a much better life than the people here. Small wonder that our ancestors emigrated to Chicago. Thomas says these people would not be poor if it were not for centuries of English oppression. That has to be true. But neither he nor I are willing to spend much money in the cause of violent nationalism. He admits to me that somebody has to rebel and kill English soldiers. But he doesn't want the blood to be on our hands. There is a conflict in these sentiments. I don't think there is anything we can do about it.

June 2.
Connemara.

Tom and I are staying several nights at a small hotel, out on this barren, desolate but incredibly beautiful peninsula. Last night I finally asked him the question. The result was an interlude in our marriage that I would not have believed possible.

"Thomas Patrick Doolan," I said to him as we lay together in bed, "who are you?"

"Pardon, my dear?"

"I said, who are you?"

My heart was beating fast, I was taking a big chance by trying to break through the wall of his reserve. The chance was worth taking and anyway, what loss could we suffer?

"When I married you, you were a stranger, an aloof but kindly stranger. Now ten years later you are still a stranger, a stranger in whose bed I sleep and who is always pleasant, kind, and considerate to me, who puts up with all my intolerable failings, and who tells me at least once a day that something is my decision. I am tired, Thomas Patrick Doolan, of living with a stranger."

I expected that he would dismiss my question as foolish, the kind of question only a woman would ask.

"I'm your husband."

"I know that. What I want to know is, who is my husband?"

There was complete silence for a few moments.

"You still think I'm a stranger?"

"Well, in some ways certainly not, but in some ways, yes, you still are a stranger. You are a man who hides almost everything to himself, behind that polite reserved exterior. It's fine in the courtroom and it's wonderful when you are negotiating with business partners or those awful packing barons about cleaning up the mess *they have made. It's not a good way to be with your wife."*

"I'm sorry," he said with a catch in his voice.

"There is nothing to be sorry about," I replied. "I should have asked this question a long time ago. It's not your fault that you are so aloof, it's my fault for not telling you how much it troubles me."

"Do you love me?"

"Do I love you? Thomas Patrick Doolan! What do you think? Haven't I said that often enough, haven't I acted that way often enough? Didn't what we just did together show how much I love you?"

"You told me before we were married that you did not love me."

"I was a silly, frivolous, immature child, Tommy. I found you a lot more attractive than I was willing to admit to myself. Haven't I told you often enough since then that I love you?"

"I know you have, Mary Louise. I thought perhaps you were simply going through the routine that you thought was appropriate for husband and wife. If I've learned one thing about you in our years together it is that you are a practical person. You do whatever is necessary in the circumstances even if it's distasteful. And you say whatever needs to be said even though your heart really isn't in it."

"I must admit that I've never thought of myself that way."

"I'm not being critical," he went on. "Rather, I admire your ability to adjust and to be in harmony with every possible situation, I wonder, however, to what extent I'm just one more possible situation?"

"You listen to me, Tommy Doolan, I haven't been pretending, you're not a possible situation. I've loved you all along, I loved you even when I didn't think I loved you. I will always love you. You're a wonderful, wonderful husband. I could never ask for a better husband. I'm not just being tolerant of you, even if sometimes I seem to act that way. When you have been gone to the office all day and come in at the end of the day looking tired and sometimes discouraged, I become weak all over in my love for you. Is that enough?"

He drew me into his arms.

"It is more than enough, my dear. Sometimes I have thought to myself that that's your way and that you do feel powerful love for me. Yet I've never really been sure."

"Are you sure now?"

"I'm sure now, Mary Louise."

"You've turned the conversation back on me. We are not lying here in bed discussing me, we're discussing you."

"I will concede to the court that I am a hidden man. I do not speak often of my feelings or my emotions, of my joys or my sorrows. I quite agree with you that that is a mistake. One of your good traits as a mother that I admire greatly is your ability to let our children talk of their feelings. I understand that this is not fashionable child rearing practice. I think it's by far the better way."

I've never even been aware that I've done that. Maybe I was the kind of person who couldn't do anything else.

"Thank you."

"It's my father. He's been dead these fifteen years now and I feel he's still watching everything I do."

I had thought that. I didn't say it, however. I let him go on.

"He said often that I was not a real man. My mother had spoiled me rotten. He said I would never survive in the practice of law because I was too soft. He said I would be a poor husband, because I was not tough enough to keep a woman in line."

"Did he keep your mother in line?"

"No. He thought he did. He thought he was the boss. As you must realize, he wasn't."

"You have done very well in the world, Thomas.

You're a good lawyer and the best husband ever. Your father was wrong."

"I've never been sure."

"Well, you can be sure now."

He drew me to himself and hugged me very tightly.

"It's hard to explain, Mary Louise my love, since the day I first saw you I've wanted you. I've always been afraid of losing you. There were several times early in our marriage when I thought I would lose you. I suppose I've been afraid that if I told you how many terrors there are in my life I might lose you. I now realize that's silly. It will be difficult for me but I promise you that I will do everything I can to drop the wall between us."

"Well, Thomas Patrick Doolan, you can depend on it I'm going to claw at that wall."

"You have my permission," he said with a light laugh. "I'm not going to change completely, Mary Louise, but I think I am now, after ten years, confident enough in love that I'll be able to share a lot more of myself with you."

It was stiff and formal, but it was enough. I clung to him in near adoration.

"Oftentimes," he said, "I simply don't know what to make of you, you astonish me, you delight me, you baffle me, but, Mary Louise, you are never dull!"

"That's a great compliment," I said, kissing him, and then kissing him again and again and again. "I hope I always surprise you."

He sighed, and then I realized that he was crying. Tom Doolan, the man without emotion, was crying as his wife just did. So I kept on kissing him.

"Why do you weep, my dear?"

"Why does a baby cry when it's born?"

June 1, 1907.
London.

"What were you looking for when you tried to salvage the ship off Michigan City?"

My husband and I were walking on the Strand, arm in arm like young lovers. Suddenly that question had popped into my mind and because our relationship is changing, however slowly, I felt I had to ask him.

He was quiet for a little while.

"Tommy?"

"Oh, Mary Louise, I heard the question. I need time to think of how to answer it."

"You will answer it, however."

He hugged me fiercely. It was embarrassing on a street in London but I didn't care.

"I am now finding myself in a phase in my life when there are questions that I have to answer."

"That is correct, Thomas."

"There were no elaborate plans when the cruise was planned. It was straightforward. The Ancient Order of Hibernians needed to raise money as I told you then. I didn't want to go but I felt that out of loyalty I had to. On the other side of the lake I encountered a man and a woman with a child. Presumably the child was Ellen and the man and woman were her parents, they were even younger than we were. They had just arrived from Ireland and they had been searching for me because they wanted to give me something. They had heard about the cruise to Saugatuck and felt it would be better to find me there than to come to St. Gabriel's, which was, I hardly need tell you, seething at that time with Irish nationalism. He gave me a box. It was not a large box, oh maybe twelve inches square. He wanted me to take it home and to keep it for an unspecified amount of time until he or someone else came back and asked for the package that I had received. It was carefully wrapped. And closely sealed. I sensed that there was some sort of metal container inside it. Yet it was not heavy enough to be gold."

"You didn't find the box?"

"No, I didn't find the damn thing. Yet I am convinced that it is out there somewhere. Perhaps someday some-

one will find it. That young man and his wife risked their lives to get the box to me. If he hadn't tried to reach me on the ship, he and his wife would be still alive and their daughter would have her real parents."

"We're her parents now, Thomas."

"You know what I mean. . . . It seemed to him to be a wise way to deliver the box. It was much better than his showing up at my office in the Exchange Building where you can't tell who might be watching. Both of them were terrified. Apparently he had stolen whatever was in the box from people who were going to sell it to get money for arms. Perhaps his days were numbered anyway. Nonetheless, I feel responsible for what happened to him."

"How did he know you would be on the cruise?"

"His people, whoever they are, must have allies in Chicago. They heard about our cruise and somehow got word to him. . . . They were so very young, Mary Louise, so very young."

"You're too hard on yourself, Thomas."

"Sometimes I know that, Mary Louise. I'm not really responsible for their deaths or for the death of little Agnes. Yet if I had made a couple of different decisions, they would all still be alive."

"I wasn't much help to you in those days, was I?" He shrugged his shoulders.

"We had different ways of crying, Mary Louise. I understood how you felt. I couldn't tell you how I felt. Moreover, in those days I thought I'd better keep the secret of the man from Detroit."

"Did he speak of his little girl as 'Ellen'?"

"I think so. We're not certain that our Ellen really is his daughter. I thought Ellen might be a nice name to call her."

"It's such a dear name I'm glad he chose it."

"It's more dear because of the person that bears the name, I think, than just the name itself."

I agreed with him.

"I'm sorry for how bad I was during that year. Please forgive me."

"I was not angry at you, Mary Louise. I knew that you would get over it and would be my wonderful wife again."

"You're not going to hide from me anymore, Tommy, are you?"

"I'll be careful, Mary Louise, I'll try not to hide. I will depend on you to prevent me from doing that."

"You knew about Timmy Millan, of course?"

"I understood before we married that you had a crush at one time on him. I thought that was over. I didn't realize until after we were married how deeply you felt. I'm sorry that he died when he did. From everything I knew about him he was a wonderful man."

"He has gone, Thomas. Just like our little Agnes. The two of them are looking down on us and taking care of us."

"So we must believe, Mary Louise, so we must believe."

— 25 —

NUALA SOBBED. I felt salt in my eyes too.

"Dermot Michael, what a beautiful story!"

"We really don't know the end of it, Nuala. They're still in their early thirties in the story and are going to live thirty more years."

"Well, maybe there are diaries all around someplace. It would be interesting to see how herself reacted to all the changes that must go on in the world. Still, the story really ends there. The story we're interested in. Now we know what the mystery was. All we have to do is to find the box."

That's all. No problem.

"How are we going to find the box?"

"Isn't that obvious, Dermot Michael. Aren't we going to go down to Grand Beach and isn't your daughter going to find it for us?"

"How is Nellie going to do that?"

"Isn't she going to crawl around on the dune and when she starts to cry and shout, then we know that's where we have to dig."

"You're going to use my daughter as a divining rod?"

"Dermot Michael, this psychic business is no fun. If you're going to have it I think we might as well use it once in a while to do something good for people."

— 26 —

THE NEXT morning Nuala asked if I would ever let her borrow the Benz for a couple of hours. She had left milk and baby food in the fridge for herself.

"Sure," I said, not looking up from my keyboard. The new novel was now moving at breakneck speed.

I didn't ask her where she was going with it. If she wanted to tell me, she would. Doubtless she expected me to ask.

"Would you ever mind if I went out to see Maybelline?"

"It's your decision, my dear!"

She thought that was pretty funny.

Fiona was disappointed that she wasn't permitted to accompany her chief.

"Your job," I told her, "is to take care of Nelliecoyne."

Reluctantly she traipsed up the stairs.

I fed the child, burped her, and changed her diaper. She made enough fuss about the feeding and burping to let me know I wasn't doing it right. Since it was not time for her next nap, I brought her down to my office and put her on the floor. I stationed the wolfhound at the door.

"Don't let her out of here, Fiona."

The child displayed no interest in crawling out of my

office. Her intent rather was to disrupt it as much as possible.

Finally a key turned in the front door. Fiona barked and dashed to the door. Nelliecoyne charged after her. I followed in the show position.

"Och, isn't it a grand welcome committee? Yes, Fiona, me darlin', I love you too. Nelliecoyne, you look neglected. Hasn't your daddy been taking care of you?"

"He has too."

She kissed me with more vigor than the situation demanded.

"You didn't change her diaper?"

"Woman, I did!"

"You didn't feed her?"

"Woman, I did."

"You didn't burp her?"

"Woman, I did."

"Isn't that grand! I don't suppose you made a fruit salad for me?"

"Woman, I did."

"Did you really! Dermot Michael Coyne, aren't you the sweetest husband in all the world!"

"Woman, I am!"

My wife put our daughter to bed. She was sleeping almost before her head hit the pillow.

"Didn't you tire her out, Dermot Michael?"

"She tired herself out."

"Crawl around your office, did she?"

"She did."

"Well, where's me fruit salad? I'm perishing with the hunger."

We settled down to the fruit salad and a "small glass" of white wine.

"Don't I need it after that terrible place? Dermot, promise me that when I go crazy you won't put me in such a terrible place!"

"I promise, though I doubt that you'll ever go crazy. Besides, how would I know the difference!"

"Brat!" she protested.

"How's Maybelline?"

"Tranquil."

"Valium?"

"No, one of the newer mood-stabilizing drugs—Depakote. And lots of it. I'm thinking . . . why didn't anyone notice she was manic?"

"Perhaps because she was always that way."

"Well, now I'm her new best friend. We're great buddies, so I suppose that's a good thing."

"What our Jewish friends call a mitzvah."

She sighed, the virtuous sigh of a woman who has done a good work.

"Would you ever do two favors for me, Dermot Michael?"

"That many!"

"The first one is to call Martha Farmer for me and ask if she has time to talk to me."

I looked up the number of NewFacts, her firm, and called her. Of course, she had a few minutes for my wife.

Nuala motioned for me to stay on the phone.

They chatted about children for a few moments. Martha said that hers were "as good as could be expected" under the strain of the last several days.

Then Nuala got down to business.

"Was there ever a scandal back in the days when you and your friends were working on the high school paper?"

Martha hesitated, perhaps wondering what was behind the question.

Then she answered, "It wasn't really a scandal. One of us submitted a story for the paper about an experience over at Rosehill Cemetery. It was wonderfully written and very scary. A parent called and said the story couldn't be true because it had mixed up the locations of certain graves. We replied that actually it was fictional and said that in the next issue. A lot of kids in the school were disappointed because it was such a wonderful ghost story."

"Who wrote the story?"

Martha didn't hesitate this time. She answered candidly.

Nuala went on to other questions about Chicago high schools, which were not of immediate interest to us, but which provided a way for her to ease out of the conversation.

So that was the way of it.

My next call was to John Culhane.

"John, do you have a record of the books and papers which were on Nick Farmer's desk when your men searched his apartment?"

"Sure, Dermot. Let me see. Hey, there's a lot of books on one subject. . . ."

"Nigeria!" Nuala said with a whoop of triumph. "I knew it. Roger Conrad wrote a prize-winning book on Nigeria. Nick Farmer remembered that he had once submitted a fake story to the high school paper years ago. He suspected that the Nigeria book was a little too good to be true. He was trying to prove it and destroy Conrad."

"After all of the stories this year about journalistic fakes! Was the book a fake?"

"I don't know for sure. Farmer thought it was. He was trying to prove it. Conrad found out, maybe from Doug Jurgens. He couldn't face the disgrace. So there's probably some fakery in it. Find someone at the University of Chicago and ask them what they think."

Culhane was silent for a moment.

"It would be a motive for murder, though it would be hard to prove. We'll roll up Zog and his crowd of Balkan commandos in a day or two. I suspect that some of them will tell us."

"You could ask Conrad himself, poor man."

"We will certainly do that. . . . Good work, Nuala Anne."

"Thank you."

She sighed after we had hung up.

"It couldn't be Martha, because she still loved her husband. Anyway, she's not a big enough player to bother with. Why would Doug Jurgens kill him? News directors are not exactly virtuous men. Still how would you rebuild your career by exposing one of them? No, he had to be after a big fish. Roger Conrad was the only big fish."

"Robin Cleary and Johnny Quinn?"

"No money there. Your FBI was already after them. Besides, they're too dumb to be killers. Then I remember what they said about fakes. Martha told us that Roger had submitted a story when they were in high school which was a brilliantly written fake. They saved him, probably because she persuaded Nick to say it was intended to be fiction. Nick remembered. When Roger's book on Nigeria was such a success, Nick was furious with envy. Then perhaps he realized that Roger was not what Doug Jurgens called a 'hard-edged' reporter, a little too lazy to take the chances the book must have involved. He set out to destroy Roger."

"How did Roger find out? From Martha?"

"Nick wouldn't have told her because she wouldn't have approved. We'll never know for sure. As I said, perhaps Doug hinted to him about it."

"It all figures," I admitted, astonished at how clearly Nuala "saw" things when she turned on whatever dimensions of herself that are dedicated to "seeing."

"They're all such fools," she said bitterly. "None of it had to happen. Why would Roger run the risk of a huge fake? Someone would have found out eventually, especially in this time when fakes are popping up all over the place. Why would Nick need to destroy an old friend? Why would Doug let himself get involved? Was a story worth that much? Poor people."

"Poor people indeed, Nuala Anne."

"Martha is an innocent, Dermot Michael, a sweet,

lovely innocent who needs a nice husband to protect her from her innocence. We'll have to find one for her."

Naturally.

"We have solved both mysteries."

"And I need a nap."

"Alone?"

"Don't be silly, Dermot Michael Coyne."

There was, unfortunately, one possibility which Nuala and I had not taken into account.

— 27 —

WE WERE sitting in the first floor of our house when the Balkan gang shot their way in. We were watching the PBS series on the Pope of which the Bishop had spoken at our dinner with Nessa and Seamus. Nelliecoyne was sleeping peacefully on the couch. The wolfhound was curled up beside her. Nuala and I, arm in arm, were watching the fascinating story. Suddenly automatic weapons fire tore apart our front door. Three men in black ski masks came bursting in. One of them had an automatic weapon and the other two had dangerous-looking knives. While the man with the automatic weapon covered us, one of the knife bearers snatched Nellie off the couch. He must not have noticed the wolfhound or he must not have thought she was important. Instantly Fiona jumped on him, knocked him to the floor, and grasped his throat with her teeth. He dropped Nelliecoyne as he fell. Nuala dove from the couch and rolled over with the baby in her arms. The man with the automatic weapon moved it back and forth as if he was going to kill the lot of us. The wolfhound's attack surprised him. Thus I had time to jump on him, diverting the weapon into the air. The burst of gunfire ripped into the ceiling of the room. The other man with the knife closed in on me. I kicked the man with the gun, yanked it out of his hand, and swung it towards the attacker who was now only a few feet away from me. I hesitated to begin firing for fear the ricocheting bullets might hurt somebody. Besides, I had no idea how to work an automatic weapon.

Then the man whom Fiona had pinned to the floor sank his knife into her side. Blood poured from her side and stained her white fur. The knife wielder had made a terrible mistake. Fiona tore out his throat. His blood gurgled out. The man advancing towards me stopped in horror. Even gangsters are shocked when somebody dies such a horrible death. I swung the barrel of the automatic weapon and hit him in the face and now it was his turn to scream. The man from whom I'd taken the weapon jumped on me.

At that point I wouldn't have given any of us much of a chance to survive. I had not reckoned with Nuala's canogi stick. She hit the two remaining invaders on the back of the head with it. A sharp bark of wood hitting bone exploded. Both of them slumped to the bloody floor. Fiona was yelping with pain. Nelliecoyne was screaming.

Then the reinforcements arrived, two of Mike Casey's Reliables arrived with drawn guns.

"Dermot!" Nuala said, clutching our daughter to her breast. "Fiona is going to bleed to death!"

"Not if I can help it!" I said, which is an appropriate line for John Wayne in a situation like that.

At that point I heard the sirens of the uniformed police of the Sixth District arriving on the scene. I grabbed a pillow and stuck it into the wound on Fiona's side to stop the flow of blood. One of Mike Casey's staff said, "I know where you can find a veterinarian! Let's get her into the car!"

So I carried the bleeding dog to the surveillance car and we sped over to Clark Street. I didn't think Fiona was going to make it. She'd made no attempt to resist being carried away, most unlikely behavior for any dog, especially a wolfhound.

She weighed 130 pounds but somehow she didn't

seem that heavy as I carried her out to the car.

"It will be all right, girl, it will be all right," I reassured her. Or perhaps I was only reassuring myself.

Somebody must have called the veterinarian before we got there because she was waiting for us.

"Good heavens!" she shouted. "What have they done to this beautiful dog?"

"A guy stuck a knife in her as she jumped him because he had seized the little girl the dog was protecting."

The vet had us put her on the operating table and quickly injected something. Fiona's eyes looked glassy. I was afraid she was going to die right there.

"It's an artery," said the doctor, "she's lost a lot of blood. I'll rig up a transfusion."

I didn't know they had transfusions for dogs.

"You stopped the flow of blood, sir," she said to me, "now let's see what we can do about stitching her up."

Fiona's large brown eyes were sad. She looked at me pleadingly as though begging me to keep her alive.

"Don't be afraid, girl," I said, "it's going to be all right, it's going to be all right."

"Good dog," the vet said as she worked feverishly. "Very good dog."

Fiona whimpered in return.

"It was a close one," the young woman finally told us as she stitched up the hole in Fiona's side. "I think she's going to make it, aren't you, good doggie?"

"Fiona," I said, "good dog, very good dog."

Fiona responded with a weakened bark.

We moved into our apartment at the Hancock Center late that night until the mess at our house was cleaned up. Nelliecoyne was fretful, displeased, upset, as well she might have been. I suggested that we might not want to return. Nuala Anne would have none of it.

"Wouldn't that upset Letitia?"

"Nuala Anne, Letitia Walsh Murray is in heaven. Nothing upsets them there!"

"How do you know?"

Then she took her daughter in her arms and sang to her.

"Dread spirits of the Blackwater,
Clan Coyne's wild bahn si,
Bring no ill to him or us,
My helpless babe and me.
And Holy Mary pitying us,
To heaven for grace does sue,
Sing hush a bye loo, lo loo lo lan,
Hushabye loo lo loo."

The next day my daughter and my wife and I, the former two much more relaxed than I, drove up to the veterinarian's.

Fiona's cage looked like a hospital room. She lay on her side with a couple of IVs hanging above her. The vet had tied her down and sedated her lest she pull on the stitches and the IVs. She looked up at us and whimpered.

"Good dog." The vet caressed her forehead. "This dog is a very special patient."

"She's an Irish female," I said, "they have their ways."

Nelliecoyne, with the doctor's help, touched the good dog's huge snout. Nuala and I petted her. She made a noise like a purr of satisfaction.

"She'll be up and around in a day or two," the vet told us. "She's one very lucky dog. You saved her life, sir, when you applied that compress."

"Didn't she save all of our lives?"

On our next visit, Fiona was up and about, a little shaky on her feet. The veterinarian's two kids, early primary school, were fussing over her. Fiona was eating up their attention. Faithless bitch.

At the end of the week, after we had returned to Southport Avenue, we brought her home. No running for a couple of weeks. She immediately went on a patrol of the house to make sure that the smells hadn't changed since she had left. Then she barked happily and insisted on kissing all three of us.

"Sure, Fiona," Nuala said as she hugged the massive pooch, "what would we do without you."

The Chicago cops had rolled up the Balkan gang at the very time three of their members were trying to kill us. On a contract put out by Roger Conrad. Martha Grimm, meaning no harm, had mentioned to him as a curiosity our interest in the faked article of their high school years. He knew that we were on to the same story as Nicholas had been investigating. When the police went to his office to arrest him the following morning, they found that he had hung himself. Doug Jurgens admitted to the police that Nick had given him hints that he was working on an exposé of Conrad's prize-winning book on Nigeria. He argued that he had not thought that Nick could ever deliver such a story. Nor did he think that Roger was the kind of man who would put out a contract on anyone. In his depressed mood he would not. However, according to his doctor, in his manic mood he would do almost anything. He had not taken his medication for several weeks.

"Two women without husbands," Nuala said with a sigh. "Why do men have to be such fools. . . . Not all men, Dermot Michael, just some of them."

"Conrad was afraid of disgrace."

" 'Tis no excuse, poor dear man. God rest him, and Nicholas too. And that poor man that Fiona killed."

Indeed.

They would all go on her nightly prayer list.

Nuala insisted that we visit Bubbly Creek, a place which I had steadfastly avoided all my life because of rumors that blacks who had been killed in the 1919 race riot had been thrown into its polluted depths. However, as we gazed at it from the parking lot of the Riverside Shopping Center on Ashland Avenue just south of Archer (Mr. Dooley's Archery Road) it seemed quite harmless, even peaceful, in the late October afternoon sunlight. Two canoeists paddled by as we watched.

"Should they be doing that?" herself asked me.

"So long as they don't try to swim or fall in. None of the larger craft use it anymore, so it's a nice place to canoe."

"Uhm . . . you know, Dermot, this is the place where for the first time she admitted to herself that she found him physically attractive, though she wouldn't have used those words."

"If you say so, Nuala Anne."

" 'Tis true. The whole story started here."

She sighed her loudest West of Ireland sigh. Sometimes that sigh is melancholy. But not always.

— 28 —

IT WAS not a bad day for November, temperatures in the upper fifties. George the Priest, Nuala, the little Bishop, Nelliecoyne, and myself were at my parents' house at Grand Beach. I thought the project was utterly mad. I don't know what George the Priest thought. The little Bishop probably thought it was delightful. He arranged himself on a deck chair, pulled out of storage just for him to survey the whole situation. He seemed quite confident that Nelliecoyne would unearth the buried treasure.

Nuala's idea was simple enough. When we had experienced the vibrations in October, that was a sign we were supposed to find the magic box. It seemed to me most unlikely that the box would be in our dune. One hundred years had passed. The winds and the waves had come and gone. Our dune undoubtedly had been shaped and reshaped many times before the house was built back in 1917. The landscaping had changed, the shape of the dune had changed, the beach had changed, it would be pure luck if the box was there at all. More likely it was somewhere out under the sandbars on the Lake.

My fey daughter was dressed warmly in a black and red Chicago Bulls warm-up suit, including a matching ski cap which, as far as I know, the Bulls never wore for a game. In fact I don't think even Dennis Rodman, aka Rodzilla, ever wore one.

And, oh yes, the wolfhound was there too, parading around as though she owned the dune and the beach and the Lake and the City of Chicago many miles away invisible in the distance.

So, after a cup of coffee and a dozen raisin Danish purchased at the Village Bake Shop in New Buffalo (the best such rolls in the North American world, according to the little Bishop, who ate three of them), we went to work. Nuala put Nelliecoyne on the lawn in front of the house. Characteristically, she decided she didn't want to crawl. Rather, she rolled over, sat up, and made faces at the little Bishop. Naturally, he made faces back.

"Nelliecoyne," Nuala insisted, "we're here to work, not to flirt with the poor man."

So it was decided that if she didn't want to crawl we would just pick her up and carry her across the lawn and down the steps of the dune and out along the beach, now utterly abandoned beneath the naked trees that leaned over us like watchmen in a graveyard.

We walked up and down the beach, Nellie in Nuala's arms, waiting for something to happen. Nothing did.

It was, I said to myself, an absolutely crazy notion, nobody is going to find a box from the missing ship after a hundred years and one month simply by carrying a possibly fey child up and down a dune and around on the beach.

After an hour and a half of fruitless search, it was time for lunch. We went back to the house and fed Nellie with baby food, much of which she endeavored to throw at the little Bishop with appropriate screams of glee. The rest of us settled for Swiss cheese burgers from Redamak's.

"Isn't the little brat going to sleep now," Nuala asked. "But she can't go to sleep until she finds the buried treasure for us, can she?"

"She's your daughter, Nuala," said George the Priest.

"You are absolutely certain, Nuala Anne, the treasure is there?" the little Bishop asked.

"Well, Your Reverence, not to say absolutely certain. It's not like some of those other things that I'm really certain about."

"I don't know anything at all about this," I said, though no one had asked for my opinion. "However, if my daughter wants to sleep, we may as well let her sleep. She's not going to be any good to us if she isn't wide awake."

Nuala went upstairs to take a nap with her, and the little Bishop, George the Priest, and I went for a walk on the dune.

"This is absolutely the craziest thing I've ever done in all my life," I told them.

"Little Bro, I wouldn't mess with those two women in your life for all the money in the world. If Nuala says there's a treasure around here someplace, I'm not going to disagree with her."

"It can do no harm," the little Bishop said wisely, "for us to continue to look."

So after Nelliecoyne woke up and I changed her diaper and put the Bulls uniform back on her, we sallied forth once again.

Incidentally, Nuala isn't the one responsible for the Chicago athletic team's clothes her daughter wears. She does admit, however, that they're darlin' altogether.

We had hardly locked the door of the house when she began to scream just as she had on those mysterious Indian summer nights.

"She knows something is close," Nuala said, confident that her predictions were correct.

"Why didn't she scream when she came out of the house in the morning?"

"Dermot Michael, you ought to know by now that this business of picking up vibrations doesn't follow any logical rules."

"I'm not sure I like the idea of my daughter being a divining rod."

"Your wife is a divining rod too," Nuala insisted. "So let's just see what happens when we put her on the ground."

The ground in November was too cold for that. But what did I know?

Though wailing fiercely, Nellie began to crawl across the dry brown grass of our front yard. I could never see why we had to have a lawn on the top of the dune. Dune grass would have been more natural. My father said the lawn was there when we got it and anyway we might just as well keep it up.

The logic of the argument escaped me, like I said, however, what did I know!

"We lost a lot of the dune in the storm in '72," George said. "Most of this is fill."

"You mean this isn't the original dune?"

"I don't think so," said George. "It was twenty-six years ago and I don't remember all the details, but I think we hauled a lot of sand and dirt in here."

So Nellie crawled vigorously across the lawn and then headed right for the edge of the dune. Did she know she was supposed to be a human divining rod?

What do babies know anyway?

They know how to drive their parents crazy, that's what they know.

Nuala snatched the child up just as she reached the stairs going to the beach. Very slowly and carefully we walked down the stairs again. Then at the very edge of the deck which was just a few feet above the beach, Nellie went ballistic.

"It's nearby, Dermot, I know it's nearby."

She walked back and forth along the platform a couple of times and then settled on one spot where Nellie's cries were loud enough to be heard across the Lake in Chicago.

"It's right below here, Dermot," Nuala insisted. "I

know it's right underneath this deck and down in the sand. I don't know how it got there but it's there."

Then, astonishingly, our child stopped wailing and snuggled into her mother's arms. It was as though whatever she was supposed to do had been done and now she could relax.

She didn't need a lullaby. Nuala sang one anyway.

"Astonishing," George said. "Absolutely astonishing."

"Uh-huh."

"Arguably," the little Bishop added.

I removed from a pocket of my Bulls denim jacket a large indelible marker I had been carrying with me for just such an eventuality and painted a great red "X" on the deck.

"What do we do now?" I asked.

"Isn't it obvious, Little Bro," said the priest. "We get a contractor to come out here and he'll move the deck and dig beneath it, right on this spot."

"How are we going to explain this to Mom and Dad?"

"Sure, Dermot Michael, won't that be easy? Won't I tell them that I'm convinced that there's buried treasure underneath the sand, a kind of Holy Grail?"

"Oh."

That's what she told them and they might have thought that all of us were crazy. However, my parents being the kind of people that they were had no objection so long as we put everything back.

Joe Anderson, our contractor, was a bit concerned about the possible intervention of the Army Corps of Engineers or the Michigan Department of Natural Resources. I reassured him that it would be a one-day task and the sand would be replaced at the end of the day. So, at the end of November, six weeks after the two ships had mysteriously appeared in the Indian summer evening, we were back with the same crew, Nelliecoyne snug in her mother's arms, Fiona as lordly as ever. Mr. Anderson and his two sons had maneuvered a front loader into position on the beach. Very carefully they removed the boards of the deck and then began to clear the sand beneath the red spot on the deck, sand which had washed in during the March storm. Some storms stole beach and dune, others restored them.

I'm sure they thought we were crazy. So did I.

We were all bundled up because even though the sun was shining, it was a cold November morning. This morning Nelliecoyne was wearing a Chicago Bears sweatshirt and was wrapped protectively in an orange and blue blanket. Her mother also wore a Chicago Bears sweatshirt and her usual jeans.

They must have lifted fifteen or twenty loads of sand and dumped it behind the sea wall. Nothing but sand.

"I think we are getting close to the clay," Joe Anderson warned us.

"Clay?" Nuala exclaimed in dismay.

"The base at the bottom of the Lake, underneath the sand, is clay, ma'am."

Nelliecoyne slept in Nuala's arms. Fiona, curled up on the beach, watched us with an air of tolerance at the human follies. Periodically I threw a stick into the water and she chased it, utterly unperturbed by the fifty-two-degree temperature of the water.

Then they hit something that was not sand. It crunched as though it were fragile. The workers grabbed shovels and began to move the sand away from whatever it was they hit. Sure enough, it was wood, wreckage of some sort.

"Something that probably washed in with the sandbars during the big storm in March," Anderson said.

"We had better be careful now," I warned everyone. "We have an archaeological find here."

The wood might have at one time been part of a ship's cabin. Or so it looked to us who were expecting a cabin.

I wondered how we would explain our "dig" to the Department of Natural Resources. I decided that we'd better not. Next summer we'd tell them that there was a lot of driftwood on the new beach which the March storms the previous year had piled up on the beach. They could dig if they wanted to. If there really was a treasure in the rubble, they would want to claim it.

Suddenly, Nuala shoved Nellie into my arms and jumped into the rubble. She kicked through the sand and shoved it away. Fiona bounded in after her and joined in the fun.

Nuala burrowed into the sand, shoving her head and the upper part of her body into it as if she were some sort of burrowing creature. Then, she pulled herself out of the sand and held above her head triumphantly a small box, just as Thomas Doolan had described it to his wife in London ninety-one years ago. Fiona barked loudly in celebration.

Nelliecoyne stirred in my arms, distracted from her nap. She opened her eyes, considered the situation, thought better of it, and went back to sleep.

"See, Dermot Michael, didn't I tell you we'd find it now?"

"Woman, you did."

"You are a wise woman, Nuala Anne," the little Bishop said.

"Maybe we ought not to open it," George the Priest said. "Maybe we ought to find an archaeologist."

"Och, Your Reverence, you're just as daft as your brother. Aren't *we* supposed to open it now?"

That was easier said than done. We had to get one of our big screwdrivers and plunge the screwdriver into the lid of the box to pry it open.

Inside were several cloths, old and dark and moldy.

Nuala tore off the wrapping and finally came to the buried treasure, stolen from violent revolutionaries in Ireland over a hundred years ago so they couldn't try to turn it into money for more violence.

"Would you look at it! Isn't it the most beautiful thing you've ever seen?"

"The Ardagh Chalice!" George gasped.

It looked to be a tarnished drinking goblet, studded with stones. But what would I know?

"I think not," the Bishop said, examining the treasure which Nuala Anne had thrust eagerly into his hands. "It's small like the Ardagh Cup, but unless I am mistaken, it may well be older and it is certainly more richly covered in jewels. Presumably those who had discovered it were going to remove the jewels and sell them."

That was that. We had discovered a precious relic of Irish antiquity for which a man and a woman and a child had died a hundred years ago, a Holy Grail that my daughter, with some assistance from my wife, had discovered again. Just as Tom Doolan had predicted ninety-one years ago.

"What will we do with it?" I asked.

"Well, what else can we do with it?" my wife replied. "Aren't we going to give it back to the people of Ireland who have owned it all along."

And so we did at Christmastime when we brought Nelliecoyne to the land of her origins. We paid a discreet visit to the National Museum. The chalice (or grail as I always called it) had disappeared during Cromwell's depredations. There were rumors that it had surfaced at the end of the last century. The curators asked no questions. The find was reported the next day in *The Irish Times*. There were no hints about who found it.

" 'Tis a lovely chalice, Dermot Michael, isn't it?" herself said as we walked across Stephen's Green to have lunch at The Commons in the basement of the house where Newman had been rector, Hopkins a teacher, and Joyce a student.

" 'Tis," I agreed, as I was supposed to.

"No matter how beautiful, not worth risking the lives of three people."

"It wasn't the chalice, Nuala Anne. It was a winter storm that came too early, an old boat, and a dangerously irresponsible captain. Ellen's parents were young and romantic and convinced that they were immortal. They were caught in an accident, just like the plane crashes that kill many innocent young people."

"Aren't they all happy that the chalice has been returned? Even happier in heaven now?"

"I'm sure they are."

"Och, Dermot Michael, aren't you the most brilliant husband in all the world!"

I wasn't and I'm not. But you take praise wherever you can find it. That I was a brilliant husband and a brilliant father became the theme of our visit.

YOU'RE BEGINNING TO BELIEVE THAT BULLSHIT.

"What matters is that she believes it."

FOR HOW LONG?

The new disc was an instant hit. I made progress on my novel. The Christmas TV program had sky-high ratings. We heard on good authority that Nessa would receive a ring at Christmas. Maybelline was quiet and smiling at our family Christmas party the Sunday before Christmas (and the day before we left for Ireland). She and Nuala were together for a good part of the time. Nelliecoyne stole the show by toddling around the party. She shouted gleefully after every successful step. Nuala had taken both Maybelline and Martha Grimm under her wing. The lines of tension around her eyes diminished. More and more she enjoyed her daughter and less and less did she worry about her. We gave the Mary Louise diaries to the Chicago Historical Society. With a few tears from my wife, we deposited Fiona with Cindy's family. She made friends instantly with Cindy's kids and pretended not to notice us when we were leaving.

Nelliecoyne won the hearts of everyone she met in Ireland. Naturally. Especially since she was cautiously experimenting with walking.

When Irish eyes are smiling, sure they'll steal your heart away, especially when they are the green eyes of a little girl with red hair who has just learned to walk and whose smile is as almost as big as her mother's.

— NOTE —

In the text of this story I have acknowledged my debt to Louise Wade and Thomas Jablonski for telling me the real story of the "Jungle" and exorcising the versions of both Upton Sinclair and my predecessors at the University of Chicago.

There are scores of books about Great Lakes shipping and shipwrecks. They are available from Northern Lights Bookstore—*www.norlights.com*. Two that were especially useful were *"A Fully Accredited Ocean": Essays on the Great Lakes* edited by Victoria Brehm and *Great Lakes Shipwrecks and Survivals* by William A. Ratigan. A beautiful book of photographs and prints is *Ladies of the Lake* by James Clary. There is an especially wonderful drawing of the graceful *David Dows,* a five-masted barkentine on which the *Charles C. Campbell* is based. The largest sailing boat ever to appear on the Great Lakes, the ship was launched in 1881 and sank in the ice off Whiting, Indiana, in late November of 1889. She did ram and sink a ship but no lives were lost.

Although Chicago was the busiest port in the world in 1870 and the fourth busiest (after New York, London, and Hamburg) at the turn of the century, there, alas, is no comprehensive history of shipping into Chicago.

The shipwreck on which the story is based was the ramming of the *Lady Elgin* off Winnetka, Illinois, by the schooner *Augusta* in the summer of 1860. God rest those that died in the wreck and all those who have died on these terrible inland oceans.

I am indebted to Robert Hornaday for the story of the wreck discovered in the dune forty years ago at Grand Beach and to John and Richard Daley for background about the Yards and Canaryville. Seamus Heaney and Nóirín Ní Rrian found Irish lullabies for me.

None of the people in the story exist outside my imagination.

Will there be more people in the Coyne family, when next we meet them? Well, isn't that up to God?

AG
Grand Beach
Summer 1998

Look out for
Andrew M. Greeley's
new Blackie Ryan mystery,

The Bishop

and the

Missing L Train,

coming out in paperback
in July 2001!

Blackie

— 1 —

"One of our L trains is missing!"

Sean Cronin, Cardinal priest of the Holy Roman Church and, by the grace of God and abused patience of the Apostolic See, Archbishop of Chicago, swept into my study with his usual vigor. Since he was not wearing his crimson robes but a gleaming white and flawlessly ironed collarless shirt with diamond-studded cufflinks, it would not be appropriate to describe him as a crimson supersonic jet. Perhaps a new and shiny diesel locomotive.

"Tragic," I said, pretending not to look up from the Dell 300mx computer on which I was constructing the master schedule for the next month in the Cathedral parish.

"And Bishop Quill was on the L train!!"

He threw himself into a chair that I had just cleared so as to pile more computer output on it.

"Indeed!" I said, looking up with considerable interest. "With any good fortune we will find neither the L train nor Bishop Quill."

Out of respect for his status among the missing, I did not refer to our lost bishop by his time-honored nickname, imposed by his unimaginative seminary classmates—Idiot.

"You South Side Irish are innocent of charity," he replied. "You have any tea around?"

Normally he would have appeared at night in my study and commandeered a large portion of my precious Jameson Twelve Year Special Reserve or Bushmill's Green Label before he assigned me another cleanup task. Auxiliary bishops play a role in the Catholic Church not unlike that of the admirable Harvey Keitel in *Pulp Fiction*: they sweep up messes. However, it was morning, a sunny early autumn morning to be precise. Banned from coffee by his foster sister Nora Cronin, he was reduced to pleading for tea to fill his oral needs.

Before I could wave at my ever present teapot, he spotted it, stretched his tall, lean frame to the table on which it rested (surrounded by the galleys of my most recent book, *There Is No Millennium*), and poured himself a large mug of Irish Breakfast tea.

"Great!" he exclaimed with a sigh of pleasure. The pleasures of being a cardinal these days are, alas, few and simple.

I waited to hear the story of the disappearance of the L train and its distinguished passenger. He continued to sip his tea, a tall, handsome man just turned seventy, with carefully groomed white hair, the face of an Irish poet, the political skills of a veteran ward committeeman, and the hooded, glowing eyes of a revolutionary gunman.

"So what was Idiot doing on an L train?" I asked, realizing that I was missing one of the lines in our routinized scenario.

"Your brother auxiliary bishop," he said with radiant irony as he played with the massive ruby ring on his right hand, "was mingling with the poor on the way home from his weekly day of ministry in the barrio. Preparation doubtless for the day when he succeeds me." Milord Cronin laughed bitterly.

"He will never be able to learn Spanish that does not cause laughter among those who know the language."

"That, Blackwood, is irrelevant to the present story. ... His limousine driver was to pick him up at the Kimball Avenue terminal of the Ravenswood Line and drive him back to his parish in Forest Hills."

"Brown Line," I said in the interest of accuracy.

"What?" he exploded, a nervous panther looking for something to spring upon.

"The Ravenswood Line is now known as the Brown Line."

"The Ravenswood Line is the Ravenswood Line, Blackwood," he insisted with the sense of shared infallibility that only a cardinal can muster and that rarely these days.

"Arguably."

"So the train never arrived." He extended his tea mug in my direction and, docile priest that I am, I refilled it. No milk. The valiant Nora had forbidden milk as part of her virtuous campaign to keep the Cardinal alive. "And Bishop Quill never arrived either."

"Remarkable."

"The chauffeur became concerned and called the CTA, which, as one might expect, assured him that the train had arrived at Kimball and Lawrence on time—that's a Korean neighborhood now, isn't it, Blackwood?"

"An everything neighborhood—Koreans, Palestinians, Pakistanis, some Japanese, and a few recalcitrant and elderly Orthodox Jews who will not leave the vast apartment buildings they built so long ago."

"Safe?"

"Much safer than many others I could mention, some of them not distant from this very room."

"Who would want to abduct Gus Quill?"

"I could provide a list of hundreds of names, with yours and mine on the top."

"Precisely. . . . Anyway, the chauffeur then called the Chicago Police Department and apparently reached your good friend John Culhane, who called me about midnight. They have determined the L in fact never arrived at the terminal. Rather it has disappeared into thin air and, Commander Culhane assured me an hour ago, so has the Most Reverend Augustus O'Sullivan Quill."

Deo gratias, I almost said. Instead I took a firm stand for right reason and common sense.

"L trains do not disappear," I insisted. "Neither, alas, do auxiliary bishops, though sometimes they are treated as if they do not exist. . . ."

Milord Cronin waved away my self-pity.

"The CTA is searching frantically for their missing train. The police are searching frantically for the missing bishop. He was the only one on the train at the last stop. The driver has disappeared too. The media have the story already. I hear there are cameras at the terminal and up in Forest Hills—"

My phone rang. The Loyola student who monitors our lines until the Megan show up after school asked whether the Cardinal was in my room.

"Who wants to talk to him?"

"Mary Jane McGurn from Channel Six."

"I will talk to her," I said, as though it were my rectory.

"Hi, Blackie. What's happened to my good friend Idiot Quill?"

"Mary Jane," I whispered to the Cardinal, my hand over the phone.

Although Ms. McGurn was Sean Cronin's favorite media person—he having a weakness for pretty and intelligent women (what healthy male does not?)—he shook his head. "I'm not available for comment, am I?"

"You're in prayer for the repose of his soul?"

Milord winced.

"What was that question again, Mary Jane?"

"Our mutual friend, Bishop Quill, has apparently disappeared. Do you or Cardinal Sean have any comment?"

"Only for the deepest of deep background, Mary Jane: like bad pennies, auxiliary bishops always return."

Milord Cardinal favored me with a wry smile.

"Is the Cardinal available?"

"I think not."

No one in the media had much regard for Augustus O'Sullivan Quill. Mary Jane held a special grudge since the day he told her on camera that she should be home taking care of her children.

"The crews are descending on the Cathedral rectory at this moment. I'll be there in five minutes. We're going to want a statement about the disappearance of Bishop Quill."

"You may quote the Cardinal as saying that we are confident that Bishop Quill will be found soon."

Milord Cronin tilted his head slightly in approval of my statement.

"Nothing more?"

"Nothing more."

"Off the record?"

"We are praying for him."

"Yeah," she snorted, "so am I!"

I gently restored the phone to its base.

"We cannot permit this, Blackwood!"

"Indeed."

"Auxiliary bishops do not slip into the fourth dimension, not in this archdiocese."

"Patently."

"Especially they do not disappear on L trains that also disappear, right?"

"Right!"

"You yourself have said that we will be the prime suspects, have you not? Don't we have powerful reasons for wanting to get rid of him?"

"Arguably," I sighed. "However, as you well know, in the best traditions of the Sacred College we would have dispatched Idiot with poison."

Actually neither the State's Attorney nor the media would dare suggest that the two of us could easily do without our junior auxiliary.

"This is not a laughing matter, Blackwood," he said sternly.

"Indeed."

"The Nuncio and the Vatican will be all over us. They do not like to lose bishops."

"Even auxiliaries?"

"We have to find Gus before the day is over." He put his tea mug on the rug and rose from the chair.

"Ah?"

He strode to the door of my study, a man on a mission.

"That means you have to find him."

I knew that was coming.

"Indeed."

He paused at the door for the final words.

"Find Gus. Today. See to it, Blackwood."

He disappeared, not in a cloud of dust, since we do not tolerate that in the Cathedral rectory, but trailing an invisible cloud of satisfaction.

I sighed loudly, saved the file, and turned off the computer. Time for the sweeper to get to work.